Three's A Crowd

A cry for help. A life in chaos. Not Everyone is who they seem.

JCP Thomas

Copyright © 2024 JCP THOMAS
All rights reserved
No part of this book may be reproduced or used in any manner without the prior written permission of the copyright owner, except for the use of brief quotations in a book review.

To request permission: jcpthomas@gmx.com

Hardback: ISBN NO. 978-1-0685455-1-1
Paperback: ISBN NO. 978-1-0685455-0-4
E-Book: ISBN NO. 978-1-0685455-2-8

Contents

Warning — v
A note from JCP Thomas — vii
Acknowledgements — ix

1. Pretty Woman Got it Wrong! — 1
2. Home is Where the Heart Is — 9
3. Aspartame - Sweet But Dangerous — 25
4. The Mist Falls — 37
5. Cardboard Shadows — 51
6. The Second Cumming (and then some!) — 61
7. Misty gets Risky — 81
8. He Loves Me…He Loves Me Not… — 93
9. Lorry Cocks Matter — 105
10. Well, That Did Not Go To Plan — 123
11. Shaken & Stirred — 133
12. The Mist Starts — 145
13. This is Trichy — 149
14. What Soberness Conceals, Drunkenness Reveals — 161
15. Houston, We Have a Problem — 169
16. Network Glitch — 177
17. Szymon Says — 193
18. Bathroom Battles — 209
19. Holidays are Coming — 221
20. Cum Drops on Titties — 233
21. Emily vs. Sam: The Clash of Sass — 247
22. Red is the Colour of Shame — 257
23. Brucie Bonus — 269
24. Porked in York — 277
25. The Nightmare Before Christmas — 291
26. Snoop Gate — 309
27. Limbo Land — 319
28. New Year Not You — 329

29. Jessie - Where Dreams Come True	335
30. Get back in your Lane	341
31. Lost in the Mist	347
32. Blue Monday	367
33. Play Dates without Lego	383
34. The Subtle art of shooting yourself in the Foot - By Jessie Newkirk	393
35. Misty Morning	405
36. Broken Boundaries	415
37. But it's a Shitehole	433
38. April Fools	447
39. May-Day! May-Day!	465
40. Misty & Friends	475
41. FML	489
42. The Truth Will Set You Free	501
43. The Sky Is Not Blue - For Me	515
Epilogue	523
DID you spot it?	527
Don't be a C.U.N.T!	529
Soundtrack - Film Producers, Take Note!	531
References & Resources:	533

Warning

This book contains adult themes, strong language, explicit scenes of sex, sexual violence, violence, trauma and a broad range of kinks.

It is recommended for mature readers only.

A note from JCP Thomas

They say everyone has a book in them. I've always loved writing, but it wasn't until a blinding moment of inspiration hit me combined with encouragement from someone precious that I finally decided to put pen to paper and tell this story. Whether anyone reads or enjoys it is almost beside the point—because I can now say I'm one of the rare few who had a book in them and took the time to get it out.

This book, 'Three's A Crowd', was written mostly between midnight and 4 a.m., when the world was quiet, and my imagination was at its loudest. Due to its adult nature, I've chosen to publish it under a pseudonym. I have teenage children and a professional career that doesn't need to be tarnished with my filthy mind. Let's face it—people are nosy bastards, and they'll undoubtedly wonder which parts are real and which are fiction. I'll leave that to you to decide.

What can you expect? A little bit of everything. Humour, distressing themes, and, yes, plenty of the hot stuff mixed in, because who doesn't enjoy a bit of spice? Jessie, Misty, and the

A note from JCP Thomas

crew have much more to share, and if this book piques your interest, I'll gladly continue my late-night writing sessions and bring you more of their adventures.

Enjoy the ride! (I hope it involves a cock! 🌭👀)

JCP Thomas xxx

Acknowledgements

The sky might be blue?

First and foremost, I owe a massive thank you to the person who lit the fire under me and made me believe that this story needed to be told. You didn't just encourage me to write, you dispelled my doubts, lifted me out of my fears, and somehow convinced me that maybe, just maybe, the sky might be blue again and I'd get to see it. Your support wasn't just for this book but for me as a whole, and for that, I am endlessly grateful. You're my Sam.

To the brave handful of people I selected to read the first draft — you were absolute legends. You read without judgement (at least not **too** much) and critiqued with kindness. Honestly, the fact that you didn't just throw it back at me in disgust at my filthy mind speaks volumes. I wish I could name you all here, but thanks to this pseudonym situation, your identities are wrapped in mystery. You know who you are, though, and you'll forever have my gratitude… and maybe a drink or two on me.

Thank you **all** for having my back, pushing me forward, and making me believe this could actually happen.

Chapter 1

Pretty Woman Got it Wrong!

"Hurry up in there" an angry gravelly voice shouts as fists hammer on the door of the disabled toilets. Urgh, for fuck's sake, I mutter under my breath... as I slip my chiffon blouse over my lacy crotchless one-piece.

"Two minutes, sorry" I shouted back.

I pull up my skirt and sit on the toilet and riffle through my kit bag, until I feel the familiar bulbous shape of my favourite butt plug, squirt on some lube and reach between my legs and ease it in, wincing a little as I do, until it pops into place and I relax around it. It's like my calling card my butt plug, always brings a smile to a face, blood to a phallus and sets the tone that I am pretty game.

Once in place, I grab the wide base of the plug, rotate it 360 degrees and give it a good wiggle... then pull it out and inspect it... clean... good. I do this once more... and now satisfied I am clean, I leave it in place, stand up, flush the toilet and go to wash my hands. "Come on, you've been ages," the voice shouts and bangs on the door again.

I put on my long coat thinking to myself, superman never had this problem. OK, granted my quick change into my slut attire is not aligned with the work of a superhero, no cape is required. I am not exactly saving the world, but I do need a safe, discreet place to change. And whilst I may not be saving the world, I am saving marriages, including my own.

I dry my hands on the manky service station, rotatable blue towel, pick up my bag, unlock the door and step out to be greeted by an old man with a walking stick, a face like fury and a good dose of short man syndrome.

"What's your disability?" he barks.

I am addicted to cock, I thought to myself.

"Use the other toilets" he grumbles and pushes past me.

A pang of guilt hits me, and my cheeks flame, but I **am** running late, and the ladies are notorious for queues, I don't tend to abuse the disabled toilet. But today, time was against me.

I had finished a client meeting at 11 am, it was a great meeting, and I am fairly confident the guy Harry who runs a small and rapidly growing business was impressed with my knowledge. I am optimistic he will sign the contract to have me overhaul his online marketing to help his team build campaigns and evergreen content that can be monetised, repurposed and add authenticity to his brand. But it did run on, causing me to be chasing my tail for my next client meeting.

I jump in the car and bang in the postcode in my phone allowing it to guide me to my client's house. My mind wanders as I drive, second-guessing what is in store at this appointment and running through what I can remember from what the client said when I asked him about his expectations.

My side hustle has been on the go now for a little over 12 months and nothing surprises me any more. I pull into a shady-looking street, shopping trolleys and burnt-out cars in the gardens, litter strewn about the place. How is it that I am a professionally qualified freelance marketing consultant and I could not afford to blow £150 on an hour's fun? The number of clients I have that

Three's A Crowd

don't work, that seem to easily manage, with surprising regularity blows my mind. Honestly, what am I doing wrong?!

I get out of my car and walk up to the front door, collecting a tissue on my heel as I go and frantically trying to shake it off, I see the curtain twitch as I approach. I take a deep breath and ring the doorbell. The door swings open, and I am hit by an overpowering stench of alcohol and weed. Standing before me is Mike (likely not his real name, no one uses their real names in this line of work). For this job I become Susie.

"Hey Susie! Come in come in!" says Mike, standing there, resting his hand on his belly with a joint between his fat digits, his beady eyes darting across my body. He is sporting a football top and shorts. He must be a fan rather than a player, as there is no way in hell he's ever running the length of himself let alone ever played football.

'Runaway runaway' jumps into my head, as I think about Emily and what she would be saying to me right now.

Emily is a good friend, the best in fact, always looking out for me and the only person on the planet who knows I do this. She is the person I tell where I am going, so I have at least someone who knows where to find my decomposing body should anything go horribly wrong. But she is also an opinionated, painfully direct cow. She and I could not be more different, we often have quite charged arguments, but it works and I love her dearly.

I smile back at Mike and say hello... he responds with "Oh looky looky, going to have fun with you, nice, very nice, very nice indeed."

To be clear, I am not a supermodel, just a 47-year-old mum of two, a bit saggy, a bit baggy. What Mike says is just standard client stuff. Can't be many clients who have the balls to turn you away and of course they are going to tell you, you're nice. I am also very careful to ensure the photos on my profile, present me in the best possible light, without becoming false advertising. As a marketing consultant, I

know too well the risks of over-promising and under-delivering, but most importantly authenticity. Authenticity counts. But of course, my face is never shown, I do not want my side hustle uncovered at the school gates and I suspect my husband may be a tad upset too.
"Where do you want me?" I ask with a smile.
"Follow me, upstairs" he says and turns on his bare cracked heels and heads for the staircase, I dutifully follow behind. Feeling my pussy drying out, I am sure you could hear it crack like a dessert under the heat of the blistering sun.
"Hope you don't mind the weed babe, you can have some if you like, just helps me you see, helps me last longer, helps me get hard." His arse is about level with my head as he talks and climbs the stairs at a pace that is painfully slow, deep wheezes with every breath he takes. He heads into the bedroom, an interesting space with themed wallpaper on each wall. One is a wallpaper of books like a library, another a field with a cow grazing on the lush green grass below a bright blue sky, and the third is fleur-de-lis patterns.
"Wow, interesting wallpaper," I say. "Yeah I'm a decorator babe, it's what I do."
"Wow, very good, never seen anything like it," (and hope to never again!) "Do you enjoy it?"
"I do babe, but people shaft you all the time, complain about this and that, never fucking happy people, but don't you worry about that babe" he says as he slumps himself on the edge of the bed and scans his eyes over me again while licking his lips and catching his breath.
"Babe come here, let me see you properly."
I put my bag down, slip my coat off and walk towards him, noticing how his stomach is resting on his legs almost halfway down his thighs. I stand between his legs, and he reaches his arms around my waist, slides his hand over my butt cheeks and squeezes them before siding them up to my tits.
"Very fucking nice babe, going to have fun with you, just what I

need, now I think you should deal with this," he says while he stands. Drops his shorts and boxers and thumps down on the bed again, spreading his legs to display his taught hard bobbing bell end just about visible under the doughy flesh.

I smile, and say something like "oooooh" and get down on my knees, spit on his cock and start working him with my hands and trying to work out how to position myself under his slab of flab and still be able to make eye contact (blow job essential 101) while taking him in my mouth.

His breathing gets very laboured, and I am just thinking please don't die on me.

I pause my handwork, look at him, give him a big smile, lift his slab of flab, take a deep breath, lean in and swallow his cock, eye contact out the window as his apron of fat rests on my head.

At the same time, I seem to swallow my brain. Depending on the client this is the norm. I just tune out and do what is needed, allowing my head to go elsewhere. And like falling into a deep sleep I just come around and time has passed without realising.

I am sensing the end, and so I come back into reality to find I am being crushed, he is on top of me, his full weight pressing down on my body, while he jack hammers his hips into me, wheezing and groaning in my ear. A few more grunts, and he stops, laying still, panting, sweating.

"Oh fuck babe, sweet, babe, yeah babe, needed that, you can come back babe."

He rolls off me, leans over to the bedside table and relights a joint. Sighing and regulating his breathing, before removing the condom and dropping it to the floor.

"Your cash is on the dresser babe," he says and waves his hands towards the chest of drawers at the end of the bed. I say thanks and stand up, get dressed, brush my hair and straighten myself out, chatting away to him as I do. I learn he is currently on 'the sick' and his wife is a bitch who doesn't fuck him, he likes 'working girls' as it relieves his tension, and then he can tolerate 'the bitch' for a few weeks.

I grab the money, thank him for his booking and he confirms he won't leave me a review.

"Not because you're bad babe, you're the best, I want to see you again, soon, very fucking soon, but I don't do reviews for anyone babe, digital footprint, doing my environmental bit babe, won't do it babe, soz."

"No problem", I say, "I understand, although I don't think digital footprint is the same as carbon footprint."

"Whatever babes, don't do it for nobody, Wife you see"

"Honestly that's fine, I understand thanks again for booking me, don't get up I will just see myself out"

"Thanks Babe, I will message you."

As I drive home, I am filled with a usual mixed bag of emotions, yes the £150 cash burning in my pocket is welcome. Tom being a typical 13-year-old boy has trashed his school shoes again and this will allow me to replace them. Since Phil lost his job eighteen months ago we have been struggling, really struggling. Our once comfortable life full of relatively few financial concerns shifted overnight to a living hell. The basics most people take for granted now have become carefully executed to ensure there is food on the table and a roof over our heads, anything else can wait. My own business is growing, but doesn't cover the basic outgoings and is variable in nature, so we have been depleting our savings while Phil looks for a job and I grow the business. I am trying to maintain as much normality as possible for the kids.

Yes, escorting may seem like an extreme side hustle, but I exhausted other options first. I considered a 'normal' job, but it still wouldn't cover the bills on my own and would essentially throw away all the time and money invested into my marketing business which is close to taking off and once it does, it will pay more than a 'normal job'. I looked at delivery driving in the evenings, but Phil is often out doing homers to try and bring in some cash and someone

Three's A Crowd

needs to be here for the kids. I explored Etsy and Amazon businesses but you need capital to buy stock, that capital is what is keeping us clothed and fed at the moment it just seemed too big a risk to fritter away on something that is not guaranteed.

So I started with selling my worn panties online, it's cheap and easy, you get £25 a pair. But I soon realised despite the good margins because you have to 'sext' them and chase the sale, wear them, do what they want to be done in them, and post them, you're not making a lot and if someone wants twenty-four hours wear, then your max earning potential gross is £175 a week. I can make that and more in a few hours of escorting.

Emily thought I was insane on the panty stuff, she kept saying, "For fuck's sake Jess, just wear them for a few hours, how will they ever know you've worn them for twenty-four hours and had a wank in them, you're a tit, if they are stupid enough to buy them, milk it you could send ten a day!".

But despite the fact I now sell my holes for cash, I do have standards and would not do it, I can't pretend I have worn panties for twenty-four hours and only do one. I am a slut yes, but an ethical slut.

One day it hit me, escorting could be the solution, I was fucking about anyway (I know, I know, I am going to the bad fire) I am highly sexed and get none at home, I tried for years to fix that, until I could not take the rejection any longer. Phil and I have a marriage of convenience and co-parenting; anything else died a long time ago. So yes I am breaking my vows, but so did he, there is no, 'to have and to hold, to love and to cherish'. He is not interested in me, and frankly, it makes me feel crap. I am not unhappy, he is great, a great Dad and a good friend, but we may as well be brother and sister. And it pisses me off that sexual desire is seen as dirty or less important than other things in a relationship...Why? With his lack of interest, he is choosing a life of celibacy for me. That is not my choice.

So for years I have carefully had my desires met elsewhere, got a buzz from feeling wanted and essentially got my rocks off. Always casual, but sometimes the guys wanted more, and it got complex, I did not want anything blowing up my life, and then it hit me that escorting gets me much-needed cash for doing what I was doing anyway, but with the rules of engagement clear, it was business nothing more.

The word 'escort' is a strange one, let's be frank, it is prostitution. It just sounds less base and probably sits better with those hiring you, they are booking an escort, not a prostitute.

What I didn't think about is when you hook up with someone there is an element of choice, with escorting they book you, and it feels rude to ask for their picture, which is why you end up in situations like today, waking up to being fucked by an Orca whale. If you operated a car wash, you would not turn away a Ford Cortina, you'd wash it, same principle in my head. Perhaps a Ford Cortina is a classic now?

So yeah, Orca sex is not my thing, but these people are humans and just as I need sex and want to feel desired, so do these clients. If I can leave them feeling good about themselves, keep them content in their vacuous marriages, get paid and get a buzz from doing well and feeling desired, it feeds my kids during this tough time... then it works... maybe I do need a cape for my costume after all.

One thing is for sure though, Julia Roberts in Pretty Woman got it wrong... there are not many Richard Gere's knocking about paying for sex with a 47-year-old milf... so Orca's it is.

Chapter 2

Home is Where the Heart Is

As I turn the corner onto my street, the familiar sight of home comes into view. It's dusk, that magical time of day when the world softens, and my house glows warmly from within. The lights in the living room cast a golden aura through the curtains. I can already hear the muffled sound of laughter as I walk up the driveway. It's a sound I both love and dread, a reminder of what I have, what I am working for and the shame of what I have just done. My heart winces at the thought of Charlotte and Thomas ever learning about their mum's secret life. They are my motivation, but it would not be viewed that way.

I pause for a moment, gathering my thoughts, burying that feeling and switching into Mum mode, savouring the last bit of silence before I go inside. Through the window, I can see Phil sprawled out on the couch, the kids, now almost adults, flanking him on either side, all caught up in some ridiculous joke. I can't help but smile. This is what I come home to. This is what makes it worth it. Yes life is hard right now and money is tighter than a tight thing on a tight day, but there's laughter every day. My heart swells with pride and sadness thinking about how my two kids have handled all the change in the last few years. I wish I could have protected them. I have failed them, they have had to deal with changes no Mother wishes for their children.

As I step inside, the warmth is almost too much. They're still laughing as I enter, kicking off my shoes and dropping my keys in the bowl by the door. The sound of my arrival barely registers apart from Ron, who always makes a fuss over me, he is wagging his tail as if he is about to burst. Ron is a ginger labradoodle, named after Ron Weasley from Harry Potter.

"Hey, guys," I say, trying to keep my voice light as I walk into the living room.

"Hey, Mum!" replies Lottie and grins, barely pausing between giggles. Thomas throws a half-hearted wave in my direction, more focused on whatever joke they're dissecting. And throws a 'Yo bro!' in my direction. It always makes me smile, how I have gone from Mummy, occasionally Mother, to Mum, briefly Mate and now Bro. Phil looks up from the TV just long enough to say, "Hey, good day?" and before I can answer, his attention has turned back to the screen and the three of them burst into another fit of giggles.

I am asked about my day most days... but it is almost part of the hello, blended into a greeting, not a question requiring a response, more a stock phrase... an extended hello, with no one interested or listening to the answer. The very definition of rhetorical. I am used to it, and it now just amuses me. I often think I must speak a different language, or perhaps my tone blends into the white noise or vibrations coming from the furniture which means literally no one can hear me. I think to myself, I could just answer:

"Well really busy actually, after potentially securing a new marketing client, which is another step towards getting us out of the shit we are in, I went to the armpit of England and fucked a man that resembled an Orca Whale. I thought at points I would die from being crushed, and I had to swallow his cum which had an unusually unpalatable flavour, quite bitter, almost like vinegar, which is

disappointing, as usually I do enjoy savouring a good deposit of cum on my tongue.... What about you? Any joy with the job hunt Phil? How was school Charlotte? Thomas, how was the rugby match?"

I swear to god I could say that and no one would hear a word of it. Note to self - I must test that one day!

I am well used to it by now, it is ok.

It is obvious they've already eaten, plates are still scattered across the coffee table, and the faint smell of dinner still hangs in the air.

What I say is "How was your day Phil? Any joy with the job hunt?" hoping to hear news of an interview or a job offer.

"Same old, same old, filled in forms, sent CVs, called a few people," Phil replies, barely looking at me. "You know how it is." His eyes are already back on the TV.

I swallow the twinge of guilt that rises in my throat again, then feeling the weight of my kit bag on my shoulder I realise I need to put it away, really can't be having anyone digging about in there thinking they might find a pen to discover a 10-inch dildo, some nipple clamps, a set of 3 butt plugs and a vat of lube. I keep it casual as I walk through the house, heading to the small cupboard under the stairs where it belongs. The bag slips into its designated spot, neat and unassuming, just like everything else in my life. No one ever questions it. It looks like any other work bag, after all, hiding in plain sight. The very best place to hide things.

Returning to the living room, I chat with them for a bit, catching snippets of their day between the laughter and the TV. But after a while, it's clear they're all too engrossed in the show, and I am just a background character in their scene.

"I've got a tonne of work to do. I am heading to the office, bring me cups of tea if you get a chance!" I say though I know no one will.

My office is upstairs and has an enviable view from the window across the trees and over the meadow, but it's too dark to enjoy it now, so I pull the blind down and settle at my desk, filing the post and then power up my laptop, catching up on emails while the sounds of the TV drift up the stairs. It's work, but it's not the work I am thinking about. That comes later, when the house is quiet, and everyone else has gone to bed. Lottie and Tom pop in to say good night on their way to bed, as does Phil. The kids hug me, and my husband just pops his head around the door and says "night". All very typical.

By the time I have cleared the day jobs tasks, it is approaching 11 pm, the house is still. Phil and the kids snore barely audible through the walls. I wander downstairs with my laptop under my arm to the comfort of the sofa. It's time to check what needs attention in my other job, the one no one but Emily knows about. I grab my burner phone to check WhatsApp and open my laptop and a private tab to log into my client booking portal. I refer to this work jokingly in my head as 'slut admin' or 'slutmin'. That is something they don't tell you when you sign up to be an escort, the coordination and admin is a relentless time-sucking job in itself.

As always I deal with the portal first, then WhatsApp. Forty-seven messages since last night... good god, I am always astounded at the volume of people seeking sex. Granted about thirty-nine are from people who I have seen before, looking to rebook or are already in conversation with about setting up an appointment. The rest are new enquiries. I fire off confirmations to some and delay others, as I try to juggle my diary. Then dive into the new messages which are always interesting.

Messages from prospective clients are always entertaining and generally fall into a mix of categories and styles.

1. The polite ones, who write war and peace and type it like a formal letter, they are usually just after a standard fuck, nothing spectacular.
2. The vague people, just send poorly written one-liners like 'wanna fuck you, now' and attach a dick pic. And I am like... yeah did you even bother to read my profile?

Three's A Crowd

The bit where I said I have a life and other commitments? That booking must be made in advance. What makes them think I am just sitting around waiting for such a message to then go *"Thank fuck, let me know where to come and I will be there, oh and see the dick pic you sent, wow, seals the deal, be there in 5!"* No chat, no information, nothing about age, or what they wish to do. These I don't reply to, the only ones I feel are fair to ignore. My profile clearly states my age range, how to book and what services I do and don't offer.

3. The fetish folk - My favourite, I love discovering people's kinks, so wide, so varied, and I have a strange drive to provide for them, as some requests are so wild or unusual I have a bit of pity for them. They likely get blanked or told to piss off by the majority of escorts, which must be awful not to have your kinks accommodated and accepted. It is bound to affect their self-esteem, so provided it is not outside of my limits, I always engage with them to find out more. I have plenty of clients who are grateful for me because I don't just go... "Oooo no fuck off." We are all the same, we just want to be seen and accepted, as us.

4. And then there are as my friend Emily would call 'The chancers'... people with a sob story about being down on their luck and needing a fuck, but can't afford my rates, so could I do just a hand job for £5 or a 'blow and go' for £15? I am a sucker for these stories especially given my own finances. I know the pain of going without. Granted more along the lines of a new bra than a fuck but still it's hard counting pennies and deciding what has to give. Emily says I am a *"fucking fool"*, but for me, if it works in with being on the way to a bigger appointment then what's the harm? I get a few

much-needed extra pennies, they are happy, and they don't take long.
   5. The direct people - 'Hi I am looking to book you to cum in your mouth without a condom, please let me know how to book you.'

Nothing majorly interesting in there tonight, an armpit fetish guy. I have had that before, but this one wants hairy armpits he can wank into... I am serious... as I say, you get a huge variety, it is another window into the world of humans, a whole different dimension, that most don't know exists all around them. You could be sitting next to a hairy armpit wanker on a train and be none the wiser. I don't have hairy armpits, but he was willing to pay a higher price for me to grow my hair. I considered it briefly, but then politely declined, not because I didn't want to help the guy out, but because it would affect my ability to secure other bookings, hairy pits are not usually something guys are into and so despite his offer of more money, I would be at a loss versus the normal appointments I could conduct in the time it took me to grow my hair.

There is also one from my Orca who must have messaged me the instant I left, thanking me again for today and asking when he can see me again. I am not sure I can stomach the stench and a crushed body again, so I decided to think about it and mark it as unread to buy me some time to consider my options. I learnt early on to mark things as unread, or some people give you dogs abuse... *"Hey bitch, you ignoring me?"* or *"Slut, am I not good enough for you? Hookers can't be choosers - Reply!"*. I even had one saying *"I hope you catch aids"*. Moron, you can't catch Aids, it's HIV!

I don't want to go back to the Orca, but I do have that warm glow, he wants me back... that feels good. I don't feel good often and I cherish those moments. The only other one that really catches my eye reads: *"I am going to fuck you slut until you fucking break bitch"*. I feel that familiar groan in my groin. I have no idea why, guess it is one of my kinks but being spoken to like a dirty bitch, especially if it's then saying they will do whatever regardless, and dominate me. It makes my pussy do 'loop de loops' and I can feel my pants getting damp. I respond and ask for more detail.

I shut my laptop down and open up WhatsApp... another 9 messages, WhatsApp tends to be people I know, have seen before and have a bit of a relationship with. Even though it's a burner phone, I am careful who gets my number. The WhatsApp chats are the ones I look forward to the most. My goal is to build a core base of good clients in WhatsApp and come off the portal. A varied client base of decent guys and couples that provide me with a range of experiences to cater to my wider sexual needs.

Most WhatsApp messages come in after 11 pm when the Wives have gone to bed and the Husbands are setting up their next unloading appointment or wanting a bit of escape from the mundanity of their life and marriage.

Szymon has text he is Polish, and we have a bit of good banter. I see him regularly and use him as a bit of a confidant, he cares about me and knows I want to provide exceptional service, that is super important to me, in all lines of work. He often asks what I have been up to and helps me make decisions.

There is no slut school, no book on 'escorting 101', no 'hookers for dummies' so having him and a few others on hand for advice is invaluable.

His conversation went like this:

> What slut tales from today?

>> No Cock'O'Thons today - met a new client, he was nice but a bit minky and so fat. I thought I was going to die under the weight of him!

> How minky? How fat?

>> House was stinking, stench awful when I went in and I would say pretty fat . Not quite needing craned out of his house fat.. but fat!

What did he want?

> Fairly standard, blow job, fucked my pussy. But I am not sure I will go back tbh

Why the fuck not? Did you let him down? Did you swallow his cum?

> Of course I did, I wouldn't not, you know I am a cum addict but his was not the nicest I have had… and no, don't think I let him down, he has already messaged saying he wants to rebook…he was minging… his pubes stank, when he was on top of me his fat was cool, clammy and wet from sweat…I know that is not a nice thing to say, but he really turned my stomach.

FFS Susie, you're a whore, you're being paid, it is not about you. How do you think he is going to feel if you ignore his messages and don't confirm a return visit? Fat fuck like that needs bitches like you, where else is he going to get it?

> There are lots of us on that site, he has his pick and a lot of them are younger and fitter than me.

Bitch - he chose you and wants you back… what kind of slut are you, if you turn away cock… message him back right now, tell him you are sorry for your slow response, that your a bad bitch who was considering not coming back, you forgot your place which is service cock and for that you'll give him 15 mins free on top of anything he books and a free pass to do whatever he wants to you. Make the guy feel good not bad. Men book whores to feel good, fucking do it. You want repeat clients, here is one asking for it FFS. Your dignity matters shit. Swallow your pride and his cum. I don't care if it's degrading and humiliating. Get it done.

> Oh god! Do you think he feels bad that I haven't replied?

Yeah, guy like that will have issues… fucking message him NOW and send me a screenshot of it when you are done.

Three's A Crowd

> OK

I open my laptop and log in again, bash out a reply to Orca and hit send, grab my phone and photograph the sent message and hit send to Szymon. By the time that is done, Orca has replied instantly, suggesting a few dates and times and wanting to fuck me in the ass. I respond and confirm the date and time and log off.

> Thx Szymon, he replied and is happy, date confirmed

> That's better bitch, now fuck off, but before you do, send me a pic of your cunt, I need a wank

I quickly lift my skirt, slide my panties to the side, pull open my flaps, snap and send.

> Good slut x

I have a quick chat back and forth with a few others when a new message pops up from 'McHorn' as he is called on my phone. That was his profile name on the client portal, no idea why, but his real name, **if** he is telling me the truth, is Sam.

If I am honest, I have found myself hoping for Sam's messages every night, sometimes they come, sometimes they don't, but he has been messaging with more regularity.

He booked me a few months ago, it took some co-ordination, as from what I can tell he is on a tight leash by his demanding and controlling Wife, plus he lives in the middle of butt fuck nowhere, so not just around the corner. He wanted to experience a proper throating, plus my other two holes. I learnt how to throat in my thirties and was happy to make that dream come true for him. I still gag a lot, some guys love this, some don't.

He is one of those anal guys, in more ways than one... he was annoyingly thorough before booking. Felt like I was applying for some Secret Service government job or something. I had to send a picture of my mouth, hands, and answer a gazillion questions plus confirm and reconfirm 20,000 times that:

1. I could throat and
2. I was happy to throat…I even had to send him a voice note saying just that, so he could keep as proof to protect himself should I ever decide to fuck him over… I was like, seriously Sam, I am a whore, you can do anything you want to me. You're paying.

I had told Emily about him, and she said I was a fool, "tell him to fucking book or fuck off."

If I am honest I thought he was going to be a bit of a nightmare client and definitely had him pinned as a fat balding, beer gutted middle-aged man. So when he walked in and I saw these incredible eyes, deep brown, with a fire in them, but also something softer I was blown away. If I was footloose and fancy-free and saw him in a bar he would have caught my eye.

It is always a welcome relief when you get a client that you are actually attracted to, it does happen, but it is very rare, most are in the fat, balding middle-aged man camp. Some clients are just money, just something to get through, and some are juice-inducing BOOM, he was juice-inducing BOOM ON SPEED.

There was quite a bit of rough foreplay before, I ended up lying on my back, head hanging over the end of the bed, eyes fixed on the target, when he told me to *"open your mouth you fucking bitch"* and ploughed his mighty fine looking fat cock into my throat, ramming it past my throat barrier and unloading. He never made it to my other holes, and we just lay and chatted for the rest of the time.

He was interesting, he told me about his Wife, how much he loved her (and you could tell he **really** did, the fondness in his manner when talking about her glowed out of him, I wondered what that must feel like to have a man who loves you so much they can't hide it when they talk to others about you), how smart and successful she was, but he couldn't live without sex (relatable), and wasn't looking to change his situation (also relatable). His relationship had been sexless for a lot shorter period than mine and I warned him about not doing something about it.

"Don't let it get to the stage mine is at, sort it before it is too far gone."

It was clear he loved her very much, he just needed to reconnect with her, I didn't want it to be too late for him, it felt sad. Madness to think she had a guy who loves her properly, and she just didn't want to simply open her legs for him. I don't understand that. OK, I open my legs for anyone, but if someone loved me the way Sam loves his Wife... my legs would be wide open, but only for that man.

We even touched on politics, a topic most strangers avoid. The conversation was easy and comfortable. When he left I sat for a bit with a terrible feeling of emptiness.

That same day I had three other clients booked. He had a long drive home and whilst I was driving to my next client I was thinking that it was such a shame that he was so far away as he would have been a great regular client. I didn't expect to hear from him again given the distance, he got what he came for. I had also forgotten to ask him for a review! I needed to get better at that, and I had insisted he not pay my full rate. I was very conscious how far he had driven and that he hadn't got full access to everything he had wanted as time ran out.

When I told Emily I discounted it for him, she was livid with me saying I was 'a tit' for not just taking the cash and then going on a rant about how he was a 'fucking cunt' for not saying 'no' to the discount. She said *"he is paying for your time, he still used the full time, his fault not yours if he didn't make use of that hour, bet he's a rich bastard... rich cunts are always tight as fuck, your skint clients tip and appreciate you, your wealthy ones try and negotiate."*

I did hear from him again, not immediately, a few days later. So we now messaged with some regularity. He revealed more about himself and so did I. His real name **was** actually Sam, he even gave me his surname and his Wife's name in time, shared what he did for a job and what she did. I think we had an understanding and empathy for each other's 'dead bedroom' situation.

Obviously I googled his Wife, she had that effortless beauty about her, you could tell she was classy, exactly who you'd picture pernickety high standard hot Sam to be with, I am sure when he is with me, he likes to imagine it's her, who wouldn't. Over time, I shared more about myself too, to a point. We sent filth to one another and had even seen each other again, but the second time he did not pay, he had wanted to get to know me and 'move past' a paid relationship.

He was on a business trip, and it tied in with what I was up to. His room was paid for by his company and I got to stay in it for free. I had tried to book my own separate room, I didn't want to take advantage, I know people tire of me and I knew he just wanted to fuck me, not spend time with me and would need to call his Wife and Daughter in privacy, but he insisted.

We had dinner together (went Dutch), chatted loads and fucked like rabbits. He had uncovered my real reasons for starting this work a few weeks prior with his relentless 'Columbo' style questioning and was accepting of it. Emily despised him. She kept saying...stuff like;

"What the fuck is he playing at? He's using you Jess, don't be sucked in, why should you fuck him for free? He knows your situation, knows your work, he is just messaging you to play you, keep you on side, so he can get an escort without the cost, tight bastard claims he can't afford it, bollocks, claims he doesn't have his own account, and he has to sneak cash out over months to be unnoticed, also bollocks. He says he likes you, he doesn't, he just wants his cake and to eat it and not pay for it and knowing you're a whore, who is also married is no threat to the love of his life, perfect set up for him - cunt! Don't go getting any ideas and thinking some random guy from 100 miles away is going to be interested in you. You'll only get hurt. At least paying clients are honest, they just want to fuck you, he's not, I'd have more respect if he just said, I just want to fuck you and not pay for you, don't fall for it."

We had fallen out about him a few times. Despite her anger and bitterness at the world, to my eternal frustration she often made sense and some of what she said was hard to argue with. I knew deep down this was the truth. And I gave up on believing in love and me being eligible for that many decades ago, so there was no danger, I didn't allow my head to wander into that headspace, not that I thought he loved me, that in itself was laughable. He was clearly head over heels in love with his Wife. But I did l enjoy his company, found him hot, so why wouldn't I want to fuck him? As long as I could still earn enough outside of that, what was the harm?

When a message from 'McHorn' popped up on my phone, I jumped on it. He was asking how I was and what I had been up to. I told him I had a client today, and had just finished some 'slutmin'. He was messaging to see when we could meet again, he had worked out there was a monthly marketing networking event he could get away with going to overnight, and it stacked against my main work too. So we were talking about that and planning our next meeting. He also asked about my slutmin and so for a laugh I shared with him a few screenshots of the enquiries I had had.... He immediately jumped on this one:

> Check out this new enquiry...knows how to treat a whore 🙄
>
> I am going to fuck you slut, until you fucking break bitch

You're not going to let him book, are you?

> Why not?

Look at the way he is talking to you!

> A lot of clients talk like that, it is just kink. 🫤

No, I don't like it, I don't want you to see him

I leave it there, I don't want an argument, he doesn't get it, I need the cash and this is not out of the norm. I have known Szymon a lot longer than Sam, Szymon knows I need the money and has my best interests at heart to ensure I earn that cash. He is used to the language clients use when messaging me. Sam, although having seen escorts plenty of times, has maybe not had that level of exchange with them. But it does make me pause and think, I like Sam and feel bad considering going against his word. I decided I will chat with Emily about it tomorrow when I meet her for coffee, see what she thinks.

Sam (McHorn) then starts texting filth to me, I don't know what it is, but his words are like a bolt through my body, even from 100 miles away on a text. We message back and forth, it's good fun, but I realise the time and say I have to get to bed. He messages back and this has become a new thing in the last few weeks, I know it's coming and I feel uneasy.

> Before you go, one last thing

I wait while the typing indicator flashes...

> You are important, you matter, I care about you, please be safe, promise me you won't see that guy, you really matter to me, even gods have their favourites, good night, sleep well x

Good night x

I head to the bathroom, to wash my face and brush my teeth. It's now past 1am and my eyes are heavy. As I wee, I consider what a strange thing to be messaging to a girl you have paid to fuck, and know she is a *working girl*. He doesn't **know** me, nobody but

Three's A Crowd

Emily knows me, I make sure of that. I know Emily is right, he *is* playing me, giving me all the bullshit and lines, to keep me coming back and avoid paying.

Men don't talk like that. 🙄

If a client you really connect with is rare for an escort, then surely an escort you really connect with is rare for a client. Difference is I get paid, whereas it costs him (well it did), so you can't blame him. He knows I have operated on a fuck buddy unpaid basis before starting this work, so think he is just after that really, but I do wish he would be straight and not imply he gives a shit beyond a low level friendship and some fucking. Regardless, I am not going to say no, as he REALLY turns me on.

I climb the stairs feeling the exhaustion in my bones. I head to bed, careful not to wake anyone. Phil is fast asleep, his back turned to me, as usual. I slip my clothes off, PJ's on and slide into the bed. It is a super king, the space between us like a chasm. We haven't touched each other in years, not since we conceived Thomas over twelve years ago. Phil is a good guy, he's funny, I care for him, but our marriage is more like a partnership of convenience than anything else. Co-parenting. He doesn't seem to notice much else about me.

My mind wanders back to my messages with Sam, what he said about wanting to fuck me and fill me with his hot sticky spunk. About what a dirty bitch I am, I lay there as my hand wanders and imagine his hands on me again, his flaming eyes boring into me, him pinning me down and taking what he wants. My fingers are sliding in and out of my pussy, curling around my g-spot and my thumb rubbing my engorged clit. I need a release. I silently and rhythmically work on myself, imagining Sam and the look in his eyes as he does a final few thrusts and empties his balls. It pushes me over the edge, waves ripple and radiate out from my groin as I climax.

After I lay there, staring at the ceiling, listening to Phil's snores, I can't help but feel the irony. They say home is where the heart is, but as I drift off to sleep, I know that Phil is not home.

Chapter 3

Aspartame - Sweet But Dangerous

The bathroom is filled with a thick, comforting mist, the sound of water cascading from the shower head the only noise I can hear. I stand beneath the stream, my body still as the hot water pours over me. The warmth envelops me, a temporary balm for the deep aches in my muscles. Orca really worked me, the knots of tension slowly loosening under the steady flow.

I tilt my head back, letting the water soak my hair and trickle down my face, mingling with the tears I didn't realise I was shedding. Each drop feels like a small release, carrying away the heaviness I have been feeling, the week, the months that have piled up on my shoulders. I close my eyes, trying to focus on the sensation of the water, to lose myself in the simple, physical relief. But my thoughts refuse to be washed away so easily.

As the steam curls around me, I think about the life I've built, piece by piece and how it is falling apart piece by piece. Sometimes I just get engulfed in sadness, a sadness at what has gone before, what is now and wondering what lies ahead. This morning it feels like the weight of everything is too much. The responsibilities, the expectations, the dreams that once seemed so attainable but now feel distant, like fading echoes of another time. I wonder if I took a wrong turn somewhere or if I missed something vital that could have made all the difference.

The water keeps running, hot and relentless, like time itself, and I stand still, lost in the flow of my thoughts. I think about the people in my life, the ones who depend on me, the ones I've lost touch with, and the ones I miss deeply but can't bring myself to reach out to. I think about the sacrifices I've made, the parts of myself I've given away without even realising it, and the dreams I've shelved, hoping someday I'll come back to them.

Will that ever be? I wonder. Will I have the time, the energy, the courage to pick up those pieces of myself again?

The water begins to cool, and I shiver, my thoughts pulling me back to the present moment. I'm tired, so very tired, but there's something in the steady stream that makes me feel just a little bit stronger, a little bit more like myself. I sigh a deep, weary breath that echoes in the small space.

As the last drops fall, I stand there for a moment longer, letting the cool air wrap around me and I start to shiver. Maybe I don't have all the answers, and maybe I never will.

But for now, I have a plan.

One step at a time, one foot in front of the other. Do what needs to be done, to keep a roof over our heads and food on the table.

Encourage Phil to understand how bad our finances are in the hope he will up his job hunt, a conversation I feel like I have had a thousand times, but the penny is not dropping for him, I am unheard, again. He is trying, but I would not say he is trying his best. I need him too.

I must focus on delivering for my marketing clients and growing my reputation to establish a secure, consistent and steady income, subsidising the shortfall with escorting until things are more secure.

Three's A Crowd

That is the big plan, but today I have 3 major jobs that need to be done.

I must put together the marketing plan for Q3 for a comfort menopause clothing range I have on my books. I have done the work on it, but now need to put it into a usable and digestible format, it will take the bulk of the day. I enjoy this stage in the process of pulling it together to make it live. I haven't booked any 'other' clients today as I knew I needed the space and time to deliver on this.

That is the constant challenge at the moment, 'other clients' put cash in my pocket the same day, while my marketing work can take months for the payment to be received on delivery of the project. I get a deposit at the start when they engage my services, but the balance is on completion. So it's a budgeting challenge.

As the menopause brand project is close to completion I have done less 'other client' work to give me the time needed to complete this and because of that, cash is low, very low.

That is the second job of the day, look at what can be afforded for the week ahead and plan it.

The part of the day I am most looking forward to is coffee with Emily. We tend to speak most days, I would be lost without her. She will be dying to discuss the details of yesterday's 'client', and how Phil's job hunt is going, and no doubt have a go about Sam, plus I want her thoughts on that client enquiry Sam doesn't want me to see.

I get dressed and drift downstairs to screams.

"MUM!" screams Lottie, "Tom is being a prick."

"That's what little brothers are for Lottie," I say as I hit the button on the kettle.

Tom grins and nods, Lottie rolls her eyes and storms off to brush her teeth. Phil has already left, heading into town to pop into some job agencies, thank god.

Lottie comes back and shouts, "Tom I am going and not holding the bus, bye mum" and she walks out the front door slamming it behind her. Tom picks up his bag, shouts bye and follows behind her.

I pour myself a cup of hot water and sit for a moment sipping it and scribbling on a pad, some last-minute thoughts I had about the marketing plan. Then I grab Ron's lead and hunt him down, he sees the lead and runs in the opposite direction. I have never known a dog like it, the laziest dog on the planet. One of the reasons people don't like having a dog as a pet is they get up early, wanting to be let out which means lying in becomes impossible. Ron is the last to get up in the morning. Lazy assed dog. I eventually catch him and head out for a high-speed walk through the fields.

Once home I head up to the office and get to work. Time flies as I focus on the different themes and treatments, and all the mediums we will use for reach and engagement. As well, as send a few confirmatory emails to the brand ambassadors I have recruited to ensure they are still committed to the proposed exposure. Mid-morning my burner phone pings... Henry...

> Hey Susie, what slut adventures are you on today?

>> Ahh, off duty today

> Well I have just been paid so can we sort a date?

>> Sure, when are you thinking?

> Sunday? Premier Inn, 3pm? I will book?

>> How long?

> Hour please x

>> That will work, what is on your Wishlist?

> I want to spank that ass of yours, fuck you real rough and have you suck me off, piss in your mouth, then cum on your tits. 😏

Three's A Crowd

> Well, that's what I am for! Your friendly local super whore! 😈

Lol, yes look forward to it.

I also want to talk to you about Busty Black another escort who is up for me booking you with her…and can you help me with a dating app bio? Plus I can get tickets for a talk on 'bondage', specifically rope work and rigging, wondered if you'd like to come with me?

> OK, well let's chat Sunday. You back at the training academy? Surviving?

Yes, kids these days, fuck wits! Honestly!

> Have fun! x

I run down to the kitchen and top up my hot water, and decide to pause the marketing plan and face the music with this week's cash. Shit… looking at £95 for food… kids need £3 a day for school lunches, leaving £65 for the week's shop. I log onto Asda and play about in the trolley until I can get it to work. Figuring out a bit of bulk cooking and repurposing, like using the mince to make bolognese and shepherd's pie bulked up with lots of vegetables. The only way it will work is if I duck out for the week. I am fine with that, I do enjoy a liquid detox once in a while. I click a few more buttons, check out and then get my head back into the marketing plan.

PING - my burner phone goes again - new message from 'McHorn'. Oh, I think to myself, that is unusual. He doesn't like to message during the day, he's made that very clear, he works in an open plan hot desking space. But more recently he has been ignoring his own rule and messaging more frequently, I have to confess I like it.

> Hope your marketing plan is going well. Got the green light for the 5th too! So will book a hotel if you can manage?

My god, how can Sam, a guy 100 miles away remember it's a big day for me finishing and submitting this plan, but Phil doesn't even mention it, and yet he sees the late nights and long hours I put in.

> Getting there thanks, it's looking good. Great news on the 5th. I will be there! x

Can't wait to slam myself into your ass again.
Shame we have to use condoms.

> My ass is in dire need today I tell you!

Will respond ASAP

> OK x

I ignore the condom comment, not much I can do about it. He is very much a germaphobe and had a scare with a previous escort when a condom broke. So I can't blame him. Getting an STD would be hard for him to explain at home. I hate it when he mentions stuff like that as he makes me feel like a real prostitute (which I know deep down I am) and often when I talk to him or message him I don't feel like I am, which is kind of nice.

He often replies by saying 'I will respond ASAP'... it makes me feel like I **do** matter, like he is saying, "I have seen this, I am not ignoring you, it **is** important, bit snowed under but the first thing I will do when I get chance is message you because you matter".

Wow, just wow.

And he has begun to respond fairly quickly, from a few minutes to half an hour. His ASAP response is probably not what he really means. It is more likely that Emily's theory is correct. It is just a text management system to shut me up and keep me controlled and contained in the space he wants me in.

My reply hangs as delivered but unread... I check a few times over the next few hours to see if he has read it, he hasn't, and I have that sinking feeling, and the dawning that I know deep down I am not important after all. I curse myself for even thinking I might be. Or even wanting to be, I know what this arrangement is.

I put the final touches to my plan, attach to the email and hit send. That feels good, love that feeling, I include a review date for next week, where I can go over anything they need clarification on, in a meeting once they have had time to digest.

Emily arrives "Hey bitch" she says, and I click the kettle, as it heats up, I lean against the counter, hands wrapped around a mug, waiting and listening to Emily harp on. The room feels cool, the chill of the day still clinging to the air, but the warmth from the kettle somehow seems to seep out, curling around my fingers, and creeping up my arms. I can feel the change in the air as the water inside the kettle begins to react. My body responds in kind, the warmth spreading through my hands and into my chest. I breathe in, feeling the coldness in my lungs mix with the rising warmth. The heat becomes more intense, spreading deeper into my muscles.

I slap a tea bag into my mug and a spoonful of coffee into Emily's. I think about how our hot beverage choices mirror our personalities. I am hot sweet tea, gentle, warming, forgiving, a hug in a mug, Emily is dark, aggressive, bitter and gives you a much-needed boot up the bum. I click 5 sweeteners into my mug and begin to pour the water in. I realise I have not been listening to Emily when her voice cuts into me.

"For fuck's sake... 5 fucking sweeteners? You fucking serious?" she barks.

"What?" I reply "I like sweet tea!"

"Yeah ... but 5?!"

"I like it?!"

"You like a lot of things Jess, not all of them good for you...just like fucking randoms...might feel sweet but still dangerous...same with this aspartame - sweet, but everyone knows it is carcinogenic"

"Well coffee, strong and black is highly caffeinated and

everyone knows caffeine increases your heart rate and can cause palpitations."

"Tea has caffeine in it too you dumb ass. You heard from that cunt Mchorn? Another example of something you enjoy but is dangerous!" says Emily.

Emily is just so black and white, no real shades of grey, certainly not fifty! She calls a spade a spade, tells it how it is and does not hold back. It can be uncomfortable, and often she can be bang on. If her opinion is the opposite of mine, I can rant as much as I like, but she just doesn't listen. I often just nod in agreement to shut her up.

I know where this is headed, another lecture on Sam incoming. Her eyes are hard, intense, cold, and angry and my chest tightens as I await the debate. I know deep down she is a softy and always comes from a good place, the most loyal and protective sidekick you could ask for.

She has been hurt by men, I don't know the details, she won't share, it's made her how she is. She won't admit that either, but I know she uses that experience and knowledge to inform those she cares about, to protect them from experiencing the hurt she has. Her default mood is angry and challenging, she is the dictionary definition of resting bitch face. She is the complete opposite to me and I enjoy her company for that reason.

It's fascinating to see such vehemently projected arguments.

Conversely, I avoid arguments and conflict at all costs.

I envy her ability to be straight and literally not give a fuck about how it lands. Content that if the message is needed, then to her, it doesn't matter, if it is needed you say it. Simple!

She is not well-liked (not that she gives a fuck!). She can be cutting, and misunderstood, but if you just look a bit deeper, you discover her motives are sound and she has a golden heart.

"Yes, I was chatting to Sam last night, actually. AND he messaged today."

"Filling your head with shite again I assume?"

"He is nice Em, honestly"

"No, he is a cunt, wanting into a cunt and doing what is needed to get that, without parting with a penny."

"He says I matter... he says he cares."

"Yeah, a guy from an adult escort site, so picky he interrogated you before deeming you worthy of his time, the guy who only cares about getting his end away despite what he says, words mean nothing Jess...you know this, you have learnt this, actions count not words, this only works in **his** favour , you don't get paid, he takes time away from your earning clients, can't you see? He is married, and he doesn't give a shit, you're marginally better than his right hand, he knows you have fallen for his crap. He doesn't have to worry about you being local, imploding his life, kicking off, bumping into you, he said himself he saw maybe three, four escorts a year maximum, and now he has got one he is aiming to see each month for free, it's a win for him ."

"Actually, he is worried about me, he thinks a new enquiry I got sounds a bit off, Sam didn't like the way he spoke to me, the new guy's message said something like 'slut I am going to break you', he doesn't want me to book this guy in."

"Hold the fuck on Jess... you serious? You are seriously considering taking this dipshit's advice, a guy you've known for a few months, a guy that underpaid you?"

"Because I **told** him to!" I protested "It was only fair!"

"Then... asks to move 'beyond a paid relationship' after a few texts... How many other escorts has he tried that on with? Struck fucking gold with you didn't he? Because no other dumb ass would believe that crap and now telling **you** who **you** can fuck... he is not your pimp Jess. You're independent for a reason, honest to fuck wake up, you need the cash, how often are you still going without food? Or cutting your own hair because you're putting every penny to the kids?"

"I am not short of enquiries... and he doesn't think it's respectable the way he messaged me, maybe he is right."

"Coming from the guy who, if my memory serves me correctly, said 'open your fucking mouth bitch'... wake up."

"That kind of chat, I find a turn-on, you know this, and he knows that too. He even messaged me today asking how my marketing proposal was going, Phil never does that."

"Because Phil the phallus, has his head up his arse... McHorn is a manipulative player...it **may** not be conscious... but he is getting exactly what he wants from this... what are you getting?"

"I like him"

"Well stop, right fucking now, open your eyes and see what he is doing. Think about his motive, he doesn't like you, not really, thinks you're alright, sure, he likes your holes and how willing and filthy you are, you're nothing but an escape from his trapped life. What qualifications does he have to comment on the quality or intent of a client message? Last time I checked he isn't a female escort who has experience receiving similar messages and going to appointments with no drama. Fuck him."

"I will fuck him, haha! So you think I should say yes to this client?"

"Hell yes, don't let some guy you just met, have seen twice, control what **you** do."

"I don't want to upset him."

"Why do you give a fuck? He doesn't. He doesn't need to know Jess, go, do the appointment, he is 100 miles away and would never ever know. He's not your partner, husband or boyfriend, you're not betraying him, he knows what you do, you owe him nothing."

"Yes, ok, you're right."

"Now tell me, has Phil the phallus got a job yet? Has it dawned on him, if you don't get some cash coming in and super fucking quick, you'll lose the house?"

"He is out at agencies right now actually, he is trying really hard, but just not having much luck, think his age and peppered CV are making it hard. I keep telling him about the money, but I don't want him to carry that burden alone and feel like I am pointing the finger, he is already feeling shit about being made redundant."

"He **needs** to do something, like don't be proud, take any job, literally anything, some cash better than none right? You've done it!"

"Yes any cash is needed, and he doesn't know I have done this, not exactly dinner table chat, but if he takes just any job his CV will look even worse and may give him a problem getting a decent paid job and explaining it... surely better to secure something with decent cash longer term than pish cash and getting trapped in that level of work, he's better than that."

"No, you need cash, any cash right now, the redundancy money is almost gone, how does he not realise this? Tell him, or do you want me to have a word?"

"I deal with the money, it stresses him out and, no...no way, he'd be mortified if you spoke to him, I will do it."

"Good, and Jess, if you don't, I will know... I know you."

"I know"

"OK, yesterday's client, is he one you're moving to WhatsApp as a potential regular? How many regulars are you at?"

"About seventy-three, oh Emily, yesterday was awful, I am a bad person, my heart sank when he opened the door, he was smelly and huge, my muscles still ached from trying to ensure my chest did not collapse under the weight of him."

"So not a regular?"

"Well I chatted to Szymon about him and he said I should see him again because, poor guy probably does the rounds booking escorts but none ever go back to him."

"Szymon... really? Are you taking advice from 'Szymon the flaccid' now?"

"Why not? He has used a lot of escorts, knows how it works and has seen and heard a lot. I'd hate to think of anyone facing that kind of rejection... imagine not even being able to pay for someone to fuck you!"

"Honest to fuck, is that your problem?"

"Well no... but I don't want to hurt the guy."

"You **_don't_** know him! Who gives a fuck!?"

"Well actually, I do... I couldn't do that to someone."

"God Jessie, you're actually like Aspartame, your far too fucking sweet and don't know the damage your doing."

Chapter 4

The Mist Falls

Emily leaves just as the kids pile in the door, the warmth from my tea fades, and I am aware that the air feels cool. The kids fight for air time as they each tell me about their day. Oh the torment of teens, you forget, it's not easy.

Thankfully tonight is no 'mum taxi' duty. No Rugby to drop off at.

Phil walks in moments later, and talks about a few things the agencies are putting him forward for, we should hear next week if he gets an interview. I cross my fingers, toes and eyes in my head and do a quick calculation. If he gets an interview, and it's a two-stage process he could, if successful, start in 2-4 weeks which means cash in around 6-8 weeks. It feels a long way off and relies on him securing the job. He's lost so much confidence I worry about how he is coming across. I try to 'gee him up' and praise his efforts and show my confidence that he is a grafter and will get something soon. His eyes tell a different story.

I fire off a couple of messages to Sam, (cursing myself as I know Emily is right). Mainly random stuff, things I think he will find funny, memes from the 90's and some filth links. I realise I think about him a lot and when something happens, like the other week when a warning light appeared on my car, he is who I think of to ask for help and he does.

I leave Phil and the kids to make a start on dinner and head down to Asda to get my click-and-collect food order, my time slot is 5-6 pm.

I pull down the side of Asda to the click-and-collect point, it's late summer and the air still has some warmth to it. I show my confirmation to the man who brings out the shopping. For once I have actually remembered carrier bags. This is progress, the number of times I have come without and had to handball individual items onto the back seat and boot, then load them into carrier bags in the drive is unreal. I am much more forgetful these days, I put it down to a busy mind and having too much in my head. I am convinced a head can only cope and store so much, then when something really important goes in, something less important has to fall out, like carrier bags. Well, today is a win, when the guy comes back with the plastic boxes filled with my shopping I am primed, bags in hand.

As he stands watching, which always makes me feel under pressure to go faster, I load the shopping into the bags and chat away with him. He is working until 8 pm and then hitting the city with his mates. Oh, how I miss that life. I don't get out these days and I miss it. I see work people on both sides, my family, Emily and that is literally it.

SHIT! I think as I put the last item into the bag and thanked the guy, who wandered off to deal with the next car that arrived, I didn't see any butter in there. I riffle through the shopping. Darn, I am right. No butter! I know we don't have any and Lottie needs it for her bagels, I need it for batch-making soup and for macaroni cheese. I know my account is down to about £1.15, not enough. Fuck, how did I miss this, I could have ditched bananas or something. I jump in the car and move it into the main car park to free up the click and collect spaces, then turn off the engine and start rummaging through the central console looking for change. Another win! I found about £1.90 in change, that should do the trick. I climb out of the car, click the lock and start walking across the car park towards the entrance, swerving a rowdy group of teen boys.

The evening air had been pleasantly warm, wrapping around me like a soft, comforting embrace. But then, as if the world had flipped a switch, the temperature plummeted with a sudden, almost violent shift.

The warmth seemed to vanish in an instant, replaced by an intense chill that cut through the fabric of my clothes. It started as a faint tingle, almost imperceptible, but quickly morphed into an all-encompassing cold that seized my body. I could feel it first in my bones, a deep, unsettling chill that seemed to echo through my core. My skin prickled with goosebumps as if the cold were trying to pierce through every layer.

My teeth began to chatter uncontrollably, and I couldn't seem to stop the violent shivers that wracked my frame. It was as though the cold was a living thing, moving through me, making my muscles tense and spasm against my will.

I pulled my jacket tighter around me when suddenly I felt a fast and tight grip on my forearm, wrapping around me with icy bony fingers.

"Help me" came a soft but panicked voice, I spun my head round to see the icy fingers belonged to a young girl, 15 maybe 16. The look of her was haunting. Her frame was frail and bony, her eyes drawn, the skin on her fingers wrinkly and dry, you could see every joint in her hand, her skin almost translucent revealing the faint blue lines of her veins underneath.

I jumped and pulled away, but she tightened her grip, "Please, please help me."

I snap into focus, "What's wrong?"

"You need to listen, you need to see," the girl said, her eyes boring into me, her eyes held a heaviness, like a storm cloud that had settled behind her gaze, casting a shadow over what might have once been a bright, vibrant light. The pain was unmistakable, a raw, aching sorrow that seemed to linger just beneath the surface. It wasn't just in the way her eyes met mine, but in the way they seemed to reflect a raft of burdens carried in silence. I felt an uneasiness, my stomach flipped and spun with nausea. The sadness her eyes contained was even more profound, a quiet, unspoken despair that filled the space between us. Her eyes held a distant, almost haunted look, as if they were seeing some- thing far beyond the present moment, memories, regrets, or wounds too deep to heal. It was the kind of sadness that wasn't just felt but lived, etched into her very core.

"See what, listen to what? Are you alone? Is there someone I can get for you?"

She gave a soft smile, it felt like a subtle, heart-wrenching contradiction that made the smile feel like a fragile mask, hiding the truth.

"Only you can help me, Jess" She said.

WHAT THE FUCK! How does she know my name? I was starting to get freaked out. I have never seen this girl before, she had a familiarity about her, but all teens these days melt into one, was it one of Lottie's friends? No, I know them all. A guy walks past us and gives us a concerned look, then puts his head down and shuffles off.

"I am sorry, I don't know who you are, you must be mistaken... I can't help you, please go home and be safe."

She grips me tighter, I start to panic, heart pounding.

"Jess, no you have to help me, you're the only one, don't you remember?"

Fuck this, I place my hand over hers, gently but firmly prising her hand off my arm, it feels like I may shatter her fingers they are so fragile. And I pull away.

"No, no please, help me, listen, you need to listen, you need to see, you can't hide any longer, it's Misty, save me, Jess, can't you see it?"

One moment, I was standing upright, my heart racing, every thought tangled in a chaotic web of fear and confusion. The next, the ground seemed to lurch beneath me, the world tilting violently as if I had lost my grip on reality itself. My knees buckled, and I stumbled, reaching out for something, anything to steady myself, but my fingers met only empty air. My vision blurred, the edges of the world dissolving into a haze of dizziness, and before I knew it, I was falling.

The impact was jarring, the cold, hard ground rising up to meet me with a force that knocked the breath from my lungs. I lay there, disoriented, my pulse pounding in my ears, the world spinning around me. For a moment, everything was a whirl of confusion, my mind struggling to catch up with what had just happened. Then, through the haze, I became aware of movement, people rushing towards us both, shadows looming over me, voices urgent and concerned.

I blinked, trying to focus, and saw a handful of people rushing toward us. Their faces swam into view, expressions of worry etched across them as they knelt down, hands reaching out to help. I felt their touches, gentle yet firm, as they tried to lift me, to check if I was alright, but my mind was elsewhere. My thoughts raced back to the girl I had just been speaking with, the one who had sparked this sudden panic. I looked around frantically, searching the surrounding faces, looking for her, but there was nothing. She was gone.

A cold dread settled in the pit of my stomach, the panic threatening to rise again. It was as if she had never been there at all, leaving me alone with my fear, surrounded by strangers whose kind eyes and soft words did little to quell the rising sense of unease. I reassured them I was fine, and I was, apart from an unnerving eerie sensation. Satisfied they left me be, and I wandered into Asda to locate the butter and found the fridge aisle at a warmer temperature than the change in weather outside.

When I climbed back into the car to head home, I still had a strange sensation. I sat for a few minutes going over and over what had just happened, searching the car park for the girl but found nothing. I don't know her, she was clearly unstable, I think she said Jess, but I probably misheard her, there is no way she could know my name. Maybe she said 'Save me Les' or 'My life is a mess.' Clearly, that is true. Poor girl, I hope she gets the help she needs. My mind drifts to Lottie. I may be failing in a lot of ways, but at least she is full of laughter and not wandering supermarket car parks scaring old women.

I get home, unpack the shopping, Phil and the kids help, I don't mention my encounter, I don't want to unnerve anyone and have settled on the fact it was just a random incident. I make myself a cup-a-soup and join them to watch a family favourite - Young Sheldon. It is a welcome distraction and slowly the uneasy feeling settles and dissipates a little.

I should do some work, but I am worn out. My knee is pulsating from my fall. So I don't go to the office.

Sam messaged me when he left work, he left me a voice note apologising for not responding to my text faster, but he had been in meetings, and then he went on to tell me all about exactly how he was going to fuck my ass, balls deep when I see him next. I replied in kind, with some filth and how that made me feel including an audio of my fingers in my pussy so he could hear how wet his voice notes made me and they did.

He messaged again at about 8 pm, saying he missed me and was looking forward to messaging later. 'Missed me?!' What is he playing at?

He was on 'books'. It seems he and his Wife rotate between one doing books and one doing bath. He has a daughter, Beth who is 7, sounds super smart and like her Dad, says what she thinks, is

Three's A Crowd

strong-willed and like all kids a bit of a handful at times. I realise he has started to message with increased frequency. I am not complaining. He now messages first thing in the morning, a few times a day or responds to me, on his way home, at bedtime and then after 11 pm. It is almost reliable.

After the house is still once more and the kids and Phil have headed to bed, I fire up the laptop and check my messages on the client portal. I use a site called, 'Grown-up Work' (GW) for short. It is very poorly built, and difficult to navigate, and their mobile site is even worse. I feel like contacting them and suggesting they get a UX (User experience) expert in. I know loads of UX specialists I could recommend, who are highly skilled at improving the customer journey on a website, making sure the UX works seamlessly. With everything online these days it is such a vital element of any website or users give up and drop off your website.

My heart sinks at the volume of messages, I know it shouldn't, it is work…and money, but it's so hard to stay on top of, and I have a weird standard about replying to every single one, apart from those that want me to 'come to suck them off now.'

I trawl through them all, confirming dates and times, cross-referencing other bookings, telling some I am booked for the next few weeks and putting them into a folder titled 'next'. I am working on this system now. I worked out that if I book too far in advance and an important high-fee-paying marketing client needs a meeting, then I inevitably have to undo all my GW bookings and rebook them. It becomes a slutmin headache.

The guy who wants to 'break me' has responded and suggested some dates and times. We settle on one and I mark him in my diary, feeling a strange tinge of guilt about going against Sam's wishes. But I know Emily is right. As much as I like Sam, and I **really** do, he doesn't totally get my situation fully and it is my decision how I organise that work. I don't tell him how to do his job.

There is also an enquiry for the dungeon gang bang I am organising. It was Szymon's idea, and he got me to put it on my profile a while ago. He knows I have done gang bangs before, and he knows I like rough sex. He has erectile dysfunction and can only get off to more extreme things. My sessions with him involve no fucking at all, as he literally cannot get hard enough to penetrate. But he can ejaculate.

He wants to see me 'brutally gang banged'. We plan to book an overnight stay at the sex dungeon in his city, well I will stay over, the guys come for 5 hours, I will need recovery time. We are recruiting 4 other guys all paying £250 each, meaning I will get a clean grand after paying for the venue, not bad for 5 hours of work. They will have me from 9 pm until 2 am. Anything goes for the event, except crossing my hard limits which are; no permanent damage, any marks must be able to be covered by clothes, no scat, no one under 37, and they can't take my lingerie off.

This guy seems ok, and not afraid of being rough. So I asked for his no. and explained I was passing to Szymon to provide more details. Szymon wants to vet everyone, make sure they are 'up to the job' but also confident they will respect my limits and things won't get out of hand. It is also to be bareback, but each person must provide tests with clean results within a week of the date of the event and bring their ID, which must match the results. I am not daft, I know the risks and mitigate them as best I can. I have a standard condom policy unless they can evidence they are clean.

I close the laptop, grab my burner phone and fire up WhatsApp. I still have a slight cloud hanging over me, from meeting that girl. Although I am now starting to think I imagined it, I am under a lot of stress and the body can react in strange ways.

I bang out a text to Szymon about 'Tigercock' who wants to be considered for the GB and Szymon is thrilled. He is excited that if this guy passes the next phase in the recruitment we will be on four guys and only one more to find. Szymon likes to message them and talk to them on the phone to ensure they are genuine. He says if 'Tigercock' seems ok he will add him to the gang bang group in WhatsApp. You'd think getting 5 guys to come and do what they want to a willing slut like me would be straightforward, but it's not. Finding the right people and dates to work for all is a challenge, Szymon is getting increasingly frustrated with how long this is taking.

Henry has sent me a load of stuff about 'side boob' and how he is going to miss it as summer comes to a close. He says he has bought some extra toys for our meeting on Sunday and wants me to come in my 'slut dress', the one from my profile on GW. He also tells me more about this rigging and shibari event he wants to go to and is looking for a plus one.

I like Henry, but I really don't want to be his plus one. He is single, not long separated from his girlfriend and sometimes I think he forgets he is paying for me. He phones sometimes (always checking I can talk first) and a couple of months ago, he said how he told his pal who was visiting from Australia about me and how this guy (an experienced Dom) said, 'Don't let that one get away' and he confessed to me that he didn't tell him I was an escort and he didn't know why.

I mean sure, if I had a life outside of work, GW work and being a Mum, he would be great to go for a few beers with. But it would never be more than that. I like dominant men, controlling, take no shit men. He claims to be a switch, but in truth he is more submissive, he tries, bless him, to be dominant, but he is quite apologetic about it, which ruins the vibe! I ask the date and time of the event and then tell a white lie that it would be hard to get away on a weekend evening due to family life. I can tell he is gutted and I feel super bad.

McHorn pings on my phone, my stomach gets butterflies and I sign off from Henry and Szymon, do a quick response to some others and check his message.

> Hey, did you get your marketing plan finished?

> Yes thx, how was your day?

> OK, couldn't stop thinking about you!

> Ha, thinking about my holes you mean!

> Naturally, but also you x

Emily's words still ring in my ears and my head goes blank. I actually don't have any thoughts and don't know what to say.

> You OK?

> Yes

Still can't think.... Fuck think, think, think, say something! I frantically scan my brain, I need to change the subject. I don't want to tell him that, I can't stop thinking about him too... I mean what's the point? Plus I know what he is saying is a lie, I am not a fool. If I protest and say, no you weren't, I look like a dick or that I am fishing, it might lead to him saying nice things to convince me he ***was*** thinking about me. I don't do moosh and I can't take compliments. I know what I am supposed to say, but saying 'thank you' for something you don't believe seems disingenuous. It also sounds arrogant. And then it is protocol to compliment back and I am shit at that.

Ha, that reminds me of a message conversation he and I had a few weeks back. He asked me how his cock compares to others I have encountered in my work.

Men like to know where their cock ranks, and it's a difficult question to answer. How do you do it and get it right? If I say, yours is the biggest fat cock I have ever seen, I would be lying. And he would know I was talking shit too. Men don't get that once you get past a certain size, it's not good, bigger is not always better. I remember a client once, his cock was scary, cockzilla sized and it hurt. Now Sam is not small, and genuinely, of all the cocks I have encountered he is a firm favourite. He is cut, and I love the head of it. I think cocks are mostly cocks, but become king cocks depending on who is attached to them, what they do with it and what the person is like. Probably why unsolicited dick pics rarely do it for women. I mean lets be honest, they are not always very pretty, although I have to confess Sam's is, his is a thing of beauty. It actually makes my mind go mushy, and my pussy liquifies, plus it just fits each of my holes perfectly, like it was designed for them, like a key in a lock.

I settled for saying 'above average' and it has become a thing between us, a bit of an 'in joke'... I was trying to hit the sweet spot of letting him know his cock is amazing and I love it without blowing smoke up his ass. He seems to find me funny and 'sexy' (whatever that is) neither of which are intentional.

> Your brain gone?

> Yes, sorry

I sent a flat-line gif.

Sam asks a lot of questions, difficult questions, he doesn't just want to know things he ***really*** wants to know things...he asks a question then drills down and drills down. Then he says nice things and all of that causes my brain to stall. He has worked that out and is patient with it. So a flat-line gif is not an unusual thing for me to send.

My brain is still searching through all the files in my head looking for a topic of conversation, every file I open contains only a blank bit of paper, then bingo, found one, with the word 'drumming' on it. That will do!

> How was your drumming lesson?

I remembered it's the night he goes each week. Go me!

Good thanks, although I had zero time to practise this week. Natasha has given me a load of jobs to do, so never got 5 mins. Honesty I am like her house servant. I literally get up, tidy up the kitchen, make breakfast for everyone, get Beth ready for school, turn her car on for her, take Beth to school, get there late as Beth is slow, get to work late, work, get home, do washing, clear crap up, run Beth to clubs, tidy up after dinner, house admin, hang things, get Beth to bed, research things that she has requested, sit for 5 mins, get glared at, barked at, told my tone is off, maybe grab a bit of TV. That's my life, FML.

> Sounds like adult life to be honest!

Yeah, but it's never appreciated or noticed. Don't get me wrong, she cooks and irons. I do everything else. Just draining sometimes this hamster wheel of life. It is like she doesn't see me, listen to me, value or appreciate me.

> I am sure she does x

Funny way of showing it!

> Maybe talk to her?

I've tried that, and I just get told I don't understand how stressed and busy she is. She just doesn't listen and it is always my fault. Do you know I went to hug her the other night, she just patted my head.

> I'm sorry, wish things were better for you

`It is what it is, anyway, are you really OK?

> Yes...why?

Just had a feeling that something was not right.
MHBB2

MHBB2 (Man has big brain too) is another in-joke, in response to me claiming to have a big brain (BB). Truth is this man really ***does*** have a big brain.

My mind is a bit blown. How is he picking up on that? I thought about telling him briefly about my encounter with the strange girl in Asda car park, but decided against it, it's just so random.

> No, all good!

I lie and hold my breath.

> In that case, show me that sloppy cunt!

> Hold...

I dutifully do as I am told, and we message filth back and forth for another hour before I say I have to turn in. Once again I get...

> OK but first and please hear me, I want you, I need you, you're very important to me. Don't forget it x

> Sleep well. Night x

> Night x

I want to message back and say, it's OK, you don't need to say this stuff, I know you're lying not out of badness, just trying to be nice, but truth is, you just want to have some filthy fun together and that's OK, just drop the other stuff, I don't need it.

But I don't say that. I am not like Emily. I rarely share what I really think. I have found when it comes to personal relationships, keeping your mouth shut is the best option, voicing your thoughts and feelings only leads to trouble.

When I slide into bed, I can't get Misty out my head, I toss and turn, her face haunting me. Who does she think I am? ***Did*** she say my name? No, I don't know her, she is mistaken. I do hope she is OK. I wonder what she thinks I need to remember. I decided to stop thinking about it, it was just a random incident. I don't need any more worries and I am certainly done with remembering stuff... Sam and his 'Columbo' style questions reminded me of some things I wish I could have kept as forgotten a few weeks back. He is a terrible man for rifling through my stuff, I have some things neatly filed away in boxes in my mind never to be opened again. Sealed and padlocked... but Sam began picking at the lock.

Chapter 5

Cardboard Shadows

Sam's lock picking started quite early on with me. I have throughout my life become skilled at body-swerving difficult questions, changing the subject, and diverting attention. But he misses nothing. Always highlighting again and again anything I have missed until I answer. Then if I answer, and he is not satisfied with my response he will recharge and go again.

He is the kind of person who seems to have an endless stream of questions, always probing, always digging just a little deeper. It's a bit overwhelming, borderline irritating as if he is trying to pry into parts of my life I hadn't planned on sharing with anyone... ever. But there's something about the way he asks, like each answer I give truly matters like he's not just asking for the sake of it, but because he genuinely wants to know.

It's a strange mix of feelings, mildly annoying, yet oddly affirming. It's as if, in his relentless curiosity, he's telling me that my thoughts, and my experiences are important. I might find myself rolling my eyes at the sheer volume and intensity of questions, but at the same time, I can't help but feel a little-seen, as if my words hold weight like someone finally cares to listen and understand.

A while back he asked some probably quite normal and natural questions. But the kind of questions you have not had to face as a married adult for a long time, these questions stop in married adulthood and tend not to be the focus of a couple's dinner party.

It was really late one night, and he asked how old I was when I lost my virginity, followed by something like 'good experience?' I had probably not been asked that question in over 20 years. Hookup and clients have no interest in that.

I don't know what came over me, but I told the truth. It happened over a few days of messages, but I weirdly didn't jump to my well-rehearsed usual stock answer this time. I had developed my stock answer a long time ago, but I am severely out of practice now, telling it. I don't know why I didn't just say the usual, perhaps it's because I ***was*** out of practice, perhaps it's because I was ready, after all this time to voice the truth or perhaps it was because I knew he would find the truth.

The messages went something like this;

> How old were you when you lost your virginity?

> 15, you?

> 17, good experience?

FLATLINE

> Was that the wrong question?

> No, no wrong questions, you can ask what you like, but I need to go to bed. I will answer tomorrow. Sleep well, night x

> Ok, night x

The following evening he picked up on it again...I was more ready for it.

> So, virginity?

Three's A Crowd

> No, not great experience, against my will

I am so sorry

> It's ok, a long time ago, dealt with, doesn't affect me. Just cocks in holes, I do a lot of that! 😉

Who was it?

> Boy from school. But it is ok, in the past and over with, not bothered. Boxed up and in storage.

I don't know why I admitted the long-buried truth to this man, a man I had only known a short few months. And that was it, he had his tool in the lock, working away at the mechanism and managed to snap open the padlock. From there, he kept on going, digging, asking, poking, prodding.

It unexpectedly affected me. I have, like a lot of things in my life, and I am sure many people do, put things away that don't serve you, or are just too painful to think about. Until that question was asked by Sam, I had almost forgotten about that box. It just didn't enter my consciousness and hadn't for a long time.

But something happened, Sam is the first person (outside of Emily, and we had not discussed it in decades) I ***ever*** told, and maybe it was that. It caused my own head to start peaking into that forbidden box. Just lifting the lid slightly and looking, then slamming the lid shut. The box started to rumble, once quiet, covered in dust and forgotten about, it seemed to be screaming for attention. This was not just when Sam asked his infuriating questions, but at any moment in the day or night, I could feel the box shaking, rattling, the lid bouncing as if it was trying to burst its contents.

Sam was gentle, but relentless, asking more and more and like Columbo...'One more thing'... it was like he wouldn't rest, or settle until he fully understood.

Most people tip-toe around stuff, especially sensitive stuff, not wanting to upset, not Sam. He wanted to know who. Where? How? When? Why did no one see? Did I report it? If not, why not? Why didn't I tell my Mum? Any part he learned about that, in his eyes had a flaw, or nonsensical element, he would interrogate further. Sometimes it felt like he doubted my truth, that he thought I had made it up and that upset me. I remember when it all happened my biggest fear was not being believed, and I was facing that fear now, it was an uncomfortable ride.

So he learnt, over the period of weeks and months that the most popular, hottest boy in my year, chose me. It was an Easter school disco, I had not long turned 15. He smiled at me across the hall while some more confident teens danced to Michael Jackson. He beckoned to me to follow him outside. I was stunned, I knew my standing in the school, fat, unpopular, geek girl, boys like Darren did not associate with the likes of me. I don't think he ever glanced my way, let alone spoke to me until that point and I still don't know why that changed that night.

I followed him outside, and he was lovely. He gently kissed me, stroked my face, and looked into my eyes, that was my first-ever kiss. His hands started wandering, and I began to feel uncomfortable and voiced it. Then he changed.

The change in his face was sudden, startling. Just moments before, his eyes had been soft, filled with warmth and a gentle kindness. His lips curved into a tender smile, the kind that put you at ease, and made you feel safe. But then, something shifted. The sweetness drained away like the light leaving a room, and his expression hardened.

His eyes, no longer warm, narrowed into sharp, focused slits, a fire igniting behind them that hadn't been there before. The softness in his gaze was replaced by a piercing intensity, driven and unyielding. His jaw clenched tightly, the muscles in his face tightening as if his very features were being pulled taut by some unseen force. Even his posture changed, shoulders squared, chest out like he was preparing for a battle. The tenderness was gone, replaced by a cold, aggressive determination that radiated from him with a palpable energy. It was as if a storm had swept across his face, leaving in its wake a fierce, unstoppable force.

I felt on edge, the atmosphere changed. And he just went for it. First pushing me down against the wall and slamming his cock into my mouth. I protested gently at first, but my panic increased in line with my physical and verbal reaction. Then dragging me across the field, kicking screaming, fighting, throwing me onto the ground and pinning me down with the weight of his body he entered me. I eventually gave up, and my spirit and fight drained. I just lay there, tears falling, longing for it to be over. He was cruel with his words, he jiggled my fat belly, and spoke about how I was lucky someone like him would even touch someone like me. How disgusting I was. To my eternal shame, I orgasmed. I didn't know at the time it was an orgasm, I had never had one before. It was some weeks later the penny dropped, and it further confirmed I did the right thing not telling anyone, as it could only mean I had enjoyed it. He made me thank him, he told me no one would believe me if I reported it. I knew in my heart he spoke the truth. And I berated myself for ever thinking someone like me could be wanted by someone like him.

I lay there afterwards, silently sobbing, sore, scared and numb. I had to pick myself up, go back into the community centre and clean myself up, remove my torn tights, clean mud off my face, and legs and try to sponge it out of my clothes. I had to endure a lift back to my parents with friends, all chatting and giggling about the great night we had all just had. I was shaken and silent, but it was just put down to the effects of the diamond white cider I had consumed.

That night as I lay in my bed, stunned, sobbing, feeling unclean, and wincing at the bruises and cuts as they brushed against the sheets, I had to make a decision. Would I risk telling anyone? It took days to clear my head and think straight, I was in a state of shock for some time. You would think when faced with something like that, the decision would be easy. It is not, especially at that age. On the day I skipped off school to go to family planning for the morning after pill, I also went to the library to look up what to do. When I read that post-attack tests needed to be done within 72 hours of an incident, I knew all was lost. Without physical evidence, it was even more unbelievable, it was fanciful. Seeing Darren at school confirmed this further, it was back to normal, I didn't exist, he ignored me as usual, and I started to doubt anything had even happened. Plus I was drunk at the time and perhaps was not clear enough to him.

Darren didn't just take my virginity that night, he took my confidence, and my dreams and changed my heart. Being attacked by Darren had consumed me, ate away at me, necrosis setting in. I was wallowing, and I didn't think anything could get any worse.

Darren never touched me again.

To this day I can't say the word, I can't type the word, I can't use the word, my body tenses if I hear the word. Madness eh? It is ***just*** a word. Saying the word would mean I admit it all actually happened, and why would I want to do that? I like to believe my alternative story, the one I have told everyone my whole life, where I lost my virginity at 16 with my boyfriend Chris. It was a special moment, although a bit of a let-down sexually. A much more typical and palatable teen story. One you could tell and no one batted an eyelid.

This stuff was 30 years in the past now, and I am proud of how I handled it alone. It was not easy, and I became anorexic for a few years, but that got sorted out via therapy when my parents clocked it. Eating disorders are often the symptom, not the cause, and I navigated this with general tales of school cruelty which were all true, that satisfied those around me without having to reveal the truth. I had gone on to get a degree and worked my way up in a marketing firm before branching out on my own. I liked to just think of it as cocks in holes, something I had done many times since and was not a big deal.

Married with 2 kids, life had turned out OK, apart from the fairly recent financial crisis. It was clear to me that I had dealt with the past, boxed it and filed it away, where it could never hurt me again.

That was until Sam started rummaging through my boxes. I kept saying to him, 'Get out my boxes' or 'That one is in a box, let's leave it there'. And sometimes he would, he would let it go and change the subject, but he'd always come back to it.

Admitting this to Sam has caused unwelcome feelings I didn't want to think about to creep in, my body became a battlefield. My chest, was tight, like a heavy weight pressing down on me, making it hard to breathe deeply. My stomach knots up, churning with unease, and sometimes it feels like there's this dull ache that just won't go away. My shoulders tense, almost as if I'm bracing for some unseen impact, and my jaw clenches without me even realising it.

I can feel the tension crawling up the back of my neck, almost like a pressure that won't let up, making me restless. My hands might start to fidget, my foot tapping out some anxious rhythm, trying to shake off the discomfort. It's like my body knows before my mind does that something's wrong, and it's reacting in these subtle but unmistakable ways. I can almost hear the pulse in my ears, quickening with every thought I try to push away as if my body is trying to keep me from avoiding what I don't want to face.

It's frustrating because no matter how much I try to ignore it, those feelings seem to anchor themselves in these physical sensations, making it impossible to completely escape.

Even when my mind is elsewhere, my body remembers, holding on to that tension, that unease, as if it's waiting for something to happen. But I remind myself, it's a long time ago, I was drunk, and it was just cocks in holes. I don't know why it is affecting me, I guess it is thinking about something I had not thought about for a very long time.

I don't tell Sam that chatting about this has bothered me, I don't want him to feel bad, and I don't reveal that sometimes as he questions, I find tears pouring over my cheeks. I am grateful for the facelessness of typed messages over video calls. Sometimes as well as filth pictures he will ask for a picture of my face. I hate that, I mean first of all, why? My face is irrelevant, I know he is really only after my holes, so why bother with my face? And secondly, if he asks for it when I have been blindsided by a random unwelcome emotion I never knew I had, what would he think? I am supposed to be his escape, his release, if I start behaving like an emotional psycho he will just recruit a new escort and ditch me, I will not be his burden, he has a nagging Wife for that, that is not my role in this. Plus he would no doubt then ask a gazillion more questions if he knew I was upset.

If he requests a face pic, I can usually dodge it by saying I am outside in the dark with Ron while he pees, or sometimes if he is particularly insistent I can quickly open up an editing app, and turn my eyes from red to white, erase the tear stains on my cheeks and send. The most important thing is he knows I am OK, I am strong, I am unaffected by my past, I am not a problem, I am filthy, I am fun.

I wouldn't want him to change how he treats me or take pity on me. I don't know where these feelings have come from, perhaps speaking the truth for the first time, but I doubt it. I moved past all that a long time ago, it is more likely I am just burnt out, fatigued, and stressed. After all, I am working two jobs, one of which is physically demanding, but combined with the day job is a logistical nightmare. I am seriously worried about money and how I can keep this family afloat. I am heartbroken every time I look into my kid's eyes, knowing what they have had to sacrifice and praying they can't see the truth about their mother. So yeah, I am entitled to be feeling a little overwhelmed and emotional sometimes, who wouldn't?

That said, occasionally I need a kick up the bum, but it's not all bad. I am extremely lucky, I have two healthy kids, and a supportive husband who is fighting tooth and nail to secure a job, we still have a roof over our heads, the best laziest dog in the world and food on the table. I am growing my marketing business and eventually that could, in time, support the entire family and all our worries are over. One step at a time, one foot in front of the other. Focus on the goal.

I just need to carefully sidestep the shadows that my boxes cast in my path and not get caught in them.

Focus on what is good. That is my mantra, find the good and there is so much good to be found, sometimes you just have to look a little harder.

Sam is a good thing in my life, he really makes me happy and able to forget all my troubles, I feel like 'me' around him, he is my escape too, away from feeling unwanted by my Husband, away from the mundane and daily stresses.

The last time I saw him, which was the first time outside the client hooker relationship, is a memory I cling to and replay in my mind if I am feeling sad. I now also have the 5th of next month to look forward to (27 days and 9 hours to go - not that I am counting!).

The thing I didn't like about seeing him last, was the hotel we stayed at. It is one I often use for clients and so it reminded me that I am a part-time prostitute, and I really just wanted to pretend otherwise for a while. But every seat in the bar and couch in the foyer, riding in the lift and doors we walked past in the corridors of rooms, held a memory of a face or event, so the truth was blatant and unavoidable.

But the thing I **did** enjoy very much was the 12 hours of multiple orgasms.

Chapter 6

The Second Cumming (and then some!)

I have to confess to being really nervous before meeting Sam for the second time, excited too of course and I describe it to him as 'nervcited' which really summed it up. This feeling was unusual, different.

For as long as I can remember, I've lived in a state of emptiness, moving through life like a machine, devoid of emotions. It wasn't always like this, but somewhere along the way, I started to notice how little I felt. It was as if I had become a droid, mechanical, efficient, unfeeling. There was a kind of comfort in it, though. Life was simple, and predictable. I did what needed to be done without the messy interference of emotions. I thought maybe this was just who I was, that I had somehow transcended the chaos of feelings, operating on logic alone. The only exception to this my children, there is a saying, 'You're only as happy as your unhappiest child' and that is true. Phil, we have been through so much together, and I worry and care deeply about him, I don't want these 3 to ever have any undue pain and I work hard to ensure that is the case as best I can, sheltering them where possible. So despite my unscrupulous actions, I do care for my husband. However I shut my own emotions off from Phil decades ago, so hurt by his disinterest and lack of effort, I just had to stop feeling, so it didn't phase me any more. It works and is a calmer way to live. I concluded many moons ago, I am not the full package and never will be. Darren would have never been seen dead with me and cared not a jot. Phil doesn't want me sexually. I don't seem to be able to have both. I accept that, it is better to be honest with yourself about who you are than tell yourself lies and be delusional.

With the very nature of driving to a stranger's house for them to pay money to screw you, you have to be a bit disconnected from your feelings. I have no fear, no worry, no hope, no excitement, literally nothing and I think that helps me be able to do this as a side hustle. The only emotional feelings I get are when I get home and guilt penetrates every pore. I know that if my secret life were ever to be discovered the pain for those three would be impossible to recover from, regardless of the intent behind it.

But recently, something has shifted. I've started to feel things again; small, insidious cracks in the armour I've worn for so long. A flicker of sadness here, a pang of fear there. It's unsettling, like a dark, creeping presence that I can't quite identify. These emotions, don't fit with the way I've lived. They're foreign, invasive, and they make everything more complicated and challenging. I cry, randomly, uncontrollably, I haven't cried in decades either, aside from really sad or happy sad films and the heart tugging Christmas adverts. I don't like this change, I have always prided myself on not being a 'crier.'

I find myself questioning the very nature of emotions. Why do we even have them? What purpose do they serve when they only seem to bring pain or discomfort? It was easier when I didn't feel when I could move through life with a kind of detached clarity. Now, every little emotion is like a wrench thrown into the gears, disrupting the smooth operation of my existence.

Happiness is fleeting, if it comes at all. Mostly, it's just this uneasy tension, this gnawing anxiety that I can't shake. It makes me wonder if emotions are worth it, if they're truly necessary. I had adapted to life without them, finding they didn't bring anything to the table. But now, with these feelings creeping in, everything feels chaotic and disordered.

I want to go back to the way things were, I don't want to keep moving forward with this newfound awareness. Emotions, are supposed to be what make us human, but right now, they just make me wish I could go back to being that unfeeling droid, to the numbness that kept everything simple.

Sam is travelling to his work meeting via train, but as I am driving and the road picks up the train route part way along my journey, we agree I will collect him at a station en route, and we will travel the rest of the way together. I have a work (real) meeting I am attending the next morning while he attends his work meeting, then I will drop him at the same station for him to head home.

I am not collecting him until around 3 pm, so I spend the morning firing off some emails before throwing my bag in the car and fitting in a GW client late morning. It's a regular so easy. I pull into his drive and walk up to the side door to be greeted by three bouncing, barking springer spaniels and him shouting at them.

"Hold on Susie" shouts Dave as he opens the top half of the stable-style door and I reach in to pat the dogs.

"Hiya," I say

Dave wrestles the dogs into the side utility and then opens the lower part of the door and lets me in.

"How are you keeping?" I ask, Dave is a mid-sixties guy diagnosed with an incurable brain tumour and is extremely lonely. His daughter lives with him most weekends and stays away during the week for work. His Wife passed away around four years ago, and he was diagnosed shortly after. He says that he is going to 'have fun' while he can and wants some companionship and action. He is saving every penny to ensure his daughter gets a good inheritance, but I am his monthly treat, for him, to bring him a bit of joy in his final months or years.

"Not bad Suz, changed drugs again, shake me and I'd rattle!"

Sometimes he is in good spirits, other times he is quite flat, he wants to talk, and he has even cried on me. I admire him, despite what he is facing, he has it mostly together.

We pause in the living room, an 'L' shaped room, very dated with an old flowery sofa, armchair and coffee table hugged around a fireplace, a dining table and chairs and off in the corner, a desk. The living room has three large almost full-length windows looking out across the countryside and there is no denying it is a fantastic view. He doesn't tidy, his house is cluttered and busy. But he is also dying and tired so you have to give the guy a break. A tidy home is probably not a priority when faced with your mortality.

"I hope the new drugs make things easier for you" I say.

He smiles and moves towards me, putting his hands on my shoulders and looking at me fondly. It's unsettling, like he is looking into my soul.

"You are a good un Susie sucks!" he says with a twinkle in his eye. He has called me that since our first meeting as he said he had never had an experience like it.

"And you're beautiful," he says. I hate when people say things like that, god that makes me sound like it happens all the time, like it's such a burden, that is not what I mean and not the truth, it's **not** something I often hear, and I don't know how to respond. Stuff like that is just so disinguous and awkward. I have a mirror, I know what I look like. And unless I win the lottery and get some plastic surgery, I can't do much about how I look, nor do I want to. I don't hate how I look, I am alright, I pass. But beautiful, I am not. I am not ugly either, all my features are in the right place, and I don't have any abnormalities, like a wart or a giant nose, but I don't have that 'magic'. You know, the spark that the truly beautiful people have, that just shines effortlessly, natural beauties. You wouldn't notice me in a crowd and that's how I like it.

I have blue-grey eyes, blonde shoulder-length hair and standard-issue features. I am average. Not stunning, not pig ugly, just average and that's OK. I don't bother about my face either way, can't do much about it. My body I can though, and I try to keep in shape which is getting harder post children and with my advancing age.

As these thoughts run through my head I think of Sam when he first asked for a face pic of me before meeting the first time as I do with everyone, I sent it with a disappearing timer on it (I am careful, I am a mum to two after all and don't need my secret life revealed). I messaged him, as I do all people who ask for face pictures.

"I won't be offended if I am not your type, you can always put a bag over my head."

Sam found this comment astonishing. But it's true, people don't book escorts for their faces, it's the other bits they are interested in, obviously a stunning escort is a bonus, and I am sure they get a lot more overwhelmed with their inbox than me, god I hate to think! Sam said I was his 'type' and he would never put a bag over my head. Not that most decent humans could answer any other way. I did have a client once who preferred to put a bag over my head though.

"Well let's see that beautiful cock" I smile at Dave and slide my hand to his crotch and can feel his throbbing cock already pulsing and screaming for attention.

Dave slides his hands down my shoulders and arms and then slips his hands around my waist, pulls me in and feels my ass, and slides his hands back round my waist and up to my tits. I am in a cup-less one-piece under my blouse and his thumbs linger over my nipples stroking them, they tighten and stand to attention.

"Beautiful," he says again.

I smile and kiss him while rubbing my hand on his cock. I pause and unbutton my blouse so he can see and feel my tits skin on skin. He fondles them for a bit and then slides one hand under my skirt and slides his fingers in me.

"Jesus Susie you're never not wet, so hot."

"What can I say, I like cock."

Then I place my hands around him, kiss him again and slowly go down on my knees, sliding my hands down his body until I find his belt and waistband and begin undoing them, all the while looking up at him, making sure I do my best to keep my ass pushed back and my back arched. I learnt that by watching porn, guys are visual, which means they can still see your ass and tits. It's not an easy position, but it is these little things that count and add up.

"I want in your cunt this time Susie," he says, as I look him in the eyes, smile and take the head of his cock into my mouth.

He always says this, it's a shame, a lot of older guys struggle to cum, but not Dave. In all the time I have been seeing him, he has never penetrated me, and he gets most annoyed about it, swearing next time he will start with my cunt, but never does. He makes the same mistake, every. Single. Time.

I start sucking, pushing my tongue on the underside and taking more of his length into my mouth then slowly withdrawing and curling my tongue around his frenulum. When I am working the head, the shaft is sloppy from my mouth, I use a hand to provide rhythm.

"Easy Susie!" he says

I give his shaft a full-length lick sit back on my knees and grab one of my tits, stroke and squeeze it and look at him.

"Do you want me to stop?"

"No," Dave says, panting a bit.

So I lean forward again and lick down his shaft to his balls, taking each one in turn and swirling them around my mouth with a gentle suck. Before sliding back up taking his full length into my mouth and bobbing with a bit more pace. Switching it up with tongue action, hand action and a mix of suction. Making sure I am doing my best to look at him.

I can taste his pre cum, and it's not long before I feel his balls and penis tense and his muffled groans begin to rise as he explodes into my mouth.

"Fuck!" He moans.

Three's A Crowd

As he shudders and the last drops splash into my mouth, I carry on sucking and gently stroking, as his breathing calms. I know that most guys need more careful handling after orgasm as their penis becomes extra sensitive. It feels wrong and rude to just stop dead.

He strokes my head and hair as he settles himself. He then reaches down and holds out his hand which I take, he guides me to standing and looks at me.

"Jesus Susie, not again, although thank you, you're incredible, but next time... cunt... OK?"

I feel a warm glow wash over me. He is happy. And I feel useful.

"Sure," I say.

"Want a cuppa?" he asks while pulling up his trousers and sorting himself out.

"That would be lovely, thanks, if you've time?"

He smiles "Of course" and I know that although he has enjoyed having his cock sucked to completion, this is the bit that matters to him. He heads to the kitchen shouting back.

"Usual? Black Coffee?"

"Yes please" I reply

I rarely have tea when away from home, I don't like to be a hassle and a simple black coffee is quick and easy for people. It also means I don't have to reveal I take five sweeteners in my tea which most people gaul at.

I pull down my skirt, button up my blouse and park myself on the sofa, he brings through two steaming cups and sits next to me. Placing an envelope and the drinks on the coffee table.

"Before I forget."

I hate this bit, especially when it's someone like Dave. He just wants a friend, and he has to pay for it.

"Dave, there's £180 in here not £150, make it £60, you didn't take long" I say as I count the money and split it.

"No way, not having this conversation with you again, this is my treat money and I want to spend it on enjoying you, worth every damn penny, and you deserve the extra, you're not just beautiful, and amazing at blow jobs, and I am sure your pussy is to die for if I ever make it in there" he laughs "but you're not like previous escorts, foreigners who can't hold a conversation and just feels like they are getting through."

"But Dave," I protested.

"No Susie, I won't hear of it, now tell me how's that dog of yours?"

We chat about dogs for a bit, and then he updates me on his daughter, hospital trips and sorting out his estate. I stay nearer 90 minutes in total, but it's pleasant and with good clients like him, well everyone in fact, it feels a bit too cold to just say right, 60 mins up, I am off. At a suitable pause in the conversation, I announce I really must run. He looks a little saddened but collects the mugs and sees me to the side door, gives me a big hug and says he will be in touch very soon. I hear the dog's claws scatter across the utility as he releases them.

I slip into my car and wind through the country roads back to civilisation, playing the songs 'Animals' by Maroon 5^2 and 'So Strange' by Polyphia[3] on repeat, singing at the top of my lungs. Sam sent me them recently and they make me smile. He even recorded himself singing along to them on a voice note and sent that.

Although Sam being a player, I am certain I am not the first girl he has done that to, including his Wife.

The Maroon 5 song sums up the physicality between us. 'So Strange' I relish in the undeniable fantasy that he does 'think of me like every night.' I enjoy that thought fleetingly and then give myself a firm virtual slap across the face, back to reality.

I stop at Asda to go into the toilets and straighten myself up and change. I can feel the butterflies in my stomach, Sam will be on the train by now, I checked and he has messaged saying just that.

Three's A Crowd

I hit the road and headed to the station. I arrive stupidly early, and we message back and forth while I wait. I am not sure whether to stay in the car or go into the station to meet him.

My phone pings it's the gang bang WhatsApp group. Discussing dates and excuses they can use to get away for the evening from their Wives, how they plan to tear me to shreds and use me thoroughly. I quickly respond with enthusiasm. But I don't want to think about any of that, I just want to focus on Sam.

But my head questions my sanity. What am I doing?! Why did I even agree to this, it is silly, Emily is not pleased. Yes, I like him, but I could have been making money from him. My standard overnight charge is £1000. But the bottom line is, I just want to spend some time with him, even though it's pointless other than the fact I will enjoy it. I can't help but wonder what he must be thinking. Perhaps how dumb I am to have fallen for his chat and given myself away for free to him. I ponder how many other escorts he has asked to 'move beyond a paid relationship' and that I am likely the only one not to have told him to 'do one.'

I can't help but think these 24 hours will be the death nail, it is not an hour he has to endure, it's far longer, and he will question me, uncover things, he will 'see me' and realise I am not worth spending time with. Then, when he goes home to his beautiful, uber-smart, successful Wife and child, he will slam the door on me and my mess of a life. It was inevitable that after spending more time with me, he would be able to see with absolute clarity what he had at home. He will berate himself for not having seen it before and throw himself full force into his real life. With my part in this, only to be the catalyst to that dawning. I have seen it before, it's my role as a slut. Provide for as long as I am needed. Super whore fixes marriages. And although I will be bitterly sad to not see him again, I will have twenty-four hours of fun, filth and someone spending time with me to look back on fondly.

I decide it's rude to just sit in the car, so I drift into the station, just as his train is pulling in. I can't get past the barriers without a ticket, so I lean on a wall, scrolling my phone and darting my eyes up to the barriers frequently to keep an eye out. Then I see him, he rounds the corner and spots me, I give him a big smile, it's genuine, I find my whole body just lifts as he approaches. He gets through the barrier, walks towards me, drops his bag, smiles and gives me a massive hug.

The moment our bodies come together, I'm enveloped in a warmth that seems to seep right into my bones. It's not just physical, it's something deeper, something that wraps around my heart and holds it gently. I can feel his arms around me, pulling me close, and the way he holds on, firm but tender, makes me feel like I'm exactly where I'm supposed to be.

Time slows down and the world outside this embrace fades away. All that exists is the connection between us, this shared moment where nothing else matters. His heartbeat is steady against my chest, a rhythm that syncs with my own, grounding me in the present. It's a silent conversation, this hug, speaking volumes in the way he holds me and I feel like I never want to let go.

I close my eyes and let myself sink into it, losing myself in the safety that radiates from him. It's as if every worry, every fear, every doubt is being melted away by the sheer warmth of his embrace. I want to stay here forever, in this cocoon of comfort and affection, where everything feels right and good.

For me, there's a depth to this hug, a meaning that goes beyond words. It's a promise, a reassurance that I'm not alone, that I'm cared for in a way that's pure. I can feel it in the way he holds me closer still, in the way his breath gently brushes against my neck, in the way his hands rest on my back as if to shield me from the world. If I could, I'd live in this moment forever, wrapped in Sam's warmth. It's a feeling of being home, of being seen. Here, in this embrace, I am whole, and I never want to leave.

He releases me and we chat as we walk to the car, I feel a tad shaky. The journey to the hotel zooms past, a comfortable easy conversation, the electricity between us charged as he plays with my sloppy wet hole as I drive, it is yearning for him so badly it aches, his cock visibly bulging in his trousers.

I notice he is not wearing his wedding ring. Common practice with clients and hook-ups. I wonder why... it's not like I don't know, and you can see the faint change in skin colour wrapped around the finger.

I imagine married men using escorts or having affairs go through the same ritual. They slip the wedding ring off their finger and tuck it away, out of sight. Even if the lady they are meeting knows about the marriage. But still, they can't bring themselves to wear it.

It's not about hiding the truth; as if the escort or girl knows exactly what the situation is. It's something else. Perhaps, in a way, taking off the ring feels like a mark of respect, perverse as that sounds. It's like acknowledging the betrayal, recognising that what they are doing crosses a line. When they wear the ring, it's a symbol of a promise made, a life chosen. Taking it off perhaps feels like separating that part, trying to keep what's sacred from being tainted by what they are about to do.

But really it's a hollow gesture, a lie to make them feel it is less wrong. As if removing the ring could somehow lessen the guilt, as if it could make this betrayal less real. I suppose it's a way to compartmentalise, to convince themselves that when the ring is off, they are someone else, someone not bound by the vows they made.

It's a perverse kind of respect, a twisted way of trying to keep the worlds apart. It's like paying a silent, warped tribute to the life they are betraying.

I never take mine off, I tell people I am married and no amount of ring slipping off can make me feel less guilty and ashamed. I am not proud of who I am.

Sam and I have discussed the challenges of a dead bedroom before. How, if one partner is no longer interested the other has a life of celibacy chosen for them. Which is quite unfair. Wanting sex within the bigger picture of a marriage that has found itself evolving into at best a friendship, is seen as base, dirty, like there is something wrong with you. Once sex is off the table, a marriage isn't a marriage. It's a working relationship like a team. But the closeness and connection are lost, sex by its very nature is intimate and provides closeness and connection. I may as well be living with my brother, although Phil is a lot more palatable than my brother, but you get my point. It's wrong in my opinion, that someone's needs are seen as dirty when all they want is to feel close to and loved by the person who said their vows and promised to be there for them forever. Love and cherish, to have and hold. People forget that bit. They focus on 'forsaking all others, until death do us part,' when things go wrong, feeling betrayed, but the betrayal started when 'to love and to cherish, to have and to hold.' got taken off the table. That is not what people signed up for. In a court of law, surely it is a breach of contract?

The remainder of the journey is an eclectic mix of laughter, chit-chat and of course filth. We arrive at the hotel and check-in, I try to block out the memories of different guys I have serviced here. I want to be fully present.

Once in the room, it's immediate, frenzied and passionate. We had been opening up a lot more in recent weeks about our kinks. And we were like two sides of the same coin. I like to be dominated and am submissive, he liked to dominate and enjoyed power and control, I liked to be degraded and humiliated, he liked to deliver that, I liked pain, spankings, impact play, he got off on that. All the things I didn't like, he didn't like, such as scat and having to call him daddy (that's just weird!). Sexually you could not get two more aligned individuals. I think for the first time in his life, he felt a sense of freedom, that he could share his porn choices without shame. And he did and everything he sent was exactly what I would search for.

He had said he wanted to lick me out and do 69. That me

Three's A Crowd

being satisfied was important. I had explained to him before oral didn't really do it for me. But he insisted, saying he enjoyed it, and to my eternal surprise he made me cum. That was the first of many.

Before we headed to the bar for dinner I must have had about five orgasms.

I enjoyed his cock down my throat, in my cunt and in my ass. His cock just seems to fit me and rub the right places. His words were like the twist mechanism on a tap causing my main fuck hole to gush.

I had a couple of beers at dinner and ate some pizza. I could do that, as it is likely not to be through me before we left the next day, meaning his favourite anal was still on the table. He knew I liked to be prepped and clean for an ass fuck. But he said it went with the territory and a bit of 'danger anal', never causing anyone any harm.

Over dinner, we had a laugh and discussed our partners and life. We seemed to have some level of trust now, not scared that either one of us would cause trouble for the other.

He probed around what Phil was doing to step up and bring in some cash to help me. Around how Phil treats me and doesn't understand why he doesn't fuck me, he said if I was his Wife, I'd have his cock in me permanently. I liked that idea. He felt most women are not that bothered sexually once they have 'snared' their man, conversely, I don't go a single day without masturbating, if I can't, I get grumpy.

He also discussed my other work, saying he understood, but he didn't like it. He didn't like 'sharing his toys'. I liked that. I know I shouldn't have, but never had anyone been arsed before. Emily would have a field day with that comment, I could hear what she would say... "See he wants you exclusively for himself, but when it suits him, when he needs to unload, he is manipulating you Jess don't fall for it." Well, giving up escorting wasn't an option anyway, I needed the cash, plus there was no way I could survive more than 2 weeks without a real cock. The reality was there was no chance with the distance and Sam's restricted life of ever getting that level of regularity with him.

I was lectured on safety and respect. And that there had to be another way to earn the money needed and surely if I was doing sex work I was missing out on putting time into my business which ultimately would be the thing to get me out of this mess.

Deep down I knew he was right, but it was also not that simple. He had no clue how tight things were, I couldn't afford a gap in income. It did enter my head though that the money I had just been left by a distant Auntie of £15K, it wasn't in the bank yet, but it was coming, could tide us over for 4 months and maybe, just maybe if I focused fully for those months I could do it, get the business to where it needed to be. But equally, if not topping up with other income, it would only last 3-4 months, juggling both sex work and the business, could buy us 10 months, by which time Phil would surely have a job! And we might have some savings remaining rather than having nothing to fall back on. This experience has taught me how essential that is. Could I selfishly give up escorting and cross my fingers my marketing business could provide in 3 months, to then discover it could not, and I would then be responsible for our family being homeless?

After dinner, we headed back to the room for more rough and dirty sex resulting in another handful of orgasms.

We lay on the bed after, recovering, both content, laughing and chatting. Sam absentmindedly slips his hand under the fabric of my one-piece, panic floods through me like a cold wave. His touch is gentle, and warm against my skin, but it feels like a fire igniting something raw and painful deep inside. My heart stumbles, then races, pounding so loudly I'm sure he can hear it. Memories crash over me, sharp, cruel words from long ago, the taunts and mocking laughter that made me believe this part of myself was off-limits, something to be ashamed of.

I can't let him see how much this affects me. I can't let him know. I try to steady my breathing as he circles and rubs his hand

and chats away, I don't know what he is saying. I am falling into a panic.

I force a mask of calm over my face, though it feels fragile, like it could shatter at any moment. My body goes rigid for a second, instinctively pulling away, but I stop myself. I can't move. I have to stay still, make him think this is nothing, that I'm okay with this. I swallow hard, trying to push down the rising tide of fear, bury it deep where it can't reach the surface.

My breath catches in my throat, and I focus on keeping it steady, even though it feels like I'm suffocating. Just breathe, just stay calm. I press my lips together to keep them from trembling, trying to hide the way my muscles tense, betraying me.

Despite my best efforts I can't hide my physical response and he realises. Sam being Sam, aware of my hard limits, one being that I can't be totally naked, had already probed on that topic. He knows it is related to losing my virginity and Darren's cruel words. But he doesn't get it. He would have to know more detail, and I am not sharing, he respectfully left it alone, sensing it was definitely a box best left for now, but he did say that before he dies, he wants to understand.

Sam pauses and soothingly tells me it's OK and then stops. I can feel tears welling and anger at myself for not being able to control this reaction. Well, that is it then. Psycho Jess exposed, he will get through the night, the car rides back to the station and be gone.

I manage to regain control and brush it off as best I can. Hookups and clients are not with me long enough for this to be a problem. They have their eye on the holes and reaching their sexual goal, they just accept my lingeries as part of my slut persona. It has never been an issue as everything I buy ensures full access to all the bits they want. I have a sinking feeling that if Sam continues to see me, this will become an issue.

It's late now, and we cuddle into each other. As I lay there in his arms his warmth surrounded me, and it felt like a foreign, almost forgotten sensation. It had been so long since anyone held me like that.

At first, I tensed, my body not quite remembering how to relax into someone else. It was strange, this closeness, this intimacy. I'd been so used to a cold, empty space beside me, to the absence of touch, that it almost felt like I was dreaming. But slowly, I allowed myself to sink into him, I let the tension melt away as his heartbeat became a steady, comforting rhythm.

Every breath I took seemed to come easier, deeper. His hand laid gently on my waist, and the weight of it was grounding. I closed my eyes and felt a strange safety in his arms, a safety I'd not felt for as long as I could remember. The years of loneliness, the ache of being untouched, unloved, fade, replaced by this quiet, profound connection.

A soft sigh escaped my lips as I allowed myself to be held. The walls I had built around my heart began to crumble. It was if his presence was dissolving all the hurt, all the coldness that's settled in my bones over the years. I felt a warmth spreading through me, not just from his touch but from a place deep inside, a warmth that felt like hope.

And then, as I drifted toward sleep, I realised that for the first time in so long, I'm not completely alone. As I let the darkness pull me under, I remind myself this is just an arrangement, it means nothing. I will be alone and uneasy again tomorrow, the wall around my heart must stay strong, but for now, I took solace in the peace and his embrace. I slept better than I had done for a very long time.

The next morning we fucked again, before he headed to the shower, asking if I want to join him. I felt a frustrating sadness wash over me as I declined. Knowing how I can never do that, how I just can't ever be seen fully naked. I hate being a disappointment and I knew this was just that, disappointing.

While he was in, my mind wandered to the fuck fest just past and felt that tension in my groin, so grabbed my wand, plugged it in and lay on the floor getting myself o#. It was liberating knowing he would be OK with that, instead of life at home where my toys are as hidden as my wanks. When he stepped out of the bathroom his jaw hit the floor and of course he helped finish me off.

We grabbed breakfast, checked out and I dropped him close to his meeting. My work meeting is a brunch with some local businesses. It is a chance to network and showcase my offering. I have been to this one before, it is usually quite good and a source of leads. I don't partake in the 'brunch' element as I have had a breakfast of cum, so I just nurse my coffee and hob nob. Not my favourite type of hobnobbing!

As I am chatting to Jules, a garden landscaper, I feel a pair of eyes on me from the far side of the room. When I look over I just about drop my coffee on the floor, I can feel the blood draining from my face. I know that guy, and I have a really bad feeling. He is looking at me quizzically through his brown floppy wavy hair and then gives me a sinister smile. He walks over towards Jules and I.

The penny drops, I know him alright, I would have clicked faster if he had been standing butt naked with his cock out.

"Hey Susie!" He says as he joins Jules and I. Jules looks confused and no wonder.

"You're in customer service right?" He says with an amused look on his face.

"Oh no, Jess is a marketing guru, she is quite exceptional" intervenes Jules.

Fuck, fuck, fuck.

This has always been a concern of mine, bumping into a GW client in my 'real' working life. Having my real name and identity discovered. I had always feared this might happen, but always expected it to be closer to home. Not hundreds of miles away.

"Is that so?" He says "what makes you exceptional, Susie...er.. I mean Jess?" His tone makes me uncomfortable.

"I will leave Jess to tell you all about what she does, I need to grab Mike, nice seeing you Jess," says Jules.

"Nice to meet you, I suspect I have a good idea of what makes Susie... er Jess, exceptional, she no doubt goes above and beyond and allows herself to be utilised by those willing to pay for her exceptional services." He replies.

Jules smiles and heads over to another group.

I am mute and dying inside, desperately thinking how to play this. I have always been scared of this catching up with me in the real world. Maybe I just play dumb.

"So, what is it you do?" I ask, trying to come across as nonplussed and like I have no clue who he is, but I am trembling.

"Come on Susie, you know exactly what it is I do...to you."

"I am sorry, I don't know what you are talking about, do tell me about your business, and my name is Jess, maybe you have mistaken me for someone else."

"I know those slutty lips anywhere, and now I know your name and what you do, so I find myself thinking... what will Jess do for me, to keep my mouth shut?"

Shit shit shit.

Before I can answer, Dylan from a local printer comes up to us. "Jessie, I was hoping to pick your brains!" he says.

"Sure," I say.

"I will leave you guys to it" says Girthygary (I have remembered his profile name) "But Jess, I will be in touch ***really*** soon and see what kind of arrangement we can come up with."

I smile back weakly and then proceed to listen to Dylan drone on about how to put across the impact of different flyer sizes on his socials. I can't focus and I don't give a fuck about flyer sizes.

Once my meeting is over, I collect Sam and find peace in him, helping me forget about Girthygary for a while. I am wondering what, if anything, I can do. One to speak to Emily about, not Sam, I am not having him know about this and tarnish our time together.

Three's A Crowd

But for now, I am focusing on the last couple of hours in Sam's company.

I drove back to the station a lot slower than I drove to the hotel. I didn't want to say goodbye. I didn't want our time to end. I was stunned by how profoundly I felt that. We chewed the fat on the drive, and he spoke of a networking event on the 5th of next month he had found out about that could mean he could escape once a month. I was not sure if he was serious or if he was just throwing me a line. Time will tell.

We embraced, and I wanted to just hold onto him, and not let him go. I watched him walk past the barrier, I turned and walked towards my car, pausing to look back once and caught him disappear round the corner. He didn't look back.

Sadness consumed me.

I got into my car and to my surprise there was a ping from 'McHorn'

> I will get the 5th sorted. Be safe x

I respond, certain the axe is soon to fall, once home and he has had time to reflect, is enjoying his Wife's company, a Wife that doesn't fuck other men for money because she has failed at life, a wife that doesn't freak out when touched in a certain way, a smart classy wife, the type you want to be seen with. He will go home and give her an I missed you fuck - I know lots of guys lie about a dead bedroom.

I head home to the usual domestic chaos and observe my children fondly. Once the house is quiet again... I get a ping... Mchorn:

> If you knew how I really felt about you, it would scare you.

Chapter 7
Misty gets Risky

The end of the week and weekend passed without much drama. I juggled GW clients, and rugby matches and got the news that the guy I met before my Orca meeting has confirmed he wants to proceed with me for his marketing campaign. Happy days. I now need to produce the contract and set up the initial meeting to collect the full and detailed spec, so I can begin developing the plan. I will make a start on the contract today when I get back.

First, though, I am seeing Billy the Chef. A regular and a local. I had a rule when I first started my GW work, never to see anyone locally. That waned over time. When you need cash in the door and time is against you, having a few on your doorstep makes it easier.

I saw Henry at the Premier Inn yesterday, and I am a bit sore, his latest fetish is rigging, but he has not yet been to his course, so he settles for tying my tits with cable ties and bolting on some bulldog clips.

I don't have the best tits in the world, if I could afford it that **is** something I may consider spending cash on but only if I was **very** comfortable and had money to burn. I would be worried though, about loss of sensation and would have to thoroughly understand how likely that was, as my tits are a big part of getting me in the mood. Can't lose that!

They are not tiny, but not porn star level. The old phrase, more than a handful is a waste, probably sums them up. It is one of my worries about my profile, photos and videos weirdly make them look bigger than they actually are, and it feels like false advertising. They look a bit like two pals that have fallen out, turned away from one another and space between them. My nipples make up for it, they can be quite protruding when aroused. Someone once said they are like fruit pastels. And they are a decent colour contrast to the skin. I am not a fan of nipples that blend with the skin.

I had to help Henry get them tied, they are not full enough really and seem to slip out easily. The only way it works is to bend over and let them hang and hold them while the cable ties pinch around the base. Henry pulls them extra tight, and it's not long before they ache, go numb and turn purple. With the skin taught, my tits feel like I imagine they would feel after a boob job, they are not soft any more but firm and hard. He adds a bulldog clip to each nipple and I squeal because it feels like they may cut and slice through my nipples.

My reaction makes him extra hard.

He then bent me over the bed and roughly finger fucked me. He is not skilled at this and his nail nick's me on the way in. He reached round and squeezed my tits as he drove his fingers in and out my pussy. He stands me back up and gives my tits a good few slaps. Slaps to tits are hot, but when tied they bruise much more easily. He then wanted me to suck him off and rub my tied tits on his dick, so he lay on his back on the bed and I began. I slid my tits across his cock and then up his torso, when I reached head level he grabbed one of my arms and placed my hand on his neck, then his hand on top of mine making it squeeze his neck. I freeze. He realised and released me.

"Sorry, sorry," he said "It's my switch side."

Three's A Crowd

"It's OK," I replied "I just can't do that, you know I don't have a dominant bone in my body."

I felt crap saying this, but it was the truth, I literally couldn't do it if I tried. The other type of client I have declined and there are very few I decline, is men who want to be pegged by a woman, or men that want me to piss on them. Again just too dominant for me. "No, no, my fault, Dom mode back on" and he laughed nervously, I could tell he felt bad. "So bitch, suck my cock."

So I did. He rotated between that and fucking my pussy until he finished spraying my face and tied tits while telling me what a dirty whore I was. We chatted for a bit after, and he asked my advice on his dating profile, then he handed me the envelope of cash including a generous tip which he always did. I released my tits and felt the blood rush back to them, got dressed and left.

So that is why I am a bit tender this morning, I have a couple of small bruises on my tits and a scratch just inside my pussy.

Once the kids have gone and Phil has set off in casual painting clothes, as he has managed to get a few days' work through a friend painting a flat, which is welcome news as there will be a few hundred pounds in the pot. I get showered and dressed, selecting my semi wet look, cut out crotchless and cup-less one piece, a short leather skirt, belt, blouse, my raincoat and of course butt plug. I make the short drive to Billy the Chef's. His Wife works at the Council in town, and he is off today. He is a traveling Chef so often away for weeks and when he is home he books me. He is not in a sexless marriage, but he is bored, he married young with little playing the field and feels he has not lived or had the opportunity to explore his sexuality. He claims his Wife just goes through the motions and it feels shit. She lays like a sack of potatoes and he says he may as well be fucking a corpse. I was his first ever escort booking and the first women he ever fucked in the ass, he's now a huge fan and a convert to anal. The first time he fucked me in the ass (condom of course) he came within seconds of penetrating me. Guess it was the excitement of something new.

I am never a big fan of going to a matrimonial home, always scared the wife or girlfriend will pop home for something and I really don't need that drama. Billy lives in a ground floor tenement flat in one of the less desirable areas of the city. I pull up on the street and walk to the close door which is open as the intercom does not work. I step into the close and knock on his door. He opens fairly instantly, I step inside and go to the living room. He is a smoker and always has to finish a fag before we start, he's always quite nervous initially but soon relaxes. I chat to him while he does his stuff. He talks about the stress of his work. All Chefs in my experience are angry, and I just can't imagine him being angry.

He stubs out his cigarette, takes a gulp from his can of Fanta and walks over to me, shoves me against the wall and starts groping me. He wrestles with my clothes and his until he is butt naked, and I am stood with my knee-high boots and wet-look cut-out lingerie. He has become much more confident since we first met, pushing himself and exploring more, discovering who he is I guess, it's nice to see. He wraps both his hands around my throat and gently but firmly chokes me, brings his face to mine and says "right you filthy fucking slut, get on your knees and suck me dry". He releases my throat and I drop to my knees and start working his cock with my mouth. I can tell he's getting close, and he pulls out, grabs my hair, pulls me to my feet, leads me to the bathroom and pushes me down onto my knees again. I know what's coming.

"Take my piss you filthy fucking bitch."

He slides his fingers into my mouth and opens it, places the tip of his cock on my lips and starts to piss.

Some guys can piss when erect, others can't, Billy can. I can't hide my facial reaction, I have done this a lot, it doesn't bother me in many ways, it's just piss which is apparently sterile. It's more the act of someone using you like a toilet, it's so degrading and I can't hide my facial expression. You get two types of guys into water-

Three's A Crowd

sports. Those who enjoy someone like me, submitting, but looking uncomfortable and grimacing through it and those who enjoy a girl who is as eager for piss as I am for cum, smiling while she is pissed on.

Despite my grimace and obvious discomfort, it turns me on, not because of the act itself, but because it is degrading, it's a man dominating and using you for his own purpose. That makes my pussy clench and get squelchy. So many of my kinks are a strange mix of love and hate, a battle between my brain and my pussy. The pussy wins...always.

I take and swallow what I can, he also sprays his piss over my face, hair and tits. And once he is finished he grabs my head and pulls it onto his cock, holding it there, and then releasing, so I can get air.

"Take that you filthy whore," he says.

Once he has repeated that a few times he pulls me up by the wrist and takes me into the bedroom, shoves me forward so I land onto the bed, my arms stopping me collapsing completely. I hear frantic rustling as he fights with a condom and then grabbing my hips he rams his cock into my ass and hammers at me. I can feel my orgasm building, an anal orgasm is quite a different thing and I cum loudly, my body rippling in waves and gripping his cock, my moans undeniably lost in total pleasure and this tips him over the edge, he speaks through gritted teeth "you dirty fucking whore."

His rhythm slows and he pulls out. He slides off the condom and hands it to me, he knows me well, I want that cum and sit scooping it out and enjoying it.

He disappears off to the living room to have a post-coital smoke and I know my job now. I go back to the bathroom, mop up the floor, grab my bag, rinse myself off in the shower, get dressed again and pop into the living room.

"Thanks, Susie," he says, "I am away for a few weeks but I will be in touch." He stands slips me my cash and sees me out.

When I get home I dive into the shower and clean myself properly. His shower doesn't feel like it cleans me properly. Chuck on some comfy jeans and a hoodie, boil the kettle and head up to the office to start on this contract.

I hit Spotify and selected a random radio channel to have as background music while I work, Billie Jean is playing, that takes me back! I pull up the template I have saved when I feel a chill sweep through the entire house. Bloody Thomas, bet he has left his bedroom window open again I think. But what a chill, it's like someone flipped a switch and made it winter. I stand up and turn to exit the office door and go check. Ron was curled up at my feet and began to growl, then whimper, as I moved, it's unnerving.

The moment I step onto the landing, a chill races down my spine. There she was, the girl from the car park, Misty. The same gaunt figure, the one with hollow eyes and a face that seemed etched in perpetual sorrow. She stood there, unnervingly still, just outside my Daughter's room, staring straight at me.

My heart pounded, the sound echoing in my ears like a drum. I tried to speak, to demand who she was, why she was here, but the words stuck in my throat, trapped by a fear so intense it seemed to paralyse me. I was frozen to the spot, every muscle tensed, but unable to move, to do anything but stare back at her.

She looked fragile, like she could be blown away by the slightest breeze, but something about her, something in those dark, empty eyes, was terrifying. I knew, rationally, she shouldn't be intimidating. She was small, weak, almost frail. But there was some- thing deeply wrong, something I couldn't understand. My mind raced, a whirlwind of panicked thoughts. How did she know where I lived? How did she get inside the house? What does she want?

Every possibility flashed through my mind, each one more unsettling than the last. What if my family had been home? What if my Daughter had been just behind that door and this girl, this intruder was standing between us? I felt the sharp edges of terror cutting into my thoughts, making it impossible to think clearly. All

I could do was stand there, my breath caught in my throat, waiting for something, anything to happen.

The silence stretched out, heavy and suffocating, as the air in the hallway seemed to grow colder. I wanted to run, to scream, to fight, but all I could do was stand there, locked in place by fear.

"You can't run any more, I have to show you," she said.

I want to scream for her to get out, to leave me the fuck alone, but nothing works, it's like I have turned to stone under her gaze with only my eyes able to move.

"Only you can help me, don't you see?"

"You can stop them, you can stop them hurting me" she says, and her voice carries despair like I have never experienced or felt before.

My brain begins to come back online, I am shivering and shaking, but thoughts begin to form. This girl is in my home, my house, where my kids and Husband live. I need to find out what she wants, keep her calm, take her home to her parents, I don't want trouble for her, she is clearly unhinged and distressed, but I can't have this.

"Misty? Right?"

"Help me Jess, you have to help me, it has to be you."

"I will help, let me get you home, where do you live?"

"NO!" she screams at the top of her voice, with a ferocity you would not expect from this shadow of a girl...her eyes change from sadness to fury and my entire body jumps.

"OK, OK… shhhh, it's OK, what do you need?" I ask gently.

"I need you to hear me" Her voice is softer now.

"I can hear you," I say.

"No, no you can't, you won't, you need to **really** hear me, **really** listen" She growls through gritted teeth.

"OK, OK… I am listening, can we go for a walk and you can talk to me?" I suggest thinking I need to get her out of my home.

"No…here…I need Darren and his friends to stop" she says, her eyes filled with desperation.

My mind races, Darren, she can't mean Darren from 30 years ago...

"Darren who?"

"Your Darren."

As she spoke, my mind began to whirl, each word she said tightening the knot of confusion and unease in my chest. She was just a child, but what she was saying, who she was talking about made my blood run cold. What if they really are going after young girls?

She mentioned a name, the name I had not heard in years, from so long ago. I had only told Sam and Emily about this. Emily had kept the sacred secret for decades, Sam was 100 miles away and knew no one I did. How could this girl know anything? A name that belonged to someone from my past, someone who was an adult now, far, far away from here. I had moved, started fresh, left all that behind. It was impossible, how could she know? My thoughts raced, trying to make sense of it.

I stared at her, trying to find some hint of a joke or a trick in her soulful eyes, but there was nothing. She spoke with the casual certainty of a child, as if this person was as much a part of her world as they had once been in mine. But it made no sense. This girl had never met them, how could she have? The geography didn't match up. It was as though she was reaching into the past, pulling out memories that she had no right or reason to know.

My pulse quickened, a creeping sense of dread washing over me. Was this a coincidence, or was something far worse at play? My mind grasped at logical explanations, but each one crumbled under the weight of the impossible.

What did this mean? And most importantly, how did she know? I felt a growing urge to push her, to put distance between myself and this girl who somehow held fragments of my past in her small hands. But I couldn't move, couldn't speak. All I could do was listen, trapped in the eerie sensation that the lines between past and present were somehow being blurred by the quiet voice of a child who should know nothing at all. Or worse, was she telling the truth, and were these boys now men, men who preyed on young girls? I needed to understand.

"What do you mean?" I manage.

"You know" she snaps and so do I.

"Look, unless you start explaining yourself in plain English this conversation is over, I want you out of my house and I don't want to see you again, if I see you again, I will call the Police, so your choice, start speaking or get out."

"You can't," she replies calmly.

"Can't what?" I bark "I can do whatever I damn well please."

"You can't go to the Police, you can't tell anyone about me."

"I can, and I will" I bite back.

"Then I will tell your children you're a secret WHORE!"

I stumble now, the wind taken out of me completely, my world spinning and crashing around me, I feel faint, sick, my eyes losing focus and everything goes black.

When I come round, I am slumped on the floor. I dart upright and look around, she is no longer standing on the landing. Ron is cowering under my desk whimpering behind me in the office. Heart thumping I pull myself to standing, take two steps to the left while keeping my eyes focused on 360 degree scanning the area. I feel for the handle to Thomas's room and open it. I reach inside and feel the baseball bat he keeps by the door and grab it. I enter his room and check it, no one is there, I open his cupboard ready to spring. I note his window is not open as I had thought. I repeat this in the office, Lottie's room, my bedroom and the bathroom. I slowly creep downstairs and see the front door swinging open, I turn into the kitchen, bending to look under the table, the living room, utility and downstairs bathroom also all clear. She is not here. I enter the porch, step outside and scan the street. I see a fragile frame disappear behind a bush and then Sandy the post man steps onto the drive. I am not sure how long I was out for, seconds, minutes or longer.

"Morning Jess" I hear as Sandy the postman walks up the path "bills, bills, bills, by the looks I am afraid" he glances at me holding the bat over my shoulder...

"Hey, don't shoot the messenger" he grins..I just stare at him.

"Hey Jess, you ok?" He asks

"Sorry Sandy, yes fine, just got spooked by something, sorry, being silly." I lower the bat and take the mail from him, wish him a good day and come back into the house, close the door behind me and lock it. As soon as the door is closed the cool air is trapped outside and the warm air of the house begins to work against it and take over.

I don't get my contract finished, or even started, I cannot function for the rest of the day. How can this girl know about Darren? How can he be hurting her, god please tell me that he has stopped and doesn't still hurt young girls as an adult. I can't face that, it would mean it's my fault, I didn't speak up and more have been hurt. But they live 200 miles away. Misty is here, and it is so wildly unlikely he has moved 200 miles north to the same location as me, to pick up where he left off with another young girl. That is just so farcical. None of this makes sense. It can't be that, it must be a coincidence. And for some reason she thinks I know this person. But how the hell does she know about my second job? Has she been following me... I suppose if someone did, they could work it out. Or she has found me online and latched onto me for some reason... but I don't show my face on my profile and I am listed as Susie, not Jess. Maybe it's a wild guess, a generalised comment, and she doesn't actually know. People call people whores all the time.

That said, I can't have her even threaten that. It can't be found out, it would kill my family and I wouldn't have it. Equally, I can't risk reporting her as she may say something. But she knows where I live... oh my god what a mess and the last thing I need. She is clearly mentally unstable, a psychopath but a psychopath knows my name and where I live. Or is she just crying out for help? Is it just that simple?

Three's A Crowd

I need time to think, I am too on edge, and I need a plan. I decide to take Ron out and go for a run, clear my head and consider talking to Sam and Emily about this.

Once, I can put it down as a random incident, but a second time at my home... no. There is something else going on, and I know this is not the last time I will see Misty. The thought makes me baulk.

Chapter 8

He Loves Me...He Loves Me Not...

I head home to the usual domestic chaos and observe my children fondly. Once the house is quiet again... I get a ping... Mchorn:

> If you knew how I really felt about you, it would scare you.

My mind races... I am not the smartest tool in the box, that is a certainty, but I can read into this message the potential intent behind it. Or could it be wishful thinking?

How do you respond to that? I had not a clue... I think he may be about to tell me that he loves me, but that cannot be likely, he is a smart guy, very smart and it is laughable that even entered my head for a number of reasons.

1. We have met twice...Spent no more than 17 hours together in person, sure chatted a tonne online and occasionally spoke on the phone. But that is it. You can't fall in love with someone like that.
2. He doesn't know me, he doesn't know I dig in my ears with cotton buds and Kirby grips then accidentally

leave them in my dressing gown pocket and clog up the washing machine. He doesn't know I eat my own toenail clippings enjoying the pain of pushing them between my tooth and gum. He doesn't know that when I am drunk I snore like a gutted pig. He doesn't know that with my advancing years, I have an alarming and vile single jet-black nipple hair that I have to pluck, it just won't die.
3. He just sees my filthy fun side, not when I am stressed or tired. Everyone looks amazing when you just see their best side. Like social media, just post after post of edited highlights, not showing the truth behind that picture-perfect photo. We are not in the mundanity of married life together, so I stand out as exciting and different. I am an illusion, a mirage.

It is far more likely he is going to say something else, something more 'us' more filthy. Like I literally can't get you out of my mind, all I do is think about fucking you and my cock is constantly hard. Yes, that's what it will be… but how to respond… I could get this wrong big time. I am conscious time has passed since he sent that, and I am battling with the right response. I need to say something, he can see I have read it.

I don't believe in love if I am honest. When I was a teen I had my head filled with the usual Disney and rom-com fantasies. They should be banned, outlawed for filling young girls' heads with unrealistic expectations leading to shattered dreams, it's not real life.

Girls are fed this stuff and it's all lies. Girls are taught to expect this life that does not exist, but they are not taught about men's needs. Yet love is banded about as if it is a real thing and no one speaks the truth. They are taught what to expect from men, but never how to treat a man. Whereas most good men are raised being told how to treat a woman, but never what to expect from one. It's a

Three's A Crowd

mess and the reason I have so many clients unhappy with married life and dead bedrooms.

I've pondered the concept of 'love' a lot. I understand the bond between a parent and child, that fierce, protective instinct that drives a mother to shield her offspring from harm, or the way a father's eyes light up with pride at his child's accomplishments. That kind of love is tangible; I've seen it, felt it, and lived it. It's rooted in biology, in the preservation of our species, in the deep, undeniable connections of family. That makes sense to me. It is unconditional love, everything else is conditional, fleeting, fake, smoke and mirrors, a lie.

This fake love, the one that people speak of between couples, the one that's supposedly the foundation of marriage, the force that drives people to claim they've found their 'other half', that I can't quite grasp and remain unconvinced it is real.

To me, it feels more like a myth, a grand illusion everyone is caught up in, like the emperor's new clothes. Perhaps the biggest con and sleight of hand of our time.

Everyone insists it's real, yet when I look closely, I see nothing but the threads of social expectation and tradition, woven together to create something out of nothing.

Take, for example, the way people talk about 'falling in love.' They describe it as a magical, inexplicable, an invisible force that sweeps them off their feet. But isn't that just infatuation? A fleeting chemical reaction in the brain, a mix of hormones designed to lure us into mating? Over time, those feelings fade, replaced by comfort or routine, or, more often than not, by disillusionment. People change, grow apart, and lose interest, yet they cling to the idea that 'true love' should conquer all. But what if there was never anything real to conquer in the first place?

Consider for a moment, the number of relationships that crumble under the weight of this so-called love. The divorce rates, the affairs, and the bitter fights that leave people scarred and cynical. If love were real, shouldn't it be stronger than that? Shouldn't it endure, unshaken by time and hardship?

Yet, time and again, I see people who once professed undying love become strangers or worse, enemies. What was once 'love' turns into resentment, disappointment, or sheer indifference.

Even in relationships that don't end in breakups, how much of what's called love is really just a comfortable routine, a fear of being alone, or a convenient partnership? People talk about 'growing old together,' but is that more about finding someone you can tolerate for a lifetime, someone whose flaws you can live with, rather than some mythical emotional bond?

To me, the idea of romantic love is just that, an idea. A construct designed to give meaning to what is essentially a biological drive, to justify the social structures we've built around partnership, marriage, and family. We dress it up in grandiose terms, write poems and songs about it, and convince ourselves it's something profound. But when you strip away the poetry, the social conditioning, what's left? A series of mutual benefits, perhaps, but not this mythical 'love' everyone speaks of.

I think we've all just agreed to believe in something that isn't really there, because the alternative, acknowledging that we're all alone, that our connections are as fragile as spider webs, would be too terrifying to face. So, we keep telling ourselves the story of love, hoping that if we say it enough times, it might actually become true.

And yes, occasionally when I am weak, I wish it were true, there is no denying it is a comforting concept. Humans want to be seen, appreciated, cared for and valued, to feel special, love is the facade we have constructed to deliver this.

Perhaps it is real, and we are all striving for it, but like the lottery only a handful get to win, the odds against you. I think of my parents, the only example of true love I have ever witnessed. They were each other's everything, you could see it in all they did, it was beautiful. But that seems to be the exception.

Three's A Crowd

And don't even get me started on the whole, loving someone and 'being in love' with someone bullshit. As if the latter is somehow stronger, more powerful. Another construct to persuade the receiver that it's a ***different*** kind of love, a way for those dipping their nibs elsewhere to justify loving two or more people, they can 'love' their Wife or partner so they are not cruel bastards who just don't care, but don't worry I am '***in love***' with you 'Mrs bit on the side'. So even though I am not with you, rest easy, it means more.

To me, the distinction between 'love' and 'being in love' is just a way for people to try to make sense of their emotions, to categorise and define something that's ultimately indefinable. It's like we need these labels to justify why relationships change, to explain why the fire of new love doesn't last. But in reality, it's all the same, just varying degrees of the same basic human connection, dressed up in different words to make us feel like we're experiencing something unique, something more special than it really is.

In the end, whether you call it 'love' or 'being in love,' it's all just part of the same illusion. A story we tell ourselves to make sense of our desires, to justify our choices, and to fit into the societal narrative that says there's some grand difference between the two. But if you ask me, it's all just one thing, an emotional experience that's far more ordinary than we'd like to admit.

Maybe I am cynical, maybe I have never experienced true love. Maybe my marriage with Phil, so far removed from my hopes and dreams, has just killed my belief. Like discovering Santa is not real, once known, you can never go back.

So when Sam sent that message, I was sceptical, to say the least;

> If you knew how I really felt about you, it would scare you.

> Ha, scared that if you lived with me, my holes would be red raw!

I am serious Jess, I think I love you.

FLATLINE

Holy fuck… what is he playing at… this makes no sense. What is he hoping to achieve? I pick out the keyword in the sentence instantly '***think***'. The use of this word is brought into play when anyone is testing the waters, it can be retracted easily. It was just a thought!

But why say it? It is not like we can ever be together, even if we both loved each other as they do in the movies, we are both trapped in our own shit-show lives. So why even go there? It will only bring confusion and frustration.

People really do have a habit of self-torture… focusing on things that can't be, wasting their energy. Another tick in the box for the 'danger of emotions motion', it just makes things worse… harder.

I ***should*** respond something like;

"Wow, that is such a relief as I have been thinking the same thing," but the truth is…I haven't. Yes, I have feelings I have not felt before, yes they are off the chart strong… but love they are not, I don't ***do*** love.

Or

A simple response that conforms with the reciprocal protocol; "I don't ***think***, I ***know*** I love you"

It is expected when someone says they love you, you have to say it back… but I can't. It's not true.

I also hate the overuse of the word. Apart from Lottie, Tom and my parents, I have uttered 'I love you'… in my entire 47 years on the planet to another man… I would guess less than half a dozen times.

If love is ***really*** a thing, then overusing it, undervaluing it… said without care, thought or meaning, it just slips off the tongue as easily as 'Hello, how are you?'

No, if love ***is*** a thing, it should be more precious than that, not easily given, not said to just anyone, then a few years later someone else.

Thinking about it... I am not sure Phil has ***ever*** said he loves me, we had a weird version of it years ago. A phrase we both knew meant it but wasn't the actual words. He doesn't even sign birthday, Christmas and Valentine cards with 'Love Phil'. He just writes 'Phil', that is ***if*** he gets me a card, which he hasn't for well over a decade...and Valentine's Day... pfft never had that. Phil told me he doesn't need a prescribed day to express his feelings and show he cares, he could do it anytime, why do it when everyone else is? That is not special.

I liked that idea... Why is Valentine's Day so special anyway?... The truth is, it is not, it is a commercial construct where Husbands, Wives and partners feel obligated to do something... not because they ***want*** to. I did try to make the point that, that was all well and good, ***if*** an effort is made at other times, and perhaps the purpose of Valentine's Day was to make people pause and appreciate the other, otherwise, life gets in the way, and it never happens. This was dismissed.

So for me, it takes the meaning away. If I got anything on Valentine's Day, he would only be doing it out of obligation to conform to the commercial pressure, it would not be about us. It would not be because he actually wanted to. So since then, we haven't done Valentine's and I don't feel hurt or disappointed (do I?)

As I predicted, Phil doesn't express his feelings or show he cares the other 364 days of the year either. Love pfft, nonsense... It sucks.

I respond to Sam as best I can, very conscious I am coming across as a bitch, but better than lying.

> You don't, and I don't believe in love anyway.

The awkward conversation continues before we say good

night. As I lay in bed, feeling rotten for not reciprocating, I find myself questioning if perhaps he could love me, maybe it's possible, maybe what I am feeling ***is*** actually love. Then I imagine what Emily would say and berate myself...and Sam... how dare he dig into long-dead childish fantasies and ignite a hope that is hopeless.

From about this point on, post our second in-person encounter things ramped up.

He messaged more frequently, during the day despite his open-plan office, he replied to me almost instantly every time I messaged him, he ducked out into quiet areas and sent me voice notes or videos. He always messaged the minute he woke up. He messaged me while he drove to work asking if I was free ***and*** when leaving work. He would give me notice and let me know, 'leaving in 10 mins if you're free?', allowing me time to get Ron on his lead and out the door. So we started speaking every morning and evening. Our longest conversation was on a Thursday when he drove to his drumming lesson after work.

At weekends he would text, and he would call when Beth was at dance class on a Saturday afternoon. He could manage as he dropped her off and went for a walk. If he got the news that he was alone any other time over the weekend, he pinged me to see if I was free and called. It felt like he literally could not get enough of me. He now had my 'real' phone number too and so used WhatsApp on that instead of the slut phone.

I adapted my routine to walk Ron at the times I thought he would likely be able to speak. It was the high point of each day, the thing I looked forward to and made all my other worries pale into significance. It made my life worth living. He shared his weekly schedule and plans, so I knew if he was on school drop-off and free after 9, or if Natasha was doing it, and he'd be in the car at half eight. He always let me know in advance when that changed. If something happened last minute, and he couldn't talk he would fire off a quick message to let me know. 'Can't talk this morning,

Three's A Crowd

Natasha riding in with me today, gutted, miss you, will message ASAP x'

We chatted about anything and everything, hopes, dreams, future, wives, husbands, frustrations, nostalgia, filth, songs, movies and jokes. We just clicked on every single topic. Our connection was undeniable.

He continued to tell me he loved me, he continued to dig, challenge and question my lack of emotion. We spoke about Darren and my past. He wanted me to learn to love myself, stand up for myself with Phil, and demand better, he always took the time to reassure me, to tell me **I mattered**, that I was important, he missed me, **he loved me**.

He raised my GW work a lot and got more and more focused on wanting me to stop that work. I could understand, I wouldn't like it the other way round. But I was trapped, in desperate need of cash. The more he put thoughts of stopping in my head, the harder it was seeing clients. It began to leave a bad taste in my mouth. He would hear about my clients, and he didn't like the positions I put myself in and the way some clients treated me. He said I was too precious, my safety mattered, and he wanted me to stop.

Soon he wanted to know when I had appointments and to message when I was done. To let him know when I was out and safe... he didn't like knowing about it... but not knowing where I was and who I was with was worse for him. I told him Emily knew where I was going and who I was with so not to worry, as I already had someone local who could act if I went AWOL. I reminded him that being 100 miles away, there would be little he could do if something awful happened. But he still insisted, saying better to have another person I could trust aware, just in case Emily was not around.

So he knew the times, addresses and appointment lengths. If I came out a bit late there was always a message from him asking for an update or saying if I didn't contact him by X he would be contacting the Police. I messaged each time I got out and within a nanosecond he was there, relieved to have heard from me, relieved I was alright. This eventually took its toll on him, and we reduced it to an update on 'new' clients only. The premise was existing clients we knew were 'OK'.

He just weirdly gave a shit, and I was beginning to think this pretence of genuinely caring would be hard to keep up with. He even refused to sign off messages at night unless he knew I was back in the house after taking Ron out for his last pee of the day.

It was all mind-blowing, I started to become convinced he did care, I had never had anyone show interest or care to this level, or bother about where I was or who I was with.

Phil didn't know where I was half the time, never asked, or batted an eyelid if I was delayed or late.

Sam and his behaviour was completely alien. I liked it.

He told me the 'sky was blue' and he was going to 'get me out my box and show it to me.' That I could have love, and that I deserved it, that feelings are important.

It became impossible to fight any more and against my better judgement I eventually caved and confessed that I thought I perhaps loved him too. And I did, so much, like no other, it was the truth.

Never had I felt this way before, never had I had such strong emotions and I didn't like it. It was scary, it felt vulnerable, out of control. I like control.

I explained I didn't like to overuse the word and I refused to just instantly reply to an 'I love you' with an 'I love you too'. I didn't want it to become overused and meaningless.

I was beginning to feel safe with him, that I could rely on him, relax a little, and think that it was OK to allow myself to need and want him.

He was ever-present, consistent and reliable. He became my comfort blanket. Lyrics in love songs hit me, as if for the first time, like I got it for the first time. I felt safer than I had done in as long as I could remember.

That said I remained petrified. Emily kept me in check, reminding me how farcical this all was. And I fought it, sometimes relaxing and enjoying, sometimes wary. Sam always clocked it when I was feeling wary and said my 'shields were going up'.

I worried constantly about having said or done something that he didn't like. I was certain it would be the moment he woke up from this mirage he had built and saw me for who I was. I struggled to share what I truly felt, wanted and worried about, it made me seem crazy, unreasonable, and infatuated. I didn't want to do anything to scare him away. Some things, most in fact, are best left unsaid in my opinion. Kept safely in your head, in a box, where they can cause no trouble or harm to others. Just your own anguish to contend with.

He kept saying 'I am not going anywhere.'

I tried to keep him out for so long, hold him at arm's length, but it became tiring. Under his persistence eventually, it was easier to just let him in.

But with that came fear, I didn't want to accept it, my internal doubt and dialogue telling me that I knew he did not speak the truth, perhaps not consciously. I had certainty he was not aiming to hurt me. But this could not be real and true, he couldn't love me, the failing female who was secretly a whore. Yet his actions showed he maybe did love me and it became harder to deny. I was trapped in a pendulum of confusion, swinging between hope and truth.

The feeling that there was more to this, never left, expecting him to reveal that truth at any moment. One thing I knew for certain was that the fatal blow was in the post I just was unsure when it would be delivered. But I literally could not live without him. So I decided I would enjoy the ride and deal with the fall-out when it came.

Chapter 9

Lorry Cocks Matter

I can feel a shift in me, triggered by Misty's visit... her visit to my home, my sanctuary. I just can't shake the feeling that she is dangerous. Now, every creak in the house keeps me on edge. Wondering when she may appear again, and I just know she will. I feel tense that my carefully hidden side hustle could be about to be revealed to the very people I do it to protect. My motives won't matter, they won't be understood. If the truth came out. It would only leave pain and destruction.

How can I ever explain this to my children? The fear of Lottie and Thomas looking at me differently is all-consuming, seeing their eyes filled with disappointment, disgust, and disbelief. It is unbearable. I need to find a way out of this job. But that seems a long way off.

School would become a playground of torture for my children, as their friends torment them about their mother - the whore. The news would spread at an unstoppable pace, annihilating love, respect and life as I know it.

Girthygary was also messaging frequently since I saw him at my business brunch, this presented another unnerving threat to my family and life as I knew it. He wanted me to provide a free hour every time I was in his town, or he would reveal my secret side hustle to my marketing clients and family. I do not have a choice and have agreed. He says he has taken screenshots of my profile. My profile was carefully constructed and does not have any identifying pictures, just holes and tits. I never posted my face and I make sure all distinguishing marks are hidden or edited out. Like my mole at the base of my left buttock.

Where I had been less careful, Girthygary included, is that once a relationship of sorts was developed, and I had a good feel for them, I happily sent further images. Either to secure a booking or provide additional wank material in between, hoping to encourage rebooking. Stupidly this Included unedited pictures of my butt, mole fully present and correct. There would be no doubt it was me. My memory is shockingly bad these days and I cannot recall what else I have sent him, but from what he describes, he has enough to sink me.

So when my children bound through the door a short while after Misty vanished, dropping bags and kicking off shoes, leaving them where they fell, my arms instinctively reached out to grip onto my huffy teenagers, they squirmed away like wriggling fish. I can almost hear the eye rolls and the muttered sighs as I try to draw them in closer and I do. As I hold onto them, I realise I can't leave this to fate. I cannot sit back and let her destroy my life or Girthygary reveal the truth. I need to find out once and for all, what Misty wants, what she knows and how I can stop her from exposing me. I also need to keep Girthygary sweet and quiet.

The challenge I have in relation to Misty is I don't know what to do. How do I find her? How do I get her to engage? I don't know where to start, I need help. I decided I would tell Sam about this. I don't want to if I am honest, he will just worry, but he always has a way of looking at things in a logical step-by-step way. He often raises things I had not considered. I am also going to talk to Emily. I am certain between the three of us we will formulate a plan.

Phil gets back shortly after the kids, he is tired from his phys-

Three's A Crowd

ical labouring and painting day. His eyes look weary, he just looks a bit defeated, beaten. It is upsetting to see. I make dinner for us all, just a simple spag bol, with no mince for Lottie. She is the world's fussiest eater and just takes the pasta, plain with nothing else on it. I often fret about getting more nutrition into her, but equally do not want to make a thing out of eating as I know all too well the consequences of that. She does enjoy fruit a lot and that is a blessing.

After dinner, I fire a message off to Sam.

> Hey, something odd happened today and I need your help, I am OK, I will explain later, hoping you will be around x

A few short moments later 'McHorn' pops up on my phone.

> Of course, I will always help you, I will be on as soon as sleepy time hits here.

Just knowing he is there sends a soothing mask over my body. I am wishing the evening away, as ever I can't wait to message him, but tonight I desperately need him.

I should really do some work, and get that contract done, but I am still a bit discombobulated, my head is darting from hypothetical scenario to hypothetical scenario. Instead, I sit with the family 'watching' the film National Treasure. I cannot recall a thing about it, but apparently it was good so I agreed and played along.

As everyone disperses off to bed I see 'McHorn' pop up.

> Hey Natasha's crashed, what's up?

> Hi, well it's a bit of a strange story, last week when I was doing the Asda run, a young girl about Lottie's age grabbed my arm and stopped me in the car park and was talking nonsense to me, saying I had to help her, to listen to see, it was creepy, I think she said my name but can't be certain as it was all a bit weird and I was in a bit of a panic, I pulled away and fell as I did it. People came to help me and when I got up, she was gone. Then this afternoon, I came out of my office and the same girl was in my house on the landing. Saying the same stuff, I was petrified Sam, she's in my home where my kids are, she said she needed me to help her, to stop Darren and his friends, I know the name is likely a coincidence, but she then said 'your Darren' to me, I panicked and said I was going to call the police... she barked at me 'that I wouldn't do that or she would tell my kids I was a secret whore'. I am really freaked out Sam.

OMG, fuck, what the hell

> I know

OK, give me a minute.

....

Do you recognise her?

> No

What are you thinking?

> I don't know, I mean I do think it's likely a coincidence, I don't know the girl. There are only 3 people who know about 'my Darren' on this planet, you, me and Emily. So how can she know? I have not seen him in 30 years, and he lives 200 miles away as far as I know. But it's the mention of my name, and I am scared she knows about my escorting. I just have a bad feeling I am going to see her again. She is clearly ill.

> Is she maybe from Lottie's school? Maybe that's how she knows your name? But you maybe don't recognise her? High schools are big places.

> I guess that's a possibility.

> It's the only possible explanation, the Darren thing has to be a coincidence and the whore thing, just an angry teen.lashing out calling you a whore. It just hit you because of your work.

> You're probably right

> MHBB2! But you need to be careful, lock your windows and doors when you're in the house, lock your car when out. If it happens again, try and get a snap of her on your phone and report it.

> OK

> You ok?

> Yeah just a bit freaked out is all.

> Understandably, I am sorry that happened. Wish I could give you a hug.

> Me too. Anyway, how was your evening?

We message back and forth for another hour and then both hit the hay. I wish more than ever I was sliding under the covers next to him, feeling his arms lock around me, like a shield that can stop anything. I crave his warmth.

I toss and turn. My sleep is fitful, waking frequently, my heart racing, and sweaty. Waking releases me from images and sounds of Misty. Misty crying, screaming, kicking. Misty with Darren, Darren's face, other faces from school long forgotten, sex, the train I used to get to school, my cello case, the cafe I worked at, my old family dog Dottie, physical pain, fear, panic. Lottie and Thomas playing and laughing as toddlers, crying as teens, GW clients.

Clearly my mind is frantically trying to sort the events of the day, intertwined with memories from the past. That knowledge doesn't make it easier to shake off the uneasiness though. I haven't dreamed in years...for as far back as I can remember, or if I do, I don't recall them. Eventually about 3 am I give up, I can't face drifting off again just to be faced with more unwelcome images. I take myself downstairs and grab a pad, and pencil and draw feverishly. I haven't drawn like that in years, it is comforting, distracting and peaceful.

In the morning I hear Phil's voice faintly:

"Jess... Jess... you OK?"

My eyes focus and my body feels heavy, I am still in the living room, pad and pencil still loosely in my hand.

"Oh gosh, I must have passed out here," I mumble.

"What's up?" He asks, "You OK?"

"Yes, just had one of those nights where your mind won't shut off, so thought I may as well get up"

"Want tea?"

"Yes please"

He returns with a mug of steaming tea which I nurse, as I feel its warmth wrap me up in a tea-shaped hug.

"Thank you," I say.

I force myself to get moving after my tea, but still reeling and edgy I decide to take Ron out and run. I enjoy running, you can just focus on the rhythm of your feet, your head empties, that said it doesn't suit me, I am out of my element, with an awkward and uncoordinated style. My arms swing too high, and my legs kick out wildly as if unsure where to go next. I am pretty sure the expression on my face is a mix of determination and discomfort, eyebrows furrowed with effort, and mouth slightly open as I gasp for air. My running style...ungraceful.

As I fall back into the house everyone is just leaving. I reply to some messages from Szymon on my burner phone. He wants me to come over to his on a weekend afternoon. He is about an hour away, and to do that on the weekend is harder, but not impossible. He is fed up with waiting for the gang bang boys to sort their shit out and so says he wants to see me fucked by some people in his home. He will pay my usual hourly rate and charge the additional men and give it all to me. It's potentially a good earner for a couple of hours. Adrian from the GB group has said to Szymon he would oblige provided he can belt my ass really hard. So we look at some dates for that and he is going back to Adrian to confirm plus reach out to some other guys he knows.

I am just considering jumping in the shower when Sam messages me asking if I'm free as he has just left for the office.

He rents a co-working space (hence the open-plan office). It works well for him, it keeps work out of the house (which I envy, I don't get to close the door and walk away, and work is always poking me saying this needs to be done!). It is low cost and also gives him access to professional meeting rooms for client meetings. As a freelance business turnaround analyst, it projects the right image. I think once my business is making enough I will look into co-working spaces. I miss the hub and buzz of interacting with people and feel quite isolated working from home; I don't miss the morning traffic and city centre parking costs. Although today it's likely a good thing I am working from home mainly, as I am half dead.

"Morning gorgeous" He beams, and it's so good to see his face, it's a video call. "How are you? You look a bit flustered?"

"Ahh sorry, yeah just been for a run and not long in the door" I carry the phone about while I talk to him and prop him up on the porch windowsill while I wrestle with my wellie boots to get them off.

"A run... in your wellies?" he asks. Honestly that man misses nothing.

"Er yes..." I say suddenly feeling embarrassed, I don't want him to know I don't have any trainers, they burst a good 5 months ago and I can't afford to invest in a new pair at the moment. Kids uniforms and food come before trainers for me, that is a luxury and way, way down the list.

"Why?" He asks... "That's not good for your feet or knees and wellies are slippy, you'll hurt yourself."

"Erm.." my mind runs a quick search to see what white lie might be passable, bingo... play the 'I wasn't expecting it' card.

"I didn't intend to run when I set out."

"Well, next time, don't fucking wear your wellies to run in OK...?" He says

"OK"

"Jess... look at me."

I raise my eyes to the camera.

"What are you not telling me?"

"Nothing"

"Jess, I can see it... what is it? You can't lie to me, your face is like an open book!"

"No, it's not, I am a most excellent liar... highly skilled" I smile.

"Not with me, you are not, I see you, so spill"

"OK, OK, I don't have any trainers"

"Well, bloody buy a pair you dumb ass."

"I will" I lie.

"You'd better or I am going to spank your ass until it bruises," he says.

"Ooof that's not an incentive not to buy them" I laugh "You know what spanking does to me."

From there our chat descends into filth, by the time we hang up he is hiding a hard cock walking into the office and I have another smell to expel in the shower other than being sweaty from my run.

As the water runs over me, I work the soap around me. I find myself wishing that Sam was standing behind me, groping and gliding his hands, pausing and squeezing my tits. Twisting my nipples and making me wince, feeling his breath on my neck and ear as he tells me; 'what a desperate dirty bitch I am and that he

Three's A Crowd

is going to fuck me hard, that he doesn't care what I want, he is just going to use and abuse me and spray his spunk up my asshole, mark his territory, like the filthy whore I am, he owns my ass'.

I imagine feeling his hard throbbing cock pressing on my lower back. I need to cum, so I grab my face wash bottle with one hand, which is just the right girth. Place the other hand on the tiles and reach down and begin to glide it in and out of my soaking wet, aching, groaning, cock hungry pussy, increasing the rhythm until I convulse and cum hard.

After all the tension of the last fourteen hours I needed that.

With a run out the way and my pussy in a rare state of rest and satisfaction I crack on with the day ahead.

Right! First thing is first, I am getting that bloody contract done, meeting with the menopause brand, and then I have a new GW client which should be quick and easy, once all that is done I plan to speak to Emily and get her thoughts on the Misty problem.

It takes me about three times as long as it should to pull the contract together and raise an invoice due to fatigue, but it gets done and is fired off to Harry, including a few dates for our first meeting.

Ping! Mchorn!

Bet you had a wank in the shower!

> Well given the state you got me into, what do you expect!

Control?... no wait, forgot your brain, is in your pussy! That's your control centre! 🐸

> Ha ha, I am pleading the 12th.

The 12th?

> Yeah you know, the thing people say when they don't want to say anything as it incriminates them? An amendment! Thought MHBB2?!

> That would be the 5th Jess... honest to fuck, pussy for a brain!

>> I will have you know, as I have told you before I have a BB, and my BB tells me a needy pussy works for you.

> But you need a hard cock for that needy pussy.

>> I do, desperately.

> See MHBB2! Don't forget to message me when you're done with your client today. I expect to hear from you shortly after 3 pm.

>> I know, will do.

> Good, got to run... pls.. Be safe x

>> I will x

At 11 am I jump on a Google Meet call with Claire and her team from the menopause brand to walk them through the plan. I answer their queries and explain things they are unsure of, and we divide responsibility for who is doing what in her team with milestones and review points. Claire is thrilled with the work and we agree on another meeting date.

By 1 pm I am heading out the door, fully slutted up in a really whore like red under-bust basque, no panties, stockings and suspenders covered by a dress and long coat. It's what Jeff had requested.

Jeff is new, married and a trucker. He didn't want anything out of the ordinary, just a standard fuck, all holes included.

Sam and I had argued about my services, he said it was usual for certain activities to warrant an additional payment, such as anal, cum in mouth, water-sports, and being spanked. I didn't see it that way, it was my marketing brain. Keeping things simple at the point of sale results in more sales, complicated pricing is just a barrier that puts people off and can lead to misunderstandings and disappointment. I had raised my prices a while back when he first mentioned this to encompass the wide range I offered. But I still believe a single set price was a better strategy. An all-inclusive price with no hidden fees.

Of course I want to make money, but I cannot abide people that take the piss or take advantage. Fair simple pricing was important to me. One thing I changed at Sam's request was removing bareback as an option on my profile. I am not a fool, I know the risks, and I only ever offered bare back to those that could prove they were clean with recent valid tests. To be honest not many wanted bareback, escorts are risky I guess for the males and with a large proportion married with kids you could understand them wanting to be safe. You didn't want an escort turning up on your marital doorstep saying she was pregnant, and it would be hard to explain any STDs to your Wife. Sam really didn't like bare back at all, like Emily he is quite cynical at times, said that tests and ID could be faked and got his knickers all in a twist about it, so I decided to remove it just to shut him up. I hate confrontation.

I pull into the lorry park just before 2 pm and await the message. Jeff messages telling me which lorry he is in. I scan the lorry park and clock it and stroll over to the cab.

I feel for truckers, many escorts discriminate against them. A regular message on GW from truckers is... 'Do you do lorry meets?'. The first time I was asked this I replied and said 'Yes, of course, why wouldn't I?' I was wondering if I was missing something. I just got the reply that lots of escorts refused to and to this day I don't really understand the reason.

I feel like we need a movement, an uprising, and I should make a placard and wave it in my fellow escorts' faces and protest outside brothels with a sign saying 'Lorry's Cocks Matter!'

To me it seemed like one of the safest options, lorries tended to have company names and phone numbers on the side, so if the worst happened you would have some recourse, compared to other meets that are in reality much more anonymous. Other clients could delete their profiles and vanish. Although Emily said I was a 'dumb fuck', because 'what good would a company phone number and name do me if I was dead?'. But I don't subscribe to her view of the world, she seems to think everyone is bad and evil and a potential murderer. I am 47 and have not met one yet.

As I walk across the lorry park, I clock the cabs with curtains drawn and wonder if the trucker inside is sleeping or being entertained by a colleague. I can feel eyes on me as I cross the tarmac, my eyes meet one guy who kind of smiles and gives me a knowing nod and wink.

As I get to Jeff's cab he jumps out, and walks around to open the passenger side door to help me up. I don't need it, I have mastered getting into lorries, but they are high up, and he probably got a flash of my sloppy pussy from below.

I close the door, and he comes back round climbs in his side and starts drawing the curtains as he talks to me.

"God I need this, 14 days on the road solid and my balls are blue, it's hard to coordinate a working girl to meet when you travel so much."

"Blue balls means a big load and that makes me very excited," I say with a smile.

"Oof, like a bit of cum do you?"

"Cum addict" I say "Sign me up to cum addicts anonymous!"

"Let's test that shall we?"

He climbs into the back behind the seats and starts stripping off. I follow and take off my coat and dress.

"Fuck me", he says as he strokes his hard cock... and reaches out to feel my tits. "Bend over" he says, and I lean onto the mattress, and he slaps my ass a couple of times, whacks his cock off it and then pulls my ass cheeks apart, bends down, spits on me and slides his spit all over my asshole and pussy lips.

"You don't need that, you're already soaked you dirty bitch." He lurches forward, and I can feel the head of his cock at the entrance to my pussy, slipping and sliding about trying to find its way in.

"Condom!" I say.

"Ahhh fuck, I didn't get any."

"I asked you too, as I told you I was out and wouldn't have time."

"I know, I am sorry, I didn't have time either, but don't worry, I am clean."

I stand up and turn to look at him. I feel so bad, I **never** don't have condoms, I totally made it clear for him to bring some. But I do understand how days can run away with you. I didn't know what to do. He is all hard, primed and ready to rock 'n' roll, I had driven 40 mins to meet him and I desperately needed this £150.

"How do I know that?"

"Look, I am married, I have a Daughter, she is 9, yes I fuck about on the road, but rarely. I have not seen an escort in months. I test regularly because I can't risk taking anything home and giving it to my Wife."

"I test regularly too, but this is my livelihood, my life, I have kids Jeff."

"So we are the same! Both sensible, it's fine."

"You promise me you're clean?" I say searching his eyes, wanting him to look into mine and realise how serious I am, that he has to be.

"I swear."

I think for a moment.

"Come on, help a guy out, I need this, and you have nothing to worry about, I wouldn't do that to someone. That would be pretty low."

So I nod, smile and bend down to suck his cock which was beginning to droop, once back up, I resume my position leaning on the bed, and he goes pussy to ass with a ferocious energy, while spanking my ass, and pulling my hair so my back arches.

"Dirty whore, fucking men in lorries, cum loving piece of filth" he says and continues to throw out a range of dirty talk until he pulls out, tells me to turn round and sprays his spunk all over my face.

"Going to spray my seed all over your slut face" he groans.

It just keeps coming!

Naturally, I scrap it off my face and scoop it into my mouth.

"Yep, you're a cum addict" he laughs as he gets himself dressed. "Thank you" he says and hands me my money. "I will be in touch next time I am passing."

He once again comes round to open my door and help me down, I climb down carefully and head back to my car, reach for my wet wipes, clean myself a little further and reapply some makeup.

I reach for my phone and message Sam.

> Safe x

He replies instantly.

> Thank fuck, thank you, all OK?

> Yeah, all fine, standard stuff x

I don't like to go into details, it doesn't seem fair, sometimes he asks though. I don't mention the condom or lack thereof.

> Good, got to run I have a meeting, love you will message later

I drive back still cursing myself on the condoms, I won't do that again, no matter what happens I will make the time for condoms and be late if necessary. I need fuel, thank god for the cash in my pocket. I pull into the retail park and go to the Tesco garage fill up, go in and pay the money. When I get back in the car Emily is waiting for me.

Three's A Crowd

"Hey Em, where did you come from!? I've so much to tell you!"

I am suddenly hit by how warm the car is. I always have the heating on full blast, I hate a cold car, but stepping in from the outside it slaps me like walking into a wall, wrapping itself around me, choking me, like I can hardly breathe.

"I am always around Jess, you know that." She says "How was Lorry man?"

I fill her in, and she does not seem surprised by any of it.

"For fuck's sake Jess! Why did you let some dirty fucker, fuck you without a condom? You know the risks, you may have caught anything, for fuck's sake and not even clean tests, what were you thinking?"

"It was awkward, I felt bad," I replied weakly.

"Well, fuck me, wouldn't want to upset a random trucker, wouldn't be at all awkward telling Phil, Lottie and Thomas you have HIV because you're a dumb fuck!"

"Oh Em don't"

"Fucking will, you total idiot, how long do you have to wait until you can test and know for certain you're OK?"

"I don't know."

"Jesus Jess, did you not think that's something you should know in your line of work? Find the fuck out and let me know and get tested."

"OK, OK, OK... thanks just add to my worries, but there is something I need your help with, something strange happened to me," I say, and I start to tell her about Misty at Asda and at home.

Her response was not what I expected and she threw me completely.

"I know her," she says.

"What!?" I exclaim "How, when?"

"Almost as long as you," she replies "she needs help Jessie."

"Well clearly, why have you not told me about this?"

Em turns on me in a flash, raging anger explodes out of her. I have seen her temper before but not like this.

"I have, but you were not listening as per fucking usual. When do I get the chance to tell **you** anything eh?"

"Woah, what, what do you mean?"

"You don't listen, never fucking have, you never ask anything, I gave up trying to get you to listen to me a long fucking time ago, it is always about you and always has been. I am just your sounding board, steps up when needed, keeps you safe, you don't even really recognise I exist, what do you ever do for me?"

"Jesus Em, what the actual fuck, what are you on about? What have I done? I hang out with you all the time! And when have you ever mentioned Misty to me?"

"I told you about her in your kitchen the other day, but you were zoned out, it's like when I speak you ignore me, until we start talking about Sam of course, then your ears prick up, you still talking to that dick?"

"Yes, of course, but Em, I am sorry I didn't hear you, I have such a lot on my mind, shit excuse I know, I am sorry, tell me about Misty, has she scared you too? You should have forced me to listen Em, this is serious, Why didn't you?"

"Because you don't fucking listen! So what is the actual point, but I tell you what, you need to start listening to her or everything will fall apart."

"You mean she will tell people about my escorting?" My heart is pounding , my head so hot I feel it melting my newly applied makeup sliding, my stomach churning like a washing machine.

"Well she knows, and she knows exactly who you are."

"Fuck."

"You want this to stop, it's down to you, face her, listen to what she has to say, it won't be nice, but it is the only way."

"What does she want Em, I really don't understand"

"Jessie, this is something you need to hear from her, not me."

I feel an overwhelming tightness in my chest, panic rising, it feels like the car is closing in on me.

"My advice Jessie, if you're listening, listen to her and wake up to the fact Sam is playing you."

I start sobbing and squeezing my eyes shut.

"Fucks sake Jessie, stop… stop being a fucking baby, crying doesn't help, grow a pair and sort this. I'm leaving."

I try to steady myself and open my eyes to find Emily gone, I didn't even hear the car door close. I can hardly hear a thing as the blood is firing round my head like a fire tornado. I hear some aggressive beeps and jolt up, check my rearview mirror, realising there is a queue of cars behind waiting to use the pump.

I start my engine and push the buttons to open all the windows in the car. I need air, I lift a hand to apologise to the cars behind and drive off.

All the way home I am questioning if I am a bad friend, I have to admit I have been a bit self-absorbed lately, lost in my own troubles with money, and the business. But was I really that bad? I hated the thought of hurting Emily. She is so good to me, she doesn't deserve that. I will be better.

As I get home, the house is still quiet, I put my slut bag away, get changed and settle down at my desk to clear some emails.

I message Sam to see how he is doing and send him some spanking porn. He says he is leaving on time tonight so I intend to walk Ron around 5pm to catch him. I have not yet decided if I will tell him about what Emily has said.

As I sit at my desk trying to concentrate I cannot shake the feeling of dread that is consuming me. It's a tightness in my chest like something heavy is pressing down. My stomach holds a dull, queasy feeling that won't go away. My heart thumps a little too fast, each beat reminding me that something's not right. It's a sense of unease, a nagging knowledge that something bad is just around the corner.

Chapter 10

Well, That Did Not Go To Plan

Home is the usual buzz and chaos, dinner time, sibling fights, picking up after teens who clearly don't understand plain english. I slip out and walk Ron, chat to Sam about his day, and he takes the piss out of me for running in my wellies.

The evening passes without anything out of the ordinary, but I still feel uneasy. I can't get hold of Emily, I don't think she is talking to me.

Once the house is calm, I check in on my slutmin duties, WhatsApp messages and of course my precious and favourite time of day, Sam O'Clock.

By the time I almost crawl up the stairs to bed I am desperate for sleep, it doesn't come. And when it does it is another fitful one, resulting with me once again waking up on the sofa, pen and paper loosely in hand and Phil looking at me quizzically.

I go away today, I have a 'proper' work client meeting tomorrow and I am combining it with three GW clients on the way and one tomorrow before my meeting. That will get me almost 1K for this week combined with the Lorry guy, minus hotel and petrol costs. But they are going through the business.

I take Ron out, catch up with Sam who asks about my clients for today. I explain I have a new one early in the afternoon, then one on the road down who is a regular, followed by another car meet that evening, an Australian I have seen a few times. Tomorrow morning is another regular and then a 'real' client meeting where I am presenting the results of the campaign we have just run.

Sam reminds me to let him know when I am done with the new client, I don't mention the fact it is the one he asked me not to go to. The one who wants to 'break me'. He also requests I let him know when I arrive safely at my hotel. He mentions how he hates this and wishes I did not have to do ***this work***. Not only that, but he starts criticising Phil, and I defend him as he is genuinely really trying.

I shower, dress, do a few bits of admin and hoover the house before packing my bag.

When I brush my teeth my 'self filled' tooth filling comes away,

leaving a sharp spike that is rubbing on my cheek and scratching my tongue.

Fuck!

Szymon broke my tooth maybe five months ago. It was a total accident, Szymon has erectile dysfunction and he can't get excited or cum unless he is being really rough. His first ever message to me was:

Looking for a whore who can take it really rough, rare to find…are you that whore?
I enjoy:
Hard face slaps… really hard! Hard tit slaps… really hard!
Aggressive hair pulling …and I mean really aggressive! Spitting on you and degrading you!
I am sure you get the idea…better to be upfront, I am not playing, I do mean hard!

Three's A Crowd

So I agreed, and I can absolutely confirm, he **did** mean hard, **he was not playing**, but he is such a lovely guy and has helped me so much. It really felt like a noble cause to provide for someone that kept getting turned down by escorts due to his wish list. He had also lost all confidence dating, because he couldn't perform and at what point do you bring that up on a date?!

"Hi, I am Szymon, a good guy, but I can never have sex with you because I am impotent, but you can play with my floppy cock and I get turned on by hurting you. Do you want a second date?" Or do you wait until date two? Or hold off until you're kissing, and she reaches for his groin to discover no reaction, and he has to say "oh... by the way..."

I feel for him, it must be so hard! Or not, in his case.

I made it clear, no permanent damage, no visible marks, and we agreed some safe words, all of which I never needed, and I know if I had he would have always respected. I am pretty tough and can handle most things, and to be honest I am a bit of a pain slut too, it sends you into a calming headspace and then when fucked after, it causes supercharged orgasms.

He never mentioned at this point his erectile dysfunction. He only bought it up about 48 hours before our first meeting. I was a bit gutted to be honest but there was no way I could pull out, it would hurt his feelings far too much. He was very upset when he opened up about his problem and how it made him feel. So meetings with Szymon did very little for me sexually, he'd finger fuck me or use a dildo and he paid well. We got on well, he likes spending time with me, and it made me feel good, as a person and as a slut. But I always had to finish myself off when he left. It is a strange experience interacting with a guy who can't get hard, giving a blow job to a flaccid cock that never hardens, not seeing any visual reaction to your hard work, until with no warning some cum dribbles out.

In one meeting, he was ramming a new plastic vibrator I had got free with a lingerie purchase in and out of my mouth with aggressive force. He liked to see me choke, my eyes water and dribble pour out my mouth. Sadly the way he rammed it in on one particular thrust must have knocked an already weak tooth and it cracked.

I didn't tell him, he would feel bad. And it didn't hurt at all, just literally cracked, but it left a sharp point which presented me with a problem. Not least the fact I didn't have an NHS dentist and I couldn't afford a private one, but also sharp teeth and blow jobs don't mix. Not only that but dentists are the devil's foot soldiers. I do anything I can to not go unless I am at the point where the pain is so bad I can't sleep or think.

So I had a good old Google and found an amazing product on Amazon, called 'moldable teeth'. It is fantastic. It's tiny cloudy looking beads, you add hot water and mix, and they gravitate together into a kind of putty, you can squeeze, mould and shape inside your mouth where it hardens and hey presto, tooth filled, sharp point vanishes! One bottle is about £6 and lasts for months. You don't need many of the beads to fill a hole. Inevitably it loosens and comes out as you eat over a period of weeks. As a result this was a fairly frequent repair job needing redone every three to four weeks.

So with my sharp tooth exposed and four clients to see in the next 24 hours, I needed to reach for my trusty bottle of moldable teeth. Ten minutes later I am sorted with not a sharp edge to be found. I throw myself into the car and head off to meet the new client who is going to 'break me'. How many times have I heard that and what exactly does it mean?!

Guys seem to like the idea of 'breaking women' but it means something different to them all. Some like to see you cry out in pain and beg for things to stop. For others, they want to see you cry out with pleasure to the point you can't take it any more and beg for it to stop. Some want to fuck you until you are done, a limp worn out rag doll, but at the core of it, it just means they want to feel like a man and assert their power and dominance over you.

Three's A Crowd

I am all for that!

People's names on GW are entertaining and revealing. They fall into a variety of categories:

The trying to be smart/promote their dicks crew:
Uwantit
Takethisandparty
Fatcock29
Heavycummer
Unloader719
12incher
Girthmatters
Hardasnails
Uwon'tbeleftwanting
Cum4aride
Holefiller
Pussylover

Then the more sensual ones:
SensualWhispers
PassionateEmbrace
VelvetDesires
TenderAffection
IntimateBliss
Letsgetphysical

And then people who use their names or some form of movie name.

My profile name was simply 'Anything for cock'.

This new client's profile name was, I think just his name, I say I think as it was a collection of letters that didn't really make a name, but looked eastern European with extra x's and y's and c's in it.

We had chatted back and forth on messages, he knew my rules.

Not completely naked, no permanent damage, no scat, and we had agreed to condoms as he was not able to provide tests.

I had also learned his Wife was due to give birth at any

moment with their first child, and he was extremely sexually frustrated. He had managed to get his mates flat, and was evasive about the exact address, he just gave me the street name via text this morning and said he'd meet me there. He would be waiting outside.

As I swing round the corner into the street, I see a figure standing on some steps leading up to a flat. It is the only person standing on the street, so I assume it's him and pull in, parking just ahead of the stairs. As I drive past our eyes meet, he has his hood up and his eyes are cold, empty, almost dead. I have a wave of unease flash through my body and dismiss it. After all, feeling uneasy is fairly common at the moment.

I step out of the car, lock up and walk up the stairs to meet him, giving him my best, brightest biggest smile and asking how he is. As I stand next to him, I am suddenly aware that I am almost dwarfed by his presence. He takes up more space than an average guy. His muscles are pronounced, even under his hoodie.

"Hi", he says, low, monotone, unfeeling but with an accent.

He taps the fob onto the door lock and steps in, and starts walking down the corridor to the flat. I scurry along behind him, teetering on my high heels, trying to chat and break the ice. It feels uncomfortable, so I am firing light small talk questions at him and making comments about the hallway and area being lovely, but it all falls on deaf ears and a stony silence is all I get back, which only causes my verbal diarrhoea to escalate.

He wrestles with another set of keys and opens the door to the flat and gruffly motions towards the living room on the right. "In there" he says.

I step into the living room, and he goes straight forward into the kitchen. I place my bag down against the wall. I wait, in silence and scan the room. I notice some strange looking things attached to the walls, mounted on wood drilled into them, with carabiners, rope and clips. It looks quite haunting, something out of place against the cosy sofa, soft cushions, and personal photos. Weight discs are stacked in the corner and I assume the wall structures relate to this.

He enters the room and silently motions me towards him, reaches into his pocket and holds out his hand with cash.

"You want this whore?" he says and as I stretch my hand out to take it, he opens his fingers, and it falls to the floor.

"Pick it up bitch" he barks.

I am a bit taken aback but just assume this is all part of the game and go to bend down to get it, when out of nowhere he punches me in the stomach. The moment his fist connects with my stomach, everything changes in an instant. It's not just pain, it's a shockwave that seems to ripple through me. The force of the punch drives the air out of me, and I try desperately to suck in a breath that won't come. The pain isn't sharp; it's deep, dull.

"I said pick it up bitch."

I struggle down and get the money and drag myself up to standing, I have lost the power of speech, he knocks the money out my hand again as I uncurl up.

"Fucking pick it up you dirty whore, it's the money you want, you'll do anything for money."

I am a bit more on edge as I try to bend a second time to get the cash from the ground, and I was right to be, as he swings at me again.

My vision blurs slightly with the second blow, and the world around me dims a little. It's not just the physical pain that hits me, it's the sickening feeling of vulnerability, of being completely exposed and powerless. I think of Sam, scared what he would think if he could see me, cursing myself for not listening.

This time he lets me collect it successfully from the floor and I wobble over to my bag and put the money away while he kicks off his shoes and clothes. Somehow I am grabbed, and he pulls my arms behind my back and wraps cable ties around my wrists pulling them so tight they dig in and nip the skin. He drags me to the middle of the room and onto my knees landing with a thud. He starts fucking my face, and I mean that, using my mouth and throat like a pussy, grabbing onto my hair, yanking it back and forth. What happens next is less clear, he is talking to me all the time. Talking about how disgusting it is, I do what I do. What a worthless piece of shit I am, I can't recall exactly. Shock, shame or panic had taken over, and I was there, but not.

Once finished with my face, he yanks me up to standing, grabs a sock from the floor and stuffs it in my mouth…then shoves me hard. With no hands for balance, heels and already being quite disorientated I fall back, thankfully landing on the sofa behind, a sharp pain erupts on my wrists as the cable ties cut in. He moved towards me, his eyes fierce and cold. He opened my legs and slammed his cock deep into my pussy. I try to speak up about condoms but I can't be understood because my mouth is stuffed with his sock. There is a glint of satisfaction in his eyes. I shut my eyes and picture Sam, I want him - his face, his smile flash through my head, guilt spreading over every pore. I feel myself being manoeuvred again, and I am placed over the arm at the end of the sofa as he then takes my other hole. He fucks me so hard the sofa travels. Finally, he explodes inside my ass. Then disappears, leaving me there collapsed over the sofa's arm.

A few minutes later he returns, and uses scissors to release my hands. We are back to silence now. I want to speak up about the lack of condoms. But I don't. The atmosphere is tense, and I am just too shaken. I've lost some clothes along the way, and I get dressed and he does the same.

Before telling me to 'get the fuck out,' he says he will be back in touch and I better respond and come back. He has plans for me, something like that, it all sounded off and sinister, it implied I would regret not coming back.

Wobbly I make my way to the car, start the engine and drive. I start heading to my next appointment. I can't think straight, my stomach is sore, my wrists nippy, and I don't want to think about my next appointment. I am running through what just happened, but my thoughts don't form or come properly.

I just feel edgy and empty and full of adrenaline. I must have driven for a good fifteen minutes before I realised Sam has been messaging, he should have heard from me by now. Shit!! I didn't mean to keep him waiting, but I was just too shaken. I use dictation to send a message while I am driving.

> Sorry, safe

Instant reply

> Thank fuck, was worried had a really bad feeling, you ok?

> Fine

> Thank God!

I carry on driving, not really paying attention to the road, I don't know why this has affected me so much. With the exception of being punched it was not that out of the ordinary for escorting life.

Was it because I felt bad even going, because Sam had specifically told me not to? Was it because he was kind of right? This guy didn't respect my rules, was it because he punched me in the stomach? Like a mini attack.

All I knew, more than anything, was I wanted and needed to speak to Sam just to hear his voice, perhaps it was a combination of the shock of being punched, feeling vulnerable, on the back of Misty freaking me out and Emily being weird. I felt bad... as I knew it would be an unfair request as he was working, but I messaged him and asked if he could ring me. I just needed to hear his voice. Moments later the call came in, but video... fuck.

I felt close to tears and seeing his face made it worse but also better, it just helped.

He asked questions, I couldn't really give any answers, he shared how sick he had been feeling and the bad feeling he had so strong that he actually hurled. He knew something was wrong.

I was so grateful for him, he couldn't talk long obviously, but he would call later to check on me.

I couldn't face my next client, so I cancelled, citing car trouble as the reason. It took me a long time, stopping and starting and pulling over, but I got to my hotel, checked in and lay on the bed. Annoyed at myself for being so pathetic. Feeling sick that it was the ***very*** client Sam warmed me about. Urgh. I thought I would go to my evening appointment, but I cancelled that too.

Natasha had a late clinic and Beth was at a friends house for tea, so Sam called me again, video again. I lay on my bed listening to him and feeling calmer, he clocked my wrist which had some small cuts/tears from the abrasion of the cable ties. I brushed it off, but he wouldn't have it and went off on one about it all.

He said how he hated me doing this job, he hated the thought of anyone else touching me or hurting me, he wanted it to stop.

When he had to go, I cried, cried for my life and how it had become this, cried for my kids, cried for Sam and what a god damn awful position for him to be in. To top off my day, bloody Girthygary messaged again telling me to give him a date for a meeting or he will post the pictures of me to my home, addressed to Phil. Fuck.

I have not told Sam about Girthygary and I didn't let on to him that today had been the client he had told me not to let book - I couldn't face the 'I told you so.'

Chapter 11

Shaken & Stirred

I am still shaken the next morning and I suffer a third night of disturbances. Sam checks in on me in the morning and throughout the day.

I had a fairly uneventful meeting with my GW client first thing then a really successful presentation of the marketing results with my big client. They are so impressed they have left me a fantastic Google review and want me to keep me on for the next quarter's plan.

I was so pleased to get home that night. I wasn't even a little irritated by the strewn shoes, dumped plates and chaos. I can't focus or sit still though so I take myself off and lift weights for 40 mins. I decide against doing any work as I fear it will be a waste, I will only have to revisit it, and check it over again as I know I am not focused. I watch some Gogglebox with the kids before they head to bed, do a bit of slutmin, WhatsApp and see Szymon has a date for going to his which I can manage. Chat with Sam and take myself off to bed for what turns out to be yet another night of disturbed sleep. I am getting a little fed up with the lack of sleep now.

The morning comes all too soon, I go running (in my wellies) with Ron as the kids scatter to school, Phil has an interview so has left. He had news he was not successful at the last one and is a bit prickly.

I talk to Sam as he drives to work, (making sure my wellies are removed!) and he tells me he can't talk on his way home as he is collecting Natasha and Beth. They are off to see a show. I knew as he had shared that with me earlier in the week. He hopes to message when he is home, depending on the time. We message on and off throughout the day.

I struggle with my emotions around Sam a lot. I just wish I could click my fingers, and we would be together without hurting anyone. And when I know he is out with his Wife and family, I long for it to be me. I guess it is jealousy. How immature is that? I genuinely want him to have a good time, and he should do more of it. He rarely takes time for himself. Literally, the only time for him is his drumming lesson, practising in between is a rarity as he is given job after job and gets glared at if he sits down for 5 minutes.

Natasha is the main breadwinner, wears the trousers and dictates his entire life. He has to ask permission to breathe and take a shit, I shit you not…at least that is how it comes across.

However, I am equally, acutely aware I am only getting one side of the story and one version of events. I am certain she would have a different story to tell and the truth must lie somewhere in the middle. He claims to love her and that she is a good person, and I am sure she is, he wouldn't have picked someone bad. That said, is it right to treat someone you love how she does? She may be a good person, but not to him.

How can he love her though and also love me? That I don't understand, but I don't understand love full stop. He is much more experienced in that department than me. He had a lot of girlfriends and lived with lots of women before he got married.

I find what he tells me such a challenge to get my head around as he definitely wears the trousers with me, it's hard to imagine him not! And then I think, god I am really just his plaything, a chance for him to express an alternative persona. I am so far removed from the successful, uber-smart domineering woman he chose to be his Wife, her qualities must be the things he desires and respects in a woman. None of those qualities I have. But let's be frank, he is not after me for my personality, charm or intelligence.

She is a neurology consultant for fuck's sake...that is akin to being a brain surgeon. The clichéd career everyone uses in conversation is a literal representation of intelligence and success. Emily points this out all the time. "Don't be fooled Jess, he would never pick you, even if you were both free and single and he would never pick you. You will only ever be his bit on the side. That is all he wants from you."

I just wish I could do 'normal' things with him, go to a show, stroll on the beach, have drinks with his friends, who I feel I know but will never meet, coffee with his parents and see if they are as annoying as he claims, pig out on the sofa bingeing on a Netflix season. It is a futile and pointless waste of my brain's energy thinking like this, but it happens, and it eats me up.

I always find a Friday now brings with it sadness, as yes, we will speak while Beth is dancing tomorrow, and message over the weekend when we can, but it's always far less than in the week and I just miss him. It can't be helped, I get it, doesn't mean I have to like it though.

He messages when he is home, but it's late and says he is 'expected to be in bed,' So no chat tonight, I occupy myself with other slutmin. My stomach lurches as I spot another threatening message from Girthygary. Cue another disturbed night, contemplating the amazing time Sam and Natasha have had, how they have bonded, rediscovered affection and are currently fucking. Along with worries about Girthygary destroying my family. I do eventually sleep, but it's filled with a nightmare.

My nightmare is not the same as the ones I have been having recently. This time it's a community hall, where I am presenting my business to the group. There are amphitheatre-style wooden seat steps inside along each wall with people sitting on them. Up at the back in the corner are Sam and Natasha, she is elegantly draped over him, their hands entwined, listening to the speakers and kissing in between. Natasha's eyes are boring into me and smiling as they pause between snogs.

I have to stand and present my business in the centre, members of the audience ask questions, I can feel her gaze, and she is stifling giggles under her breath as she sees me squirm and fail, unable to satisfy the audience. I sit down on one of the wooden blocks, defeated. Natasha has a satisfied smirk on her face. I feel worthless, beaten, and foolish for ever thinking I would stand a chance in this league, a league I clearly don't belong in, I feel less and out of my depth. I am a weed among flowers, so screamingly out of place.

As all the talks finish, I am sitting packing my bag, Natasha and Sam walk towards me headed to the door just over my shoulder. Natasha pauses, smiles at me and says "foolish girl, look at you, he would never have picked you, how could you ever have thought that you are nothing to him."

I wake up from it, tears flowing. I get up and draw.

I heard from him the following morning, apologising he could not message, telling me he had a good time, but he missed me. Also he said that today he had been told by Natasha they were off to the beach after Beth's dancing, and so he would have company at dancing. This meant we would be unable to speak, he also informed me that it would be harder to message today. Whenever they do something he always pitches it as if it is her decision, not his. As if that makes it more palatable. Hinting that he doesn't want to. I know this is a lie.

I understood, wished him a good day and didn't ask if he fucked his Wife last night. Partly because I didn't want to know and partly because it's an unreasonable thing to enquire about... I mean I can't very well ask that he does not fuck his own Wife! And as much as it would hurt, he did marry her for a reason, he is happy, and life is perfect apart from the sex.

I provide that...for now, if he rekindled that with her, he would be completely happy and have no need for me. He would have everything he wants. I want nothing more for him than happiness, he deserves happiness and if that means I have to let him go, I would.

The definition of a dead bedroom, clinically is sex less than ten times in a year. So a little less than once a month. I do not consider that dead. It is alive, just pretty terminal, serious and on life support. But there is still hope as there is still some action. Like when someone is in a coma if there are some vital signs, there is hope, they still might wake up. Sex ten times a year with your partner is hope, not dead.

My dead bedroom is Dodo dead... extinct, gone forever and there is no hope that it will come out of the coma and sustain life. No vitals registering. Better just to pull the plug. And if you told me, there had been some scientific discovery that could bring the Dodo back to life... I would have to politely decline.

I wonder if Sam shares my definition of a true dead bedroom being no sex at all or does he fuck Natasha a few times a year and class that as dead?

So Saturday drags with my mind wandering to Misty, Emily who is still not talking to me, guilt over the 'break me' client, anxiety about Girthygary and wondering what Sam is up to. Will today be the day he realises he is not 'in' love with me and wants to put his all into his Wife?

Sam messages when he is home. Later once his house is quiet he starts requesting pictures of my pussy, ass and tits. I hide my fatigue and worries well. I have not told him about my disturbed nights and I won't mention how manic I am when he is unable to keep in touch, or how much it affects me. It is unfair as it cannot be helped. Sharing would make me look like a psycho and I would move from the 'fun exciting box' to the, 'urgh here is another nagging woman box'. He has one of those, he does not need another, if anything would kill us, that would do it. Besides, I am genuinely not a nagger, I am simple, easily pleased, and I don't like drama and confrontation, but when it comes to him, these feelings of uncertainty and jealousy are new ground. We have a good laugh and top-level filth before turning in.

I drift off quite quickly for once, it is welcome and deep, until I wake, aware I am clawing at myself. I have an insatiable itch just inside my vagina. It's like there's a tiny, persistent fire just beneath the delicate skin. I can feel it, a sharp, nagging itch that demands my attention, making it impossible to fall back asleep. As I scratch it, desperate for relief, the sensation shifts, spreads, and intensifies. The more I scratch, the worse it gets, like trying to put out a fire with turps. I head downstairs stopping in the bathroom for a wee on the way. It burns...fuck, I think, it is probably thrush. I have never had it before but I know the symptoms. I know I am also at increased risk of thrush as it can be aggravated by increased sexual activity and friction, with any micro tears providing the perfect environment for candida to thrive. Additionally, the use of lubricants and spermicides can disrupt the vaginas natural environment making it easier for yeast to grow.

Knowing this was a risk when I got into this I thankfully bought a tube of Canesten ages ago, I seek it out and rub it on. It soothes instantly, but the relief is very short-lived.

That is how the rest of my weekend goes, slapping on Canesten cream, enjoying a short spell of relief , messaging Sam, doing a bit of work, walking Ron, chatting to the kids, playing some Uno.

By Sunday evening I am starting to worry about this itch, there is no improvement which there should be if it was thrush. I am wondering if it is bacterial vaginosis. I am due my twelve-week STD test anyway so I decide I will order one online. It's a discreet home kit and I pay for upgraded delivery. All being well it will arrive on Tuesday. I have to cancel this week's GW bookings. Until I know what I am dealing with I can't really do that to anyone, it would be terribly unfair. I don't contact anyone I have been with, as no point until I know. So that is **_another_** week that I am down on revenue, combined with last week's cancellations due to my stupid upset over 'break me' boy.

The words *fuck my life* (FML), spring to mind. Can anything else be piled on me?!

Monday is slow to come but also fast. I am out early to see Harry to discuss the brief and get the project moving. We are meeting at 9am at a hotel about forty minutes away, I carefully suggest a hotel that is **not** one I use for fucking.

Sam and I chat as I drive to the hotel, and he heads into the office. It's now down to twenty days until we see each other. It can't come quick enough. His idea of this monthly networking event is genius, it should mean we are guaranteed to see each other every month, for an overnight. We plan to attend the actual event every second month so we have tales to tell on returning home to our respective partners. The other time not we will skip the meeting and just spend time together. Although it likely won't be every month, as school holidays and the like will no doubt get in the way. We chat about the upcoming meeting and I mention how hard it will be in the months when it's not possible. I also mention the fact his holiday means this is the last time we will see each other for two long months. He is off on a safari with Natasha and Beth in October. I don't want to think about that right now.

"I can't not see you, I need to see you." He says "We just have to find a way, Jess."

I walk into the hotel foyer at the same time as Harry, we chat about our weekends as we order coffee. I don't bother mentioning my itchy vagina, which I am still being driven around the twist with. I am certain that would not paint me in the best light.

I have my questions prepped and collect everything I need, delving into the heart of his company, his ethos, the product, target audience. I am already building a strong picture of the ideal customer - what their pain points and interests are. We discuss his goals for the marketing plan in detail and what measures should be put in place. I am in my element, this is what I love, and I already have so many ideas of where to take this campaign.

The hotel is buzzing with business people and probably whores revving up for the working week. We order more coffee, when it arrives Harry needs sugar and the pot on the table is empty. I go to the next table to grab some for him, and rummage amongst the sweeteners and other pots badly organised with sachets of ketchup, vinegar and salad cream. Despite the number of bodies milling about it feels chilly, the warmth of my coffee has left me, and I am convinced someone has left a fire door open. I return to the table and we continue our discussion.

As the meeting is coming to a close, I put my coat back on and wrap my arms around my body while Harry moves onto a more personal rapport-building type chat. He shares where he is going in the October holidays. I am listening but begin to drift, feeling like someone has their eyes on me, I glance around, trying to not look like I am distracted, but I am. I glance over his shoulder and I see her, Misty, alone, staring at me glassy-eyed. She looks so out of place amongst the suits and dresses. Frail, drawn, almost skeletal. My eyes widen and then I regain my composure. The last thing I need is a scene with a client I have just signed. I need Harry to leave and then I am going to calmly talk to her, get to the bottom of this, I am in a public place. I am safe.

Thankfully Harry starts making moves to leave and gathers his things, we both stand, and Harry shakes my hand.

"You're freezing" he exclaims.

"Cold hands, warm heart as they say," I reply, forcing a smile, but deep inside dread is filling my body from the toes up. I catch her movement from the side of my eye, gliding towards us.

"Thanks so much, Jess, looking forward to seeing the plan."

As I look at him, I lose sight of her, my heart is thumping so hard I am sure it can be heard above the chatter.

"I am excited about this Harry, you have something very

special here, and I am thrilled to be a part of it. I will be in touch at the beginning of next week."

I am willing him to leave before she reaches us. He turns to walk away and as he does, I almost hit the ceiling, as his body steps to the side and walks off, she is there, right behind where his body once filled the space .

Some relief hits me as Harry disappears into the distance, thank god he is away. But it can't counter the overpowering sense of doom.

I sit back down and Misty, never taking her eyes off me, descends painfully slowly into the seat Harry was sitting in, her gaze fixed. She sits unnervingly still, as if frozen in time. Her posture is rigid, her back perfectly straight, hands resting flat on her knees. The way she holds herself feels unnatural, too composed, like a mannequin positioned by an unseen hand. Her head is slightly tilted, eyes unblinking, watery and fixed on me. There is an eerie stillness, contrasted against the remainder of the room which is full of energy.

"Can I get you anything?" I ask "No," she replies.

"How do you know my friend Emily and what do you want with her?" I ask

"She is my friend too"

"Please don't hurt Emily," I beg.

"You don't hurt your friends" She says coldly. "I needed Emily to help me make you listen."

"I am listening, and maybe we could be friends?" I try. I am thinking if she considers me a friend and 'friends don't hurt each other', then maybe she will keep my side hustle secret.

"That is down to you" She says and as she does, her eyes fill and overflow with tears, and they just pour from her eyes. I hand her a tissue.

"How do you know me? Why do you need to talk to me?"

"I have always known you, you need to understand"

"If I listen to you, will you leave my family alone? I don't want my children hurt, please, I am begging you."

"It is not about them, it's only about you, but if you continue to ignore me, I can't stop them from being hurt," it feels sinister.

"What do you mean?" My voice rises in frustration and fear and a few people spin around to look at us.

Someone shouts over to me. "You ok?"

I nod back and calm myself. Why are they asking me!? I am not the one sitting here with tears running down my face.

"Sorry, I just want to protect them and to help you, are you at Rysden High?"

"No, I am at the Dames Order School."

My head spins, I have not heard that in decades, that's the name of my school, but it's not in this town, it is hundreds of miles away, she must be so far from home.

"That school is not local, do your parents know you're here?" I say. "Where do you live?"

"They still hurt me Jessie and I want it to stop."

"Who, who hurts you?" I ask, trying to be as gentle as I can.

"Darren's friends" She replies, and my blood literally drains out of my body.

"Darren who?"

"Your Darren!"

"Darren and his friends are not at school any more."

"They found me Jessie."

"I am sorry, I am confused, Darren and friends are adults, you're a child, that school is a long way from here, so why are you here? How do you know anything about Darren from my school?" I can feel my frustration building again. I feel sick, are they paedophiles?

"You won't understand until you listen, really listen, hear, feel, see."

"Well I am here, listening, so talk". I feel sick, but feel like we are just going round and round in circles and I just want her to spit it out, whatever it is.

Her shoulders take a huge heave and her sadness seems to visibly intensify before my eyes in response to my words, I didn't think that was possible, I don't think I have seen anything exude such sadness.

"This is.... is what I mean, you just won't allow it to happen. I will never be free unless you stop pushing me away, I can't carry this any longer."

She spoke in a voice that was barely more than a whisper, her words heavy and laden with exhaustion. Her shoulders slumped, and her eyes defeated. Each syllable felt like a slow, reluctant surrender, drained of energy and purpose. It was the voice of someone who had fought too long and had nothing left to give.

I could see, I could feel her, and her desperation hit me.

Here was a girl, practically the same age as Lottie, lost, scared, broken and for a reason I may never know or understand, she has latched onto me for help. I thought of Lottie, and how I would hope that if she was lost and lonely in this world and reached out to a stranger, they'd help her. My heart ached.

How could I not help this girl? Sure, it is absolutely the last thing I need, I have more than enough on my plate. But that doesn't warrant me not helping this frail girl who looks like she is close to the end.

That's the only way I can describe her, like the light was going out. I couldn't bear the thought of being part of that final curtain falling, and for what? Because I am busy? Because I am scared she will expose me? Nothing she can do to me would be as bad as that burden which would haunt me for eternity.

I concluded that she was really no threat. She is a child after all. Her clothes hung loosely off her skeletal frame as if they were draped on a wire hanger. Her collarbones jutted out sharply, and her wrists were so delicate that a bracelet would have slid right off. She was brittle as if she might shatter with the slightest touch.

Yes, I was confused and had a tonne of unanswered questions, but asking them was getting me nowhere. She is telling me to listen. That's what I will do, two ears, one mouth and by doing that, I hope the answers will reveal themselves.

Once I know more, I may be able to guide her to the right professional help, the Police, or at least discover who her parents are and talk to them. If I listen as she wishes, and I just let her talk, then she will have no reason to expose me. The more information she shares through talking, the easier it will be to prove to her that my Darren and hers are not one and the same. Unless they are. I feel sick at the thought. Hopefully, she is confused, and I can then also discover exactly how she knows about my Darren, what she knows and who betrayed me, Sam or Emily?

"I'm sorry, I want to help, I am listening, tell me what to do."

Her shoulders drop as if some tension has been discharged from her.

She leans forward. Reached for my hands and pulled them into hers, wrapping her wiry stick-like fingers over mine. I am already cold, but her touch is like an icy wind that hits my skin and radiates up my arm. I can feel myself trembling lightly. She looks me in the eyes, takes a long deep breath, slowly closes her eyes, like delicate curtains being drawn, and her eyelashes rest on her cheeks, she begins.

Chapter 12

The Mist Starts

Her voice is soft, pained, shaky, barely a whisper and I sit in silence as she speaks:
Drama club at school-finished walk down the lane to the train station Mark and James,

Leaning on a wall, near the garages they looked at me and smiled

I smiled back stunned

Never looked at me before I am invisible.

kept walking

"Hey, wait up!" It was Mark stopped, confused

They caught up with me.

While Misty talks I feel my head begin to spin... I know that lane, I know those garages, I know those names, this is insane. I start to pull back and then resist the urge, I have to listen. Misty continued:

'Hello' I said

'So' said Mark, 'we know!' And he smiled. 'Sorry! You've lost me, what do you know?' 'About you,' said James.

'Well can't be much! Not much to know about me!'

'We know you're desperate for cock'

'Oh yeah, we know everything,' I turned to continue walking.

Mark ran in front of me blocked my path, stopping me.

'Uh-uh-no you don't', he said.

'We know you begged for cock, we know you don't get it. We know that must make you sad'

I try to push past

Grabbed from behind, linking his arms under mine behind my back.

'Fucking listen to him' hissed James. 'Let me go!'

'Whack'

Slapped across the cheek face pulsed in pain 'Shut. the-fuck up.'

'We need to talk, we want to help you, let's go for a walk.' led off behind the garages

'I don't know what you think you know, but it's not the truth, I'd like to go, I just want to forget everything please, and I'd like to go home!'

Shoved against a tree trunk hand over my mouth

His weight against me his face in mine

'Shut the fuck up and listen. We know you begged to suck his dick, he pitied you and let you, you then begged him to fuck you, he did, even though he felt sick doing it, he got over that and tried not to think about the blubber bulging beneath him. He gave you a gift, he gave you something you'd never get.'

I shook my head

'Whatever story you want to tell yourself, crack on, we know the truth.'

'That's not true, please, that's not true.' slammed his hand over my mouth again.

'You're fucking delusional, look at you, who'd want you, we should give you what you want because you'll never get it otherwise. But you say a word to anyone, we'll make sure we tell the truth about that night, then everyone will know, because I saw you come onto him, I saw you in the disco, hands all over him, whispering in his ear.' 'Yeah I saw that too, I also saw you lead him outside by the hand!'

'No! I screamed under his hand.'
'Calm down, it's OK, we can make it all better.'
Arm grabbed pulled over the undergrowth. shoved onto a fence
Held
Dress pulled up, pants pulled down.
I try to kick.
I feel something slip into my vagina and out again.
'He was right, she's gagging for cock,' laughed Mark.
It hurts
My skin tore from rubbing against the fence.
He groaned, shuddered then still.
They swapped
James now hammers into me
Mark was talking.
'This is what you want, you begged for it. You're a lucky bitch, we don't fuck fat bitches but we feel sorry for you so we will keep doing this for you. But we can't have anyone know, it would be embarrassing, but far, far worse for you, no one would ever believe you and we'd make damn fucking sure of that.'

James moans and empties inside me. released
Slumped over the fence sobbing. Mark bent down and grabbed my chin, raising my head to look at him. I can hardly see him through the tears.
They made me thank them
He stroked my hair.
'Don't cry, it's ok, the best is yet to come.'
She stops talking, although the hotel bar is busy, and I know there is noise, silence is all I can hear. My stomach lurches in waves as if I am about to heave. I am shaking violently, my eyes tightly shut. I can't think. I feel her bony hands slip away from mine. I

don't know what to say, it is as if I have just lived what she said, I can't describe how shaken I am. I feel scared. I regulate my breathing, in and out and as I calm and open my eyes. There is no Misty. She has gone. I swivel my head around and can't see her anywhere. People at the neighbouring tables are looking over at me.

Shit, shit, shit, I think, fuck! I need to help her, she needs to report this. I leap to my feet and dash to the table next to me to speak to the couple enjoying tea and croissants.

"The girl, where did she go?" I ask.

"Sorry, what girl?" The guy replies.

"The one that I was sitting with!" I say in exasperation.

"Sorry, I don't know," he replied.

Infuriated, I ran out of the hotel and scanned the car park. She has vanished. Nowhere to be seen. I go back to pay for the coffee and ask the girl behind the bar the same question.

"Oh yes, I saw a young girl leave the bar a few minutes ago."

I walk out to the car, plonk myself in the seat and rest my head on the steering wheel.

If Emily had not met Misty I would be questioning my sanity. I feel so badly for Misty, if what she is saying is true, then she needs help to stop these boys, but why me, why have me help, and what does she want me to do? Where are her parents?

I am haunted by the names all familiar, but I guess common names. I knew these people 30 years ago, they would be men now, not hanging about at my old school, and that school is 200 miles away for god's sake, but this girl is here.... This makes no sense.

I did what she asked, I listened, and it got me absolutely nowhere. I don't have any answers to any of my questions and I still don't know how I can help her.

Chapter 13

This is Trichy

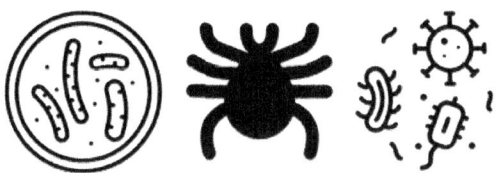

It takes me some time to get home. I am floored, drained, done. And when I do get home I am useless. I can't focus, I cannot get a thing done. My mind is empty but busy. I get Ron when I get home, take him for a wee in the garden and then lock all the doors and go up to bed.

I don't sleep, I just lay cuddling Ron in a trance, like a coma but awake. Periodically I respond to texts.

Phil:

> Interview went well I think, but you never can tell.
>
>> Glad to hear it, you can only do your best, you will get there
>
> Yeah - I am going to go see Dave, he said he might have some work
>
>> OK, take your time, see you later.

Sam:

> How was your meeting?
>
>> Great! How's your day?

> Busy! You home?
>
> > Yes.
>
> You OK?
>
> > Yes
>
> Sure?
>
> > Yes
>
> You're not saying much 😕
>
> > Sorry, bit busy
>
> With what?
>
> > Just the usual
>
> OK....
>
> > Sorry, will message later x
>
> Ok, love you x

Shit, I am aware I am not engaging, but I literally can't. I cannot think properly. God, he probably thinks I am being weird.

I know my day is goosed, I set an alarm for 3:50, so I can kick myself into action before the kids get home. The alarm is not to wake me from sleep, sleep won't come with my mind as it is. It is to alert me that I need to put my game face on.

I wish Emily was about, I hate it when she goes in a huff with me and even worse when I don't really know what I have done. I just lay staring into nothing for eternity, unable to organise my thoughts which are just jumping all over the place. No thought completes or finishes. Early afternoon, I decided to be the bigger person and text Emily.

> Hey Em, I am sorry I upset you, How are you?

Three's A Crowd

She replies instantly:

Fine

> What did I do?

Doesn't matter.

> It DOES!

Forget about it, move on.

> OK, but I can't be a better friend if you don't let me know.

Just try and listen

> OK, what's happening with you?

Usual

> What does that mean?

Nothing

> Em, why don't you ever answer my questions, I know you're bothered by something but I can't help you unless you tell me, I am not a mind reader.

I don't need fucking help

> Stop being so tough

I am tough

> I know, but you don't have to be with me, what's wrong?

Nothing

> Oh FFS Emily, you tell me to listen, but then you don't talk!

Well fuck off then

> Emily! God! Come on, I am trying.

It's not me you need to listen to.

> Is this about Misty?

Yes

> I saw her today

And?

I fill her in with a quick voice note.

That's just the start Jess.

> What do you mean?

She has more to tell you.

> How do you know?

I have met with her please Jess, just listen to her, please.

> You know it makes no sense, any of it.

It will, if you keep listening.

> Em you're scaring me. Did you tell her about Darren?

No

> WTAF is going on!!!!!

Talk to her and find out!

> Can't you just tell me, I am scared Em. When can I see you?

Soon, got to go . And I can't tell you, that's up to her.

> Don't be a stranger x

Three's A Crowd

My mind continues to race until my alarm shocks me out of my thoughts. I brush my hair, splash my face and make a cup of tea.

Lottie and Thomas burst in, fighting over who gets to fill me in on their day first. Lottie wins and Tom wanders off, he comes back and fires a Nerf gun hitting Lottie just by the ear. She bursts into tears and goes nuts, the two of them fly at each other. I can't even muster the energy to sort this out. I just half-heartedly check she is ok and tell Thomas that was silly and never aim at faces. He claims it was an accident.

I just keep looking at Lottie, thinking to myself the contrast between her and Misty. How I would die if anything like what happened to Misty happened to Lottie.

They disappear off to their rooms and I head out with Ron. I can't even face talking to Sam. I message and tell him I am not free. When I get back Phil is home and quite upbeat about his chat with Dave. I smile and nod and say the right things in the right places. I take myself off to the office where I just stare blankly at the computer screen.

Once everyone is in bed Sam messages:

> Hey, you ok?

> > Yes, you?

> Fine, but worried about you…

> > Nothing to worry about here.

> I feel like your shields are up? Why? Have I done something?

> > Sorry, no you haven't and no they are not, just ran into that girl again today, it just floored me

> Where? What did she say?

> She was in the hotel where my meeting was. She told me about a sexual attack, two boys, she mentioned Darren again, my old school, and the two names of the boys are names I know from my old school, and somehow she wants me to stop it for her. The attack was horrendous.

Fuck! That makes no sense, your old school is miles away. Poor girl, how did she know you'd be there?

> I don't know.

I think you need to contact the Police.

> And say what? I don't know her full name, I don't know anything.

She has grabbed you in a car park, come into your home and now a hotel. Tell them, there will be CCTV.

> But what if she does something and reveals my other work? Plus it turns out Emily knows her and says I need to talk to her.

WHAT?!

> I know…My head is spinning. I have been thrown all day. And it's like I have not thought about Darren in 30 years until I mentioned it to you and now this, and now I can't get that stuff out of my head too, I have been dreaming about it.

J Babe, I am so sorry. Do you think and don't bite my head off, you are not over what happened with Darren?

> No, I'm over it, I dealt with it a long time ago.

Dealt with it , or ignored it?

Three's A Crowd

> I dealt with it, and I have functioned perfectly fine, if I had not dealt with it, I would not have had relationships, held down a job etc It doesn't bother me. It was a cock in a hole, I do plenty of that! No biggy!

But you're dreaming about it.

> Yeah because of Misty probably and telling you, just my brain processing the day's events. Nothing more.

OK. Listen, I think you should get some sleep. I will give all this some more thought.

> Thx and Yes, you're probably right, sorry.

Don't ever apologise to me for this babe. You matter, I love you, sleep well and speak tomorrow.

> Love you night x Oh before you go… you've not told anyone about my past, have you?

Ofc not babe, I swore I would take it to the grave and wtf would I tell?

> OK, sorry, ignore me, love you x

I'd never betray you, go to bed, love you, have pleasant dreams, night x

Of course, I don't go to bed immediately. I wrestle with my thoughts trying to get them to align into something that makes any sense. Plus my pussy is driving me wild. God, I hope that kit arrives tomorrow, and I can find out what the fuck is going on.

I slap on some Canesten just before turning in, and pray I will drift before its short-lived relief wears off. No such luck. Eventually sleep does come, but unsurprisingly it is disturbed by the day's events, flashes of Darren and even Mark and James from school. Brains are crazy!

The rest of the week goes without a hitch, well by a hitch I am referring to Misty. Phil's at home more the rest of the week with no interviews or homers lined up. On Thursday he gets news that he was unsuccessful... again. He is not the type to lay about and is doing some much-needed DIY jobs around the house. I talk to Sam every morning and night when walking Ron, and we message as usual in the evening. Emily is still being a little weird, but we are texting. Sleep still evades me due to itching and a full mind. I fire off proposals, campaigns and have numerous online meetings. With no clients to see this week due to the itch, I am more productive. I tell Sam I am just seeing old clients.

My test kit arrived on the Tuesday and I rapidly pricked my thumb, filled the vials with blood and took it straight down to the postbox to return it, using the prepaid box. They should get it on Wednesday, results Friday. I have almost emptied that tube of Canesten and had to invest in another, which I can ill afford, especially after the two weeks of limited clients and reduced income.

I am helped along by that inheritance coming in finally, which is welcome, but it certainly does not mean I can breathe. I am being very strict with it and will only take the minimum to survive and cover costs. I just don't know how long Phil will be out of work and my business income is not reliable or steady. I am doing everything I can to preserve that money just in case. I do however blow about £30 treating everyone to a McDonald's (would not have been my choice, but the kids love that stuff). It breaks my heart to see how excited Lottie and Thomas are when I announce it. I remember a time when a simple McDonalds would not have raised a concern or excitement. Now it's like I am saying to them, I am treating you to a 5 star gourmet meal. I have been squirrelling away a little cash each month in anticipation of Christmas. I am a complete Christmas fan. It is my favourite time of year. We used to make Christmas a big deal, Christmas markets and shows, it's not like that now. Gifts are tricky for the kids, as being teens it's all about the brands, and so I am grateful for Vinted.

I feel like such a failure.

There are only a few short years left before they both flee the nest, they won't recall when times were good, and we took them all over the world and did things together. They will only remember the exceptionally rare excitement of a McDonald's and that all their mum did was work. I wish this had happened the other way round, when they were younger and couldn't remember. Sometimes I get panicked thinking about driving lessons and university, praying I will be out of this mess by then. It is not fair that my finances prevent them from reaching their potential. Then I have to give myself a shake, or I would spiral.

One step at a time I remind myself, just one foot in front of the other. I find the best way to keep sane is to choose something to challenge me, something I can control when everything feels so out of control. It helps. With the lack of cash in the last fortnight, I decide for the next ten days I shall just live on juice. I do this periodically, mainly for the feeling of actually having a grip of something and the bonus is, removing me from the weekly food shop helps the budget too. So I include a bit more vegetables and fruit in the shop and batch make juices for the next 10 days. The first three days are always horrendous, headaches, fatigue, extreme hunger, dizziness, but once past that it's like flicking a switch, no hunger, bags of energy and an accomplished feeling.

On Friday morning I get a ping on my phone, it's my test results... I don't want to look, I feel exceptionally nervous. I enter the access code on the website, my hands shaking, and it feels like the page takes forever to load. I peak through scrunched eyes as the results load. I scan down the list, feeling sick as a dog, I **hate** doing this.

Hepatitis B	-VE
Hepatitis C	-VE
HIV	-VE
Chlamydia	-VE
Trichomoniasis	+VE
Syphilis	-VE
Gonorrhoea	-VE

FUCK FUCK FUCK....
WHAT THE FUCK IS
TRICHOMONIASIS?

I google, and calm, OK, OK, it could be ***far*** worse, not great, but could be worse. Main thing is it is curable and easily treated. It's a little bastard parasite. I need antibiotics. I have to take them for seven days and then retest.

My mind jumps into practical mode.

1 Get treated, fast. No way I am going to the doctor, I don't need awkward questions. Plus the likelihood of getting an appointment any time soon thanks to the 'NHMess' was slim. So I lose another £30 by ordering antibiotics via Superdrug online. They should arrive tomorrow, meaning I will finish the course next weekend. Then there should be just about enough time to test (another £29) before seeing Sam. At least I don't need to repeat the full STI test, just the trichomoniasis bit.

Three's A Crowd

1. I am now only 12 days away from seeing Sam. I need to act fast. Yes, Sam and I use condoms, which you can understand, I guess I am quite the risk. But condoms don't really protect from trichomoniasis (Trich) for short. So I need to be clean and clear before I see him.
2. Incubation of Trich is 3-28 days… shit a brick, so I now have to contact everyone I have been within the last 28 days, as I may have had it and not known. Thankfully Sam is outside of that, as this is a 5 week gap for us this time.

I can't do any GW work for another 7 days minimum, until I get the all clear. The money I earned from Mr Lorry Cock is basically wiped out on testing and antibiotics, to say nothing of the loss of income for a week, and risking my time with Sam. Lesson learned, always use condoms, no matter what they claim. Seriously, what else can go wrong?

This is going to be Trichy.

Chapter 14

What Soberness Conceals, Drunkenness Reveals

So on top of all the shit I am dealing with I have to message a lot of people, some are OK about it. Some are not so. I knew it would not be a great thing to have to do, but it would be far worse to keep quiet. Whilst it was not life-threatening and curable, it could break marriages if someone took it home to their Wife.

It took a few weeks, most were kind enough to let me know their result, all where negative, except Jeff, the lorry driver who had to have a difficult conversation with his Wife. But frankly, that was his own fault, he gave it to me.

When that came out and I told Emily over coffee, she went nuts at me. Things had been better between us, but I got both barrels from her on this.

We met at a favourite coffee spot of ours, I had told her already about testing positive and having to inform everyone, she kept asking me and asking me which 'cunt' I thought had given it to me, which I was unable to answer until now.

I knew she would ask about it again and could feel the heat rising up my neck as I waited for her. I had ordered drinks and sat waiting. It was a cool day but the tension in me was like a furnace.

"You worked out who the cunt is yet?" She asked as soon as she arrived.

"Oh Em, why does it matter?" I replied.

"I have my suspicions"

"OK smart arse, who?"

"The lorry guy, Jeff"

"How the fuck!"

"I know everything and worst part is you believed him, when he said he was clean and not fucked a whore in ages, why can't you see when people are playing you?"

"Hey, that's not fair could have been anyone and condoms don't always stop the spread."

"You really are a dumb bitch, you should have said no the moment he could not produce a condom...but you just can't say no can you?"

"Em, don't be mean to it's been a tough few weeks, Misty, cash, Girthygary, pissed off clients over this news, Szymon is frustrated we have had to postpone the weekend thing he wanted."

"Oh diddums, poor Szymon, the wife beater who has **stiffiulties**? Why do you give a fuck?"

"Emily, that's not fair... plus I am not his Wife, and he doesn't beat me!"

"No you are not, thank fuck and yes he does."

"No he doesn't, **it's no** different to any other person with a sadistic kink."

"Yes... actually **it is**."

"No... **actually it is not**... Some guys like to spank, some belt, whip, cane, whatever, they need and want to see a bit of pain and that gets them off, Szymon just does that with face slaps, no bloody difference."

"Really? Face slaps? Face slaps like Sam does?"

"No"

"Why not Jess... what's the difference?"

……

"I'll fill you in will I?!" She barks after my silence.

......

"Sam slaps your face hard, it makes you wet, you feel controlled, and it's a bit of a shock, but you enjoy it. Szymon with his 'limber timber', slaps you, and you get knocked off your actual fucking feet. Sam slaps you because he knows you and knows what you like. Szymon and his cold spaghetti dick gives you headaches, and dizziness and your vision goes white... see the difference?"

"Look Szymon is a broken man, he is sad, lonely, yes he slaps hard, but I am alright, he doesn't bruise me, does not cross any of my red lines. You almost sound like you like Sam?"

"No I **don't** like Sam, not one little bit, he is going to rip your heart out and leave *me* to deal with it, you need cash, he doesn't pay, wake up Jess, seriously, what do you get from this with Szymon? And **don't** say cash."

"Friendship and I feel wanted, useful."

"He is not your friend, friends don't throw each other under a bus, sending them off to fuck a fat Orca for his amusement."

"But he looks out for me, keeps me right."

"He manipulates you, knows you have a 'need to please' and takes advantage of that."

"Urgh, I am not arguing with you."

"So you don't have a need to please?"

"Why do you always have to have a go, Em?"

"Because I care, because I don't want you hurt, and for me it's not so much Szymon's slaps, it's him gaslighting you into thinking he gives a fuck, when he doesn't and then when you eventually realise he is just using you, your world will end, just like it will with Sam."

"Don't say that."

"Truth hurts, doesn't it? But you know deep down it is the truth."

"Whatever Emily."

"Tell me you didn't tell that guy that was going to 'break you' and ignored your wish for a condom about getting Trich?"

"Of course I did!"

"I would have not said a word, served the cunt right if he passed it to his wife after ignoring your boundaries."

"Em that is horrible, I would **not** do that to anyone, you know what, maybe you're the problem! Constantly criticising and interfering." I regret my words as soon as they fly out of my mouth.

"Fine, see how you cope without me. Oh and by the way, I got 'Girthygarys' info, found out his Wife's name, and threatened him with the same he has threatened you with, that shut the cunt up, so fear not, you won't be hearing from him again, you're fucking welcome, like I said, see how you cope without me. Good fucking luck."

And just like that she left. I am annoyed at myself for barking at her, but eternally grateful if she has sorted Girthygary out, time will tell. However, ***I am*** starting to think Emily just enjoys having a go and making me feel crap. She has been particularly bad since Misty came on the scene.

I wish I knew more about what Misty had said to Emily, as she has changed since then, more prickly than usual and seems to be supporting her more than me.

I go to gather up our coffee cups and return them to the counter, but only mine is there, she must have taken hers up on her way out, she can be considerate sometimes, but why not take mine up too? Probably to make the point, which is petty.

I feel like I am more irritated with her than usual and perhaps being unfair, but with her constant criticism, I am growing tired of her.

The same evening I caught up with Emily. I had a charity quiz night I had to go to. Frankly the last thing I needed as it had an inevitable cost to it, turns out the cost was not just financial.

I was in a team with some local business owners I knew. Despite not wanting to go, it was a good laugh and took my mind off everything. Isn't that the way, things are never as bad as you build them up to be in your mind. I had a few beers and that combined with an empty stomach and the feeling of being 'out out' which is a rarity, I went a bit nuts and had a few more sherbets than I could afford or needed.

A guy I knew from a local mortgage broker firm was on another team and while queuing at the bar I was chatting to him, his pal interrupted us, saying to Neil the broker:

"Who's this?" While looking at me.

He introduced me and I chatted to Neil and this guy Graham for a bit. He was a gardener. He kept making sexual innuendo jokes, he was fun.

Then he said something strange and mentioned it a good few times throughout the night.

"Next time Neil, get Jess on our team, I can tell she's up for anything and filthy."

This kind of thing happens to me on occasion. I am convinced men can see a slut when she is in front of them, and they ***just know***. I have mentioned my theory to Sam a few times, and he tells me, men cannot see sluts.

I know that sounds crazy, but I am sure they can. It's nothing to do with how I am dressed. Tonight I am just in some black leather trousers and a casual cosy off the shoulder jumper. It's classy. Not slutty. No flesh on show to speak of. I often wondered if I gave off excessive pheromones, sometimes I can smell my own pussy. Or is it that they can just 'see me'.

My standard dress for both GW and normal life is what I like to call 'Classy Slutty.' It leaves people questioning, is she a slut or a classy bird? But there is a hint of slut to it.

Throughout the quiz night I message Sam, but I am too drunk to type properly. I send questions from the quiz and other random stuff.

Didji kkii ethe flf wis red, yellow bkue?

Eh?

What glaf foes not have red whote and bkue?

You drunk?

No

Heohns i am s slut

What?

I realise messaging is no good, so I nip outside and send a slurred voice note telling him, I am right, he is wrong, and this guy tonight can see me and knows I am a whore.

Sam types a reply saying it is not true, then becomes focused on me getting home safely. I argue back via voice note, telling him it's the way it is, you get women that are proper women and then people like me. I continue educating him that men can tell and that's why, when I am in bars or away with work I end up fucking people because they can see it. Then you have to go with it, and that men just know they can use me and do what they like to me, just like that, new client you didn't want me to see.

He jumps on it:

Did you see that client? The one I told you NOT to?

Shit...

I try to explain, try to apologise, but I know I have hurt him, badly hurt him. Sam goes cold... short replies, makes sure I get home and then says he can't speak to me, and signs off for the night.

No late-night chat.
No 'good night, love you.' No 'miss you.'
No 'you matter.' Nothing.
He is gone.

Three's A Crowd

The alcohol and fear hits me and I hurl, but only lager and bile come up.

I spend another sleepless night, but this time not tormented by dreams of Misty or Darren, but thoughts of 'this is it, he is done with me, it was only a matter of time.'

I wrestle with the fact I always knew this was coming, so why be upset. But I am, I can't bear the thought of him not being in my life. I curse myself for being a tit. But it is done now. I can honestly say it was one of the longest nights of my life.

He does eventually message the next morning, but not, first thing as usual. He punished me, made me wait. He sent a voice note rather than ringing that morning on his way into work, expressing his pain and disappointment. I messaged back instantly apologising and trying to explain again. But it didn't matter what I said, he was too hurt that I had gone against his wishes and worse not been honest about it. He had worked out that it was the day I asked him when at work, to call me and he saw I was upset. He now wanted to know more about what had happened. He said on that day he had a horrible feeling, like he could feel every thrust and he was actually sick himself in the toilet. He and I both seem to be able to sense each other's discomfort, not always but often.

The next few days were awful, he got more and more details out of me, the weekend came, and we could not speak, he had ***another*** family day resulting in Natasha joining him at Beth's dancing so they could hit the road quickly after. I wasn't sure if that was a lie, and he just couldn't bring himself to speak to me. So we only messaged, it was infrequent and hard to judge what he was thinking. It felt like he was assessing if I was worth the ongoing hassle, before allowing the axe to fall.

He also told me what had happened was r*p@. I disagreed. Truth is, I don't think you can r*p$d be when you have agreed to 'anything' but your limits ***and*** **paid** for you. I knew he was going to fuck my holes and he did, ergo, consent. But Sam claimed not using a condom, when it had been agreed that was required, classed as r*p@. He said that is the law. He sent me links supporting his definitions of r*p@.

For me, r*p@ is penetration **against** your will, I had agreed to penetration, that's what happened. Therefore **not** r*p@.

I eventually gave up arguing, it wasn't doing me any favours. I would just quietly keep my thoughts to myself and see if this could be solved.

When we did eventually speak, things got sorted out. I learnt over time that with Sam you could fall out and he then addressed it head-on. He would not let it fester, no matter how uncomfortable. A level of relief spread over me. I confessed how worried I had been about his frostiness, he confirmed his disappointment and hurt but reassured me it did not change anything, he still loved me. However, he did raise, yet again, how much he hated me doing 'that job'. He dug into my finances more and more in an attempt to come up with a plan that could get me out of it.

Emily was quick to use his reaction to crucify him, again, saying how cruel it had been to leave me worried, that he knew fine well how much I worried. If he really gave a shit he would have not done that. She reminded me this was evidence he was not interested in me, in any other way than being the 'bit' his perfect Wife refused to fulfil. I knew she was right, but I prayed she was wrong.

My itch began to subside around three days after starting the antibiotics, I finished the course and had the new test ready to go on day eight, the results came back three days before I was due to see Sam, just in the nick of time, I was in the clear. I didn't want to have to have that conversation with Sam, especially on the back of what had just happened. With that hanging over me on the run up to seeing Sam, my usual excitement was shrouded in apprehension which only subsided when I knew I had tested negative.

I was also relieved I could start earning some much needed money again. I got busy booking clients in and had managed to get a few booked in for the day before I was meeting Sam.

Chapter 15

Houston, We Have a Problem

This latest drama accelerated Sam's 'Inspector Clueso' streak, and he began digging more and more, he brought up the topic of me 'not having dealt' with my past again.

Why can't people just believe what you say? I have nothing to gain from lying about this, I just wish he would accept my truth. Not every survivor of a sex attack, that isn't sleeping, is because of that!

I have slept fine my entire life, it's only recently that has gone haywire and is it any wonder with the worries I have on my plate? Combined with a random eerie girl effectively stalking me. I would challenge anyone not to be a bit unsettled. If my past was an issue I would have had sleepless nights long before my late 40's.

He bought it up on a video call.

"Jess, you look shattered, done in, not yourself."

"Gee, thanks!" I jest.

"I am serious, you sleeping ok?"

"Not bad," I don't know why I do this and not tell him the truth. That I am hardly sleeping. But I don't, I think I just don't want to be a mood hoover.

"The truth Jessie" and I can tell he is serious. It's quite hot when he gets all serious and stern, but sometimes I get the impression he has had enough and I am crossing a line.

"OK, I am not sleeping great."

"Why?"

"I don't know, stuff on my mind."

"Like?"

How can he be asking that? He knows I am skint, he knows Misty unnerved me, he doesn't know I have been itching my pussy red raw.

"Just cash worries and a bit unnerved by Misty."

"So you can't fall asleep? Maybe we need to stop messaging so late, so you can wind down?"

He's said stuff like this a few times, and it makes my stomach flip with sickness, he was getting tired of me, getting bored by the routine of calling and messaging me. This was his out, disguised as concern. A way to not be tied down to the routine of messaging.

"No I can mostly, I usually get off no problem."

"Then what?"

"Dreams I guess."

"About?"

"Oh, everything really."

"Jess, stop fucking being evasive, what is going on?"

"OK! I am having nightmares, and then I struggle to get back to sleep, but it is fine, it's just my brain dealing with all that is going on, processing the day's events."

"What are the dreams about?"

"Mostly Misty to be honest and her story she told me and then weirdly dreaming about Darren a lot, but hardly a surprise, given I have spoken to you about it recently and that is the first time in over thirty years."

"Jess, have you ever considered you may have PTSD from the way you lost your virginity and because you have told me it's all coming to the surface?"

"No, I put this all to bed a long time ago, and I don't do things like PTSD."

"Uh huh, yet you're having nightmares about it and by the way, you can't decide to just 'not do' PTSD."

"I am dreaming because you and then bloody Misty have reopened a box that was all neatly filed away, I mean it's not surprising to have a reaction to some crazy chick sharing her assault story, she's a similar age to me at the time of mine and if she is to be believed, she goes to the same school I did. Plus the name of the attacker happens to be the same, common name I guess, so yeah don't think that is abnormal, it's natural."

"Or maybe, you never processed it properly, you just ignored it and having chatted to me and her it's all coming to the surface after you buried it."

"Or more likely I am freaked out by a random young girl appearing in my home, on my landing!"

"But there is more Jess, like have you ever thought about why you got into escorting?"

"You know why Sam."

"You could have done so many other things for money, why this?"

Urgh, I think he is trying to add to his case for me to stop 'that work'. Emily is convinced of it, says he weaselled his way into my life. By stopping he can use me exclusively for free without the hassle of condoms. She says it works for him, 'everything about this arrangement works for him Jess, not you.'

He had uncovered that even before escorting I was still sexually active outside my marriage, having arranged hook-ups with people on hook-up apps. He had discovered on work trips if I was approached, I usually ended up fucking the guy whether I was into it or not. I had joked about my cock addiction, he had said this was all not normal.

"You are not and were not in my shoes, tell me what other

thing pays well, and is flexible allowing me to not lose the money I had put into my startup marketing business?"

"Look, hear me out, I think this is all related and I think you are hyper-sexual."

"Psychologist now are you?! Look I like sex, you know this, it just works as a side hustle, don't overthink this, why is it when a woman likes sex it's got to be a problem, but for men, it's just accepted as being natural?"

"You liking sex is not a problem for me!"

"See! So there you go, nothing to see here, move along."

"Uh-huh"

"What?! What does that mean?"

"I've just been pondering some of the things you have said over the last few months. Shall I tell you what I have seen?"

"I am not sure I want to know."

"Well, I'm going to tell you, you're not going to like it."

"Oh god is it bad? Is it to do with us?"

"No"

"OK..."

I am feeling really on edge, wondering what he is going to say. Has he finally realised I am just a slut and wants nothing to do with me?

"OK, let me ask you this, when I see you in like 36 hours and I can't fucking wait, what would you like?"

"What do you mean?"

"From me, Sexually. Tell me what you want, what turns you on, and give me the keys to the castle."

"You know I like everything, just stay away from my red lines."

We had agreed on our red lines a while back, if either of us crossed any red lines, we were done.

Mine: No naked, no permanent damage, no scat.

His: Now had no 'new' clients, no one outside of my work and telling the truth.

Three's A Crowd

Both of us are allowed to fuck our spouses if by some miracle that ever happened.

"Yes, but tell me what you want to happen? Like you want me to fuck you in the cunt or the ass, or mouth first?" He asks.

"I love them all"

"I know but what do **you** want?"

"All of them!"

"But what turns you on?"

"Whatever you want turns me on, just being used how you want, you know this!" I am getting frustrated with these questions, most guys like it when they can do what they want, I don't understand his problem and I enjoy it. He can literally do anything he wants to me and I would be as happy as a clam.

"OK, let's try this, you have to choose, would you like me to spank or cane your ass?"

"Whatever you want! I love them both!"

"So this is my point, remember that film 'Coming to America'?"

"Yes"

"You're like that like you can't think or choose when it comes to sex, you'll do whatever I want, I can ask you to get your tits out in public and you'd do it to please me. In fact, get your tits out now, then pull up your skirt and show me your soppy wet fuck hole."

"Of course"

I lift my tits out of my top and bra, slide my skirt up, move my panties to the side and pull my pussy lips apart to reveal a glistening, wet mess."

"I rest my case."

"Why is this bad?'

"Remember you have told me about ending up with guys if you are away with work or pubs like you just shut off and don't stop it, I think you can't say 'no' to cock." He says.

Flatline

"I want **you** to choose, when I see you, should I cum in your ass or pussy the first time? And don't use that bloody coin flipper app!"

He knew I did this when I had a sexual decision to make, and found it funny, but now had a bee in his bonnet about 'choice.' When messaging if he asked me something tough I would often say hold on, let me flick the coin.

"I don't like making choices Sam, I like to be submissive, why don't you understand this?"

"Being submissive does **not** mean **no** choice."

"Well I don't like it, it makes me uncomfortable"

"I know, which is my point, you can't say no to random strangers, you can't go a day without wanking off, you fuck for a living and before that, you fucked anyone who asked. You let people like that new client rape you and you say nothing, I think you have PTSD, and I think you are hyper-sexual, it's a common reaction to sex attacks. I think in some weird way you have a program running, installed in you, from when you were younger and you just follow the program without thinking. Like all you are, is holes, that is all anyone wants from you. This is why you never believe my truth, that I care for you and want you more than anything. To you, it doesn't compute 'bad gateway, syntax error.' And it is like you are scared of choice and you don't actually know what really turns **you** on because you will do whatever anyone says."

FLATLINE

Well semi flatline, my brain is working and thinking, but I can't say what is in it, as he will say that makes his point. But I am thinking, well yes, because that's exactly what men want from me.

My life and evidence support it. I am not the whole package.

It's one or the other with me.

My husband loves and likes me as a person, but finds me repulsive sexually and won't touch me. Everyone else has only ever wanted me for my holes. They don't want to know me outside of that. I accepted that a long time ago and I am fine with it. I can get both feelings validated, being desired by providing my holes in a no-strings-attached or paid way because they don't want any strings. Then being liked by friends and sort of Phil.

I say sort of because I am not sure he is even interested in me as a person any more. He never wants to do anything together and like sex, I gave up on asking for that an eternity ago. Men just can't stomach me for any length of time, I either turn them off physically or they tire of me as a person.

Sam weirdly acts like he wants both, but I have seen that before. (Phil - case in point) and so it is only a matter of time before he becomes fed up with one side of it. Or perhaps like Emily says, it's just him playing a game to get my holes. Who knows, but the bottom line is I know, with absolute certainty he will never pick me to be in his actual real life.

He has expressed many times how he wishes he could, but that is nothing more than words and wishes. People part with their words so easily, without much thought, receivers tend to grab onto them like starved animals receiving scraps from a table. Words are so often released with no actual intention of following through on them.

I have tried to hold conversations around **how** it might happen that we end up actually together. But it's always met with a 'I don't know' I don't want to hurt people (neither do I) and we just have to trust that 'life will find a way.'

So that is 100% categorical evidence he doesn't want me, not really. I know our life is complex with spouses and children. But plenty of people do it and work through it. Nothing in life just 'happens' because it is what should be, and is the right thing. If you want something badly enough, you don't leave it to chance or fate. You make an action plan and follow it. He won't engage on this so there is no plan, proof that it is not what he wants deep down. So for all his bluster about loving me and being important. I am not loved or important enough. I am not wanted enough. If I was, he would be prepared to at least discuss an action plan.

I am not enough.

If I was, our conversations would be different. So he makes the right noises but without action, it's just that - noise, meaningless.

"OK," I managed.

"Well just think about it please, I am not trying to hurt you, I am trying to help you, I still love you, but I am going to rewrite your code and show you the sky **is** blue. You are worth more than just holes. But don't be mistaken, I am still going to fuck you senseless and destroy your holes in around 36 hours, and punish your ass for being a lying bitch about that client, I can't wait to see you."

"Just try it!" I say tongue in cheek.

"Oh don't worry, as soon as you see my cock, I know you'll be so desperate for it, you will crumble and do exactly what I tell you."

"Well, you do have a very delicious cock."

"Above average." He laughs.

"Yes!"

And with that, he gets his rock-hard cock out on camera and I am hypnotised, brain turned to mush, as he would say 'Your brain has gone into neutral.'

He edges himself and talks filth to me, describing every thrust, every single thing he plans to do to me, how he is going to restrain me and cane me, then fuck my ass dry going balls deep in one thrust and watch me wince, because 'I am a dirty bitch, who fucking deserves it.'

My words don't form and I just wank myself off on camera and have a powerful orgasm. He holds back, he's saving his cum for me and I can't wait to taste him again.

Chapter 16

Network Glitch

With the all clear on my trich, I have booked in a couple of clients for the day before I see Sam, it feels too weird booking anything for a day I would see him. I am desperate for the cash as well. Lottie has a couple of friends' birthdays coming up and Thomas has a few away games for rugby meaning more petrol than usual. Both mean additional cash is required and I am already well behind what I need having been unable to earn.

I have had a couple of deposits for my marketing work, but I can't take it all out of the business account and live on it as there are costs I have to cover in that business, software, accounting, and insurance.

I have not seen Misty since the hotel. I am hoping that is it, that she's got off her chest what she wanted to say, and for some reason she thinks I am the one that needed to hear it and this is now over. But Emily's message about this 'just being the start' niggles me.

Both of today's clients are 'outdoor' ones. They claim it is a 'kink', they love the thrill of fucking outside. Emily thinks that is bullshit. She says they likely can't host as they have wives and they are too tight to pay for a venue and me. I don't know.

The first guy is a new client, and the last new client Sam is ok with me seeing him because it was already arranged. I say he is 'OK' with it, the truth is he is not really, but he has agreed to it. After this no more 'new' clients were allowed and I had promised. He really can't cope with it. At least with existing ones we knew I had been before and it had been ok. Emily is raging about this, saying he has no right to interfere.

Once again I don't give him as much detail as he may wish, as I know he won't approve. Plus he is a natural-born worrier and there is nothing he can do.

He is doing a new thing with me now. Which he calls the 'Lottie test'. When discussing if what had happened around the guy that punched me in the stomach and fucked me without a condom, even though I had stated a condom was required, he would ask..."If that was Lottie, would you see it as acceptable thing to do?"

Urgh he is so annoying sometimes because clearly there is no argument to that. I wouldn't want Lottie exposed to half the stuff I am, so I can't win this. But he doesn't see it's not the same, it's comparing apples and pears. I am not the same as Lottie. I am a slut for use by men, she is not. This is my purpose, not hers. I am good at being a slut, it is part of me and I like it. Truth is she is better than that, I am not. And that is not me doing myself down. It is just a fact, plain and simple.

I often say to him I wish he could just teleport into my head, I don't have the words to explain, but if he was in my head, he would understand it instantly.

So this client, Adam aka 'Pussypounder' wants to meet me in the woods and get a blow job and fuck me against a tree. He wants to 'find' me looking slutty. So he has given me a location using the app 'what three words' and I am to be there at 11 am.

I can imagine what Sam would say, you can't go meet someone in the middle of some woods you have never met, yada, yada. He has learnt a fair bit about my clients over the months along with previous hookups, and he has concluded my 'risk sensor' is broken. I can also imagine he would try the 'Lottie test' on this one too, and it would of course fail. So I tell him he wants a blow job and to fuck my pussy, I just miss out the 'what three words' and woods. It's not lying, so not crossing his red lines. Thankfully he does not ask the venue this time or for an address, he is obviously busy clearing his desk before coming away to meet me.

So I head into the woods, tectering on high heels and a very skimpy dress with a long coat. I get to the 'what 3 words' location, take my coat off and wait. Thank god there is still some warmth in the air even though it is now September. The guy finds me and does exactly what was agreed. The only point that nearly went astray was when he tried to lift my dress completely off and over my head, which gave me a panic as I was naked underneath. He was fine about it and apologised. He came in my mouth and his cum was pretty darn good.

I let Sam know all was fine when I got back to my car. As usual he messaged back, relieved and also thankful that was the last time he had to worry about it.

Early afternoon I met a regular Graham, it turned out to be a mix of a car and outdoor meet. We met at a community woodland car park where people go to walk their dogs, but being midweek and early afternoon it was quiet. I sucked him off in the car and then he wanted to fuck me in the ass, which yes, I have done in cars before, but he is a big guy and being over 40 it's not that easy any more, so it was outside, me bent over his car boot. A brief pause to let some dog walkers past then off he went again drumming me against the boot of his car before finishing.

With £320 in my pocket and enough money to fill the car for my trip the next day, get Lotties' two friends a gift, get to the rugby match at the weekend and get the weekly shop, I feel a lot more relaxed. Plus I had a lot booked in for after seeing Sam, so I would easily be on £2K by the middle of the following week.

Once home I packed my bag, always better done when the kids

are away and Phil is out the house so I can retrieve all my toys and slut attire without risk. Phil is home shortly after and starts doing some garden- ing. He is doing tons around the house, I think being out of work has affected his self-esteem so badly he just needs to feel he is contributing something. I admire his work ethic, he is a grafter, never still and whilst I see flashes of despair across his face, in the main he doesn't complain and just keeps himself busy rather than wallowing in self pity.

Lottie piles home shortly after, stressing and moody over how much homework she has, Thomas is staying at school for a Rugby game and needs to be collected later.

I take Ron out and chat with Sam as he is leaving work. He has had a frustrating day dealing with people who 'don't deserve their share of oxygen.' But he sounds genuinely excited that we are seeing each other tomorrow. Just hearing his voice my pussy responds like Pavlov's dogs but dribbles pussy juice rather than saliva.

The rest of the evening is standard, I collect Thomas, they have dinner, I am obviously nil by mouth due to knowing I would be having my ass fucked today and destroyed by Sam tomorrow. The family don't bat an eyelid, they are well used to my crazy eating habits. I do some 'proper' work scoping out my ideas for some campaigns. I am just about to shut my laptop down and head downstairs for an hour to watch something when a new email pings up:

Subject: I am not done

Jess

I have more to share. We need to talk again, you're not getting it. There was a glimpse at the hotel, but there is more.

I will find you again soon.

X

Three's A Crowd

My heart pounds, head spins and nausea rises. FUCK!

I check the account it came from to see if it reveals any clues, the email address simply says yj@gmail.com. That does not help.

I reach for my phone and message Emily.

> Emily, she's emailed me

Knew you couldn't survive without me

> Don't be like that, I don't want to survive without you, you're my friend. Did you give her my email address?

No. But you message when you need something, ignore me the rest of the time.

> It's not like that. So where did she get my email address from?

Seems like that. Jess - your website maybe? Hardly hard to find. 🐌

> Fair point, I am sorry if that's the impression you have, I know I am not the best at the moment but a lot on my mind. I never got the chance to say thanks for sorting girthygary, I have not heard from him since. How are you?

Dealing with your friend.

> Misty?

Yes. You need to speak more to her Jess. Just listen to her.

> I did!

There's more.

> But why is it relevant, why me? What's she been saying to you? What does she want with you?

She wants me to help her reach you.

> Well, right now I am focused on seeing Sam, I am not having that ruined. Not a chance. It's my only bit of joy. How can I reach her? How do you reach her? Do you know more about her?

Not my place Jess, I have promised her, all I will do is encourage you, but it is all hers to explain. She needs to explain. Just let her speak when you see her.

> She can't just turn up random places. We need to co-ordinate. Em, I am your oldest friend and I feel like you're siding with her over me.

No, I am doing what is right for you both.

> Tell me, how are you really?

Pissed off at being stuck in the middle of this mess.

> What can I do?

When you see her, listen.

> OK, I don't understand, but ok.

"MUM!" I hear from downstairs, you coming? "In a minute!' I shout back.

> I have to run, sorry, I will be in touch when I am back from seeing Sam, see what we can do for me to meet with her ok?

OK, and remember, Sam is only ever going to hurt you, you're just a wank rag, don't get any ideas above your station.

> OK

I can't be bothered arguing with her and I need to go spend some time with the kids. We sit and watch Brooklyn 99 before they

Three's A Crowd

head to bed and Phil goes too. I am present but not really, as my mind runs through the email and what Emily has said. I need this to stop.

I decided to push this from my head for now. There is no way I am letting it aRect my time with Sam. I am not talking to him about Misty, my past, my 'program', my GW work, money, it will purely be me and him, enjoying each others company and fucking like its going out of fashion. I know if I stand a chance of keeping him in my life, the little time we have together needs to be as fun and care-free as possible. That's what he needs, not a barrel load of grief.

I crack on with some slutmin and WhatsApp messages while I await Sam being free.

He eventually messages and we both get ourselves all excited about seeing each other tomorrow and head to bed. This time sleep evades me because I am too excited about seeing him. Annoyingly, as much as I try to push it away, Misty's email is still playing on my mind too. I haven't responded, I will do it when I get back.

Morning comes and everyone departs, I walk Ron, Sam and I don't speak as he has gone into the office early. He has some work he needs to clear before leaving early in the afternoon.

I do a few emails, make a few phone calls and have a meeting on Zoom with a new enquiry, before jumping in the shower. I always ensure I am smooth, creamed, bare and fresh for guys, but for Sam I take extra care. I even decided to video myself shaving my pussy and send it to him. He is grateful, he has never seen a pussy being shaved before.

The day drags and when it is finally time for me to head off, I throw my bag in the car and hit the road. Sam left a while ago, he has further to travel, and we talk all the way down, with the exception of him having to jump off the call to talk to Natasha and Beth about 6pm. Once again I find myself 'nervicited.' This feeling is maybe even worse, as tonight my real world and his collide. I know a few people at this event and we have decided to pretend we don't know each other and will meet for the 'first time' there. He is hoping to tell Natasha about meeting me in a professional capacity with a view to being able to legitimately meet more often for work purposes. It feels weird that he will get to see me in action in the real world, not slut action. Although the slut will be out in full force once the meeting is over.

He calls again as he is coming into the car park, asking where I am parked, we are a bit early for the start of the event. He says he sees me, but I am looking all round and cannot see him, 'behind you' he says. I spin my head and there he is in all his glory. God I love him, I am just flooded with emotion and relief, he is here, in the flesh, not 20 ft away and all I want to do is run over to him and feel his arms wrap around me.

We wait a bit, talking away, sitting in our own cars, until it's a suitable time and both wander into the meeting a few minutes apart.

I head to the coffee stand and make myself one, my hands actually shaking. He is comfortably working the room and is already engaged with the main man and organiser of the event. Sam just has a way about him, it's like everything is just easy for him. I spy Scott and Andy, two PR guys I know and in contrast to Sam speak away to them, with my shaking coffee in hand and garbled words, as my verbal diarrhoea sets in. All the time I am talking to them, I am glancing at Sam, it's horrible having him so close, when I can't just kneel down and suck him dry.

The first thirty minutes are literally networking, before the presentations start. The first speaker discusses the power of AI for marketing and how he has implemented it in his business. He has seen time-saving efficiencies that have allowed him to focus on more revenue-driving tasks which have resulted in a 13% rise on his bottom line. I am usually an early adopter of things, but AI doesn't sit well with me. Part of what makes my business good is the human and personal content, I don't believe AI can achieve this...yet. I do however make a mental note to test it out as there is no denying the results are impressive.

Three's A Crowd

After that talk, there is a fifteen-minute coffee break. Sam once again seems to have latched onto important people, I glance over at him as casually as I can, as often as I can. He never seems to glance at me. I suppose he is thinking about his business and will 'deal' with me later.

I head to the coffee station, waiting for the huddles of people to step aside, some people are making a night of it and have beer in hand. As I slide through the people I get a waft of cider, I can't stomach that smell these days. As the last group ahead of the coffee station steps aside to let me pass, I am caught in the draft of the air conditioning and feel my body prickly with goosebumps. As the path clears, my jaw hits the floor and I freeze on the spot. Misty is there, perfectly still eyes set on me, watery, desperate, begging. She looks out of place in her oversized sweatshirt with GAP written on it and stonewashed jeans. Her clothes hang off her, hiding her slightly bony frame.

Fuck, fuck, fuck, I think, what the actual fuck. I am ninety minutes from home, how the fuck did she get here? How the hell does she know I am here? Of all the nights she picks this one, when I am hobnobbing, working and don't need a scene. Plus it's ***my*** night with Sam. I change from fear to simmering anger and tension. I am ***not*** having this, this stops now. This is not the time or the place.

I walk right past her and out to the corridor and round the corner, I know she will follow, and as I turn round, she is right there, on me, inches away.

'Misty - this has to stop! You can't just turn up places, how did you get here? How did you find out I am here?" My tone is calm but firm, I can't make a scene, but I want her to know this is unacceptable.

"Listen to me," she whispers.

"Not now, not here," I bark back.

Like a coiled spring she lurches forward, her eyes change from distraught to fierce, fiery and angry. She grabs me and wraps her hands around my wrists, glaring into my eyes, face torn and screwed up and screams at the top of her lungs.

"LISTEN LISTEN LISTEN LISTEN LISTEN."

I try to pull away, unable to escape her grip, for one so weak looking she is wiry and strong and as I try, she digs her nails deep into my wrists. Pain shoots through my wrists as her nails puncture the skin. I close my eyes and wince. As I do, she releases me and when I open my eyes she has gone.

She is so loud I expect people from the meeting room and reception to dash into the corridor to see what the fuss is about, but nothing. I run frantically down the corridor and back into the room, and back out into the corridor, the foyer, I pop my head outside searching for her. I was petrified she had gone into the meeting and sought out Sam or took centre stage to start shouting off about me, but she was nowhere to be found.

I am shaken, stunned and cursing her. My wrists are nipping, red, swollen bumps on either side of where she dug her nails into me and the skin is broken with a little blood. I nip into the ladies wash the blood away and dab them until the bleeding stops and they now just look red.

I go back into the meeting, trying to shake the feeling and focus on the night ahead. Sam clocks me coming back in and looks at me quizzically.

Everyone is encouraged back to their seats for the second speaker who is presenting on their start-up journey and what they learnt along the way. I wish I could focus, there would be a lot of value in this. When it ended, and it was the question and answer session, Sam asked a question which I didn't even really hear or understand as I missed big parts of the talk, but it seemed to have made the presenter stumble a bit.

I smile to myself, typically annoyingly smart, critical thinking, not frightened of the hard questions Sam. He really is quite something. That thought kicks my brain into action. I am not letting her ruin my night. I get to see him once a month, *if* I am lucky. This meeting by the time it ends means we won't be at the hotel until around 10 pm and as much as we would like to fuck all night, we are both over forty. We have to be up the next morning, so really it's a couple of hours tonight and a couple in the morning and that is it.

Sam had insisted on paying for the hotel, saying he will put it through his business, but it doesn't sit well with me, and he was having none of it.

With a new found focus and forcing Misty out of my head, I just want this meeting to end and to get my hands on Sam. I fire off a text to him under the table.

> Make this meeting end, I need your cock x

Finally, it is over, and I dash straight out to my car and put the details of the hotel in my phone. Sam hangs back and mingles a bit. I am willing him, in my mind, to 'get a move on.'

I was almost at the hotel when he rang, he has just left, got my message and told me it would soon be mine.

When I say hotel, it's actually a Travel Lodge. So basic and nothing fancy, and one I have frequented with other work before. I always think it's daft paying crazy money for hotels, you are literally just laying your head on a pillow. Plus Natasha is like a hawk with money. He cannot spend a penny without it being questioned. Apparently (and Emily says that is the biggest load of bollocks she has ever heard) they only have a joint account, so every penny is spotted, he even has to justify his business spend. She would not want him wasting money on a better hotel. But then she got all concerned about him sleeping with bed bugs in a Travelodge. I couldn't help thinking that comment was a bit snobby, but then I think she is used to the finer things in life. Seriously. The mind boggles. Still none of my business, just find the entire set-up very odd. Emily obviously tells me that's because everything he tells me is a lie, and he does have a separate account, he is just tight.

The rest of the evening is like a dream, just like every time I have seen him. He wanted me to give him a lap dance which after downing a can of lager I do awkwardly, and we descend into the inevitable fuck fest including a bit of caning, and it's just so hot.

He always talks about how he is really going to punish and hurt me, but he always seems to hold back. I wish he wouldn't. He is overly concerned with consent and not going too far, despite me telling him a thousand times, he has blanket consent and can go as far as he likes. I mean it is not like I have not done it before.

His cock is a dream, pops down and fills my throat perfectly. I love having cock fill my throat, it is so dominating. You can't breathe, and it is that level of control the guy has, if he holds you onto his cock and you have to tap out, gasping for breath, eyes watering, makeup running, dribbling. It turns me into a sloppy wet mess. He gets to unload a few times. The chat is filthy and just adds to the tension between us.

"Fucking take my cock, you dirty bitch, I am going to fuck your face like it is a cunt"

"You fucking dirty whore being fucked in the ass."

"Take my fat cock in your fucking ass bitch."

I am usually confirming his actions;

"I love the feel of your cock, slamming balls deep into my ass, fuck my like the fucking whore I am."

I love being fucked, its the best thing ever, I don't think I would ever tire of it and I plan to be doing it until I die, in fact, fuck it, at my funeral, it should be my send-off, everyone can have one last go at me before my coffin descends into the fire.

It's not just the physical sensations, it helps me mentally more than anything else I can think of. But being fucked by Sam is like nothing else. My favourite part is when the bellend of his cock, pushes into my pussy or ass, there are no words, it is just perfect.

We laugh and fuck, does it get better than that?

Three's A Crowd

At one point he takes me totally off guard and gets down on one knee, takes my hand and says, Jess, if we ever get the chance, I would like you to be my Wife. I laugh it off but he says he is serious. I find that very hard to deal with, but disguise it well, I don't want to hurt his feelings, he wouldn't understand. I have told him before I am not convinced I would ever marry again, and I am not. The intent is sweet, but I know, as clearly as we know the earth is round and that is a fact, this is an empty request. He is safe asking it, as he will never have to make good on his request.

It makes me warm inside that his intentions are sweet, but so bitterly sad too, he doesn't mean it, and it will never happen. Life feels unfair, I have never been 'in love'. I don't think I ever loved Phil, I may have thought I did, but now with these feelings I know I didn't.

What I feel for Sam is so different, it highlights how wrong I was. But I will never be able to experience living with love. Sam's proposal is a thousand times better than Phil's, who I had to break down in tears to get him to notice. After being with him for almost a decade and no sign of him popping the question, I was so rejected. I eventually broke down, he then reluctantly asked when drunk and vomited straight after. Like a fool I said yes.

I wouldn't change anything really, but only because Lottie and Thomas would not exist. But the truth is I should never have married him, the signs were there long before I forced him into proposing, and our sex life had gone before marriage. I raised the lack of a marriage proposal for all the wrong reasons, feelings of rejection and desperately wanting him to want me, desperately wanting anyone to want me to be honest. Not just my holes (although Phil didn't even want them). I have always wanted someone, just someone to actually want me, fully, totally me. Someone so desperate to be with me, **because of me** and didn't need to have their arm twisted to pop the question, spend time with me or take an interest in me.

I think I also pushed it due to societal pressure and embarrassment. We had been together so long and people would ask all the time when we were getting married. It was embarrassing and added to my shame, it further crushed me and confirmed what I have always known. I am not wanted. If you ever wanted proof of that, that is it. Forcing someone into asking for your hand in marriage. There is no one before or since (including Sam) that has felt enough for me to do whatever it takes to have me. I don't completely know why or what is wrong with me, but the truth is clear. It just feels like I am not meant for that.

What I am experiencing with Sam is probably the most painful thing I have ever encountered. I now 100% understand that saying 'love hurts.'

Loving Sam feels like this constant ache in my chest. It's not sharp, not something I can pinpoint or cure, just this dull, nagging pain that never goes away. Every time he speaks kind words, it's like he's giving me exactly what I have been desperate to hear my entire life, exactly what I need to keep holding on. His words are so perfect, so convincing. They make me want to believe that everything is real between us. But they hurt too.

But deep down, I know it's not true and even if it was, so what, what's the point, we will never be together ever.

I hate it because I want to believe him so badly. I want to hold on to every 'I love you' like it's the truth, but there's always that little voice in my head (probably Emily's) reminding me that he's just telling me what I want to hear.

And still, I stay. Still, I hope.

And that's the worst part—the hope. It's like I'm torturing myself with the possibility that something could happen between us, that is real. It can't ever feel real how things are. And how things are will never change. Hope is dangerous. Hope leads to disappointment.

It's exhausting, loving him like this, fighting between what I feel and what I know deep down. He knows I remain unconvinced of his feelings, I feel for him, and it must be beyond frustrating for him. This is another thing, that may be the end of us, eventually, he will get fed up trying to convince me that what he says is true and who can blame him. However one of his red lines is lying, and if I said I believed what he said, I would be lying. I cannot win!

I try not to express what I really think for this reason and more. I would love to have a full conversation with him about all of this, but he would avoid this particular topic, probably the only one he avoids. It is such a big topic, we don't get the time. I do not find it easy to talk about difficult things, it takes me time to speak up. I fear the consequences of speaking my truth. It is a bit of chicken and egg, I can't speak up unless we have the time for me to bravely tip toe into the conversation, before feeling less petrified, but we can't have the time unless I speak up.

I don't want him to think I am forcing him to leave or blow up his life, or being that 'other woman' who puts pressure on him. I am not in a position to be free yet either, and I would never ask him to leave his daughter. He says to me that even if he was free, I am not. But I would love to know that if I was free, if I left Phil tomorrow and was available. Would that then make him take action and choose me? Would he then leave his life for me? I know it would be silly for him to do that now, he gains nothing. But if I was free, would he? I think not.

Neither of us is leaving our marriages at the moment. The only way he would leave is if Natasha made that choice for him. But if in some alternative universe or by some miracle he **does** love me and wants to be with me, and he decides to take action to make that happen, it can only ever be because **he** chose to, **really** chose to, chose me and a life with me, free of all pressure. Otherwise, I am just setting myself up for another Phil. He needs to decide if he is staying with Natasha or making a change with me, that decision needs to be **for him**, not with either Natasha or I in mind. I feel he needs to decide, but the truth is, he already has.

Despite the impossibility of this, seeing him once a month and getting the scraps from his table when he can message and call, I can't seem to let go. I am trapped, I love him, and that's the part that hurts the most. Loving someone who says all the right things but will ***never*** act on them, because the truth is he doesn't want me, not in that way, not how he wants his wife.

At the moment, I have to accept I am trapped. I can't get enough of him, enjoy the ride as best I can and not let my feelings consume me.

It would really help if Emily was not adding fuel to the fire too.

Chapter 17
Szymon Says

Waking up next to Sam the next morning feels like slipping into the warmest, safest place in the world. The moment my eyes open, and I feel the heat of his body beside me, everything else fades away, the worries, the noise, the rest of the world. His arm is still draped over me, his breathing steady, and for a moment, I just lie there, not wanting to move, not wanting to break this perfect bubble of comfort.

I can feel his heartbeat against my back, this quiet rhythm that makes me feel like nothing could ever go wrong. The soft rise and fall of his chest is the dictionary definition of peace. Despite the intrusion by Misty I actually slept. I don't want it to end, I don't want to face the reality of waiting outside this bed. But I know he has to leave, and it will be two months not one before I see him again due to his upcoming safari.

I can already feel the clock ticking, pulling us away from each other even though we're still tangled together. It's this bittersweet feeling, knowing I can't keep him here, knowing that soon, the warmth of him will be replaced by nothing. I cling to this moment, savouring every second, wishing time could stretch out just a little longer.

I don't want to let go. Not yet. Not when this feels like home. He comes to, we kiss and I feel his cock bobbing on my thigh, and we start the morning, as all mornings should begin, with a fuck. That should be the law, failure and the sentence is five years in prison. You can get out for good behaviour if you allow the prison guards to fuck your ass, whenever they want and leave you gaping.

As we lay there together talking pish and laughing I absent-mindedly rubbed my wrist where Misty dug her nails in, he clocks it and asks what happened, thinking it was him. I explained. He was, as to be expected, mad at me for not telling him and had he known he would have come and helped me find Misty, had a word with her.

Sam gets mad when I leave things out or don't tell him things he feels are important, but he doesn't understand that all I was doing was with us in mind, not allowing her to steal time from us.

We fuck some more and I store to my memory every curve of his cock, every vein. Then we jump in the shower, one after the other because I am a weirdo and I curse myself for my weirdness, but there is no choice, it must be this way.

The Travelodge doesn't have a restaurant so we go over to the service station and grab something. I really don't eat breakfast and certainly should not be spending on overpriced service station food, but I don't want to raise any concerns or questions.

Over breakfast, brought up my GW work again, trying to persuade me that it would be better if I stopped. He feels as if I would be able to earn more by focusing on my business. He has a go at Phil again saying 'There are two directors in your household, not one, he needs to step up'. I defend him, pointing out how hard he is trying. He asks me about what clients I have coming up, I tell him and he jumps on Szymon. He knows a fair bit about Szymon, and he doesn't like him. I share that I am due there this weekend and about the gang bang that is planned, the date is to be confirmed. His eyes turn to thunder and a big debate ensues. He does **not** want me to do the gang bang.

"Jess, no, your life is worth more than any amount of money, I am not letting you do this."

"But I know them, Szymon is a good guy and will look out for me"

"I don't care, you're **not** doing it."

......

"I mean it Jess, you do this, we are done, you won't see me or my cock ever again."

"OK, OK" I say "I won't." Feeling defeated, "Szymon won't be happy."

"I don't give a fuck, you don't have to do everything Szymon says, what the hell possessed you to agree to this in the first place?"

"It might be fun and it's good money"

"What the actual fuck Jess!"

I am stunned at his reaction. I have done plenty of gang bangs and group sex before with no problem at all. But I know this is not worth arguing about, his foot is well and truly down and I won't do anything that risks losing him, he has maybe not totally grasped this yet, but he has got me, hook line and sinker.

I wish more than anything I could give up the GW work for him, I cannot imagine how hard that is, but I have mouths to feed, and I just can't. I feel like I am failing him by being unable to just do as he wishes. Plus I don't want to leave him today and have any bad feelings especially when I won't see him for two painfully long months.

He has also requested that I not see any clients at all while he is in Africa, he says he won't be able to bear it, and he will be out of contact for days on end due to Wi-Fi, he does not want to be worrying about me. I have agreed, but I know I need to see a lot before and after to make up for the loss of earnings, but I don't mention that.

He continues with a 'Szymon' rant and I listen. He also dives into my profile on GW criticising it saying that the way it is written, combined with my prices it's no wonder I attract 'dicks like

Szymon.' Again he says I don't need to do what 'Szymon says.' what Sam fails to grasp is this is a paid service, so in reality you do have to do what they say.

We have a heated discussion about my inability to say 'no' and my stance that if they are paying it is their right and him having a wildly different view. He begs me to at least consider stopping GW because it hurts him so much. I say I will.

I don't think my profile is bad, I actually think it is quite good. I read and researched a lot of other escort profiles and they all sound like a bunch of moaning minnies. 'Can't do this, can't do that,' they don't come across as friendly at all.

For example:

Sexy Sofie

Do not contact me unless you have read my profile in full, paying particular attention to my 'how to book' tab.

I am 43, curvy, chatty, flirty and squirty! Available for in-calls* and outcalls*.

5ft6" Blonde with natural 38DD natural breasts.

I love oral but not 69 as it is hard to receive pleasure when concentrating on giving it. Happy to see crossdressers and ladies, can offer pegging.

I don't do pain, either giving or receiving and no water sports. I do anal play but not penetration. Happy to rim. I can be submissive but only mildly. Please review the full list of services I offer and don't request something I have not ticked.

I can give a full GFE* (no bareback so don't even ask) but I won't do rough sex or PSE* and won't accept this type of behaviour in a booking.

-I expect you to be polite, well mannered and above all else clean

-No haggling

-No time wasters

HOW TO BOOK

It should take a **maximum of 5 texts** to secure a booking, any more than that you are wasting my time and will be barred.

I am not sitting around waiting for you, I need notice to manage my diary, so if you think you can text me and walk in instantly or I will come and see you instantly don't waste your time or mine.

I do not respond to messages such as 'hiya', hya,' 'you free babe?','you're fit' or any other pointless communication.

I do not want to see your dick unless in person, no dick pics.

It is quite simple, approach me as you would any other professional service, arrange a booking and be clear about what you want to get out of it.

*GFE = girlfriend experience
*PSE = Porn star experience
*In-calls = You can come to my home
*Outcalls = I will come to your home or other venue.

I mean Jesus, I would be scared of upsetting the woman if I was the guy. Not sure what you could and couldn't do. Hardly a customer-centric advert that makes you feel like she is approachable.

Mine on the other hand is very honest and I hope, authentic and welcoming:

Anything for Cock

I am 47 Bi woman, married and I do this as a side hustle. If that bothers you, move along. No, he does not know. I have a family and work around that, discretion is key. As such I cannot be available at the drop of a hat.

I do this for the genuine love of sex. You'd be hard-pushed to find anyone filthier.

I am 5ft4" Blonde and my tits are smaller than they look in the pictures, for some reason pictures make them look bigger - false advertising really.

As my name suggests I will do anything for cock, I enjoy rough sex. I am BDSM and fetish-friendly. I challenge you to find a sluttier slut. I can take pain and in general take quite a lot.

I am submissive and love to be dominated and controlled. I don't have a dominant bone in my body, so if you're looking for that, it's not me.

I am more comfortable in lingerie and therefore prefer to keep that on during sex, my lingerie is always full access to all the bits needed.

My only real limits are no scat, no permanent damage, no marks I cannot hide, not totally naked and no photos or videos.

You can literally do anything to me. Message me and let's chat.

I mean seriously, who are you going to message me, honest, open, friendly or her?

After breakfast, the heat dies from the conversation and turns to more affection and dread, we both know this is it for a long while.

"God, I am going to miss you," he says.

I just can't speak. It's not that I don't want to say the same back. I just am literally about to break and cannot form the words. We have not firmed up a date for the meeting post-safari, I don't think he likes to think too far ahead and has to assess the atmosphere at home. He needs to pick his moment. I don't like not knowing when we will see each other again, it makes me feel like it may not happen as nothing is set.

I manage to say

"Will we manage November?"

"I can't not see you Jess, I can't bear to be without you, I will find a way."

He hugs me in the car park, and it feels like he wants to hang onto me, but I can't stand it. I need to rip the plaster off fast and go, this is too painful.

"I better go," I say, holding back tears.

He hugs me one last time and I turn and walk in my car and begin driving. He calls me instantly, I can't speak to him, I am too upset. I call him back in five minutes once I am more composed, and we talk the whole way home about how awful this is and it is.

He says 'Love Again' By Dua Lipa[4] reminds him of me and that the sky *is* blue, I listen to the lyrics, and he is right, and yes… god fucking damn he got me in love, not again but probably for the first time ever. And I didn't ever think I would hear my heart beat so loud.

I get home and life is on the same trajectory, no one has really noticed I have been away other than Ron. I tell Phil and the kids about the AI speaker, but I can tell no one is interested or listening. I realise that is something else I adore about Sam, he actually listens to me. Sam misses nothing, my lot miss everything. Sam was worried Phil or the kids would notice my wrists, I reassured them they wouldn't, and I was right.

Sam lets me know he has arrived home safely and then is quieter than normal, which makes me worry, but I try to tell myself it's because he has been away and has to play nice for a bit.

A wave of panic and heat washes over me.

Emily messages:

I hear you saw each other again and pushed her
away, she's upset.

> SHE is upset?! SHE turned up at a work event, not
> the time or the place

She is desperate Jess, she can't control it

> Who's side are you on? She needs to fucking
> control herself.

Let her get it out

> I will, but at the right time and place.

I will pass that on. I can't help her, you have more
empathy and patience, I just lose the rag and tell
her to get to the fucking point, so what, you were
fucked, just a cock in a hole. Move on. Anyway,
how was Sam the snake? And I don't mean how
did you get on with his cock.

> You'll be annoyed to hear this, but amazing as
> ever, he even said he would marry me given the
> chance, and he wants me to consider stopping
> GW.

Jessie, I am not annoyed, I am glad you had a
good time, I just remain highly sceptical of him. I
don't want you hurt, you've had enough of that
and I worry you have fallen for him and this will be
too much for you.

> So you do care!

Ofc I do you silly bitch. Just keep your wits about
you. He can't control you Jess. If he wins, and you
stop GW you will never be able to be faithful to
him, you need cock more than once a month,
you'll fail, you know you will.

> Well, I am not giving up GW, I need the cash.

Good - keep it that way, but remember. You need
cock too. You go round the bend without.

Three's A Crowd

That night Sam and I message briefly, both feeling flat, and he heads to bed early as he is tired after his early start the day before and the hours of frantic, frenzied fucking.

I stay up and fire up the laptop, respond to some work emails, some slutmin and WhatsApps, as the house cools due to the heating being switched off I wrap a blanket around me and then ping.. An email arrives in my inbox... Misty.

<u>Subject: You turned me away</u>
Hi
You have made me sad, I am lonely. I won't stop until you listen.

See you soon.

Sickness takes over my sadness about Sam, I am not sure which feeling I prefer, neither in truth. Another tick in the 'feelings are a pain' box. I reply this time, I want to tell her to fuck off, leave me alone, but I know now I can't, she is not giving up, lets just get this done.

<u>Subject: RE:You turned me away</u> Hi
You turned up at a really bad time. Let's sort a time and I will listen.
J x

She replies instantly:
<u>Subject: RE:RE:You turned me away</u>

It doesn't work like that, I will see you soon.

I don't even bother responding to that and take myself off to bed, although, why, I really don't know. I can't fall asleep, I am worried about when she might appear again and what she has to tell me next. If she has been in my house, two work meetings with people about, what is to stop her from turning up here when my kids are about. When sleep does eventually wash over me, it is uneasy and disturbed, images of Misty and being attacked prevent my slumber.

The days that follow are a 'normal' mix of work, GW work, mother duties and grabbing chats with Sam when we can. But life isn't quite normal any more and I wonder if it ever will be again.

Wondering when Misty might show is like living in a constant state of suspended animation. Every rustle in the bushes, every creak of the floorboards, sends a jolt of fear through me. I find myself scanning my surroundings obsessively, searching for signs of her.

The simplest tasks become Herculean feats. A trip to the shops feels like navigating a minefield. Every noise, every stranger, becomes a potential threat. My mind races with thoughts of her appearing, leaving little room for peace or relaxation.

My body is a prisoner of this constant state of alert. My muscles are tense. Sleep is elusive, as my mind refuses to shut down. Even when I manage to drift off, nightmares haunt me.

It's an exhausting existence, a relentless battle against fear and uncertainty while maintaining the ability to function and not alarm those around me. Every day is a terrifying one, unsure of what awaits.

When Sunday rolls around, and I am heading off to see Szymon and Adrian I am really not in the mood. I am shattered. I prepped my bag and headed off. Phil is taking Tom to a rugby game and Lottie is studying, so I am not missing anything much.

I had chatted with Szymon a few months ago about his impotence and had suggested he try Viagra. He was so upset and ashamed by his condition, I wanted to help. He said there was no way he could go to the GP and ask for it, he is far too embarrassed.

Three's A Crowd

When I told him, he didn't have to, he was astounded. I told him about online pharmacies. The downside was that if he got over himself and went to the GP it would be free. Online pharmacies you had to pay, but he would not have to face the shame. Although there was nothing to be ashamed of.

He gave a thousand excuses why he could not do that, like what if he had a boner for the rest of his life? What would people think? What if he died taking it? What if it didn't work and he then knew that was him forever, flaccid with no chance of ever fucking someone, ever again.

He was being ridiculous, but I felt for him.

He did eventually buy some but was scared to try them, so I suggested he try them when he saw me next. He didn't have to be embarrassed because I already knew, plus he would have someone on hand who if he did take a funny turn or felt ill, could help. He felt like a failure having to look to medication and I reassured him plenty of my clients relied upon the same. That was the truth.

As I drove down to him, I voice noted him, saying "Have you taken it yet?"

"No," he replied.

"DO IT" I messaged back.

"Jeez, thought you could not be dominant"

And I can't, except when putting my foot down to try and help someone. So he did, he popped half (too scared to take a whole one) about fifty minutes before I arrived.

I pulled into his street and buzzed his door, I was let in and climbed the stairs to the first floor. He answers in his pants and takes me through to the 'second bedroom' which also has a dining table and chairs in it as well as a TV. I don't ever get into his main bedroom. The second bedroom is a spare for his son when he has him. The room is cold and old. It reminds me of staying at my grannies. The walls patterned wallpaper in sun-bleached tones of yellows and browns. The table and chairs are dark mahogany. The pictures on the walls are dated oil paintings. The bed, more like a camp bed than a full bed, it does not have a real mattress, it is hard and lumpy, with a yellow candlewick thrown over it. The only thing that makes it remotely modern is the #at-screen TV on the wall, which of course is showing some porn. That too is vintage and grainy, a mass line of naked women somewhere dark, being herded, beaten and fucked.

I sit on the bed and Szymon offers me a drink, I ask for water and he comes through. He seems flat and I know why. I can see his cock.

"I am just broken," he said.

"Come on... half the battle is psychological and you have been so worried about this, have you felt anything?"

"A little."

"OK that's great, so pop the other half, I am here now, you're safe and try not to focus on it."

So he does.

He then goes on a rant about the gang bang and how he can't fucking believe how hard it is to get four other guys to fuck me. He said he even advertised it on Locanto and got a few bites but they were all-time wasters. He said he also had another guy lined up for today, but he wanted to talk to me on the phone. Apparently, they all want that, to check I am real and this is not some trap. Honestly, people's cynicism amazes me.

He phones this guy and says to him; "Hi, I have the bitch, I will put her on" He hands me the phone.

"Hi," I say.

"Hi, so you want fucked?"

"Always" I reply.

"How old are you?".

"I am 47."

"I like fucking older bitches, what do you like?"

"Anything."

"Anything? Really?"

"Yes, you can do anything to me, just don't mark me permanently, take my lingerie off or shit on me, other than that, anything you like."

"Sounds too good to be true, I want to fuck your ass until it gapes, choke you and ram my cock down your throat, hold your nose so you can't breathe bitch, that ok?"

"Of course."

"This is a set-up."

And he hangs up! I am baffled, I was telling the truth and Szymon is annoyed.

Given this and the Viagra vexation, I don't have the heart to tell him that I am not allowed to do the gang bang any more. He was so flat about his lank cock, it felt cruel to reveal that when he was so low. I would do that when he was a bit more than him.

"So it looks like it's just you, me and Adrian."

"That's fine" I said "Oh I asked Adrian about you watching him belting me, and he says he is fine with that, as long as he gets me privately for 20 mins as well."

'Oh... OK' says Szymon. "Anyway, it's Sunday, you've come a long way, I had better make use of you. Stand up bitch."

So I do and put the glass of water on the table. I know what is coming and I brace. He walks up to me and grabs a fistful of my hair, yanks it, pulls me closer and gobs in my face.

"Worthless fucking whore" and then he swings at me, a very hard slap across the face which unbalances me and I stumble a little, my ear is ringing and I feel my brain rattle. I compose myself and he does it again. As I straighten myself up he spits in my face once more. Then grabs my hair again and forces me hard down to the floor, drops his pants.

"Suck my cock bitch, I know how much you love sucking cock."

And I do, on both counts but sucking a flaccid cock which does not respond is not as rewarding. But I don't mention that. Then I nearly squeal because I feel a twitch in his cock, I have never felt that. I look up at him to see if he has noticed but he just opens his mouth and gobs on me again. He pulls away and takes both hands and slaps my face like a cat bashing a ball, one side then the other, fast, hard. I feel disorientated. He yanks at my blouse and pulls my one piece apart and grabs a full tit in his hand, squeezing it like it's a stress ball, with such force you can feel the bruises form instantly. This is followed by all the usual Szymon stuff, squeezing and twisting my nipples, pushing me down, climbing on top of me with my arms trapped underneath so he can slap my face and tits and gob on me, reaching round and roughly finger blasting my pussy. All the while he is telling me what a filthy worthless piece of shit I am.

Eventually while straddled over me, his flaccid cock spurts some cum, in a very undramatic fashion, and it dribbles out onto my cleavage. He scoops it up and smears it on my face mixed with his saliva. He gets up and leaves to make a cup of coffee, returning a few minutes later with the coffee and some polish vodka.

"Still nothing," he says flatly.

"I felt a twitch," I reassured him.

"A twitch is nothing." He says grumpily "can't fuck someone with a fucking twitch can I?"

"It's your first time, you were nervous, it's bound to affect it." Just then the buzzer goes, it must be Adrian. And sure enough, it is. Szymon answers the door and I hear Adrian say. "Where is the slut?". Szymon replies "down there."

Adrian walks in "On your hands and knees whore."

So I do, and I can see from the corner of my eye he is pulling his belt out from the loops around his waist. He comes closer and rubs his hand over my ass, stroking it, then takes a step back and begins belting my ass. Szymon is leaning against the doorframe watching and playing with his limp cock. Adrian is not gentle, and I wince and squeal with each impact, feeling the welts form. After maybe 15 or 20 strikes, I can't recall accurately as I kind of zoned out, I heard him ask Szymon to leave.

Adrian then drops his trousers, pulls me off the bed and lays down on his back. I knew what was coming, he wanted me to wank him off, but not in a normal way. He liked what he called a 'danger wank', really hard and fast to the point I should be worried and so should he, that I would rip his foreskin off. The only way I could do this for him was if he spoke to me during it in a commanding tone, telling me to wank his cock harder or he'd belt my ass again.

In contrast to Szymon, his load was plentiful, and I caught most of it in my mouth. As abruptly as Adrian arrived, he left again, handing Szymon cash as he went.

Szymon slapped me about some more, roughly finger fucked me, used my dildo in my pussy, ass and mouth and trickled his load into my mouth.

Before leaving, Szymon excitedly gave a run-down on some of the activities for the 'brutal gang bang.'

"You won't know what hit you bitch, there will be no holding back, we are going to break you, whore like you fucking deserves it. That dungeon has so much kit, but first we will jump you and wrestle your dress off you and then drag you to the spanking bench and clip in your wrists and ankles. Some of them might fuck your ass and face. I will slap you about and ram your head back and forth on any dicks that come near your mouth. We will lash you with whips and paddles, use the stocks and each one will fuck all your holes. Maybe use the medical area and open you up with a speculum. There will be not a moment's rest for you for five fucking hours, you will be like a rag doll. And if we need a piss, we will use you. Piss in your mouth, cunt, ass. Use the range of giant dildos to fuck your ass and cunt. Have you spit-roasted and air tight. You will be begging for fucking mercy, but we won't stop, not unless you use your safe word. We will leave you like a piece of trash to sleep there caked in cum, piss and bruises. Fucking slut."

I can tell he is getting turned on by this and I feel horrendous I won't be able to deliver this for him.

I got £430 for two hours, it should have been £280, but Szymon said he was paying for the two hours anyway and that Adrian was paying for an hour so that's what it was all combined. I was chuffed, Szymon was always very generous with his cash.

As I drove home I felt so sad for him, what Szymon had said about his impotence, knowing him and his tone I was actually worried. I checked in on him later that night, and he was so flat, one word answers, just not very Szymon at all. I did my best to reassure, explain and encourage, but nothing got through to him and I went to bed worried about what he might do.

Chapter 18

Bathroom Battles

Monday felt like forever to come, the night was long, haunted by my thoughts and disturbed with dreams. I literally trudged through the day with the highlight being speaking to Sam first thing and on his way home.

I was as productive as I could be, I had a couple of easy GW clients and some good progress on some of my proposals.

I was beginning to find night time was a double-edged sword, wishing it to come so I could message Sam, but praying it would not end so I didn't have to face sleeping and finding myself upset and pacing the house.

Sam and I messaged mainly about filth as usual but he also mentioned how if I were his wife, I would be in constant use. We bantered back and forth, and it made me smile. I loved this time, we just **got** each other. We fantasise about what life would be like if we were together. I reminded him again I would likely never consider marriage again and didn't want to get into a heavy chat about that, so diverted it to marriage connected with filth, saying I would want our vows to contain 'obey' which has been dropped in modern times. I can't say that to many people because these days being a woman who has had her rights hard fought for, it seems disrespectful, but the truth is I would like that.

Just a simpler life where the man is in charge. I'd swap all my worries for that life in a heartbeat. I joked with him that the only way I would marry would be if I could construct the vows, and they would look like this:

'I, three holed slut Jess, take thee, Sam the man, to be my wedded master, to fuck and to suck from this day forward, whenever, wherever, for use and abuse, wether in sickness or in health, to drain and to worship, and to obey his every command, till death us do part, according to God's holy ordinance; and thereto I pledge thee my holes.'

'With this ring I thee am owned, I give thee my body, and with eternal consent all my fuck holes. I thee endow: in the name of the pussy, and of the ass, and of the eager mouth. Gluck Gluck.'

He agreed these were the most excellent vows.

We agreed it would probably have to be a low-key private ceremony as it may not go down well with parents and elderly relatives. That suited me as I would not want a big fancy wedding, and actually don't want a wedding at all, but if by some miracle we were given the opportunity, these are the **only** vows I am saying. He thinks I am joking, I am not.

We say good night and as ever he tells me he loves me, he misses me, I matter, that I am amazing and like no one he has ever met before. We have an undeniable connection. I can't argue the last point, we do.

The rest of the week is a blur, work, other work, grabbing Sam when I can, every day that passes brings us closer to him going away on Safari with his family, where there will be almost zero contact for twelve long days. I want that to come so it can be over, but I don't because I don't know how I will manage without him.

Phil has a second interview and we are all holding our breath.

Three's A Crowd

Lottie has fallen out with a friend and is upset, Tom has hurt his knee in rugby so can't play this weekend. We decided to spend the afternoon doing a Harry Potter marathon, an afternoon is not enough to watch them all, but we could all do with just switching off and chilling. I have splashed out and got a few bags of popcorn, Phil has put the movie on and we all grab blankets and curl up on the sofa watching and chatting. Phil barks at the kids periodically to be quiet, he gets so irritated when people talk when the TV is on. I am watching but fighting sleep as having sat for a bit I find my eyes heavy. I drift off for the second half of the philosopher's stone and the first half of the chamber of secrets.

About twenty minutes into The Prisoner of Azkaban I say I am heading to the kitchen to fill up the popcorn bowls and bring another jug of juice through. I am filling them up for the kids and Phil, not me. I have had half a bowl and have that horrendous feeling I always get when I have eaten too much, my stomach feels huge and I feel disgusted with myself and angry. As I leave the stifling heat of the living room, the cold hits me in the hallway like walking into a brick wall and I shiver as I head across to the kitchen. I place the bowls on the counter, open the cupboard with the crisps and popcorn and bend down to dig about. As I grab the popcorn and curl myself upwards to standing I see a pair of boots with Grolsch bottle tops on the laces. I think to myself when did Lottie get those, I've not seen anything like that in decades, but as I scan up the body in front of me, I quickly realise it is not Lottie. It is Misty. Once again in her GAP oversized sweatshirt and stone-wash jeans. I physically jump and recoil in shock.

My skin prickles, my heart thunders, and panic is too mild a word to use. My kids, Phil are just across the hall, this cannot be happening. How the hell has she got in here again and how do I explain this to her, I can't have her kick off and start shouting like she did at the networking event, my home is not a bustling busy hotel where that noise would get lost among a sea of other noises.

"Misty, please, not here, not now" I plead.

"Yes here, yes now."

Fuck

"I am not being pushed away again, now or I walk in that living room and tell your family you're a hooker."

Shit, shit, shit... think...I have no choice.

"OK, give me one minute."

I grab the bowls and take them through and place them on the coffee table, Thomas looks up.

"Mum, you OK? You look white and you're shaking bro."

"Fine, just feel a bit funny, going to sit on the toilet for a bit, carry on, be back soon."

I come back into the kitchen, gently grab Misty's hand and pull her towards the bathroom, with pleading eyes and a finger across my lips, begging her to be quiet. I let go of her hand in the bathroom, and closed and bolted the door behind us.

Misty grabs my hands, and together we sink to the floor, sitting crossed-legged opposite each other. We sit her skeletal fingers still wrapped around mine. I am trembling and on very high alert knowing my kids are just through the wall, I need to comply, keep things calm and get her out of here.

Leaning together using her sunken glassy, red eyes she fixes me in place. I notice the huge bags under her eyes and her protruding cheekbones. She just looks ill.

"Ready?" she whispers.

I nod slowly knowing I have zero choice, I tremble as she begins to whisper to me, its stilted and bitty, part sentences. I shut my eyes and try to really focus as I strain to hear her.

My friends - sleepover parents and brother away raided the drinks cabinet.

Watching dirty dancing- laughing fun, doorbell -friend answered

The boys - she let them in - friends excited - it's the cool boys at my house - they didn't know

Bad- fear - be normal - play ball join in truth or dare game.

On edge - feeling sick.

Maybe I am wrong-seems OK Darren, Mark, James.

Dare - go to bedroom give Mark and James a BJ my stomach churns - head spins,

"Oh my god, you OK" says Jo. too much to drink

Darren "Mark, James, take her up. Anne, get her a basin, and bring some water."

"No, I'm fine" I shout

Laughing - accused angry drunk can't walk - voice frozen

In my bedroom - door closed,

James - leaning on my wall, staring at me undoing his jeans. Stroking his cock shaking my head - try and walk to door music thumping downstairs

"Where are you going?" wading through water.

Almost there - bang door opens - Mark basin and water

"You don't look well, go back sit on the bed, we'll look after you, see I got you water and a basin.'

Frozen, confused.

Mark - strokes my hair gently "Why don't you just lie down" slowly edge down onto the bed

BANG -SLAP fists of hair grabbed, pulled to feet

As Misty talks and my eyes are shut I can feel her gripping me and shaking uncontrollably, I open my eyes a little and just see what can only be described as a broken and petrified girl. I find myself feeling so much pain for her, thinking of Lottie and seeing tears roll down Misty's face like a conveyor belt, unstoppable. Even though she is talking in staccato I can feel tension, and almost see what is happening as if it was real. I close my eyes again, I really don't want to hear any more, I can feel where this is headed. I am less conscious now of being home and the danger of my family being through the wall. I am sucked in.

"stupid bitch, you know what we want." Thrashing, punching

Thrown on desk face down things fly.

James on my back

Holding arms, holding head

Stuffng my mouth with hairs scrunchies Mark - yank up nighty and pants down. wriggling - fighting

Pinches nail in my ear whispers in my ear

"Stop moving and shut up"

Try to scream - scrunchies in mouth two fingers in my nostrils pulling them James pulls my legs the opposite way "I'll rip your nostrils"

Stop struggling. James - opens my legs fingers me squelching.

Laughing

"Look how wet this stupid bitch is."

Fingers come out - cock in stare at Jason Donovan poster

Cum dribbles out Mark's turn spun onto back

rRps shirt nighty open exposed

Enters, thrusts, stops withdraws - punches wardrobe

Cock soft - not seen a soft cock - ugly

Suddenly I am brought back into the bathroom as I hear Lottie banging on the door.

"Mum, mum, you ok? Who you talking to?" My eyes fly open and panic sets in.

"Yes, fine, just feeling a bit ill, just me moaning as I feel ill, won't be long sweetie."

"OK, if you need anything shout" she replies.

"Thanks Lottie."

My voice is shaky, I feel like I have Parkinson's I am trembling uncontrollably. Misty's eyes have flown open, but she stays silent, her shoulders shuddering as her tears fall. She closes her eyes again and grips my hands tighter, I close mine and she continues.

Mark pushes my head into the desk - waves his floppy cock Slaps me repeatedly

"You stupid fat ugly bitch, look what you've done. I don't ever want to see that fat fucking pile of blubber again. You turn me off again, fucking well make sure no one ever has to see that or do something about it, I don't ever want to see that again. Pussy and mouth. Only thing I ever want to see. What a fucking waste of a Saturday night. James had the right idea fucking you face down. Do you know how fucking lucky you are we'd even bother dipping our cocks in someone like you. I should punch your face in for this."

I cry silently

I pull my nighty over my body ashamed they leave.

Lay for a bit

Hear them exit the house lay on bed

Anne comes, checks on me. mask on, hide it.

She makes me a sandwich mop up the booze

Cheese and salad cream

Misty stops talking, she grips me and we both sit there silently, I want to reach for her and wrap her in my arms and tell her I am sorry this happened. But I can't, I am too shaky, unable to move, every part of me filled with adrenaline but paralysed. I feel her pain so acutely, tears pour and I hear them splash onto the floor between my crossed legs. My stomach is churning, sickness rising. I don't know how long I sat for.

My trance is broken by Lottie bending down to me. "Mum, what's wrong?" She sounds panicked.

I open my eyes, fear washing over me thinking she must be wondering who the hell the girl is, but Misty is nowhere to be seen. I looked around the room, confused, I locked that door, how did she get out without me noticing, how long have I been sitting here?

"Mum, mum, answer me," says Lottie staring down at me.

"Oh Lottie, sorry I just feel really ill, I am OK, sorry didn't mean to scare you."

My stomach churns again, my head gets hot and it rises within me, I realise I am going to be sick and spin and dart to the toilet lifting the seat and emptying the popcorn into the toilet. Lottie disappears and comes back with a glass of water, Phil and Thomas come and check on me.

"I am fine, honestly" I manage "That popcorn didn't agree with me, I feel better now I have been sick."

I do a good job convincing them and they return to the movie. I return to the kitchen and find Lottie shutting the kitchen window which I was certain was not open earlier. She helps me carry the popcorn bowls through again. We rejoin them to watch the end of the Prisoner of Azkaban. They are all very sweet and keep checking on me. By the end of the Goblet of Fire, I am almost back to normal. Well as normal as you can be having had a young girl break into your house, threaten to tell your family you're a hooker and then tell you a truly horrendous story, who then vanishes and you don't know how to help her or when she will appear again. I am 'normal' enough to pass as normal, but inside my mind is tormented.

Once everyone is asleep, slutmin and WhatsApp are done and Sam messages, he picks up instantly that I am not myself.

I tell him what has happened, I tell him she has been emailing, I tell him I am scared and worried and I want to help her.

> You need to report her Jess, for your own safety and to get her help

>> I can't risk her telling anyone about GW, it would kill Lottie and Thomas and my family would implode

> But this is dangerous, you need to do something, report it please

>> Would you want Beth finding out Natasha is a prostitute?

> No and don't EVER call yourself that.

>> Then don't make me report it. And it is what I am. Emily seems to have a way to contact her. I will talk to her and see if I can get more sense from either of them on what this is about.

Three's A Crowd

> OK, please be careful Jess, I couldn't bear losing you

>> I don't think she is that kind of a danger.

> She hurt you last time you saw her

>> I know but think that is because I pushed her away

> Doesn't fucking matter Jess, it's not on. I won't have you hurt. She needs told it's not acceptable, you'll help but only if she starts being clear on what the fuck she wants.

>> OK

I can feel myself shutting down

> You OK?

>> Yes but I think it's best I go to bed, I am done in. Sorry

> That's ok, I love you, this will be ok, you will get through this.x

>> Night, love you x

I don't go to bed, I just haven't got it in me to message. I know there is no chance of sleep for a while. I fired off an email to Misty.

SUBJECT: You OK?

Hi
You vanished, I am worried about you, are you ok? Do your parents know about this? I really think you should report them, I can come with you if you'd like? How else can I help... Just tell me.
Jess x

She replies instantly

SUBJECT: RE: You ok?
Hi
You heard, so it was ok for me to leave. It makes me feel better when you listen.
Parents don't know and it's too late to tell them or the police. Just keep listening, that is all you need to do.
X

OK, I think, for now, I will keep listening, and maybe when she trusts me more I can help her admit this to people that can help and she can move past it. I consider messaging Emily, but I can't bring myself to do it. It's been a tough day and god knows what kind of mood she will be in. I will catch her tomorrow.

I just sit for a few hours going over and over what Misty shared, filled with a sadness so deep it's unshakable. She is skin and bone. How can they even say she is fat? But I understand the devastation of words like that, I think about my Darren and what he said. Difference is my Darren was right, I was fat at that age, but it still wounded me irreparably.

Misty is the opposite, far too thin, she needs to gain some weight and fast, she looks like she is on death's door. In the years following Darren, I did lose weight, but have never felt comfortable in my own skin. If only I could see myself as I was at the time, I would have so owned that body, I would kill for that now, over the 47-year-old mum body I now live with.

I get to the point where my eyes are beginning to shut themselves and I jolt awake, so I reluctantly take myself up to bed, half wondering what the point is, I will be back down for sure in a few hours, and I was not wrong. I dreamed of Darren and his words, I faced images of his cock down my throat, dragging me into the field, I was also haunted by images of what had happened to Misty, her experience far worse, walking home from school, in her own bedroom, scrunchies in her mouth, fighting, crying and their words.

It's one of the worst nights I have had to date and that is saying something.

As I sit up in the middle of the night terrified of falling asleep again, I recall Misty mentioning Jason Donovan posters. I must ask her about that, she is clearly a retro kid with her GAP sweatshirt, Grolsch bottle tops and Jason on her wall. If she has a love of Jason Donovan then that is something we have in common. Although these days I love a bit of Zach Effron, Ryan Reynolds and of course, Pascal, from Pascal's Subsluts.

I do eventually drift off again and am a bit more settled, when I wake in the morning on the sofa once more, this time using the excuse of my tummy still being upset to Phil which justified my sofa surfing, I am groggy and tired. The first hour of the day is like dragging myself through quicksand. A walk with Ron, a shower and the feeling passes. I am stunned how well the body copes with change. If you told me eight weeks ago I would have to survive on three to five hours of sleep for the following eight weeks I would have claimed it was impossible. Yet it is not. My body seems to have adapted and a bit like doing a fast and your energy improves after day three, sleepless nights your energy improves after a few hours.

Chapter 19

Holidays are Coming

The week progresses as weeks do, filled with the usual, I do reach out to Emily about Misty, but wonder why I bothered, she is angry and evasive. I don't get her sometimes and she just repeats all she has said before, 'listen to Misty'... yeah I know, got that message, loud and fucking clear.

The end of the week is far better with news that Phil got the job, the downside is it doesn't start until the New Year and the pay is beyond crap, but it's something. There are still three and a bit months of the year to go which means four months until a pay check. But at least we know it's coming. He will continue to pick up odd jobs painting, building furniture, anything he hears about that he thinks he can do, and he will be keeping the job hunt up in case he can secure something with a better salary sooner.

Sam jumps on this news and starts really pushing for me to stop the GW work. I want to continue, not because I really want to, but just because I don't want to erode what little money we have left and yes that £15k is now in the bank, but it won't last long and if my marketing business is not being consistent come January, Phil's earnings won't cover our outgoings, not by a long shot. I have already stripped away every unnecessary bit of spending, there is nothing more I can do to reduce our outgoings. I don't think Sam really gets it.

I really am not enjoying GW any more. Did I ever? It feels like something to get through now. I have never felt bad about it before, it has always given me a sense of achievement and satisfaction, but I find myself dreading it more and more and feeling guilty for doing it because of Sam.

It takes Sam a good few weeks of persistent questioning, challenging, nagging and arguments until one night I finally crack and delete my GW profile. I have my regulars on WhatsApp and I will see them out until he goes on holiday, make as much as I can in that time, then trial stopping.

He didn't want me doing it while he was away anyway. He is pleased he can go without being distracted with any worries about me. It will be school holidays which makes things much more difficult for me to juggle as well, so I would have been doing less GW work anyway. I have some major concerns about upsetting and letting down some of my regular clients, ones that really rely on me, Szymon, Henry, Dying Dave to name a few. The thought makes me feel sick. I feel utterly terrible about it. In a weird way, I will miss them.

Sam's mind is blown over this, he does not understand why I give a shit about these people, but he still helps by constructing a message I can send to all to let them know my decision. I will send this just before he goes away. He also suggests I delete WhatsApp for business on my burner number, so I am not tempted to take pity on them. He knows me well, if I saw something from Szymon feeling down or Dave needing me, I would struggle to say no to that.

He is over the moon, but I make it abundantly clear if I need to, I **will** go back. I am not having my kids homeless and starving. He makes it abundantly clear that if I do return to GW, he can no longer be with me as he cannot handle it. He hopes it doesn't come to that, we both do. I am scared I will have to make the choice between feeding my kids or losing him. The kids will win, how can they not? It would not be my free choice, but as a mother unconditional love trumps everything, meaning you constantly sacrifice your own needs and desires.

Sam is thrilled because it means I can test in thirteen weeks' time and then provided I am clean we can ditch the condoms. He explained HIV can show late, up to thirteen weeks after unprotected sex, I never knew this.

Emily is all over this like a rash.

"See that was his plan all along, he has no fucking clue how badly this will affect your finances, how would he feel eroding his savings, fucks sake and all so he can use you without the inconvenience of a condom, cunt."

Sam updates his rules now to be, I can't fuck anyone once I stop GW work but him, he has learnt about my wayward past and how if I find myself being touched up by a man (which doesn't happen often, I am hardly the bell of the ball). I suddenly find myself with a cock in a hole. He claims this is down to my 'program' and he won't accept that kind of behaviour.

That prospect is scarier than giving up GW to me because it just kind of happens and that is hard to explain to anyone. The good thing is, with cash so tight I don't go out these days. I miss it terribly but I can't afford it. Plus I am constantly filled with anxiety about Misty turning up, so I tend to stick to home and essential in-person meetings only.

This anxiety is not unfounded, since she appeared in my kitchen I have seen her another five times. I have not told Sam, I don't want to worry him, especially with his holiday coming up, I will handle this.

I have been unable to sit and listen to her, it has always been the worst time. She came into my office when I was on a Zoom call, she signalled me over when in a cafe with a marketing client, and she appeared in the driveway while getting into the car when the kids were about to come out of the house.

Each time she grabs me and I try to pull away, she digs her nails in and screams, like at the networking event. On my driveway instead of shouting "LISTEN LISTEN LISTEN" she screamed "WHORE WHORE WHORE." I am now having to wear multiple hair bobbles over my wrists to hide the damage, and they nip all the time.

It is a constant worry, so going out is not an option.

I have emailed her and told her, I am not being difficult, I want to help, I want to listen, but we have to find the right time. I explain it can't be when I am with people or working. She responded by saying 'it doesn't work like that, when I need to tell you, I need to tell you, I cannot hold it back, and you need to listen.'

Emily is no help, she basically repeats what Misty says and won't tell me any more. I feel like they are ganging up on me and my lifelong friend is slipping away. She seems angry with me all the time and is so negative about Sam.

In my darkest moments, I feel like things are falling apart, money, letting GW people down, Misty, Emily being weird and Sam about to leave for his holiday. I feel very alone. Emily being a pain about Sam does not help my already worried mind. With Sam going away and going pretty much no contact, I could do with feeling good about him, feeling safe and confident he will want me when he comes back. Confident he won't have an epiphany having spent nights under the stars with Natasha, realising that he has missed what is right under his nose. Emily stokes the embers of doubt.

Because the weeks leading up to his departure are busy. Filled with GW clients to try and bag as much money as possible, marketing work, Misty, and chatting to Sam at every opportunity the holiday is upon us before we know it.

His holiday, which sounds like a trip in a lifetime, consumes my mind and fills me with a sickness that cannot be expressed and I can't voice how I am feeling to him.

When I think about it a coldness settles deep in my chest,

spreading through my veins like a slow poison. He tried to reassure me, "Just a holiday," he said like it was nothing. A simple getaway with his wife and child. **_His wife_**. The woman he still shares a life with, the woman he gets to do things with, not the woman locked in a chat, he can't speak to freely, do anything with and hardly sees. Yeah, it is 'just a holiday,' sure.

I try to show interest and encouragement when I speak to him. He deserves a break, it will be amazing to switch off, and spend time with them. The things he will see. It's an expensive and fancy holiday, a luxury safari, touring all over Africa, gala dinners and dances in the desert. Days crossing the desert away from civilisation, a chance to totally switch off from the world (and me).

But inside, everything is shattered. The idea of them, away together, laughing, maybe even... reconnecting. I can't stop thinking about it. Them strolling hand-in-hand, the sun setting, Beth running in front of them and his smile, his beautiful, perfect smile, being hers, not mine. I imagine her in that space where I wish I could be, feeling the warmth of his skin, hearing his laugh, and it twists something so deep inside me that it hurts to breathe.

What if this trip changes everything? What if the distance between us grows beyond miles on a map, and I lose him? What if the silence I already dread stretches into something permanent? I try not to imagine it, but it's impossible. I fear he'll come back with that spark, that look in his eyes, the one he used to have for her, when she was the centre of his world back on her and not me. What if she becomes that again?

Jealousy and worry claws at me every second, poisoning even the moments we still share. I hate myself for feeling this way, for being so consumed by it. How can I trust the space and time they will share? The chance that being away from the chaos, just their family no distractions will pull them back together.

And then there's the emptiness. The silence that will engulf me while he's away. Every morning without his texts, without his voice. Every night without the comfort of knowing he's thinking about me. I'm not sure how I'll fill those empty hours, there will be no slutmin for a distraction either. I wonder if he is asking too much of me, to stay off GW and cope with his absence, it is a big change. The thought of it is suffocating. I can already feel the breaking in my heart and the overwhelming loneliness that will stretch on endlessly until he returns. He says he will miss me, even if he does, he will not experience it the way I will. His days and nights will be busy, and full, mine will stretch with emptiness.

What if he doesn't come back to me the same? What if the pieces of him I've held onto so tightly slip through my fingers, like sand, irretrievable? The pain of that thought, of losing him, of losing 'us', is unbearable.

I hate that I feel this way. I hate that I'm not the one he can choose to spend his time with, to escape with. I hate that I'm left here, waiting, wondering, aching. Always aching.

All I can do is wait. Wait, and hope, and pray that this trip doesn't tear him away from me, that it doesn't rebuild something between them that I'll never be able to compete with.

I can't say any of this to him, it would be too much and I don't wish to make him feel bad. It's not like he can't go. And despite my feelings, I do want him to have a good time, but I pray the veneer he places over me does not slip.

On the Friday after seeing my last (hopefully ever client) as he drives back from the office, we speak for what will be the last time for two long weeks. I project an upbeat response, saying I will miss him, but have a good time, focusing on all the exciting things he will do, see and experience.

He says he will miss me, but he will still message me and although they won't send for days, as soon as he is somewhere with a Wi-Fi connection and signal, I will be inundated with his messages.

He has sent his itinerary, so I know when he will be at stops that might have connectivity, so I know when I might expect to hear from him. I have to move the subject along as I am barely holding it together, and I don't want him to know how distraught I am, that is unfair.

He says to me before we say our final goodbye; "You don't have to be so ok about it you know."

I tell him "It is what it is" while I fight back tears.

We say our goodbyes and hang up, I break down and ball my eyes out for a good forty minutes delaying my return home with Ron, messaging Phil and the kids to say he's gone AWOL chasing a pheasant, (not unusual) to buy me time to compose myself.

That conversation is not the last time I hear from him before he departs UK soil. When he comes on to message that night, he sends me link after link to songs of love. I save them all to a playlist. It includes some of the cheesiest songs ever written, but their words previously meaningless hit hard, and I cry as I listen to each:

She's so lovely - Scouting For Girls
Fill My Little World - The Feeling
Just the Way You Are - Bruno Mars
I'll Stand by You - The Pretenders
Love it When You Call - The Feeling
I'll be There For You - Bon Jovi
I Don't Want to Miss a Thing - Aerosmith
It Must Be Love - Madness
It Was Always You - Maroon 5
I'm Your Man - Wham
Ain't No Sunshine - Bill Withers
I Wanna Be the Only One - Eternal
Lean On Me - Bill Withers
I Just Can't Stop Loving You - Michael Jackson

It's possibly the most romantic gesture I have ever encountered and that breaks my heart even further.

I told him something I heard once that I loved, that although he will be thousands of miles away, and we will be unable to reach each other, we can both see the ***same*** moon. So if at night he looks at the moon, I know he will be too.

Eventually, we head to bed, he no doubt sleeps, I don't, but what's new.

In the morning, he keeps me updated when they leave, arrive at the airport and are boarding. He messages again when they land, and once more as he is leaving civilisation and his signal goes and that's it... for the first time in six months... there is no Sam to message, there are no calls, voice notes, there is nothing just darkness and the abyss.

The void is worse with having put GW on hold, I have no slutmin and no WhatsApps to look at. I am at a loose end, filled and fraught with emotion. A physical pain like no other.

I conclude I have it worse, his time is filled with excitement, safari and meals, dancing and entertainment. Mine is filled with nothing, nothing and oh yes, nothing.. His time will fly, holidays always do, and mine will last an eternity, every second dragging and refusing to jump into the next one. He will be in my thoughts constantly, I won't enter his, apart from fleetingly in between all the fun he is having.

It's been days now with no messages, but it feels like weeks, maybe even months. Sam. I keep saying his name in my head as if somehow it will summon him, bring him back into my world. But the silence remains.

I miss him in ways I can't even put into words. It's like this ache, this heaviness that settles deep in my chest and won't let go. I keep checking my phone, knowing full well there's no signal, and no way for him to respond, but I can't stop myself. I send messages, hoping, praying that by some miracle they'll go through. But they never do. Just that little undelivered notification, staring back at me like some cruel joke.

It feels like a part of me is missing, like I'm only half a person without him. I didn't realise how much I relied on those small things, the random texts, the quick calls, the way he'd send a simple 'thinking of you' at the exact moment I needed it. Now, there's nothing. Just the quiet. It's unbearable.

Three's A Crowd

I can't stop thinking about what he's doing, and where he is. Is he happy? Is he thinking of me? Or is he so wrapped up in the moment, ***in her***, that I've completely faded from his mind? The thought gnaws at me, relentless. What if he doesn't miss me the way I miss him? What if being away from me makes him realise how easy it is to slip back into that life?

I try to distract myself, to stay busy, but everything reminds me of him. Every song, every place I go, even the quiet moments when I'm supposed to be resting. It's all him. His smile, his voice, his touch. I replay our last conversation over and over, analysing every word, every pause, trying to find some reassurance. But instead, all I find is this creeping anxiety that won't let me rest. It wraps itself around my thoughts, whispering that maybe I'm losing him. Maybe this distance is more than just physical. Maybe it's emotional, too.

I can't reach out, I can't hear his voice, and it's driving me mad. The not knowing. The uncertainty. It's like standing on the edge of a cliR, peering into the unknown, not sure if I'll fall or if I'll be caught. What if something shifts while he's gone? What if he comes back and things are different? What if 'we' are different?

I'm scared. Scared that this space, this time apart, will change things in ways I can't control. Scared that I'm not enough to hold onto him, not when he's away, not when she's there. It's not just jealousy any more, it's fear. Deep, gnawing fear that I'll lose him, that I'm already losing him, and I'm helpless to stop it.

I wish I could talk to him, even for a minute, just to hear his voice, to feel that connection again. But instead, I'm left with this empty silence, and it's crushing. It's like screaming into a void, knowing no one will hear you.

I can't contain my emotions, I can't contain my constant thoughts, and worries and so I decide to write to him, each evening, pretending he is there and I am just messaging. So I do. It is raw, honest and it helps. I write openly as if he will never see it, so I am safe to say whatever I feel.

On day three, just as he says, randomly about 7 am a flurry of pings happens, and I leap for my phone, heart in my mouth, wondering what news he has, perhaps I am having the best time ever and sorry but I won't be in touch when I am back, or perhaps he will say he is missing me like I am him. It is the latter and I feel the tension lift from my body briefly.

And this is how I exist for the next fortnight in a constant motion between relief and doubt. Joy and fear. Literally living for the next ping. It is a miserable existence and not helped by Misty continuing to turn up in random places and me pushing her away. There is no way I can cope with her at the moment.

About midway through when a flurry of texts come, it brings mixed emotions. He shares that he and Natasha had a huge argument, Beth had been a bit naughty and his reaction had accidentally caused something to fall and hurt Beth, not badly, he felt terrible. This resulted in Natasha going nuts at him and Beth acting out even more. It is apparently all Sam's fault. I hate the thought he has had an argument and his break has some tension, but deep down the bad evil part of me, I am ashamed of, is quietly smiling and satisfied. Maybe Natasha is not all that, I wouldn't respond like that to him, ever. And I wouldn't. But he will never get to experience that, and I will never have the opportunity to show him.

Over the holidays, I feel terrible guilt for Lottie and Thomas, I am having to work and we don't have the cash to do much at all. I drop them at friends and we go visit the grannies but that is the highlight of their holiday. Their friends' Instagram and Snapchat stories are filled with beaches and cities as they are all away with their families. Failure and guilt consume me.

To occupy my mind I try to focus on Christmas Shopping. I have been saving as best I can, but the budget is small and won't go far. I do everything I can to stretch it by buying second-hand and seeking out bargains. God bless Vinted.

I go on a juice-only phase for the entire time he is away. It feels like something to divert my focus on, to feel like I am winning at something.

The night before he is due home he is in contact, he is in a hotel and he asks me to send what I have been writing. I was in two minds, but I do, and all 140 pages of pure emotion are sent to him, which he says he read all at once, that same night.

He gets back late on Saturday, tired, and we message briefly, I want more, but I know that is unreasonable, and he heads off to bed. I am disappointed but understand, I am just thrilled that I can message and he responds within minutes not days.

We don't actually speak until Monday on his way to work when he video calls me. I am on edge and nervous, desperate to speak to him, and petrified of what he might say.

When Sam's face finally flickers onto my screen, it's like a jolt of electricity runs through me. My heart lurches, and for a second, I forget how to breathe. There he is. Sam. I've been aching for this moment for two long weeks, but nothing could have prepared me for how it actually feels, to see him, to hear his voice again.

His smile is there, and he seems genuinely pleased to see me. "Hey, so good to see you, I've missed you so much, it's been awful," he says, his voice crackling through the weak signal. The sound of it hits me in a way I didn't expect, like a missing piece sliding back into place. It feels like he's close again like the distance between us isn't so unbearable.

The uncertainty remains in my mind. The questions I'm too afraid to ask dominate my thoughts.. How was the trip? How were things with the two of them? Has he rekindled his love with her? Have they fucked? Is he working out how to end this with me nicely? I don't say any of it. I can't. Instead, I focus on every little detail of his face, drinking him in as if this moment could somehow make up for all the time we've been apart.

"I missed you too," I say, the words tumbling out before I can stop them, raw and unfiltered. My voice is shaky, and I wonder if he notices. I feel exposed, and vulnerable, like I'm standing on the edge of something fragile.

I try to ignore the flickers of doubt, focusing on the warmth of his voice. I've been craving this, his presence, even if it's just through a screen. But it's not the same. It never is. I want to reach through the glass, to touch him, to feel the solidness of him.

The questions I want to ask sit at the back of my throat, unasked, because I'm too scared of the answers.

The call is brief, too brief, and when it ends. The screen goes dark. For a moment, seeing him, hearing him, felt like a balm to my raw, frayed edges. But at least I can now reach him when I need to and if that's all I get for Christmas, I will feel like I made it to the good list.

I don't ever want to go through that again. I jokingly say to him, please never go on a no-contact holiday again, it's said with projected jest, but I actually mean it. I need him and love him too much for that. It is bad enough being 100 miles away and restricted in communication, but that was another level and I do not ever want to experience it, ***ever again***.

All I want for Christmas is to be able to reach him, and have him there, on tap, like he has been. I am so grateful he is home.

Chapter 20

Cum Drops on Titties

Life feels better with Sam home, we slot into our regular routine and focus on early November when we plan to meet at the next business networking event. This is one we don't plan on actually going to, so we get more time together. It feels an eternity away. 17 days to go.

It is chilly outside as autumn has truly descended, the house is constantly cold, and I am working at my desk with a coat, scarf and woolly hat on. I am even going to bed with my woolly hat on. Phil isn't bothered, not like he looks at me anyway, but I wonder what Sam would make of me over the winter months if we lived together. He wouldn't have his free access so easily, it would be like a never ending game of 'pass the parcel' before he got to the prize.

I have been cold for what feels like eternity and I don't put the heating on in the house when everyone is out, it is a waste of money we don't have, heating a house, when it is just me, and I am using one tiny corner of it. But today I needed it, I was particularly cold. It's right into my bones, almost sore, so when I get back from walking Ron I put the heating on in my office, go make a cup of tea and head back up to start work. In the time it takes me to boil the kettle and brew the tea, the office seems to have gone into overdrive on heat. It is positively stifling. Honestly I think to myself, never happy, too cold, too hot.

"Hey bitch" I hear, and recognise that monotone sarcastic voice instantly, Emily has obviously let herself in as she does and now joins me in the office.

"Hey, want a drink?" I enquire.

"No."

"Didn't your mother ever teach you manners?" I jest with her "It's no thank you! P's and Q'S cost nothing! Why is it called P's and Q's anyway? Should it not be P's and T's?! I must google that!"

"Manners give people the wrong idea," she says.

"How are you?" I ask.

"Fucked off."

Oh joy I think, here we go, what lecture am I getting today. But my mood cannot be dampened, Sam is home and I get to see him in 17 days. When I am in a good mood I find Emily and her manner entertaining, I have an affection for her harsh exterior, a respect for her straight talking, no social filter approach, and can see what others can't, although abrasive, it all comes from a good place.

"Dare I ask why?" I enquire.

"I'll fucking tell you anyway."

"I know, I am all ears" I smile.

"Two things, one, you, ignoring her and two, that cunt Sam. You're causing me grief and I can't be fucked"

"Oh, we are doing this again?"

"Damn fucking right bitch."

"I assume by her...you mean Misty?"

"Who the fuck else Jessie, don't be smart... every single time you ignore her, who does she run to? Me! I have enough on my bloody plate, be a fucking friend for once and speak to her."

"She comes running to you?"

"Yes, I have **told** you this."

"Not really Emily, you haven't told me much at all."

"Fucks sake, I have, but your not listening to her **or** me."

Three's A Crowd

"OK, well, tell me now."

"Every single time you turn her away she finds me, she balls, moans, cries and is a pain in the ass. Harps on about you and how it **has** to be you, you know me, can't be arsed with shit like that, I just tell her to get a grip and speak to you."

"Well, I am all for speaking to her, but I am **not** for her just turning up whenever she bloody well likes, letting herself into my home, that reminds me, I need to remove the key from the lockbox, she chooses the worst times, I have no choice but to turn her away, I have emailed her and told her this, she is unhelpful and refuses to agree a time to meet, so what am I supposed to do?" I reply with an annoyance in my voice rarely seen.

"Jess, just fucking sort it, whatever is going on next time, excuse yourself and see her, I am demented with it, for me Jess, please."

Emily never asks me for anything and she looks both fierce and weary.

"OK, OK I will unless it's around my kids, I am not scaring them."

"Right....cunt face, you need to end it."

"What, why?"

"I can't sit back any more and watch this, he is going to destroy you."

"Jesus Emily, that is a bit dramatic, he happens to make me very happy and why do you have such a bad view of him? You have never even met him and I tell you nothing but good things about him."

"Do you believe I have always had your back? Do you believe I am your friend? Do you believe everything I ask for has your best interests at heart?"

"Well, yes, but sometimes you're wrong."

"When Jess? When have I been wrong? Give me one freaking example of when I have been wrong?"

I think for a bit and can't think of anything.

"But you might be wrong this time" I say "'he has not done absolutely nothing to indicate he is bad."

"Jess, stop being so fucking naive, when will you learn? You meet someone on GW, they want you for one thing. I have seen this with you a thousand times, where you get it in your head someone may like you, they don't."

"Am I that unlikable Emily, really? Thanks."

"No but I know men and I know the likes of him. He has this hold over you and I don't like it, I know you have fallen for him, the longer it goes on, the worse it is going to be when it all comes crumbling down which it fucking will. You are acting like a fucking love sick teenager."

"What hold? And yes I have fallen for him, why is that so bad?"

"Come on Jess, search your heart, do you really believe he feels the same way as you?"

"I think so."

"That's not a certainty, is it? So deep down you doubt it?"

"Yes, but that doesn't mean it's not true," I say limply.

"Let me tell you a story... imagine this is me... what would you say to me? Right now, you've what...given up your **only** decent income stream, for a guy that you have met three fucking times, and the first time **he paid** for sex with you. Not really the foundation for a real relationship is it? A guy you can see once a month **if** you're lucky, a guy who lives over 100 miles away, a guy who is married to some high-flying smart beautiful professor, you're batting out of your league Jess and you know it, a guy that is so controlled by his wife, it will only ever be a few hours once a month. A guy that now has you exactly where he wants, with no payment and no condoms as soon as you're clear. A guy that has worked out what a compliant thing you are, that you will never demand he leaves his wife, turn up on his doorstep, scream and shout or cause trouble for his real life. Not a bad deal for him is it? A guy that says he loves you, but **also says** he loves his wife, a guy that is probably still fucking his wife, no matter what he tells you, and probably fucking escorts on his doorstep, do you see how nuts this sounds Jess? "

She is not done…

"Lets try the fucking 'Lottie test' on that will we? Is this how you would want her to be treated? He gets everything he wants, you won't ever dare ask for more, you will always be last on his list, you will feel that, it will erode your self-worth, even further and if you think I am wrong. Remember how he avoids **any** real talk by saying; 'if only, I wish it too, the universe has a plan bollocks'. You're being sucked in by his words, his attention, it won't last, he will tire of you. And that is not to mention, when did you last manage to go more than a week without cock? Let alone a month, or longer. And now you think you will manage months at a time? I know you, I know you need it, both physically and mentally. He can't give you that, so it is inevitable you will fuck up… and then he will be done with you anyway. Let alone the fact he doesn't know everything you have done from your past… if he did, he would run a mile and not touch you, I know it and you know it. That **will** come out at some point… this will end Jess. Whether it's him realising its too complex and going back to local escorts, or re-finding proper passion with his wife, or you fucking up, or him learning more about your checkered past. This has no legs, it will die, and the result… **you**…taking a final crushing blow. Plus you are not free, you are married to Phil the phallus who never uses his fucking phallus. You won't leave Phil, until the kids have left home, at which point you will be over 50 years old. Beth is half your kid's age, so he will then have a child mid exams and won't leave either, you're 10 years away from being together and would both be approaching 60. The entire thing, even if he did **actually** love you, which, news flash, he does not, is totally unviable. He just wants his cake and to eat it. After everything you have been through, I am not convinced you will ever recover from realising he just wants you as a fuck hole. This stupid idea of you having a life with real love, is farcical, that shipped sailed for you a long time ago, accept it. I can't sit back and watch it happen any longer. It will be me left to pick up the pieces, again, and I think this time there will be bits that won't be able to be put back together. Wake up Jess! Dump his ass and let's go out this weekend, you and me and find someone to fuck us, like the good old days."

I am silent, fighting back tears, I don't want what she is saying to be true, but so much of it makes sense. I know I have been wrestling with all this myself, I am not in his league, I do have a past, so chequered anyone who discovers it would never want me, he does love his wife, he has never hidden that, he has told me, she couldn't be more opposite to me, he chose her to marry, he probably is seeing escorts, he is still on the GW site after all, I checked, he does avoid any real talk about him and I, I ***am*** last place, I do have a need for cock, I can't say no to men, I will fail and fuck up, I do need the cash, he is over 100 miles away. We are both trapped in unhappy marriages we cannot escape due to children. Would I want this for Lottie? No. But I am not Lottie, it is too late for me, and Lottie deserves better.

"Sorry Jess, cruel to be kind, dump him or I will intervene."

"Emily, please, don't, let me think."

"I am not having it Jess, I love you too much and I am the only one who will ever protect you from men fucking with your heart, he is fucking with it big time. I have always protected you Jess, you know this, who are you going to trust? The man you've known five months and met three times or me, who you have known 29 years?"

"What if I just look at it as a bit of fun? Box up my feelings a bit, accept it for what it is?"

"I would have no issue with that, ***if*** I believed you could, but I fear you're too far gone, another example of you not listening, earlier, and I would have no issue if you'd not gone and got yourself into a dumb ass exclusive situation, when you can't manage it and need the cash. Don't get me wrong, I would prefer you didn't do the GW work, as some of those bastards I don't like, and I happen to agree with Sam on his view of some. But I know how dire things are for you. But you **can** get your need for cock elsewhere, without having to rely on **him** deciding he can spare you the time and dictating how much money you can earn."

"OK, give me a chance, give me time to see if I can get more chill? And perhaps talk to him about how we should just be fuck buddies? I don't want to lose him, it would break me."

"I know, but if it's inevitable , why not rip the plaster off now before it gets even worse? And fuck buddies with no tie in, he can't expect fuck buddies that don't fuck others, given how unavailable he is."

'Please don't interfere, I promise I will deal with this."

"OK, you'd better, or **I will**."

With that she takes herself off and I feel very uneasy. Problem is I know she is right, I just don't know what to do about it and I so wish she was wrong.

That night when messaging Sam, he picks up on a change. I had very consciously tried to be as 'normal' as possible, sending him filth links and other chat, but he said he can tell I am being weird, slower to respond, shorter answers, and he can 'feel' it, he says he know my 'shields are up,' and he wants to understand why. I convince him I am fine as I am not prepared for this conversation yet, and we start talking about seeing each other. It throws him ffR the scent, for now and he lists a few things he wants to do to me when he sees me next, he mentions tying me up and spanking my ass.

I respond saying those are a few of my favourite things... and it makes me think of the song from the sound of music! I joke it would be much better written with a filth angle, he agrees and I quickly pen a version of it.

Cum drops on titties and Balls fit to burst

Bright red spank marks and Pussy's with a thirst
Held down with force and tied up with string
These are a few of my favourite things
Cream-coloured fillings and crisp hard whippings
Dirty talk and filthy talk, butt plugs and clamps
Cock in my ass and when my cunt sings
These are a few of my favourite things
Canings that leave me with pretty red gashes
Choking on cock so my eyeliner smudges
Silver white fountains that are sticky and cling
These are a few of my favourite things
When the day bites, when the world stings
When I'm feeling sad
I simply remember my favourite things
And then I don't feel so bad!

Sam confirms these are also some of his favourite things and we have a good laugh. Honestly if kinks were made for each other, mine are the glove, and his the hand, it just fits. Perfectly. But even more this cock has been tailored to fit my pussy, ass and mouth exactly, we are perfectly aligned on filth and body parts, it is quite uncanny.

The next 17 days drag, the only thing that gets me through it, is counting down the days and talking to Sam whenever we get the chance.

Christmas gifts begin to arrive, and I wrap as I go. I hate any last minute rush and like to be organised. I am getting more marketing client prospects and have several meetings to pitch for their business. I am crossing my fingers, toes and eyes that I win them. I need to.

Lottie is in full prelim stress mode, they start in January so she has cut herself off from everyone and locks herself in her room, studying and occasionally coming out to bark at us all. Thomas is focused on rugby, constantly outside doing drills, the boy is obsessed. Phil is managing to get bits of work here and there so he is out of the house quite often. This works for me as I need my wank time and I am not sure how whipping out my wand and putting on some Pascal's Subsluts would go down. Although to be honest, he'd probably just walk past me and not notice.

Some mornings I am mid-wank when Sam calls on his way to work, and he helps me finish by directing me and telling me what he is going to do to me when he sees me.

Emily pops in regularly, reminding me to have the 'chat' with Sam and to sort shit out with Misty, to stop running from it. Misty is still appearing at difficult moments and digging her fingers into my wrists, they are now quite bad. I keep emailing her, asking her to actually arrange a time and place, but she ignores my requests and turns up anyway. It is a constant worry and one that keeps sleep at bay.

I find myself thinking of my ex GW clients often, getting to 10 pm autopilot kicks in, and I reach to do my slutmin and look at WhatsApp. Then I remember, I don't do that any more. It is a bit of a void and I have nothing to do. I wonder if Szymon has tried viagra again with any success, if Dying Dave is still alive and if yes has he found anyone who actually takes time to talk to him, or maybe he has finally made it into someone's pussy. I think of Henry, hoping he is OK, and if he had to tell his Australian friend we have 'broken up' and he did 'let that one go.' Or maybe he has landed himself a proper girlfriend, that would be super. I think of the no condom anal, stomach punching guy and if he ever saw me again what he might do.

I suddenly have this hour I never used to have between my lot piling off to bed, Sam being online, and I fill it with porn. My pussy is angry, I am approaching 5 weeks without any sex and I feel like I could literally jump on every fence post that I pass when walking Ron and ride it silly. I don't because I don't want a pussy full of splinters.

I don't feel anywhere near as useful or wanted any more, I kind of realise how much GW work boosted me. I grab onto every word Sam says to fill the void, but I can't fill my pussy how it once was, and that is hard.

On the Saturday before I see Sam, I am dropping Thomas at a Rugby game in the afternoon. Sam and I talk while Beth is dancing. I love talking to him so much, we didn't talk about much, just him telling me about some work stuff and having a rant about some argument with Natasha. Something to do with her ordering four (yes four) pairs of boots to try and make a decision on which she was keeping. Sam had not done something right about returning them and she was livid. I was more blown away by being in a position to order four pairs of boots at once. I imagine she doesn't buy £30 Asda boots, more likely a brand, maybe £70 a pair. So the ability to just spend £280 without it impacting and it not being a problem to wait for the postage return and refund was mind-blowing to me. Not to mention the fact I could not understand how any of this was Sam's responsibility to sort out her returns.

I sometimes stay and watch Thomas play, sometimes I don't. Today is utterly miserable weather wise and I can't bear the thought of standing in the pissing rain and wind. So I head off to do the weekly shop. I tend to do it online, sometimes delivery, some- times click and collect. I like online, as you can see every penny spent and make adjustments without the pressure or temptation of being in the store. This week I have not had a chance but I will use their scan and shop to keep an eye on costs. Nothing worse than standing at the till to discover the total is more than you have in your account and having to request some items be removed until the total matches what you can spend.

I drive off, planning what I am going to get, passing the field with the fairground being set up. I am praying my kids don't spot it or hear about it as it's cash I can ill afford, then feel like a bad parent for even thinking like that.

The car heater is just not clearing the cold air, and it feels like the inside of the car is no different in temperature from the outside.

I turn up the dial, and the air blasts icy cold and attacks my body. I take a shortcut down a quiet residential lane, and as I turn and round the corner, the road narrows down to a single lane due to the badly parked cars on one side. Out of nowhere, a figure steps out from between the parked cars. I slam on the brakes and come to a sudden halt.

Misty - motionless in the middle of the narrow road, her frail figure barely visible in the dim grey overcast light. Her clothes are, hanging loosely on her slight frame, her Gap sweatshirt patterned with rain, and her long, tangled wet hair obscures much of her pale face. But her eyes, wide, hollow, and unnervingly fixed, lock onto mine from just ten feet away. Her expression is cold, almost vacant, sending a chill through me.

For a moment, everything is still. My hands grip the steering wheel tightly, unease creeping up my spine. Then, with a sudden purpose, Misty begins to move. Her steps are slow, deliberate, as she walks straight toward the car, her gaze never wavering from mine. I can feel my heart pound faster as she approaches, fear rising in my chest.

Without warning, she reaches the car and slams her fists down onto the bonnet with a force that reverberates through the vehicle. The sharp sound of her fists striking metal cuts through the air, and I flinch, instinctively pushing back into my seat. Her hands come down again and again, frantic and aggressive, her pale knuckles reddening with each impact. A mother and toddler walking along the pavement, glance over , the mother looks concerned at the sight infant of her, shields her child and steers him round the corner at speed.

Panic takes over, my breathing quickens, and I fumble to throw the car into reverse. My fingers tremble on the gearstick as the car jerks backwards. The tyres screech against the tarmac, and I try desperately to turn, but the street is too narrow. I can't control it. The rear of the car slams hard into a metal post with a sickening crunch, jolting me forward in my seat. I freeze, shaken, my mind racing with fear and confusion.

I glance up, heart pounding in my throat, expecting to see Misty still standing in front of me. But she's gone.

A car peeps at me as I am now blocking the road, I gather myself and drive off and when I get to Asda, I park up and inspect the damage. Fuck, one giant dent in the boot of my car. It is a leased car and a shit heap, but it will need repairs. I still have around 26 months to go on the lease so there is time to save for it and in 26 months I pray I will be in a better place to afford it. But it is the last thing I need.

I am really getting fed up with Misty now, it's beyond a joke. I can't go anywhere without risk. It's freaking me out, she seems to know my every movement. I decide I am going to speak to Emily and **beg** her to tell Misty to come to my home, when everyone is out and we can talk there. I am not having this any more. I am not being unreasonable. If I have to help the girl I will, but on my terms. That's the deal, I can't be having car accidents, I can't be having her interrupt my work. And I want to sleep again and while I know she could appear at any moment I seem unable to.

After the shop which was hard to get through due to feeling both shaken and annoyed at the car damage, I head back to the game and catch the last 20 mins in time to see Thomas score a try. His team has won, and he is buzzing, his coach is over the moon with him, and he chats all the way home, giving me a blow-by-blow account of the game from start to finish.

Once home I confessed to everyone about the car damage, claiming I was stupid when reversing and hit a post. Not a complete lie.

I fired off a message to Emily saying how this was totally unreasonable and if Misty wants to talk to me, she needs to bend and if Emily wants me to deal with it, then she has to encourage Misty to play ball.

She replies instantly:

Three's A Crowd

So yet again it's down to me to handle your shit

> I don't know what else to do

FFS I will try.

> Thank you

Spoken to Sam yet?

> No, let me enjoy this visit with him, please

Chapter 21

Emily vs. Sam: The Clash of Sass

When I get home I head to the office, catch up on emails, message Sam some dirty thoughts I have been having about him, restraining me with hands cuffed to my ankles on a spreader bar and delivering some rough 'painal,' with some links to make the point.

As ever he responds rapidly, and I can't help but feel safer with him than I have with anyone or for a long time. It's odd to feel safer than you have done when your world is crumbling, but he can be relied upon, he is mostly consistent, he responds, he listens, he is there. I don't have anyone else that is there like he is, even though most of the time he is actually not here at all. So whilst I don't feel secure in his true feelings for me, or what the future may hold for us, I do feel secure knowing I have someone I can reach out to. Even if I choose not to, which in relation to today's events I choose not to, I really don't want to lose that safety net.

He is out tonight, going to neighbours with Natasha and Beth, so he won't be able to message apart from a quick, I am home and goodnight. I hate nights like that. But understand them, and it's definitely not the night to bring up today's incident, I don't want to ruin his evening.

Sunday and Monday come and go. I have been nil by mouth since Saturday, laxatives taken Sunday night meaning all will be good to go come Tuesday morning, pipes empty and clean. I pack my bags when the house is empty, I wank myself stupid in anticipation. I try to focus on work until late afternoon when it will be time to go. I am not all that productive, it has been ***nine*** weeks, ***nine*** bloody weeks, ***nine*** weeks of no Sam, ***six*** weeks of no GW and no cock. My pussy knows what is coming and is gnawing at me all day, twitching, aching, dripping.

Sam and I don't speak as normal in the morning, as once again to allow time for me, he has gone into work super early. He messages when he has left the office, again he is leaving ahead of me as he has further to travel.

Finally it is time for me to leave. As I drove, my hands gripped the steering wheel a little tighter than usual, my heart pounding. The anticipation was a mix of excitement and nerves, creating this fluttering sensation in my chest that I couldn't shake. It felt like electricity in the air, crackling with every mile closer I got to Sam. My mind was racing, replaying our last goodbye and imagining what it would be like to finally see him again.

I played songs from my playlist, as I do every day, but today they felt stronger, making me smile one second and feel this overwhelming longing the next. I kept glancing at the clock, willing time to move faster, yet also trying to calm the storm of emotions building inside me. My stomach was doing flips, like that feeling you get just before something amazing happens, equal parts thrilling and nerve-wracking.

I kept wondering how it would feel when we finally locked eyes after all these weeks. Would it be the same, or even better? What would I say? My mind ran through all the things I wanted to tell him, but at the same time, I knew that the second I saw him, words would not come. He has that effect on me.

We spoke for the last hour of the journey and it settled me. But as the familiar landmarks came into view, signalling that I was almost there, my heart felt like it was about to burst. I was so close. I could practically feel him already, and it was this beautiful, overwhelming rush of hope, relief, and love all wrapped into one. I couldn't wait to see him, to finally be near him again.

We ended up meeting on the road, driving close to each other, and he followed me into a village where I was leaving my car. The plan was I would jump into his and he would then drive us to the Premier Inn. We planned to check in, fuck and then go out for dinner.

Parking was awkward, and I was distracted being in a village that I was known in, for a few reasons. So I wasn't able to be as free as I wanted to be when I first saw him. But I felt it, it felt like my whole world paused for a moment. My heart raced in my chest, and every nerve in my body seemed to light up. He didn't even have to say anything, just seeing him there, standing a few feet away, looking at me with that familiar smile, sent a rush of emotions flooding over me.

I was excited but also a little nervous, like I was seeing him for the first time all over again. It felt surreal. I'd been counting the days, imagining what it would be like when we were together again, but nothing compared to the real thing. I could feel tears welling up, not out of sadness but pure relief and joy. I hadn't realised just how much I missed the little things, his laugh, his eyes, the way he looks at me, how being near him instantly makes everything feel right again.

The moment we hugged, it was like time sped up and slowed down all at once. I didn't want to let go. All the waiting, the missing, the lonely moments, it all disappeared the second I felt his arms around me. There was this overwhelming sense of peace, like I could finally breathe again, and all the tension I was carrying just melted away. Being with him felt like home. After all, home is where the heart is.

We drive the short distance to the hotel, hardly able to contain our excitement, him telling me how much he has missed me, how good it is to see me. Then his phone rings and I see 'Natasha' flash on the screen. My heart jumps into my mouth. He motions to me to be quiet. My phone is on silent, it always is and I freeze. I don't think I move a muscle for the entire five-minute phone call.

As soon as I heard her voice, soft but strained, sadness crept over me. She sounded tired, like the weight of the world was pressing down on her, and I couldn't help but feel this sharp pang of guilt. She didn't know. She was just living her life, maybe too consumed by the pressures of being a high-flying professor or whatever it was, that had taken the spark from her voice, and here I was, sharing something with Sam that she had no idea about. It felt cruel, like I was hearing a part of her that I wasn't supposed to.

Her words were ordinary, talk of schedules, logistics , but the exhaustion in her tone was hard to miss. It was like listening to someone who had slowly become detached, not just from her life but maybe from herself and Sam, too. There was no joy, no lightness in her voice. I felt sad for her, for both of them, really. It was obvious that something had drained her spirit, and as much as I wanted to hold onto Sam, at that moment, all I could feel was sympathy.

But along with that sympathy, I could sense why Sam had sought me out. It wasn't just about fun or escape, there was something more. Maybe the life they'd built together had taken more from her than either of them had realised. Maybe all her success came at the cost of the connection they once had, and now she just sounded so... done with it all. It made me wonder if being at the top of her field had come at the expense of her happiness, her sense of life.

And there I was, sitting next to him, playing a part in it. The guilt dug deeper, but so did the understanding. It didn't make what we were doing right, but it made sense in a way that made my emotions more complicated. She sounded like she had long ago lost her lust for life, and Sam was just trying to find something he couldn't get from her any more. But as her voice faded from the speaker, I felt the weight of it all settle on my chest, the reality that no matter how we felt in this moment, there was a sadness here that couldn't be ignored.

I gave myself a shake, I would ignore it, I had waited nine long weeks and at least for the next twelve hours, he would be mine. I mentioned to him how sad and tired she sounded. He agreed, you could hear the frustration in his voice as he explained how hard she worked, how he had tried to make her see and to slow down, but to no avail.

The topic changes back to a more lighthearted nature as we check in, then it turns depraved and dirty as the hotel bedroom door closes behind us, and we fuck like it's a drug. Over the built-in table, where the tea and coffee maker and TV are. Him forcing his cock dry into my ass, pulling my hair to lift my head telling me to look at myself being fucked by his fat cock in the ass. To look at what a dirty fucking slut I was. I don't like looking in the mirror when being fucked (or any other time to be honest) but he loves to see that shame on my face and explodes, spraying my insides.

I was concerned I had built up how good his cock and cum was in my mind as it had been so long, I hadn't, it was better. Each time I see him it's better. I didn't think that was possible. We don't do vanilla sex, neither of us are into it, but he does some vanilla things sometimes and to my utter surprise, shame and disgust, he makes them work. Like when he nuzzles into my neck and kisses it and nibbles on my ear, it's like my legs don't work and I begin to drip to the floor.

By the time we head out for food, my pussy is a lot happier having had several orgasms, but it's not done.

Over dinner we do actually talk about work, he needs something to go back with so he has information to share with Natasha. So he takes his book out and makes notes as I share some of my knowledge about marketing campaigns and securing clients.

He is so serious when he is in 'proper work' mode, it's hard to focus, it turns me on. He challenges, enquires, questions, explains, listens and looks at me intently. I am enjoying a beer, he is driving. I manage to come across as if I know what I am talking about, and he seems impressed. I am unsure if that's an act or real. He is not the type to be impressed.

He talks again about how he will drip feed information about me to Natasha over the coming months in a professional capacity to pave the way for more frequent meetings in the future. I am all for that. And at this moment, I can't imagine what Emily says is true, he seems so genuine. Or is it that I want it to seem that way?

As we talk and standard marketing terms and acronyms come into the conversation I just hear filth. That's what happens when I am cock starved, scrap that, it is simply the way my brain is wired:

Three's A Crowd

Example of the sentence	The real acronym	What I hear
A CTA should be well crafted	Call to action	Cunt to Mouth
We want to keep CPC low	Cost Per Click	Cum Pussy Cock
The LTV of a customer	Lifetime Value	Lick That Vag
Keep an eye on the ROAS	Return on Ad Spend	Rim Oral Ass Sucking
SEO is essential but a slow burn	Search Engine Optimisation	Suck Each Orb (applicable to balls or tits)
I operate on the principle of ABM	Account Based Marketing	Anally Bang Me
Need to speak to the PTB	Powers That Be	Past Throat Barrier
I use a DB for CIM	Database for Customer Information Management	Dirty Bitch for Cum In Mouth

When we get back to the hotel, a lot of those acronyms are born out in practice and much more.

The night was off the scale amazing. I don't know if I had allowed something to fade from the last time I saw him, I knew we connected, I knew our time together was off the charts, but the reality, in person, just brought it home quite how off the charts it was.

If Carlsberg did connections... this would be it.

And there didn't appear to be any part that didn't work. The sex - amazeballs, the filthy chat - incredible, my desire for him - unmeasurable, none sex chat - engaging, atmosphere - fun, tenderness and care - present at the right moments, my love of him - deep and bottomless.

It just seems so unbelievable. And of course cruel.

Falling asleep with him his warmth enveloped me like a comforting blanket, a shield against the world's uncertainties. As I drifted off to sleep, nestled in the crook of his arm, I was at peace, calm, happy. It was a feeling I don't think I had really felt before. Especially at the moment when the night usually brought a mix of anxiety and unease, a constant undercurrent of worry. But with Sam, it was different, I wasn't scared to go to sleep. I felt safe, and protected, and when the nightmare came, he soothed me, and it passed, allowing me a quality of sleep I had forgotten was even possible.

In the morning emotions were mixed, overjoyed to be waking with him, but internally distraught that the nine-week wait, culminating in around nine hours of awake time with him, was close to the end. It didn't feel enough, I wanted more, but I wouldn't dare mention that.

Of course, first breakfast was a fuck, and we suddenly found ourselves in, god forbid missionary... Sam said.

"Oh, this isn't very us!"

"You're quite right, hold on," I said and swung my legs up, one either side of my head so they could rest on his shoulders and he could push his weight down on them, allowing him to get really deep inside me, filling the condom.

Second breakfast was me scooping cum out the condom he had used to fuck my pussy and enjoying it, Sam didn't fancy the second breakfast.

Third breakfast, we headed to the restaurant.

Just as we are about to eat, my phone rings. It's a client wanting to ask a gazillion questions about the proposal I sent through, I signal sorry to Sam and get up leave and stand outside chatting with Oliver. I hate people talking loudly on phones in restaurants.

I also thought it would give Sam the chance to call or message home.

I was on the phone for a good fifteen minutes before I went back in, even though it was November, the sun seemed to stream on me like I was centre stage under a spotlight and I started to sweat. As I opened the doors to the hotel, I was stopped, dead in my tracks by what I saw. Emily, striding towards me smiling, giving me the finger and saying…

"Sorted."

And walks past me and the other customers entering the building and heads to the car park.

I feel like I am about to die, physically like my body is about to give out, my life literally flashing before me. Hysteria building… What has she done? I am torn, do I run after her and find out what the fuck she has said, has she said anything? Maybe it's just a coincidence that she is here. No, she said 'sorted'. Fuck she has spoken to him, fuck, fuck, fuck!

God, what has she said…Emily is not someone you just meet for the first time unprepared. She has either gone full-on attack or told him things he won't like. Either way, Sam's view of me will have changed forever. She believes he is a threat, and she will not have held back, I have seen it before. Fuck.

Part of me thinks I should just go to the room, get my things, and leave. It is bound to be over anyway and this way I don't have to look him in the eyes. FUCK! I can't even do that, my car is in the next village and the room key is on the table.

I walk back into the restaurant, he doesn't look up, he is focused on cutting up his bacon.

I slide back into the seat silently welcoming the cooler air. He looks up at me… his eyes look pained.

"You want to explain that to me?" he says cooly.

"I guess you met Emily," I state.

"She is a fucking delight," he says.

"What did she say? Or do I not want to know?"

Sam then tells me blow-by-blow what happened and while he speaks I can't read him.

He tells me how she said to him, he is a manipulative bastard, playing me, a liar, that he needed to fuck off and fuck with someone else. That she won't allow it, just to be honest, tell me I am nothing more than sex for him, be straight about how he actually doesn't give a shit, just be honest and stop being a dick. It's someone's life he is messing with, how dare he stop me from working. That if he didn't grow a pair, and be straight, she would take it out of his hands, take me out and get me fucked, maybe even organise a gang bang for me. How she knows what a slut I am, she knows what I have done, gang bangs included, and how I've loved doing them. How if presented with multiple cocks, I wouldn't be able to resist. She said she had enough dirt on me to scare him away for life, make him see even more clearly, that even as just a set of holes, I am not worth the hassle. He said that every time he tried to speak, she told him to 'shut the fuck up', every time he tried to ask a question, she said she 'didn't have to answer to him.' That he must end this or **she would.**

My jaw is on the floor. I am upset inside desperately trying to contain it, so hurt that she, my friend, would treat someone I care about deeply with such cruelty and disrespect. That she, my friend, would do something she knows will break my heart.

Despite that overpowering worry, I am more concerned about Sam, what he is thinking and what he is feeling.

"And?" I manage quietly, unable to meet his gaze.

I wait for him to respond, his silence the loudest thing I have ever heard.

Knowing the silence is a ticking time bomb, a countdown to the inevitable end.

Chapter 22

Red is the Colour of Shame

Emily is my oldest companion, I have trusted her with everything in my life, there is nothing she doesn't know about me and at that moment I felt nothing but hurt and betrayal. My life is a shit show, falling apart at every turn, and she adds to it by speaking out of turn with the guy I happen to have fallen in love with. If things were not hard enough between us due to distance and our circumstances, she has cast more shadows over the prospect of any continued future. I am finding it very hard to see how she thinks this has come from a good place.

I am in total panic. The proverbial swan looking calm on the surface but working away underneath trying to figure out how the hell I can resolve this.

"You tell me?" Sam says.

"Can you ignore it?" I ask.

"The fact I am thought to be a devious bastard just here to use you? Or the fact you would go out and fuck someone else? Or the fact you have done gang bangs before? Or the fact there is more in your past I don't know about?"

"I won't fuck anyone else, I wouldn't jeopardise us" I reply.

"But you can't say 'no' can you?"

"I do struggle with that, I can't lie, but I am not in those situations any more, and I removed myself from those for you."

'That's your program Jess, we need to rewire you. And do you think I just want you for sex?"

"Sometimes," I say weakly.

"Why would I be here in a hotel, having spent an evening laughing and talking with you if all I am interested in is sex? I can get that from any escort in my own town tomorrow... so newsflash, there must be something else going on... like.... Oh, I don't know, the fact I love you?"

I don't want to tell him what's really in my head, it will only make things worse. I want to believe he loves me, deep down I have always wanted to be loved, but how can he love me, and be ok with how things are? Not even contemplate how to move forward.

"OK," I replied.

"You're just going to have to accept it, I don't know what else I can do, other than tell you I love you, if I won't take my word, what else can I do?" he says.

Show me I think. But keep quiet.

"I am trying to trust your word and believe you, It's just hard to understand."

"There is no try, there is only do," he says.

I laugh a little, he does love a wise Yoda quote.

"I am sorry that happened, she's all about keeping me safe, I know it's hard to believe but she comes from a good place," I reply.

"Safe from what? Me?"

"I guess."

"I am not going to hurt you Jess, ever, I need you in my life, I can't be without you, part of me would die."

Yeah, but you can't be with me either I think. I pray that what he says is true, I don't think I can survive his loss.

I smile weakly at him, he reaches for my hand.

"Look at me" he says "Look me in the eyes and hear this, I love you, you matter, I want you."

Three's A Crowd

I am close to tears but hold it together, I wish I could believe this fully. What the hell must he be thinking about my crazy bitch friend?

"Come on, let's go back to the room, get our bags, we have to go soon and I want in your ass one last time."

I am stunned he is not more unnerved by this, but relieved. And pleased we won't be leaving each other with a bad feeling, but I can't help thinking when he has time to think more clearly he will see things differently.

We get to the room and he fucks my ass doggy style over the bed, before whipping off the condom, grabbing my head, pulling it into him and holding his throbbing cock down my throat where he unloads. God I love that feeling, although I am always a little disappointed when it skips my tongue and I don't get to taste it, but I adore the feeling of being taken and used, like I don't matter and he can't help himself.

We get ourselves sorted and head out to his car, as he drives me back to my car he says;

"Have you done a gang bang?"

Shit...it's not over.

"Yes," I say.

"When? How?"

"A year or so ago, client, Manchester.'"

"Fuck Jess, tell me it wasn't bareback?"

"It was, but they were all tested."

"All? How many?"

"Oh.... only three, it was supposed to be more but only three could make it."

I see his hands grip the steering wheel a bit harder.

"Only three!" he exclaims "I am so fucking glad you're not doing that work any more, what else have you not told me, I should know about?"

"Nothing."

"Really?"

"Not that I can think of," and it's the truth. I don't know why he wants to know anyway. It's in the past and I am only with him now.

We get to my car and we hug and say our goodbyes, me fighting tears. Leaving Sam today feels like such a heavy weight, the difficulties of distance and uncertainty pressing down on me. It's not just the usual sadness of parting for another month, but the sharp edge of fear that cuts deeper after this morning's revelations. Everything feels fragile now, like the ground beneath us has shifted in ways I can't yet fully understand.

As I walk away, I can't help but wonder if this might be the last time, if the moments we've shared are somehow slipping through my fingers. Each glance back feels heavier, each goodbye harder to swallow. It's like a shadow hangs between us, making the weeks ahead feel like an eternity. I used to count the days until I'd see him again; now, I can't shake the cold whisper in the back of my mind asking if I ever will.

We drive up the road together, him at my rear following, he calls and we talk, he is saying he misses me already, and how this is the worst part, seeing me leave. I am fighting back emotion when the road splits and he veers west, it breaks me to see his car vanish out of site.

As soon as I am home I message Emily.

> How could you?!

It needed done, you'll see in time, you will thank me

> Well it didn't work

It will and if need be I will go further

> Emily, please I am begging you

Beg all you like, I won't let him hurt you.

I don't bother replying. I am too angry at her. Too hurt.

Three's A Crowd

That night as usual when Sam gets back from seeing me, he is less responsive, spending time with Natasha and Beth. I understand it, but it feels awful like he has served his time with me, ticked that box and now his attention is elsewhere. When he does eventually jump on to messages, he starts his incessant questioning. The gang bang thing has clearly eaten away at him and he digs and digs until all details are revealed. He is shocked to learn how little (in his eyes) I put in place to keep me safe, meeting three guys I didn't know, being drunk, being taken to their apartment, and not knowing how I was going to get home.

> Your lack of regard for yourself, your lack of risk analysis, scares the shit out of me

> It worked out

> Luck

It's harder to tell what he is thinking and feeling over a text. He comes across as annoyed and cold. I don't know if it's real or my paranoia. But I don't like it and of course being tired from his early start, long day, fuck fest and journey home, he goes to bed early.

I sit up pondering life, where it's going, what's happening. I feel like I am losing Emily, she is spending more time with Misty than me while being an even bigger bitch to me than usual, like she is tired of me, and done with me. Despite my jealousy, it is a relief Misty is talking to at least someone and has some support. I had tried to encourage Emily to persuade Misty to go to the Police before, Emily agreed she should have, but Misty was having none of it.

I can't help thinking that maybe like men, friends don't want me either. I think of Sam and what he must be thinking, how the hell he could want to have anything to do with me? He has met my mental friend who told him he was a bastard. He learnt that I am not just a slut, but in his eyes a stupid super slut who has done gang bangs. It forms in my mind that he will never want me completely.

Sure, he will enjoy my filth side and take full advantage of that, but you don't want someone in your life and on your arm with my history. Fact.

Although he is right, he could just go book an escort locally. What he spends on a hotel to see me, he could use for that , less time away, less hassle, less of a tramp. Maybe that is my appeal, I am filthier than most.

I think about Lottie and Thomas and how desperately I want life to be back to 'normal', better for them. I can't even give them the basics. I think of Misty and if and when she might show up. Would she rock right up to Phil and the kids and tell them I have been selling my body.

Life feels like death row, like I am just waiting for the end, for it all to fall apart.

Despite my racing mind, I too feel tired and head off to bed just after midnight. I fall asleep instantly, but unlike lying next to Sam I wake, shaking, having just dreamt of Darren again. I just don't understand where some of this comes from, it's so long ago, and I am so over it. I feel like it's real, the type of dream when you wake, you still feel its presence, sending prickles across your body. I get up and go downstairs and grab my pad and start to draw.

Car lights seep through the curtains brightening the room for a few seconds, and the chill of the night when the heating is off creeps over my skin, giving me goosebumps and shivers. I reach over the back of the sofa and lean on it, bending down to the floor behind to grab a blanket and as I slump back down on the sofa, Misty is there, right in front of the TV, staring at me.

I literally jumped out of my seat and had to slap my own hands across my mouth to stop me screaming. I blink a few times wondering if I am just overtired.

But there she was, so painfully thin in the middle of my living room, her eyes wide and haunted. Her frame is so fragile like she might shatter with the weight of what she is carrying. She didn't say a word, but the air between us felt thick.

Three's A Crowd

She looked pained, distressed as if she'd been carrying a burden too heavy for too long.

My mind raced with the thought of the rest of the house waking up. What if they saw her? The confusion, the questions, the disruption that would ripple through everything. I wanted to get her out, to push her back out into the night, to demand how she got in, how long she'd been there, standing like a ghost among my things.

But I couldn't. I knew, at that moment, I couldn't run any more. Something in her eyes stopped me cold. The fear, the desperation, and maybe something that mirrored my own. I didn't know why she had chosen me or why she kept coming, but I knew this wasn't going to stop and I knew I had to listen. I had no choice.

"Listen," she says quietly I nodded.

She reached for my hands and took them gently in hers. Never taking her eyes off me, a tear fell from her left eye.

As she looked at me she gave me one slow nod, as if to say… 'are you ready'. I took a deep breath and gave her a nod back. My stomach lurched in anticipation of what she might tell me next.

School bell

I know I have to vary my route exit at the back, over a fence just need to get to the train station in sight now

Pass the bushes, rustling two of the boys block me "tut tut, wrong way" "Please I need to get home" "I don't care!"

Try to move - to walk around them,

They step in front of me, again & again.

"Are we doing this the hard way or the easy way?" group of sixth formers walk past.

"Hey Ben, would you Fuck her?"

Ben ignores them - keeps walking.

Whispers "will we tell them what you do for us?

Let the whole school whisper about you?"

"Didn't think so, let's go for a walk?"

One in front - the other staggered a bit behind.

I can't run forward or back, I'll be stopped, I know this. but I try
"Nice try, keep walking."

Into the nature reserve its quiet shoved in the direction they want looking for an escape

Can't find one.

Silent tears - shaking "Pathetic" one spits.

Shoved up against a tree hard my back slams into it

Feeling my tits through my top batting their hands away

Pain through my foot he has stamped on it "Fucking stop"

I stop, I freeze.

Reaches up under my shirt feels me

"What the fuck is this, Jesus, your pussy's got fat, what the fuck, hold her!"

Held - skirt yanked up, tights down.

I feel sick tits groped

Cock out

"Stop please, you can't." hand slides up my leg

I kick

Face slapped, neck grabbed, squeezing

"Fucking. stop that right. now." I stop finds the top of my pants

Slides his hand down panic

He can't. it's too late.

"What the actual fuck!" He barks removes his hands

Holds hand in front of my face, covered in blood.

"Fuck sake."

Smears hand all over my face dives into my pants

Rips my sanitary towel out rubs it over my face

"What the hell, that's disgusting" released

"She's fucking disgusting."

My eyes have been shut and they dart open, I can feel this as if I am there, the shame, the embarrassment, totally humiliating. I feel for her so much, having to endure this. I go to pull my hands away, I want to talk to her, to tell her it's OK, to tell her if she tells me who these people are or her full name or her parents details I can help. She doesn't have to put up with this. But as I pull away, her eyes dart open, she digs her nails into my already bruised and cut wrists, and she hisses at me, face twisted.

"LISTEN!"

I stop pulling away, another panic rises in me, I am at home, my children sleeping peacefully upstairs, I can't have her kick off, I need to contain this. I shut my eyes again and she continues.

Grabs my hair

Pulls me down to his belly

"You've fucking done it again, soft as fuck." they walk off

Spit into my hands clean my face

Get new towel from bag pull up pants and tights grab used one of the ground roll it.

Can't leave it - animals

Catch the train

A long silence follows, only broken by her soft sobs. She releases her grip on my hands and lays forward placing her head in my lap and she gently weeps, her bony shoulders shuddering.

I don't speak, I place my trembling hand on her head and stroke her hair. Her hair is thin, wispy as if she is going bald. Her whimpers are soft but pained, my eyes fill and my own tears fall on top of her head. I want to help her, but if she won't tell me anything, what can I do? I try questioning her;

"Who are they?"

"What's your surname?"

"What is it you want me to do for you?"

"I think we should maybe speak to the Police, I would come with you."

She darts upright, eyes wide, petrified, I have never seen fear so wild in someone's eyes, head shaking wildly, I think she is about to scream.

"OK, OK, not now, maybe one day, when you're ready, but we have to find a way to stop this Misty."

"You'll stop it" she whispers.

"How Misty? If you don't tell me more, how can I? What can I actually do?"

She does not answer.

She places her head back on my lap and continues to tremble and let all this emotion out. Time stands still, eternity passes and we stay like that for what feels like hours. She quietens and stills. She sleeps. I rest my hand on her soft hair and my own head lolls back and I sleep.

"Jess!" What the fuck!" Barks Phil.

I spring up, head groggy. I don't quite know where I am, or what's happened.

"Jess, the back door is swinging open!" He barks.

"What?" I reply a bit croaky rubbing my eyes.

"The back door, it's open."

My mind is still battling to work out why I am in the living room, what day it is, what time it is.

The fog begins to clear... Misty! Shit, where is she?

"Oh god Phil, sorry I don't know what happened."

"Jess! Seriously, what is going on with you? The door has probably been open all night, anything could have happened."

"I am so sorry, I don't know," I am trying to think of a reason the door would be open, one that is believable.

He storms off marching round the house. I get up and follow.

"What are you doing?" I'm scared he is going to walk into a room and find Misty.

"Checking the kids are here! Checking no one is in the house for fuck's sake."

I skulk behind him, relief passing over me as we find Lottie and Thomas and no Misty. Ron is lying on our bed, bingo that's my excuse.

"Oh god Phil, I think I know what happened, Ron was nudging me in the night, wanted out, so came and let him out, he was taking forever... I was shattered and came through here to sit and wait on him, left the door open and must have passed out, I am so, so sorry."

"Fuck's sake Jess" and he storms off. That's me in the bad books, if there is one thing that makes Phil mad, it's home security.

I am lax at it, granted, but he is the other extreme. But frankly, him being in a huff is the least of my worries.

I don't think things will ever be the same with me and Emily again, I am not sure things will be the same with Sam again either. The two people I need in my life, drifting, and changing.

Cash pouring out the door faster than water through a damn. Even if things haven't changed with Sam, there is still the very real prospect I may need to return to GW and that marks the end of us anyway. I am now three long months into almost every single night being devoid of sleep. I am tired, I feel almost done. But I can't be done, I have my own children to think of and Misty needs me. I don't know why, and I don't know what to do, but I know she needs me.

The 'Lottie test' I can't abandon her.

Chapter 23

Brucie Bonus

I've come to realise that when it comes to wishing, hoping, or believing that Sam loves me and wants to be with me, I'm all doom and gloom. It's like I can't let myself fully trust in the possibility of 'us', not when he's married, I am married, not when we're so far apart, not when we can't communicate totally freely, and not when I have never experienced someone actually wanting anything much to do with me. It seems impossible to fathom. Combined with the fact we can only be together fleetingly, only ever infrequent moments. It's hard for me to believe in something that feels so fragile, temporary, like it's always just one step away from crumbling.

What hits me even harder is how much this contrasts with who I usually am. In other parts of my life, I'm annoyingly optimistic, I take on challenges and believe things will work out. Sam would say that's half my problem, I just blindly believe all will be fine, like going to a gang bang or a BDSM client. But when it comes to Sam, I'm the opposite, I'm filled with doubt, constantly bracing myself for the worst.

And I hate it.

I hate that this situation turns me into someone I don't even recognise.

But if I'm honest, it's because Sam is ***that*** important to me. I've never cared about losing something this much before. The thought of losing him... it's devastating. It's like my heart has already prepared for the fall, just in case it happens, but the truth is, I don't think I'd ever be ready for it. That's why I can't help but wrap myself in all these fears, like a protective layer so it won't hit so hard when it comes.

Sam has become a part of me, and losing him would mean losing a piece of myself.

I actually worked out the percentage of time we spend together in person, and it's tiny.

If an average month has 30.42 days x say 17 'awake' hours.

Then 30.42 x 17 = 517.14 possible available Sam Hours (SH for short).

If I see him in person once a month and we paint the best case where we don't go to a networking meeting I get around 8 awake hours with him.

So in one month 8/517.14 = 1.54% of SH's.

That's it! I am 1.54% of his 'in-person life', but let's be fairer, 8 hours of those on say 20 days a month he would be working, so no one really gets SH's other than work. So there are 160 unavailable SH's to anyone.

517.14-160 = 357.14 True Sam Hours that are actually available outside of sleep and work (TSH's)

8/357.14 = 2.24% of TSH's are available to me. And that is being optimistic, ***if*** we manage every month and ***if*** we don't go to the meeting. So the reality is far, far less.

If I was to factor in messaging and phone calls, at an optimistic 2 hours a day, averaged to account for slightly more during the week and a lot less at weekends and not take into account holidays and other times when he cannot communicate at all.

Then in addition to 2.24% TSH's. I do get some NRLSH's (None Real Life Sam Hours).

2 x 30.42 days in a month = 60.84 NRLSH's 60.84/517.14* = 11% of NRLSH's

*we message during work so working off SH's not TSH's.

So a ***very*** optimistic view is I get 13.24% of ATASH's (All Truly Available Sam Hours).

However, the quality and weighting of NRLSH's are far less than TSH's, so it's really not fair to combine them. They are not equal. So let's divide that by 3 to counter the equal weighting. A fair refection is I am 4.41% part of Sam's life. **That is it.**

So no matter what my secret hopes and dreams are, I am such a tiny part, a part that if lost would not be missed because the other 95.59% is where his life ***actually is***. Where it matters, where his attention is and he would never give up his 95.59% that contains his daughter, a wife he loves and cares for, for the 4.41% ex-hooker, who has a program running that means she would struggle not to leap on a cock and fuck someone. Add in an abusive mental friend, no money and a stalker who follows me places, you can understand why he would not swap his life to include me.

Being objective, unless he has a screw loose, it is not happening and never will.

When you see it laid out like that, you can't help but think maybe Emily is right after all. I don't think it's intentional by Sam, I hope and pray it's not. That would make him not the person I think he is. But maybe, he just hasn't given it that much thought, not really assessed it in the way I have. Not admitting to himself that he is actually going with the flow, saying what he feels but not identifying that the words are actually empty, meaningless and have no intent behind them.

So when he messages that he has been given a pass to attend an extra event we had spoken about, I am beyond thrilled. We had spoken about it for a while.

How he would slowly work into the conversation with Natasha

about my existence. That we met at a business networking event, that I am married, that I seem to know my stuff when it comes to marketing and I am well connected. I am a good business contact and our two knowledge bases could help and compliment each other.

I used my old burner number so we could send 'none filthy' messages about business arrangements so he could show her. On my burner phone we messaged about me taking Sam to meet Gavin, a contact of mine that could really benefit Sam's business.

My agenda and cover story to Phil is that, if I develop a relationship with Sam, as a business analyst he could refer lots of marketing clients my way.

So when I got the news that it was a go, I was fit to burst with excitement. I felt like he had really pushed things, ***for me***, like I mattered, like I was important enough, like he had prioritised our time together, like he really wanted to see more of me, as much as I did him. And on the back of Emily's shit show, it reduced my uneasiness. I contacted Gavin straight away and set it up.

So this month my TSH was doubled! I couldn't be happier.

So instead of the countdown to our next meetings starting in the thirties, the countdown began at just sixteen days.

Even though it was sixteen, it still felt as long as thirty. I swear ISSD's (In Between Seeing Sam Days) works in a different space-time continuum to normal days, each one dragging. Where as SSD's (Seeing Sam Days) went into some kind of warp-speed machine and were over in a nanosecond.

Home life continued as normal, Phil pottering about the house, painting, drilling, nailing, digging, weeding, occasionally out doing odd jobs for people and filling the cash pot in the kitchen. Those days allowed me to get my toys out and wank freely, releasing my tension from the lack of cock, orgasming without holding back and screaming the house down.

One thing I hate is when I don't get the space and time to satisfy myself and have to resort to the shower, the woods, the car or silently when lying next to Phil. Sam often made me cum when we messaged at night, even just his text words, a flash of his hard cock and I would leak like a holey bucket. But again, late at night with a house full, I have to contain myself.

Lottie's stress levels were through the roof, I hardly saw her, she got home from school and studied, on weekends she barely saw sunlight and studied all day. I tried to discuss balance and doing things with friends, but she would not budge. You had to admire her work ethic. Thomas played rugby, practised rugby, watched rugby and scrappily did his homework on the morning it was due while running out the door to get the bus. How can two children, raised under the same roof, be so wildly different?

Misty's appearing randomly got worse, it was daily now, but you never knew when, you never knew where. I would be driving somewhere, and she would be standing at a junction, staring, I can't stop because I have the kids in the car. She'd appear at the kitchen window when I was cooking dinner, chatting to Phil, he spotted her once and went into the garden to see who was hanging a round. She popped into the office during Zooms, she stood in cafes as I talked to work contacts. It was unnerving. Sometimes she'd grab me, pinch me, other times she couldn't get close to me. I continued to email my plea for arranged times, that I had a lot to get done, and she needed to pick her times better. She continued to ignore this.

Three times over those sixteen days, she grabbed me at a time I could listen. One where she found me walking Ron through the park. The roundabout was still spinning since being abandoned by some kids like it still wanted to play and no one was up for it, lonely. It was bitterly cold and she grabbed me. I have not gotten used to it , despite her frequency, it always takes me o# guard, it always puts the fear of god into me. But in the park with no colleagues, family or friends I could listen and let her talk. She told me of a time two of the boys trapped her on the train, between 2 compartments, she had her cello with her, she got pushed into the toilet, hit and then they attacked her - r*p$d her.

The second time she got me when I was free to listen as I pulled into my drive, it was a clear night sky with a handful of clouds rolling over the moon, the frosty cold air penetrating the car as she jumped into the passenger seat. I turned the engine back on to give us some heat, it never seems to make a difference in that car. She told me about the time the boys forced her to suck their cocks and critiqued her all the way through, slapping her if not happy and being cruel about her weight. I can't understand this. This part makes me think she is making it all up because she is not fat, she is scarily skinny. Then I chastise myself , I remember that feeling for me after Darren, the fear of not being believed. She has no reasons to lie.

The third and final time during that period was in my kitchen during the day. I was making a cuppa soup listening and singing along to the radio, thinking it funny that the song playing 'You're justified and You're ancient' *is* actually now ancient. As my mum would say she must 'be born in a barn' and left the door open as she came in because it turned baltic. This time she told me about one of them coming to her house, late at night, entering through the low living room window, threatening her to be quiet, which she did as her parents slept upstairs. He fucked her mouth, she had been out drinking beforehand and was sick.

Each time I see her I want to know more, ask more, help more, but she avoids the questions and disappears. She sobs and wails, it leaves me upset, exhausted, zoned out and unable to get on with my day for a good while.

Paul and Christopher are new names she has not mentioned before, I am wondering who these people are. She makes it sound like they are possibly from her school, but maybe they are adults. She can't be going to school anyway, as she is constantly about... it's not like she only comes to me after school hours and her school is supposedly over 200 miles away. She can't go to my old school, it's impossible.

I decided in a mad moment one day to phone the two high

schools in my town and ask if they have a pupil called Misty, about 16 years old. They won't tell me for data protection and child safeguarding reasons. For fuck's sake I am trying to safeguard the child. I decide I will have to spend a few hours lurking outside each school at the end of the day and see if I can see her coming out. I have to find more out about her if I am going to help her.

As for Emily, she has not visited me since she saw Sam, but she gets her message across via text, constantly telling me all the reasons Sam is bad news. She asks questions that get me thinking and highlight how much I am picked up and dropped, but I don't admit that to her. She is just trying to ruin things for me. I take great pleasure in telling her I am getting a wee 'Brucie bonus' trip with Sam, and we are staying somewhere super posh in York (where Gavin lives) because he got a deal. I hope that sticks in her throat.

Despite the deal Sam has got for the hotel, I am feeling really uncomfortable with how much money he is spending, he has paid for all the hotels. It is not fair. I have tried to discuss it with him, but he will not listen.

I may not be in a position to pay at the moment, but I want it known I am keeping a tab and will repay my share as soon as I am able. I won't have him waste his money, money that could be used for Beth, Natasha or himself on me. Plus I know he has bought me trainers, he saw me once too often on video call having been running in my wellies which led to the mortifying admission I don't have any because I am so skint. So he pushed and pushed to discover my shoe size one evening on messages, after we had spoken in the morning and he had clocked my wellies, again.

What size are your feet?

Why?

Because I want to know

But why?

> Just tell me

>> No

> Fine I will speak to your pal Emily next time she jumps me.

>> Urgh…OK fine , size 4, but please don't go buying me anything, I am fine in wellies and will get trainers when I can.

> I am getting you trainers, I want to help, end of conversation.

He did, and he didn't just buy a pair of Asda trainers, he bought New Balance, saying they are good quality and designed for running. I am grateful, I really am, but I also want to die inside. How have I ended up here? I don't want to be a burden financially or otherwise. I have always stood on my own two feet, getting my first part-time job at age thirteen and I have never had to rely on anyone for anything. **I don't like it.**

One day when messaging me, I was flatlining and doubting his feelings, he came back with the fact doubt was natural, that he had doubted my motivations. The thought had crossed his mind that *I* was playing him, because he had money and I didn't. I was crushed he could think that of me and it's now even more important I prove that wrong, that I will somehow save up money to pay back the hotels *and* the trainers. I also planned to skim some cash off the Christmas budget to get him a gift. I wanted to anyway but stopped myself as it would be so crap and next to the lavish gifts Natasha could get him. It would only serve as a visual representation of the difference between us. But I desperately wanted to show him I do care, that Christmas will not go past without me showing him he is in my thoughts and Brucie bonus evidence, that I don't need his money.

Chapter 24

Porked in York

The week leading up to me leaving for my Brucie bonus, I decided I had to try and do something to work out where Misty hung out. She was definitely of high school age, and given the two high schools were no help when I called, I decided my idea of hanging at the school gates was maybe a good one. I also went to the train station too. So I did two days at each school at home time and one day at the train station.

High schools are busy places and I positioned myself as best I could to get as broad a view of the sea of evacuating children as possible. I didn't spot her once. So many kids, that it might be possible I missed her, she seems the type to hide or blend in. I had to hide and blend in at my children's school or they would have wondered what the hell I was doing at the school gates. I then rushed home so I was back before their bus got back. When I thought about it, perhaps she didn't go to school at all, considering some of the times she showed up to see me. Given what she is going through, I would not blame her for skiving off. On Friday I tried the train station and waited from 3:40 to 5.20pm at the main entrance, again with no sign of her. I was certain she had mentioned walking to the train after school, so I had concluded she must not live in this town. None of my efforts bore any fruit, I would try again next week once back from seeing Sam.

I told Sam what I was up to and he was getting increasingly concerned. So was I. He kept pushing me to go to the police. But with what!? I knew nothing about her really, her full name, actual age, where she lived, where she went to school, when she would turn up. And whilst I wasn't actively doing GW any more, there would be a digital footprint, that if she wished to cause trouble for me she could. I could not risk that.

Finally, the day came for me to head off to see Sam again. I am not sure I will ever not be 'nervcited' about seeing him. He just does something to me. I have a client meeting at 4 pm on Zoom. If I stayed home to do that I would be late getting to him, so I decided to go to the hotel early and conduct it from there. Plus I liked the idea of being in a posh hotel, I mean who wouldn't!

I planned to just do my Zoom from the foyer or bar, as Sam would not arrive until a bit after 5 pm and the reservation was in his name. When he discovered my plan, he said, "Just check in, give my name, say you're my wife and your husband would be joining you."

"I can't do that!"

"Yes you can and if there are any problems, call me and put them on the phone to me, I can verify."

I had a flashing thought of how amazing it would be if that was the truth, then I remembered I don't believe in marriage any more so who cares, followed by feeling guilty for even contemplating impersonating his wife when his actual one had no clue what Sam did.

I pushed those thoughts from my mind. Sam, as usual, had gone to work early to make up for the lost time, and by the time he hit the road at 3 pm and called, I was almost there. We chatted for a bit, mostly about how he was going to impale me to a wall with his cock, but also how he wanted to make me cum and when I am with him, I will always cum first.

Three's A Crowd

As I approached the hotel we hung up, so I could go and get checked in. I was to call him if there was a problem and once in the room.

As I drove up the long, winding path toward the country house hotel, I couldn't help but feel a sense of awe creeping in, mixed with something heavier. The gravel crunches beneath the tyres, and as the trees open up, the view hits me in waves, a sprawling estate, too perfect to be real. The manicured lawns, the old stonework, the kind of place that could only belong in another life. My chest tightens. I haven't seen anything this beautiful in years. Not since life took a sharp turn into survival mode. Not since everything fell apart.

The hotel stands like a monument to a life I used to brush against but never really owned. Back when it was all work trips, dinners were paid for by the company card. Even then, I didn't fit in. Now? After everything? I feel like I'm trespassing like this place should come with invisible barriers that people like me can't cross any more. Yet here I am, pulling up to the entrance, the grand front doors towering over me as if to say, 'Are you sure?'

I park and step out, my legs feeling like lead. I walk toward the entrance, half expecting alarms to blare, for some unseen security system to shout 'WHORE' at the top of its lungs. Maybe even a spotlight to come down from the sky, highlighting exactly how far I've fallen. Once upon a time, I might've stood here with purpose, head high, on the company's pound. But now, after what life's thrown me, after turning to things I never thought I would, this feels dangerous. Like I don't belong.

I push through the heavy, carved wooden doors into the foyer, the smell of polished wood and expensive candles hits me like a punch to the gut. The sheer elegance of it all is enough to make me want to turn around and leave, but I can't. Chandeliers hanging high, the rich glow of soft lighting on marble floors, the hum of quiet, refined voices. Every detail whispers luxury. I feel like I'm walking into a world that shouldn't be accessible to someone like me any more. Not after everything I've done to survive.

My heart races as I approach the reception desk. I feel my throat tighten, and my palms sweat as if the receptionist can already see right through me. Like she knows. Like she can tell that I'm not the kind of woman who should be here. I imagine her looking me up and down and calling security, telling them I don't belong, that I've made some kind of mistake.

I clear my throat, my voice shaking as I give my surname.

"Miller… I… I have a room booked. My husband will be along soon."

The words feel foreign on my tongue, he is not my husband this is a lie. I'm waiting for her to look up, her eyebrows raised, waiting for her to say, 'Not possible. You're not wife material.' I brace myself for the rejection, for the buzzer to go off, marking me as an intruder.

Instead, there's a pause, a split second that feels like an eternity, before she smiles politely, violently taps something into her computer keyboard, and nods.

"Yes, Mrs. Miller, we have you booked in. Let me just get your key."

Relief washes over me, but it's tinged with disbelief. How am I here? How did I make it through the doors without being found out? As she hands me the key, my hand shakes slightly, and I can't shake the feeling that at any moment, someone will tap me on the shoulder and tell me it's all been a mistake. That people like me don't get to stay in places like this.

The bedroom is beautiful, I place my bag down, get my wand out and lower the tone of the place by having a quick wank thinking about Sam impaling me with his cock. I freshen up, and throw on my Jack Brown (about the only semi-designer thing I own) green corduroy dress with zip and voice note Sam to say I got in OK.

On the way into the hotel I clocked the cosy bar at the

entrance, it was so inviting looking. I thought fuck it! This is like a mini holiday. I will take my laptop and do my call from the bar using my headphones. Pretend like I am important, doing **very** important things. I don't get out often, so why not? I could have a beer at the same time, perfect!

My Zoom meetings went well and if anyone was listening in, then I definitely sounded important, **very** important, doing **very** important things.

When the call is finished, there are voice notes from Sam, he is frustrated, stuck behind tractors, and lorries and running late. He might not arrive until after 6 pm and we have to be at dinner with Gavin at 7 pm a twenty-minute car ride away.

I decide to get another beer and while waiting for it at the bar, a big burly guy with a mid-length beard pipes up;

"So, you are here for work?" he enquired and I clock his USA accent straight away. Maybe he heard me being important! I consider saying, I am not really here for work, I am mainly here to have the best fat cock on the planet impale my throat, hammer my holes and feed me the tastiest hot sticky juice on the planet.

Instead I settle for;

"Yes, you? Or does the accent mean you're on holiday?" I smile back

"Ha that obvious eh? Not quite a holiday, more of a tour, I have ancestors from here so travelling the area for a couple of months while writing"

"Oh wow, lucky you, writing what?"

My beer arrives, and I stand with it at the bar to continue the conversation.

"Another book, I am an author" he replies.

At that, he has me, an author, how exotic and travelling too! I pull up a bar stool and chat to him and the barmaid who is at university here about what he does, what he has written, how he got published and where he has travelled to, we also touch on American politics. He is fascinating and I am enjoying the conversation. He buys me a third beer. I am now really very tipsy.

Sam messages:

> Nearly there, 10 mins , honest to fuck traffic, where are you, in the room?

> Great, no, in the bar

> What?

> Yes in the bar chatting to peeps, see you soon, can't wait x

I continue chatting to Mr USA and Miss University, and then I see Sam out of the corner of my eye, crossing the gravel driveway, he sees me through the window, and I wave and beam at him. Jesus...clamping eyes on him is the **best** thing ever and instantly I feel my heart thunder and my pussy ooze.

Sam enters the bar and I enthusiastically introduce him to Mr USA, we chat for a bit and then Sam says "Shall we?"

So we head, I say bye to my new friends and I lead him to the room.

"Did you want to fuck him?" He asks. "No, I want to fuck you."

"But if I had not turned up, you would not have been able to say no."

"Well you did turn up and I know the rules. I wouldn't risk us." This satisfies him, and I genuinely hadn't even thought about fucking him, I just enjoyed the chat and found his background interesting. Plus you would have to assume he would want to fuck me and there was zero indication of that."

"You are mine, remember that." He says and my pussy seeps.

Once inside the room, as soon as the door closes, he hugs me, kisses me, unzips the front of my dress and gets my tits out. I am hungry, eager and drop to my knees, get his cock out and swallow it, he impaled me, hammered me and came all over my face. Pure heaven, and tasted like it too. My own personal cum vending machine. Just wish it wasn't a travelling vending machine and I had it installed at home.

I did not cum first. I am not bothered in the slightest, I far rather it when he cums, I fucking love it. Pleasing men turns me on, doing whatever it takes to satisfy them, turns me on. Even though we didn't have time to do more and have him bring me to orgasm before dinner, we made up for it later, and I certainly wasn't short of orgasms.

He also produced a pair of stunning purple New Balance trainers. I **_knew_** it! I protested but it was too late. I felt ashamed and embarrassed but grateful. I loved the thought of every time I put them on, it would remind me of him. Not that he was ever forgotten for a moment. There is now denying it was hard to run in wellies, not that I would admit that and literally a game changing gift for me that would make a real difference to my daily life.

I washed the dried-in streaks of cum I had not scooped off and devoured from my face, he changed his shirt, and we headed out to meet Gavin. During the drive over horny as fuck, I just couldn't take my eyes or hands off him. I was still on the tipsy side and most frustrated that we had to endure dinner and work talk for a few hours, when all I wanted was for Sam to bust into my holes.

I nipped to the toilet before we were seated at the table to empty my beer bulging bladder. Sometimes you do a wee that you think will never end, this was one of those, felt like I was there for a couple of hours.

As I walked back to the table and saw Sam at ease just chatting, laughing with Gavin, my heart grew a couple of sizes, like it just gained a few pounds. Just seeing him, being him filled me with both love and lust.

The meal was good, the chat was useful and productive. Sam

eyeballed me with amusement as I chose to order two starters as a main meal, rather than one main dish. Gavin is one of the good guys in this line of work, a real genuine guy, not the type to wax lyrical about his own achievements and churn out the buzzwords. Just real.

Halfway through, Gavin disappears off to the toilet. I slid my hands under the table and reached inside my sloppy wet pussy and pulled out a pair of pants, warm and very moist. I had stuffed them up there when we arrived at the restaurant. I wanted Sam to see the effect he had on me, by just being near him. I handed them to him and his jaw fell, but his eyes flamed, I couldn't tell if he was happy and intensely turned on or a bit shocked and annoyed at how brazen I was.

By the time we piled back into the car to drive back to the hotel, I was pretty damn drunk, and I can't recall the details, but I was all over him, I just couldn't help myself. My hand wandered to his crotch and felt his throbbing cock, my pussy pulsating, clenching and screaming "feed me, feed me Sam!". As we drove back to the hotel I told him, that I was a 'filthy slut, desperate for his cock, cum and how I wanted to be fucked in every hole, used and abused and thoroughly punished, put in my place, at his feet.'

A fuckfest followed once the door to the bedroom closed behind us, no holes barred, rough, primal with some canes, belts, spanks and restraints playing their part.

As always, morning came too fast. Once again, with Sam, sleep was easy, and I felt more refreshed than I had in months, even in spite of the alcohol.

After showering, I was in the bathroom putting my makeup on. I was suddenly aware he was not moving about any more and was just standing watching me. I looked at him in the mirror, smiled and said:

"What?"

"Nothing, carry on," he replied. I did, but felt very self conscious. "What?" I asked again

Three's A Crowd

"Just enjoying watching you," he replied and smiled.

"OK.... well I am half makeup-less and look like shit" I replied.

"You're beautiful and I want to freeze this moment."

My stomach flipped in a sicky way, I just don't know what to say to that. I think I unconsciously roll my eyes. He has said I am beautiful a few times. It feels like a line, like a trick, because whilst I know I am not pig ugly, beautiful, I am not.

It's like being handed a Rubik's Cube and told to solve it. But not knowing how to solve a Rubik's Cube, I would just stare at it, hoping the answer would magically present itself and not really knowing what to do with it. I don't know what to do with this. I change the subject and we move along.

We have a final fuck to finish off the fuck fest, and then we make our way down the hallway to breakfast, the faint hum of quiet conversations and clinking cutlery grows louder. The atmosphere is serene, soaked in luxury. I feel Sam slip his arm around my waist, pulling me gently toward him. The warmth of his touch catches me off guard, sending a jolt through me. I can't ever remember anyone doing this to me before, ever.

It feels so foreign, almost unnatural. I've seen it before, of course, couples walking like this, arms around each other or hand in hand, but never me. Phil has never done that. It always seemed like a sign of something more than affection, almost like a silent claim: 'She's mine, and I want everyone to know it'. It represents something I've never experienced, pride, ownership, a lack of embarrassment. It's like they're saying, 'She matters.'

My mind starts to wander. What must it feel like to have someone who does this naturally, without thinking, in front of everyone? As if it's normal, like I belong to him. I imagine it for a moment, allowing myself to sink into the fantasy that I'm the kind of woman who has that, that I'm the one being held like I matter, like I'm important. How safe, secure and loved you must feel if that were your life. But then reality catches up, and I think of his wife, Natasha. How lucky she is to be that woman and how cruel it is she rejects him. She has everything I want, literally. I shouldn't be thinking these things, but for just a few seconds, I enjoy pretending.

We step into the restaurant, and I'm snapped back to the present. The smell of fresh coffee, baked pastries, and sizzling bacon fills the air, making my stomach growl. The breakfast buffet stretches out in front of us, and it looks incredible. There's everything you could imagine: steaming scrambled eggs, glistening sausages, freshly baked croissants, and a whole table dedicated to fruits and yoghurts, arranged like art. Even the plates are warm, waiting to be filled. I usually skip breakfast at home. I want to skip it here too, It's far too expensive, daylight robbery really, £13 a head! But looking at the spread, I can't resist.

I grab a plate, telling myself it's worth it, just this once, and start loading it with food, the kind of food I don't let myself have too often. Maybe it's the environment, or maybe it's the way Sam's hand had lingered on my waist, but for a moment, I feel like I'm allowed to indulge. Like I can pretend I belong here, with him and in such beautiful surroundings, even if it's only temporary.

After checking out, it's the sad walk to the cars, almost making it deliberately slow in the hope the inevitable does not come. We hug and he holds me tight. I don't want to release him, but it's easier to just make it quick. I peel myself off him and turn and walk to my car and drive off, tears are beginning to fill my eyes, as the fantasy world I have just lived in begins to crumble, when the phone goes, it's Sam. He has called so fast I pick up, thinking he may have a flat tyre or something and needs me.

"Jess, can you come back a minute?"

"What's wrong?"

"Just come back"

I turn the car around and drive back and walk over to him.

He puts his hand in his pocket and takes out some cash. SHIT! I think. I had slipped £50 in his pocket when I was hugging him goodbye. I knew he would not take it from me if I asked, but I wanted to contribute something to this hotel and all the others he had paid for. It hardly touched the surface of how much I had cost him, but I wanted him to know I was not taking advantage.

I protest and argue, but he won't have it, he says I can pay him back when I am in a better position and if I pull a stunt like that, he won't see me again. I don't want that and reluctantly take the cash, we say our goodbyes again. He phones as we both drive home, the money debate continues as we drive down the road. I need him to understand, to see it from my perspective, I don't want to be a burden and I don't want to feel 'paid' for. Been there, done that. He doesn't relent and I lose, as always, there is no arguing with that man.

Whilst leaving is the same painful wrench, I am comforted by the fact it's not an entire month again. We will see each other at the December networking meeting, one we are going to have to go to the actual meeting, but nevertheless, we will see each other in a little over two weeks.

I was starting to feel less like 'we' were impossible, starting to entertain the idea that he ***may*** actually really love me. He had pushed to get time away from home because a month without me was too long. I started to think we could have a future, starting to feel like I may even be brave and bring that up with him, see what he is actually thinking. I was becoming a little less scared of saying how I felt and what I wanted. A long way off from being totally honest, but more honest than I had ever been with anyone. This had to be down to the fact he was not like anyone I had ever met. Plus credit where credit is due, he was responsible for making me feel this way, making me feel more comfortable, less edgy, and less doubtful.

There is no question it was not easy on him having me in his life, I was needy and difficult.

Over the last six months, I had freaked out when I didn't hear from him, worried when he was away, panicked when messages went unread. He didn't freak out when I freaked out, never made me feel bad. He seemed to understand and was always happy to reassure me, he adapted to what I needed, consistent, dependable, present and steady. He was as certain as the sun setting in the West, I needed that. It made me feel safe. And that was the only thing that was eroding my disbelief in us.

He did what he said, and he kept me involved, and informed, if he felt anything was wrong or off he tackled it head on and we sorted it out. He was patient with my lack of confidence and belief in us. He did all he could to reassure me, he must have found it hard and frustrating but he never gave up. He listened. He was reliable, I knew when I could speak to him, when I could expect messages from him, when I would see him, he was quick to respond, and rarely left me hanging. Being apart, having him live life with another woman, not me, this contact, reliability and consistency was what I needed. Without it, I would be tortured.

I realised I am a bit like a child, having never been in a true love 'relationship,' I needed help navigating it and it was made all the harder with the distance. I had expressed several times my view that things were stacked against us, distance, Wives, Husbands, kids and why communication was ***the*** most important thing we had. Really the only tool we had to help each other understand what we meant to each other. Without it, we have nothing. It is one thing being apart, but being apart and knowing the person you love is with someone else is another strain.

The communication needed especially for me ***is*** more hassle, more effort for sure. It would be far easier if you're coming home to someone everyday, seeing them everyday. But if he was to be believed and I ***was*** important, then he would understand it was needed, that I needed it. More than that, he would want to, because he wanted to engage with me, as much as I did with him, because I mattered, he prioritised what was important to me. Without it, we would lose each other.

Communication was our only lifeline. In a long-distance relationship, (let alone one where there is another party spending the bulk of the time with the person you love) words are the only tangible connection we have the majority of the time. They're how we share laughter, filth, hopes, dreams, support and comfort each other. Build a foundation of trust. Without consistent communication, it's like trying to navigate a stormy sea with a faulty compass - you're lost, unsure, and filled with fear.

Consistency for me at least was the anchor that could keep our ship steady. It is reassuring, essential, the pulse. It is like the heartbeat that sustains life. Our life.

But when communication falters and consistency wavers, pain and heartache inevitably follow, especially for me. Uncertainty creeps in, leaving me questioning Sam's feelings and intentions. Doubts gnaw at my heart, loneliness sets in. It's like calling out into the void, hoping he will hear.

Effort is everything. It takes conscious dedication. It is my view we must make time for each other, even when our schedules are hectic. We must be open and honest, sharing our thoughts, feelings, and dreams. Without it love won't be enough to bridge the distance.

Sam had helped me feel safe **because** of that routine and clear communication. For me to trust and believe him, especially with him not being in my life, I needed to know what was going on, to have a routine, to feel secure. His consistency was beginning to feel safe, my guard was falling, for the first time ever I felt like that was ok, not so risky. I could count on him. He maybe did not realise it, but it was this that allowed me to let him in. It was that, that was defrosting my heart.

However I didn't see the darkness looming on the Horizon.

Chapter 25

The Nightmare Before Christmas

After being porked in York I was excited for the forthcoming festive fuck with Sam. Last fuck of the year! But Christmas would of course, also mean massively reduced communications.

With every last penny spent on trying to cobble together a passable Christmas feast and gifts, we were not planning to visit family or go anywhere at all as even a tank of petrol was outside the realms of possibility. Sam had visitors and activities planned for almost the full two weeks of the holidays, so there was an inevitable dread mixed in with the excitement.

Christmas is my absolute favourite time of the year, well at least it used to be. I adore the build up, the lights, the music, everyone just seems happier. I remember fondly yet tinged with some sadness, when Christmas was good, ice skating with the kids, visiting the Christmas markets, sometimes a city break to a cold festive European destination. Nights out with friends for drinks. None of it was possible now.

December just reminds me of my failings.

I shared with Sam how I was feeling about the children's gifts when I wrapped them in late November, a small sparse collection.

Christmas morning would last about twenty minutes. He reassured me the kids would understand, and they did, but it doesn't make me feel any less shit.

Neither did seeing photos of Beth's Christmas haul the year before. Even at my very best I wasn't in that league. She got a lot.

I feel slightly bitter too, that if I had carried on with GW, I could have done more. Emily made that point regularly too.

'Don't complain, you allowed him to cut off your income, maybe you could just do a few blow jobs and get a few hundred extra?'

I wanted to, for the cash, but couldn't as I would lose Sam. Emily said he would never know, I was tempted, very tempted, but it felt like a betrayal. I also feared he would see it in my face. He is the only guy that has been able to see through my white lies. Life would be intolerable without him. He was my only bit of pleasure and happiness, take that away, what have I got?

Nothing.

People often churn out things which are stock answers to difficult situations, all said with the best of intentions:

'As one door closes another opens.'

'What's for you won't go by you.' '

Everything happens for a reason.'

'What doesn't kill you makes you stronger.'

Well, what if I don't want to be stronger and being killed is the more appealing choice? Sam says the right things, but with the best will in the world, he doesn't get it. He can't possibly, some things you have to experience to really understand and this is one of them.

He doesn't have to look his daughter in the eye and say sorry we can't go visit your grandparents because we can't fill the car with petrol. Sorry, we can't spend at the Christmas market because the drinks there are £4 each, but it will be nice to wander and look. Sorry, I couldn't pay for a brand-new version of the top you wanted, so I got you this second-hand one.

Three's A Crowd

So my usual excitement over December is absent, not helped by Emily continuing to be a bitch. Her latest thing is, if Sam is paying for the hotels, and you're not contributing, you're basically still his hooker, it is just the hotel gets the cash he spends, not you. And Misty seems to be around every corner during December. It is far worse than it has been. I have had no luck tracking her down or finding anything out about her. But at the same time, she is everywhere, standing on a street corner, part of the crowd of Christmas shoppers, and in the hallway at the school Christmas show. Banging on my kitchen window. It feels like every day, everywhere I turn she is there, often a few times a day. If she gets the chance, she grabs my wrists and hisses at me, chanting "You're not listening, you have to listen" before I break free of her.

In the main, she is finding me when I can't bloody well listen, but sometimes I can, and she has revealed details of some of the assaults on the train including one where she got away but was so panicked she fell while getting off at the station and broke her ankle. Another time shortly after that were now, on crutches they took advantage of that as she couldn't run. I have continued to encourage her to let me help her report it or at least talk to her parents, and get her moved schools, that together we can make it stop, but still she won't allow it, saying it's too late, and it would never be believed.

I am on tenterhooks the entire time, looking over my shoulder, checking the house, and painting on a smile for Lottie, Thomas, Phil, and Sam.

It is hard work, exhausting.

December is also my fourth month of disturbed and haunted nights. Out of a possible one hundred and fifty nights, I have had about seven undisturbed. I have mastered it now. I don't go to bed until I literally can't stay awake, or I won't fall asleep, petrified of what it will bring. Once woken, I come downstairs and through tears and shaking I draw and draw until I calm, until once again sleep becomes inescapable, so I can quietly slip back into bed unnoticed. My nightmares are all about Misty, her stories, her finding me, her speaking to people and Darren.

I am tired of this, I feel like I can't carry on. If I could sleep and stay asleep right now, never wake up again, I think I would take that option.

Shortly after I see Sam in December, the strangest thing happens to me. Quite out of the blue and I put it down to extreme tiredness. I am working at my desk on a new proposal when the doorbell goes just after 9.30 am. I run downstairs, it's a 'signed for' parcel, probably gifts from granny for the kids. Sandy the postie is chatty and starts telling me a story about a grumpy householder he delivered to, who had installed some post lock box for when they were out to receive parcels. Sandy had mentioned to the man that the lid was heavy on it and he struggled with it. The householder went nuts and said he needed to be taught some manners, he should be grateful, to say thank you.

While Sandy was talking, for no reason at all, my entire body ran cold, I thought I was going to be sick, I made my excuses, and had to cut Sandy off, apologising.

The last thing I remember is closing the front door.

The next thing I remember is finding myself hugging my knees under the desk in my office, repeating words over and over.

"no,no.no.no.no,no,no,no.no.no.no.no,no,no,.."

From my head to my toes, I am almost convulsing, trembling, uncontrollably, I have been crying but don't recall it. I slowly become aware of things around me, and notice my rapid breathing begins to slow.

I am just hit with this strange knowledge , a kind of understanding, a clarity, I always knew I lost my virginity by force, I have never hidden that fact from myself, but now, it was like I ***really*** knew. I understood, I could see it, the doubt and questioning I have always had vanished.

When I climbed back into my chair, the computer said 11:03am. I had lost ninety minutes of my life and missed a work

Three's A Crowd

Zoom meeting. I fired off an email apologising and sat for another ten mins, shaken by this revelation. I had no idea what had just happened. I was unnerved, scared and so my first instinct was to message Sam. When I opened my phone, he had not read my filth message to him just after 9 am. But I still sent a second, I need him.

> Something weird just happened

I make a cup of tea, and go back to my desk, trying to shake off the feeling I have and the nagging concern that I am potentially finally losing my shit.

After feeling more secure than I ever thought was possible with a guy, a slight change has creeped in over the last few weeks.

I have seen a gradual reduction in Sam's communication. Nothing that can be raised as it would seem unreasonable. He doesn't respond instantly any more, it can be hours. He doesn't always tell me his week's plans or any changes to them. He doesn't message good morning, every morning any more. It's not all the time, but the change is there and it hangs over me like a big question mark.

I gently raise it on occasion. Like 'you took a while to respond,' and I get.

'Open plan office , not easy to message.'

I just reply, 'I know,' not wanting to cause trouble. But the open plan office didn't matter before. I wonder what has changed, and does he think I can't remember when he would message all the time, in spite of the open plan office. Maybe I imagined it. But deep down I know I didn't.

Or I try to ask about his movements, mentioning that if I don't know, it's hard for me to be available. He tells me I know he drives into work either 8:30-9am or 8:45-9:15 am depending on school drop off , he tells me I know he tends to leave the office at 5 pm. It is true, I do know all of that, but truth is it varies, it can be 4:50 pm he leaves or 5:20 pm. So I tend to head out with Ron at 4:45 pm just in case. Without information, what else could I do? If I wanted to speak to him, and I did, I need time to exit the house. If I was to wait until 5 pm, our call would potentially be cut down by half. So it's my only option, or we don't get to talk.

Phil is about the house a lot more at the moment due to his job starting in January, and less people wanting odd jobs with Christmas on their mind. So I can only really talk when walking Ron. I could go and do that anytime, but without knowing Sam's movements, I don't know when **to** do it. So I head out at a time that gives us the best chance and seven times out of ten, it works, he is reliable as ever, but sometimes and more frequently of late, I am walking around in the wind, rain and cold for twice as long as our call, just to ensure I have a big enough window to catch him. Sometimes the call doesn't come at all. Just a message.

> Got company, dropping Natasha at her Christmas night out. Speak later.

I don't understand, that is something you know about upfront and he doesn't take the time to let me know. I thought I mattered? I am flexing and bending to accommodate him, and he doesn't show me any courtesy by keeping me informed any more. I just have to guess.

Emily is in my ear.

'Jess, he has tired of you, everybody does, this is the slow decline, wake up!'

Deep down I fear this is true but like a screaming toddler hanging onto their mothers leg, not wanting her to go, I try to push those thoughts out of my head and hold onto every scrap of attention he ***does*** give me, holding onto the words he says when he messages that he loves me and misses me. Praying they are true.

I am conscious I am being a bit moany about it and try to reign it in. I don't want to push him away more than I clearly already have.

The day I found myself under my desk, coming out of whatever that was, he didn't respond until 4pm. I spent those 5 hours checking my phone every few minutes. Silly because if he messaged it would pop up, but I wanted to see if he had even read it or if somehow the notifications had stopped working. They were working. He had just ignored the notifications and not bothered to read them.

I was scared and **all** I wanted, all I ***needed*** was him. I didn't want Emily and her cold manner, I wanted Sam, I needed him, I wanted some kind words, some reassurance and ideally an explanation for what had just happened to me.

> So sorry, you ok? I have been in meetings.

Relief pours over me and for the first time that day, I felt calmer, safer. It niggled me that he had not checked his phone during lunch, or done his usual before a long meeting and let me know he was headed into one so not to expect him to be around. But I figured he had not had a chance. And how was he to know I'd had a fright and needed him.

"It takes two seconds Jessie, you weren't a priority, you never have been, if you were, if you ***actually*** mattered like he says, he'd take those two seconds, especially when he knows you worry. No one is away from their phone for that length of time, he saw you had messaged and chose not to look. You can't rely on him, you need to get back to standing on your own two feet. Don't make the mistake of sharing stuff with him, relying on it and it being taken away." said Emily when I told her a few days later.

At 5pm I go walk the dog, willing him to call me. The messages letting me know he was leaving work had stopped, and changed to once he was in the car. 'You Free?'

I had no idea if that would be 4:45 pm or nearer 5:30pm.

The message comes at 5:18 pm, I am soaked to the skin and shivering, in my twenty-eighth minute of wandering.

> You free?

And of course, like a desperate fool, I am, and reply yes. We speak, he is kind, he apologises again, saying he had to work through some big proposal and needed to focus (different story to the text, which stabs my heart and I file away in my brain under, the list of reasons not to trust him section). I keep my video off saying it's wet, windy and I need to keep my phone in my pocket, it's not a lie, but the real reason is if I look at him, I am scared I will see his disinterest, and that thought makes me fight back tears.

I am confused, hurt and still suffering from this morning's events, so I am quite short with him, not on purpose I just can't speak because if I do, it will all come pouring out. I will shift from a 'fun bit of side filth' to a 'high maintenance pain', not worth the hassle. He puts my short responses down to me being affected and concerned about this morning, which I am.

"Jess this is my point, I have been telling you this, you've been dreaming about it and I think today is some form of memory or your brain trying to file away what happened with Darren because you ignored it, it's a good thing, your brain is processing it, I am just grateful it happened when you were safe and at home."

"OK, possibly" I say. But what I want to say is 'You're hurting me, I don't feel safe any more, you said that you would never hurt me. Today you have hurt me and you have changed your story so I know you are lying. You have been hurting me a lot in recent weeks, I have never felt more alone, never felt less important, I really needed you, and you were not there.'

But I don't, because it's unfair and unreasonable, it's just the emotion of sleepless nights, Misty fears and worries, a change in him, but I know he does his best, when he can. I can't ask for more than that. I don't want to be a crazy over emotional, irrational bit on the side, that is not what he needs or wants.

Later that night, when messaging he didn't mention or ask about this massive thing that had just happened to me. He wants pussy and ass pics, so I oblige. It helps take my mind off everything and I have a wank on the sofa while he talks dirty to me.

The next morning devastating news came, the job Phil had secured, the company had gone bust and as a result, there was no job. He is broken, distraught. I hate to see him in pain like that, he has tried so hard and we thought it was sorted. Granted it did not solve all our problems but it would have stemmed the flow from the leaky bucket.

I reassure him as best I can. It ***will*** be ok, we ***will*** find a way and he got the job, because he is a grafter, loads of experience, someone will see that.

Deep down I am in a panic, but he doesn't need to be made to feel bad. I put on my new trainers and ran. I run for over 2 hours up and down a hill I like to go to. Poor Ron ends up just sitting and watching me. It takes about twelve minutes to run up this hill, and he just waits and watches me pass like I am a nutter.

It is a quiet place, you rarely see anyone.

Every time I get to the top, I scream at the top of my lungs, and then cry while I run back down. When I can't run any more, I find Ron and just sit with my arm round him, in the pissing rain, head on my knees and sob. Consumed by a sea of worries.

Once the fog lifts, I can think. I look at the money we have left and what is coming in from my marketing business, we have three months left.

I now have no choice but to seriously consider returning to GW. The thought turns my stomach, I know that means the end for Sam and I.

I talked to Sam about it. He has a go at Phil, saying that he should just take any job, I agree. He confirms if I do decide to return to GW. He is gone.

It is an impossible situation. Feed the kids and keep a roof over their head or keep Sam.

Phil starts the job hunt again. You have to hand it to him. He just carries on, but sometimes I catch him looking o# into the distance. Sometimes he tells me he just feels so worthless. It's heartbreaking.

I am a big believer in mindset and manifestation. It's much harder to practise when things are headed south. But you have to check yourself to get back on track.

I do just that.

It is December, a busy month for most, so Sam is likely just off because of that. He still says he cares and wants to see me at the meeting. He often says when I mention my frustrations of the distance between us and finding each other too late in life;

"It is what it is" and "I tend to not get bothered by things I can't change."

I find this quite hurtful and dismissive if I am honest. How can he be so blasé? I thought if you loved someone, it was impossible to not be bothered, this tells me a lot. What I hear is, we don't matter enough to be bothered about, and he has no interest in changing things, now or ever. But I decided to take a leaf out of his book and go with 'it is what it is'.

Enjoy it and if it's bothering me in a few months time, I can reassess. No biggy right!?

Phil ***will*** get another job.

My Marketing business ***will*** begin to generate consistent income.

We are all healthy and my kids are, in the main, a joy. I am proud of how they have coped with all the changes. In awe of the small people they have developed into.

It may take time, but I ***will*** help Misty.

Emily, although snippy and mean. I know she really does care and is still around. I would be lost without her.

A major bit of good news lands just before November spills into December. My STD tests came back and despite my heart being in my mouth I got a clean bill of health. I sent Sam a screenshot of the results. He was overjoyed and relieved, he and I both. This meant when we met early December, no interrupting proceedings to wrestle with a condom. Full sensation skin on skin. I could not wait.

Sam and I met early in the evening, 'nervcitedness' coursing through my veins, I still can't believe he continues to make the effort to meet me, I feel like the luckiest woman on the planet. He could have anyone, why he bothers with me, I will never understand.

We checked into the Travel Lodge and had to rush to the meeting. I got to sit at the same table as him during the meeting this time, as we had now 'officially met' and no one would bat an eyelid. Some of the networkers had Christmas jumpers and earrings on. It was a welcome change being at this type of event and being able to speak to him. But really as ever I wanted it to finish and get back to the hotel. There was a cock with my name on.

When we got back, he said he had a gift for me, he said not to panic and feel bad as it wasn't a Christmas gift. We had already said we were not doing that. Although I had got him something, it hadn't all arrived, and I planned to post it. I wasn't telling him that though, as everything around gift giving and receiving is awkward. I hate it. I had cobbled together some money by reducing even further the Christmas dinner, I'd gone for cheaper crackers, a crown instead of a full turkey and other reductions that meant I could do it. I mean why spend a fortune on something you're just going to shit out anyway!

I wanted so desperately to give him something. I know he can't open it on Christmas morning, but perhaps when he opens his other gifts on Christmas morning, he will remember I got him something and think of me for a brief moment. He will know I thought of him, took the time to find something **_for_** him and got it to him. He will know he is always in my thoughts.

Sam's gift was a remote vibe, one we can both have the app on our phones and means he can play with me from 100 miles away. I love it and know they are stupidly expensive, I am embarrassed but grateful, he says it is for him, as much as it is for me.

We don't have a lot of time before having to be sensible and go to sleep. But as ever it is a cumtastic experience. All holes thoroughly dealt with, balls drained.

He had come up with a game for me, knowing how hard it is for me to make decisions, sexually he wanted to try this out. Using a deck of cards. I had to draw and the colour, and number dictated what I would be receiving. If it was a 'red' card, it would be light, 'funishment' level, black, harder, more brutal. He was trying to make me take on some choices, I could in some circumstances stick or twist.

It was fun and hot. He enjoyed seeing my tormented face, trying to make a decision combined with my expression when I saw the result of the cards I was drawing, it made him hard. He loved to make me squirm.

Three's A Crowd

Left Tit	Right Tit	Cunt Cropped
2,3,4 = Hand 5,6,7 = Belt 8,9,10 = Whip Ace = Cane	2,3,4 = Hand 5,6,7 = Belt 8,9,10 = Whip Ace = Cane	Left Inner Thigh 2,3,4 = Hand 5,6,7 = Belt 8,9,10 = Whip Ace = Cane
Left Inner Thigh	**Right Inner Thigh**	**Left Ass Cheek**
2,3,4 = Hand 5,6,7 = Belt 8,9,10 = Whip Ace = Cane	2,3,4 = Hand 5,6,7 = Belt 8,9,10 = Whip Ace = Cane	2,3,4 = Hand 5,6,7 = Belt 8,9,10 = Whip Ace = Cane
Right Ass Cheek 2,3,4 = Hand 5,6,7 = Belt 8,9,10 = Whip Ace = Cane	Red = Funishment Black = Punishment Joker = Draw again x 2 multiplier	2 Lifelines, draw again, stick or twist Ace = 11 not 1 Jack = Mouth Fuck, draw again; Queen = Cunt Fuck, draw again; King = Ass Fuck, draw again

All my worries vanish when I am with him, it removes my doubts about us, money worries drift away. It's a rare moment of peace.

Sleep comes easily wrapped in his arms, but doesn't last.

I woke up suddenly, freezing cold, shaky and upset, I was dreaming of Misty. When I open my eyes she is there, standing over the bed, staring at me. The air prickles with tension, fear, despair.

Holy fuck, how the fuck did she get in? All I know is I need her to get out. I carefully slide out of bed so as not to disturb Sam, placing my finger over my lips to indicate to her to be quiet, she nods.

I thought about waking him. But this would scare him to bits, it scares me to bits, but I am more used to it. He has had Emily kick off at him and now my psycho stalker breaks into the hotel room when he is sleeping. He would for sure end this, he can't have a psycho risk finding out who he is, or get involved, if this ends up a police matter, how would he explain being called to court as a witness to Natasha.

I throw on my long coat, gently take her hand, grab the room key and lead her out into the corridor, noticing the hotel bedroom door is not properly shut, the latch is holding it open. When in the corridor, Misty holds both my wrists and starts to talk, whispering pained.

Park & drinking with my friends
Christopher, James, Mark arrive
I am OK, with my friends -safe
They need to use my ID
They want me to go with them
I know
I protest
My friends say go
Awkward

Misty I say… "Please stop, just a moment"… I am conscious I don't want a scene, conscious it's the middle of the night, conscious Sam is sleeping just the other side of the door. Concerned she is wandering around at 3am.

Three's A Crowd

She looks at me with the saddest eyes, I feel terrible, but on edge.

"Please" she says quietly.

"We can't talk now, I really want to hear Misty, I do, but it's 3am. I am worried about you being here, 73 miles away from our town in the middle of the night. How did you get here? We might wake people up, then we'd have to explain all this, that would be worse right?"

Her eyes turn to fire, she tightens her grip on my wrists, forcing her nails into the skin, her eyes flame through me and tears pour, she hisses at me and stretches herself up to full stand- ing. I feel like she is going to full on attack me, I clench my eyes shut, bracing for impact and pull away. When I open them, she is gone.

I am not running after her in the middle of the night. I slip gently back into the bedroom, softly closing the door behind me. Adrenaline coursing through my veins. I grab my pad and duck into the bathroom. My mind is racing and still trembling from my dream and Misty in this bedroom.

I can't sleep. I don't want to sleep. What if she comes back? What if I dream again? I place a towel on the floor and sit drawing. The next thing I know, I wake up sleeping on the bathroom floor. Shit. I stealthily put my pad away, climb back into bed and try to sleep.

Sam stirs and mumbles;

"You ok?"

"Yes I reply," and snuggle into him.

In the morning when we wake, he asks if I had another bad dream. I admit I did. He says he saw the bathroom light on and thought I was doing a wee or something, that I was in there for ages. He didn't want to intrude. I explained I was a bit unsettled, didn't want to disturb him and so went and did some drawing to quieten my mind.

I didn't share that Misty had been in the room and I didn't share that I had concluded I couldn't depend on him. He may be here now, at this moment, and he may want to be there when I need him, but he actually can't be. Combined with his recent distancing, I had realised he could not be banked on.

It is easier having no one than having someone sometimes, or worse it being taken away completely. I can't become reliant on him. It makes the times when he is not around, and I need him a thousand times harder than they would have been if I had never experienced that support. I wish he had never supported me, then I would not feel like I had lost something. I won't ever forget that day, petrified having found myself under the desk, I really needed him, and he was not there. Granted, how was he to know, he was busy, he can't just be sitting waiting around and jumping whenever a drama happens in my life, so I don't blame him. I am not angry at him. But I can't rely on him. It is what it is.

That day, under my desk, it hit me hard. I was acting like he was properly in my life, and he is not, and he won't be, so some parts of my life, I can't let him into as it is too painful to need someone and not be able to reach them. I am better off alone. I don't need the pain of his absence highlighted in neon adding to my woes when upset. I had decided I wasn't going to share as much of that stuff with him any more.

"You should have got me, told me, last time you had a bad dream with me, I was able to settle you really fast," he says.

"I know, but I did not want to be a pain," I replied.

"You're not, I want to help, to be there, let me be there for you. If it ever happens again when you're with me, you get me ok? You wake me, please. What did you draw anyway?"

"Just a Christmas scene."

"Can I see?"

I show him. I am not a talented artist, but I enjoy it and it is extremely captivating and soothing. I can draw better than that, but when tired and unsettled it's hard to concentrate when on edge, the way you would sketching normally.

Three's A Crowd

. . .

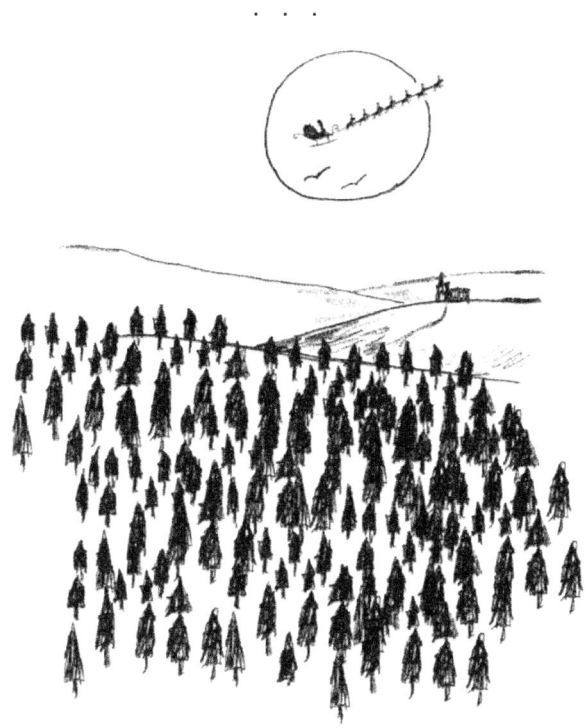

I struggle to shake what has happened in the night, who can blame me, it's not every night your teen stalker pitches up in a hotel bedroom scaring the living shit out of you. But I do a pretty convincing performance and once we start our farewell fuck session before checking out I am almost settled. I enjoy him slapping my face and pinning me to the bed, using his body weight to keep me in place while he fucks me in the ass pro-bone. That is one of my favourite positions, it makes you feel helpless and the angle is sensational.

I don't know why, but this felt like one of the hardest goodbyes.

Perhaps it was the pain of recognising I can't risk relying on him, or maybe, it being December, the month you want to be with those you love, thus underlining the point I am not with him. Never will be.

We drove up the road, tailing each other until the road split. I couldn't speak, I was too upset. Made worse by listening to the song 'Happy Ending' By Mika. It was as if it was written for us and it was just so heartbreakingly accurate and sad.

I ball and ball listening to it and then send him the link. We just won't get our happy ending, I **do** feel like I am wasting everyday. We **do** love like it's forever, but we ***will*** live the rest of our lives ***not*** together. We ***can't*** have it without devastating sacrifice.

Life is cruel, life is unfair. Fuck life.

Please someone give me a break, I am not sure how much more I can cope with.

He voice notes me back, saying "why do that to myself? Why listen to it? It's a very sad song."

That is the beauty of music isn't it? Not that it's sad, but it can talk to you in ways like nothing else. It makes you feel heard, understood, like someone, somewhere understands, whether that's excitement, joy or the heart crushing sadness of no hope, no love, no glory, no happy ending.

I didn't think December could get much worse... how wrong I was.

Chapter 26

Snoop Gate

I posted Sam's gift a few days later with a next-day service when I knew he would be in, but Natasha was out. He rang when it arrived and opened it in front of me on camera. I had got him a chocolate bar with the outer wrapper saying 'Dickhead' using the fonts, styles and letters of well-known chocolate bars like Snickers and Mars. Just a daft thing, but I had also got him wooden drumsticks, engraved with his initials (SAM) in a nice presentation box. I loved the fact his initials also spelt his first name, very clever parents, but also worked as SAM, Sadism AND Masochism, which definitely applied to us.

Suddenly as he opened it in front of me, I felt like such a fool. I mean the chocolate, cheap and shit, and then the drum sticks, he may not like; wrong wood, weight, size, I was no expert on drum sticks. He was bound to have a thousand of them and with his initials on them, would never be able to use them as questions would inevitably be asked.

I can be such a tit sometimes. But what else could I get him? I didn't know what aftershave he wore, his favourite brands, and music is all downloadable these days. I couldn't get him tickets to anything. How do you explain that?

He was very sweet when he opened my shit gifts, and I prayed he just took it as confirmation I had thought of him and hopefully didn't think too much about how crap they were.

Lottie and Thomas were in full festive swing, so aside from work for me, I was running them to friends and to Christmas parties. Phil was back on the full-time job hunt. Work for me was beginning to quieten, the big campaigns almost complete, just the festive greeting messages, blogs and New years stuff being scheduled, Q1s campaigns already produced and the companies teams scheduling and uploading the content.

I saw Misty every day, but made no progress and my wrists were very bad from her hurting me. Hiding them was getting harder.

I thought about dying Dave, Szymon, Henry and a few other clients that would be vulnerable around this time of year and hoped they were ok.

Sam's communications continued gradually fading, it had been a few weeks since we had seen each other… And one day, tired, worried and fed up, I lost the plot, which was very unlike me. I had been chatting to Emily about it and I felt so hurt I burst, it had been building in me for weeks and Emily gave me a firm shove over the edge.

She had said I needed to 'Stand up for myself'. And it was 'Not OK, for him to just pick me up when it suited him.' That it is 'common courtesy to let people know if you are hoping to talk to them, not just expect they will always be there, he knows Phil is at home and you have to duck out, but just expects you to be on hand, without notice, thoughtless fucker. He is taking you for granted, a text takes five seconds, your not even worth five seconds Jess, **five fucking seconds**, speak to him or I will and you *know* I will.'

I eventually burst following a few days of really bad communication. Two days before I had been out first thing, again, walking Ron hoping he would call, but not knowing for sure. He didn't

Three's A Crowd

even message good morning that day, he had not told me if he was on drop off or not. He didn't call. I got a message once he was in the office;

> Sorry mental morning, hope to speak when leaving work tonight, will message and see if your free

So I went, like a fool, and walked Ron, again at 4:50 pm, and again no call... again no message saying no call, and again no responses to my messages in the day, they had not even been checked.

A message came about 6:30pm

> I totally forgot about Beth's school event, so had to get Natasha, leave work early and go to that, so sorry, speak tonight, love you x

He thinks so little of me, it doesn't even cross his mind I have arranged my day to hopefully get him. He doesn't care. I am out in a fucking field freezing my tits off waiting for him... again. Like Emily says, he takes it for granted. He gets in touch, I am there, I am never not there. I wonder what would happen if I just didn't bother ducking out. I know what would happen, we would never speak, and I question if he would even be bothered by that. How can he not see how this has changed? Or maybe that is the point, he is telling me to fuck off, in a subtle way. How can he think a 'love you x,' solves everything. Do what you like, say that all is forgiven.

He sent a message later, once Natasha and Beth were asleep. It was filthy and fun, we used the remote vibe, now a regular addition to our late evening messaging, usually on a silent video call.

The next morning, it was repeated, no morning message, couple or very short messages once in the office.

> God nightmare morning, Beth wouldn't get her shoes on, late for school again. Chasing my fucking tail FML. 😶

> Kids eh?! 😅

> How are you?

He has not asked this in about a week.

> All good, you?

I lie, but what am I to do? How do you bring this up without sounding like a nut job.

> Will call tonight x

I message stuff throughout the day as usual, again it is not seen for hours, later on a couple of reaction emojis or one word answers. It is something I guess.

I headed out with Ron, no phone call, for the 50 minutes I am walking, freezing my hands, so frozen my Raynauds sets in, leaving them in seething agony for the rest of the night. No message to say something had come up.

I just knew at that point Emily was right. There is no excuse for it, he could have let me know what was going on, it takes nanoseconds. It hit me hard, I was nothing to him, and when I was out heading to the shops and he actually sent a flurry of messages to me, I gave short replies. Not because I was trying to be mean, but because I was trying not to burst. He eventually asked what was wrong. Sam being Sam, he pushed me on it. The damn burst, I sent a voice note saying everything that was in my head.

I can't believe I did it, bursting like that is so very out of character for me. I usually bury my pain. I do with Phil. It never helps saying how you are feeling. It only serves to make the other person feel bad. For me, it always ends up being my fault anyway, your original reasons for being upset become highlighted as silly and invalid as the receiver defends themselves.

I was shaking, hurt, angry and scared.

"I have said before that long distance we have to make an effort, you know how much I worry, this has been like this for weeks now and it upsets me, I have raised your reduced communications and distancing gently a couple of times yet you still don't hear me, I get things happen, I am not an unreasonable bitch, but if you gave a shit, you'd take the 5 seconds to let me know, this is evidence I mean absolutely nothing to you, and you have got your work cut out convincing me otherwise."

Fraught voice notes get sent back and forth. Sam, full of all the things you'd expect. "You do matter, I am only human, I have been busy, I work in an open-plan office, I have been in meetings, I didn't know Natasha was joining me" etc etc.

So then I end up feeling like a tit, that *I* am in the wrong, unreasonable, we eventually speak rather than voice note. He requested to call me, I didn't want to speak to him, I was full of rage and hurt. For some reason, Natasha and Beth were out, so he could call and he did. He looked genuinely upset, eating bags of crisps and a bit watery-eyed. I feel awful, like the worst person in the world. As I expected it is me that ends up apologising for being crazy and unreasonable. Maybe I am.

Later when thinking about this, I wonder what is wrong with me. Am I unreasonable? I never, ever win this kind of argument with anyone. I just never win arguments full stop. The conflict, followed by witnessing the upset in the other person, makes me want to reverse time and undo all I have just done and said. I feel foolish. But equally frustrated, how am I never able to get anyone to see things from my perspective? I am so good at seeing things from other people's viewpoints, and if anyone is hurting I bend over backwards to help them, but no one ever sees my perspective and no one has ever bent over backwards for me, to make me feel better.

There is only one conclusion to draw from that. I am the problem. It is always me that is the problem. At least I am self aware.

I recall similar things with Phil in the early days. I gave up then too. Christmas and birthday presents being a prime example. We got stuff for each other in the beginning. Once the kids came along he said, "let's just not do it any more, it's silly, save the money and spend it on the kids." I argued it was not, it was a time to get something for the person in your life, a time to show you had thought about them. It's not like we bought anything for one another at other times in the year. It didn't need to be big or lavish, just a token. It felt like it would be the start of just not bothering with each other, and I was right.

He just stopped getting stuff, I couldn't do that, I had to get him something, often small, but something. He would then be all embarrassed and annoyed that I had broken what we had agreed not to do. It made him feel bad. I always ended up apologising.

I was very hurt the first few years he didn't get a gift. I couldn't say anything because we had agreed not to, in a way. I can't really say ;

"Hey, you know how we agreed, not to get gifts for each other? I did and you didn't and now I am upset!" That is a lost argument before it starts. Plus I don't give to receive, I felt like raising it would undermine the intention behind my gift, like I had only done it to receive something in return.

However, in my head I didn't think it was unreasonable to get a gift from your husband at Christmas. Turns out I was wrong. I could not work out how to win that argument without causing tension. I cannot handle tension.

Once again at some point over the years I did gently mention it with some success. He now usually gets me something small, but I know he doesn't want to, if he did, he would never have stopped. It's an obligation, I wish, I had never said anything, as getting something forced to avoid an argument that the person doesn't want to give, is worse than getting nothing.

Just like messages and phone calls from Sam, as soon as you raise it , it becomes '***a thing***.' After my outburst he did go back to how things had been for the first few months for about four days.

But then it slipped again.

It didn't matter, if he wanted to message because he wanted to message me, he would be doing it. It is better him not doing it, than it being a forced obligation.

It made things a lot harder for me, emotionally and practically, but better than him feeling forced to do something he didn't want to do.

I learnt a long time ago, perhaps in my teens, you are better not speaking up, no need, no point.

Usually, the bleeding obvious is right in front of you. Actions are the biggest clues, not words. You don't need to raise it, you have the evidence. It serves no purpose. And on the rare occasions I break my own rule and speak up, I always end up in the wrong and apologising. So, to smooth things over, I pack up my hurt and store it in a box in my mind, wrap it in 'feeling repelling balm' and hope that it is strong enough to prevent inaction from penetrating, making me numb. It is safer. Less painful.

I wish I could make myself numb to Misty. When she comes the feelings are so intense, I don't think I ever want to feel again.

The final week of work before Christmas break I can feel the trepidation building. I remember Sam's October break, no exaggeration it was traumatising.

I don't want to face another 10 days of that. He will message when he can, I know that, so I might hear from him everyday which is better than October. I will miss him so much and my mind will be pained, painting pictures of him doing all the things I want to be part of and can't.

Evening chats will no doubt be curtailed too, as family and friends will be around, staying up and drinking. We make the most of our last few nights, by talking filth and playing with the vibe.

We speak for the last time as Sam leaves work on the Friday

before Christmas. I wish him the very best of times over Christmas and I mean it. He needs a break and Christmas is fun, he says he will miss me, he will message when he can and if he gets any peace, he will message to see if I am free to talk.

I started writing to him that night. I like to write to him when we can't speak, like I did in October, I will not send it, but it helps, makes me feel like he is there.

On the Saturday before Christmas I send him a load of fun and filthy would you rather questions early afternoon.

Would you rather;

Have strangers watch you have sex or watch strangers having sex?

Extremely loud sex forever or silent sex forever?

Blowjobs everyday or anal sex once every 6 months?

Have sex with a cow and no one finds out, or not have sex with a cow and everyone thinks you did?

Sneeze or fart or burp every time you orgasm?

Watch your sister have sex everyday for the rest of your life, or join in once to stop it?

Would you rather have penises for fingers or a vulva for a mouth?

The last one has to be vulva for a mouth. Cocks are floppy most of the time, you'd never be able to hold anything.

He messages back an hour or so later, saying these needed some thought, and he would get back to me ASAP.

I don't hear anything. That night I was taking Lotties to a friend's birthday at the bowling alley. I sat in the car while she was in, with my laptop doing some work. The place is buzzing with rowdy groups of teens. It was so chilly, I ran the engine to keep warm.

As I looked across the car park, I swear I saw Misty. But if it was her she vanished. But when I glanced over to the other side of the car park, she was there again, standing behind a parked car, only her head and shoulders visible. I blink, she is gone. I looked straight out the front windscreen, she was in front of my car, hands on the bonnet. I jumped and screamed. She vanished, I looked all around, I couldn't see her, checked my mirror, she was at the back of the car. My heart thundered, this wasn't possible, how was she moving so fast, like teleportation. I shook my head. She was gone. I checked my car doors are locked and I spent the next five minutes scanning the car park. Nothing. I concluded I was losing it.

I am getting so little sleep, perhaps I am starting to go around the twist or hallucinate or maybe I actually just nodded off.

I messaged Sam:

> Hope you're ok, waiting on Lottie coming out of this party, rock n roll Saturday!

I can't focus on work now, I am still on edge and scanning the car park. I am praying for a text back from him, I need to stop this, but if I am on edge and I message him and he responds, I feel better almost instantly.

I don't have to tell him what is going on, it can be any old pish, but just seeing his name pop up helps. There has been no reply from him. I check to see if it's been delivered. It has **and** it has been read. No response though. That is unusual. He usually always gives a thumbs up or something if he has seen it. I have seen them delivered and unread, but never delivered, read and no response. I figure maybe he was about to respond when someone walked in, I was sure he would reply soon. It was Beth's bedtime, so likely in the middle of bath and books.

Another ten minutes passes and I check again, still the same. I carry on with some work, though I don't really focus as I am still checking the car park for Misty. It's about 10 minutes before Lottie is due to come out, I close my laptop and check again, still nothing. 5 minutes later it pings.

> What time did you send that last message?

>> About 8:20 I think, why?

I find this an odd question as it shows the time on the message.

> I think someone has been on my phone.

SHIT...

Chapter 27
Limbo Land

Lottie jumps in the car and I drive home, she chats all the way and I don't hear a word, my heart is thumping and blood firing through my ears. I am wondering what this means, it can only mean one thing, Natasha has been on his phone. My stomach churns at how far she may have scrolled back, what she may have seen, what is being said in his house right now. And worse, thinking of Beth, two days before Christmas.

Sam messages briefly, I clarify if he is sure his phone has been looked at, he is certain. It was charging in the kitchen, while he was doing books with Beth. He says nothing was mentioned when he went back down, but the atmosphere was strained, and they ended up having a chat about life, the universe and everything. The main point being, how they had become close best friends rather than Husband and Wife.

On that Sunday I knew his in-laws were arriving. I didn't hear a peep.

My thoughts - tangled. I keep glancing at my phone, the message screen open, my fingers hovering above the keyboard. My heart's a heavy weight in my chest, and I can't stop wrestling with this agonising decision: Should I reach out to Sam?

It feels like their entire world has been turned upside down. Sam's wife knows about us, and the fallout must be catastrophic. I can only imagine the chaos and pain they're going through right now. I don't want to add to their suffering, and I certainly don't want to become another source of stress. They're already dealing with so much, and the last thing I want is to make things worse by putting additional pressure on Sam.

Yet, there's this persistent ache inside me, a fear that by staying silent, I'm abandoning Sam. Is he feeling isolated, cut off from the only person who truly understands the situation? Or is it better to leave him be? The thought of him believing I've disappeared from his life. I did not want that. Equally given this has happened and his life would be falling apart, perhaps that is exactly what he wanted.

I'm torn between wanting to reach out and offer some sort of comfort, some reassurance that I'm still here, and fearing that my message might only add to his burden or be unwelcome. I worry that my words could come across as intrusive or as an unwanted complication in an already overwhelming situation.

The silence between us feels like a gaping void, growing larger with every passing moment. I don't want to come off as insensitive, yet I can't shake the worry that by not saying anything, I'm letting Sam down.

Each moment I spend debating whether to send a message only deepens the ache in my heart. I want to be there for Sam, to remind him he is not alone, but I also need to respect his space and the gravity of their situation. It's like being trapped between the desire to offer support and the need to step back and not interfere.

So here I am, caught in this painful limbo, my mind a whirlwind of conflicting emotions. I don't know what the right choice is, only that I wish there was a way to ease his burden without adding to it.

Guilt engulfs me, this is **my** fault, I should never have messaged at bedtime. Had I not done that when his phone was charging in the kitchen, we may never have been discovered, at least until we wanted to be. We could have moved things forward at our own pace and perhaps planned a future together, with careful consideration for damage limitation, not now.

That was not a priority now.

Sam messages quickly updating me that night, still nothing has been said, the atmosphere extremely tense, he thinks she is getting through Christmas for Beth's sake. I try to reassure Sam that he doesn't know what she knows, how far back she went, damage limitation could still be achieved. Say it was just sexting. Nothing actually happened.

I didn't tell him, but I knew that it meant it was over for us. He needed to focus at home before that kind of conversation.

His texts are understandably brief and he gives nothing away about what he is thinking, and very little about what is going on. He asks for us to move to another messaging platform, one with only me in it he can hide in a password protected secret folder on his phone, so we do.

Christmas day comes, I message him wishing him a merry Christmas, and hoping it is a good day for Beth. As good as it can be anyway. He messages late that night hoping the same for me.

Christmas day here is fine, apart from Misty showing up at the kitchen window and dragging me into the garden to tell me about another attack at school. I am shaken and upset, concerned about why she is at my house on Christmas day and not with her family.

Lottie has used her own money to make me a hamper basket and Thomas wrote out a favourite quote for me and framed it. Phil even made me a makeshift demo board for my marketing gantt charts.

The kids coped well with their modest pile of gifts and were grateful. We walked Ron, had a basic Christmas 'feast' and watched some films. I got face creams from my mum, which was amazing as I really needed them and they are so expensive. She also gave me a bit of cash to 'treat myself.'

On Boxing day I visited my mum, using the cash she had given me. I let Sam know that is what I am doing, just in case I am in his thoughts. He always wanted to know if I was travelling far, and to let him know when I arrived somewhere. I didn't know if that was still relevant and felt a bit silly telling him.

Sam messaged that night, extremely brief, but longer than we have had. He reveals nothing of what is going on, just that it is frosty in the north. I feel for him so much, the tension, walking on eggshells, her behaviour clearly shows she knows, but she doesn't maybe know, he knows, she knows. I am sure he is having to stick to her like glue to almost prove he is not doing anything he shouldn't be. I feel for him, he never had much freedom, he has lost even more of it now.

I stop keeping him updated after boxing day, no point, he has bigger fish to fry. I send an occasional message so he knows I am thinking of him. I also sent a short video message, just in case he wanted to see a friendly face. After I sent it, I decided that was stupid, I am likely the last face he wants to see.

I braced on the 27th for news, as the in-laws were departing, and he had a few days before the cousins descended. He went to Panto with Natasha and Beth and told me it was good, but the atmosphere was chilly.

I don't know what to do, how to behave, I don't want to message normal daily minutia, I don't want to send filth or how I have managed to fit in my daily wanks with everyone around, I don't want to message about my dreams, sleepless nights, Misty, Emily, money worries, or the fact I fucked up on my January dates and couldn't meet on the date we had discussed. That was not relevant now, as I knew we would not be meeting in January, if at all. All my usual chat seems irrelevant now.

Sam had mentioned before he broke up for Christmas he might be going to a drumming lesson between Christmas and New year. I message and ask about that, hoping he may be willing to speak, and may need a friend. But I didn't hear from him that day.

Three's A Crowd

Emily popped over, despite the cold outside the living room was like a sweat box with the fire roaring. Phil disappeared when she arrived, he is not a fan. She was full of glee, she told me that was it, it would be over between us soon enough. I told her to 'shut the fuck up', because me, in this didn't matter, there was a family falling apart, and stop being so callous. She went off in a huff.

I didn't care.

On that Friday, a week since we last spoke, Natasha went to the shops with Beth to get supplies for the cousins coming. So Sam had a bit of alone time and we messaged, he sent me a picture of himself and a couple of voice notes.

He was like a broken man, exhausted looking, clearly not sleeping (welcome to my world). His voice was flat. Still nothing had been said, but the atmosphere at his home was unbearable. He spoke about all he had to lose, being in Beth's life full time, his home, the history he and Natasha shared.

It was clear his mind was made up. I made no comment, these were his choices to be made, part of me thought, god the hard bit is done. He should make his break now, not for me, but for him, because if he stayed, he was choosing a loveless, sexless life with no fun, and what had happened held over him, for forever, no trust, no value, no love.

I understood talking to him, that he put his sense of duty and responsibility above all else. He would not turn his back on that ever, even if that secured his own eternal misery. For him, he had invested too much in his unit. He was never going to leave them, ever. If Natasha chose for him to stay, he would accept that, but he would never choose to leave.

He soon had to run, in case she came home, I understood.

I knew now that he and Natasha (when she eventually raises it) will likely paper over the cracks, settle for their lot, like many marriages. They would have, not a bitterly unhappy life, but not a full and content life. But pleasant and tolerable enough. His life would have memories, fun, holidays and a sense of belonging as a family.

I knew that meant I was out, with a tight leash and the little freedom he had, now lost, seeing me would become infrequent, if not impossible. That is if he even wanted to continue to see me. Surely he couldn't continue this as is, It would be cruel to all involved to carry on.

That would mean he would continue to betray Natasha, having witnessed first-hand the pain he caused her. I felt that witnessing her pain, the woman he loved, would be intolerable for him, and he would be unable to carry on. He can't be focused on repairing things at home **and** focused on me. Having me would make it harder to fix things at home as it would only highlight his unhappiness, not serve it. Not to mention, if discovered a second time, I hate to think about the impact it would have on Beth and the narrative, that she would learn in time. He would not risk that. Then there is me, the least important part in all this, but still a part. If he continues to paper over everything and see me when it suits, it is probably not very healthy for me. It would be categorical evidence his heart lay with Natasha, he would have done the hard part, revealed his unhappiness and not chosen to get out.

I decided to make this easier on him and voice note this epiphany. I keep my feelings out of everything, not sharing how this will tear me apart, that would be unfair. I understand that knowing the effect this is having on me, may make things far harder for him. I made it clear it is not what I had hoped for, but understood there was no choice. Weirdly he was there and messaged back instantly that he did not want to lose me from his life.

I feel so sad for Sam, such a special person and yes he has done a bad thing and hurt his wife, but the problems were there long before I was on the scene. I am the symptom, not the cause.

I cannot fathom how she is torturing him for so long, not revealing she knows. She even mentioned me to him and suggested he set up a business meeting, she would like to meet me. I wonder

Three's A Crowd

what the hell she is playing at? Does she want to meet me and humiliate me? Does she want to destroy my life too? Is she thinking why should it just be her and her family that suffer, that Phil has a right to know?

Sam is concerned she may reveal all in a public flogging when the cousins arrive.

I get she is hurt, possibly irreparably so, but she is being cruel and manipulative. Sam says she will have made her mind up and there will be no budging her on it.

I am astounded that she would allow her pride to lose her Sam. She does not see what she has. Despite her constant rejection, not just physically but emotionally. He has stayed, supported, loved, protected, done her donkey work, been ignored, picked up, put down. She gives nothing back. Sam has raised with her how he feels before, even before me. He has told her of his unhappiness, and it has fallen on deaf ears, and then she is surprised and hurt by what happened?

She rejects him on every level, rejecting his value, his worth, thoughts, opinions, and needs both sexual and non-sexual. The worst part is, he just accepts it all.

Natasha's games continue, conversations around their relationship, but never revealing she knows anything. They spoke about the four things that they felt were missing and gained agreement on them (attention, affection, friendship and sex). She raised things long past from ten, eight and six years ago and pointed the finger firmly at Sam.

The cousins arrive and there are a few nights out ahead for Sam and Natasha. He sends an ominous message but one I have been expecting, saying;

> I have a wee bit to think about, torn between duty and love, but I do love Natasha, she is a good person and mother of Beth, we have history.
>
> Blowing up my life hurts 5 people.

I can do the maths... I will be the collateral damage here. Two boats sinking, do you save the boat with five people on it or one. You choose the boat with five, there is no choice. It is me that will be the one to be hurt.

As New Year approaches, Sam starts to tell me he loves me again, that he misses me and that he can not have me absent from his life. He asks for reassurance on how I feel about him. I can't lie. Perhaps I should have, it would make his decisions easier, and he could focus on the woman he ***does*** love without me muddying the waters. I reassure him. It is like he wants to know one part of his life is not falling apart.

He has no clue the impact this has had on me, I won't raise it, as it is cruel , he is going through worse, but doesn't mean I have not felt this, in a way he will never be able to comprehend. If and it is a big if, we somehow get through this and continue to see each other, things will never be the same for me. In the spare five minutes he can spare me every other day, while giving me little to no information, he wants me to reassure him in the thirty seconds before he vanishes to make him feel better, with no thought for what is going on my end. He doesn't even ask.

Another time he messages he mentions I could come to his town on a Friday, he has less meetings on those days, and we could fuck. He confirms he will no longer be able to travel. I am left thinking, ok so that's it, we never get an overnight, we never get to spend time together. Ever again, and he expects me to just come and be fucked for the day. It is likely he won't be able to message or speak as much now. He knows my background, he knows my anxieties and he thinks this is going to be OK for me? It hurts. It really hurts. If ever there was evidence he just saw me as a fuck, there it was.

At the moment I cannot afford that distance in petrol, let alone book a day-use hotel. I used to use them a lot when escorting, a cracking idea for a working girl. You can get massively reduced room rates for the day. But my clients more than covered that expense or often paid for them, themselves.

This Christmas holiday is the longest I have ever known. When the final day of the year arrives, I am glad of it. I am praying the next one brings better things for me, Phil, the kids and for Sam. Sam texted me wishing me a Happy New year about ten minutes past midnight. I replied saying the same and letting him know I may be out of action tomorrow as I was headed to the hills.

    I doubt it matters, he won't be able to check anyway, I will be home before he can look.
    I don't know what is going on, he has 'the cousins' to see in the new year. I wonder if he and Natasha always kiss at the bells.
    I go to bed, I do not sleep. Misty comes, great fucking start to the New year - cheers!

Chapter 28

New Year Not You

I actually can't cope any more, Misty had me up for hours last night, she threw stones at the bedroom window. It was a bitter night and I shivered heading down the stairs. I quietly let her in (I removed the lock box key a couple of months ago).

She looked thinner, almost like she was dying in front of me. I was so utterly exhausted and weary, I begged and begged her to just let me be for a week, I needed a break.

"I don't get a break," she sobbed.

"Then let me help Misty, by telling me something I can work with."

"You do help, when you listen it helps."

"I can't listen now Misty, I have to be up at 6am, I am taking my kids to the hills to sledge, it's the only activity we are doing. I have used the remainder of the cash my mum gave me for Christmas to fill the car, they are excited. I have not slept yet, I am physically and mentally exhausted."

"So am I," She hisses.

"I know, but I can't listen now, it won't go in, I can't think."

She just curls up and sobs softly, we both fall asleep, she has vanished when I wake.

If I got two hours sleep I am lucky, but the day in the hills is exactly what was needed. When I get to the hills I am dumbfounded to have a message from Sam, wanting me to let him know if I was 'protecting myself' or 'just not into him any more'. I message back and reassure him. If only he could see the fifty handwritten pages I have scribed in a little over a week all about him, checking the messaging app every fifteen minutes or so. So yeah, my feelings have not changed.

The limbo days roll on with maybe a message a day. The cousins leave and Beth is heading to her grannies soon for a few nights. It's dangerous territory, just Sam and Natasha, Christmas and New year out the way, now is bound to be the time she may raise her discoveries.

Sam mentioned he did not like the distance between him and I, and how he wanted communication to be more 'normal'. It feels like I'm being accused of not communicating. Is he serious? I think. It is not my doing. I listen though and message more frequently, having not done so because I didn't want to add to the pressure. I get nothing back in return, he does not increase his communications and I feel pathetic for it. Yet whenever he messages, he gets a response. I am a punching bag.

I remain hopeful Sam might want to talk on the phone tomorrow as he heads back to work. Nothing is said. I head out and walk Ron just in case, and he does call eventually. Seeing him is so mixed, he looks tired, broken. His tone was flat, no spark, not at all happy to see me or talk, clearly and understandably mind else- where. Sam just vents, and I can't believe the stuff he is telling me. We had to cut the call short as his pass for the car park was not in his car so he had to go to sort that out.

Sam told me that Natasha was still off work that morning, but made Sam do all the jobs making him late leaving for work. She even said in front of Beth 'We better let Daddy get to work, he will be desperate to get away from me.'

Shocking, no matter what is going on you don't bring a child into it, it's confusing for them.

He shares a gazillion other snipes and demands that happened over the break. It has been horrendous for him. And still, nothing had been said about her discovery. His mind was fucked, trying to understand what was happening and where it was all headed. It was obvious Natasha was hurting, but this was getting silly, it was cruel, border line abusive. Raise it, or don't.

When Sam hung up he said 'Hope to talk later' but I didn't know what that meant. Later on the phone when leaving work? Or later on the phone going to his drumming lesson? Was he going to his drumming lesson? Or text late tonight? I had no clue. I couldn't clarify because based on my pre-Christmas communication rant, I would be seen as too demanding, especially with what was going on. More so now, he held the trump card of pain and stress.

I send a couple of messages in the day, I don't do many, maybe two, as I'm conscious it's his first day back and he will be busy, but I had hoped with the opportunity more available than it had been for the last few weeks, he might take it and be keen to communicate with me. He doesn't.

I just don't know where I stand, I am not fluent in silence.

I head out in the dark, cold wet night hoping I might get a 'just leaving are you free?' It doesn't come. My mind drifts to perhaps something is wrong, perhaps something has happened and Natasha has finally burst.

He eventually sends a voice note and sounds in the depths of despair, he has lost one of his big work contracts, plus dreading going home and I just wonder what else can be piled on top of him. I wish I could help more.

When he messages after 11 pm, he is so flat and confesses he is really feeling it, the pressure, it is all too heavy for him, scared of losing everything he has worked for.

After he goes to bed, I can't help but jump into help mode. I spent a couple of hours writing out some positive things about his life with Natasha and life in general. I have found that in your darkest, it helps to visualise what is good. I also covered some advice on how to handle Natasha. As someone who has never had the kind of treatment women wish for or are fed via delusional romantic movies, I have a bank of creative ideas which would in theory 'wow' any woman. I have always listened to my friends and studied it in a way, like a special interest topic.

I doubt it will help, he may not even look at it but it makes me feel like I am contributing something and shows him I care.

I also suggest as Beth is away, to invite Natasha out for dinner, he does listen to that and suggests it to her and she agrees.

This is self sabotaging behaviour, I know that. It is one of my many talents.

The next morning, I go out early, again, just in case. Sam is late leaving the house but does call. He has had another bad morning, another rant, Natasha has said and done some cruel things. But she is clearly hurting.

When he got in from work last night, despite her being off work still, she had already eaten and cooked him nothing. There was nothing to eat in the house and he had to go to the shops, she didn't join him while he ate and he ate alone. She rejected a hug.

Understandably she is extremely hurt and upset, but seriously, tackle it… this is infantile, and mean. She is behaving like a primary school child. She is an adult and a smart one.

He lets me know half way through the day, Natasha has messaged him, dinner out is off, she has a sore tummy. She told him she would bring home an Indian. Strange thing to do with a sore tummy.

Each night he and I are on tenterhooks, wondering if this is the night the axe falls. Clearly, Sam is in the thick of it, living it, and I can't imagine how awful that would be. It is not easy being in the dark either. I have a very bad feeling tonight, I think this is it. I message:

Three's A Crowd

> You ok? I have a bad feeling.

> It's happening. Very bad, can't talk

I feel physically sick, his world is falling apart.
I don't sleep, he messages with an update in the early hours:

> It is terminal, separate beds, both WFH tomorrow. Told her all it ever was, was just chat. Damage limitation. She is hurt because you got the attention she should have got.

I can't get the image of him lying alone in a separate bed and crying out of my head. I can't understand how she can be annoyed at the lack of attention when ***she*** has ignored him for years. I can't believe her reaction to what she believes is just sexting, god help him if she was to know the truth. But I equally understand this is the most fraught time when she will be lashing out from pain.

I message Sam late morning to check on him, I don't want to over-message. I keep checking my phone, it's been 8 hours and no response. I am petrified for him. I am petrified for Beth, who is due back home today.

Sam had been waiting for Natasha to deliver the final death nail. In tandem, I had been anticipating Sam delivering mine. It came just after 11 pm that night.

> Shit day, lots of chat not good

> I am so sorry

> I need to be here for Beth & Natasha

> I understand

> I can't do both

> I know

> I want to stay friends and keep in touch. Be nice to have someone there for me.

> I hope it works out, I will support you.

> I will message now and again

> OK

And that was it, five lines, ending everything. Undoing all the promises, of always being there, he would never leave me, he loved me, I mattered. Confirming what I had always suspected, they were empty promises and total lies.

Actions, not words, he finally took the action. He has shown me how insignificant I am.

I was stupid. Emily was right.

Chapter 29

Jessie – Where Dreams Come True

Emily believes I am stupid on a number of levels, this latest event involves getting far too involved with 'Sam the cunt' just another one to add to the list.

As I sat staring at my phone, scrolling back over Sam's death nail, it wasn't a complete shock, part of me knew this was coming. I had braced myself, but still, when the words hit, there was this wave of disbelief. A mix of, "Wow, this is really happening," and at the same time, a strange calm, because deep down, I already knew.

It's such an odd feeling, being surprised by something you've been expecting all along. Like the pieces were already there, but until someone actually said it out loud, they had not slotted together.

This is more evidence of my stupidity. I was shocked by something that I always knew was coming.

Emily has always said I lack two major skills. The first, never waking up to those she deemed to be 'cunts' and the second, risk.

I knew Emily would now hate Sam for eternity. He would never be anything but a cunt in her eyes. I on the other hand will never agree with her on that, and it will drive her round the twist. I will never hate Sam.

Yes I am hurt, but him not wanting me does not make him a bad person, he just doesn't want me, he is entitled to make that choice. He does not deserve the title of 'cunt'. I don't even put Darren of all people in the 'cunt camp'. He must have had his reasons. People who do horrible things, often have their own pain to carry.

On the risk side, she and I differ. She sees danger in everything and everyone. She keeps people at arm's length. She is not a people person, I am. I find them fascinating.

I find myself remembering a client from Doncaster, she was concerned before I went, thought I was stupid for going and when I returned with broken ribs I got a lecture.

He had contacted me, being very open and honest about what he wanted. He was a sadist and was quite clear he wanted to 'hurt' me.

I am a masochist so this did not alarm me at all, it excited me, better than someone asking for a 'girlfriend experience'. In my experience very few people who claim to want to 'hurt' you actually follow through to a scary level.

We spoke on messages for a long time before he booked. He wanted to make sure I was 'up to the job.' That my profile was the truth, that I could take pain and he could do 'anything'. He would set me challenges, like pegging my tits, pussy, wearing nipples clamps for a certain length of time and evidencing with pictures and videos. He wanted bareback, he provided clean results just before seeing him and I did the same. Safe words and boundaries all agreed up front. Nothing stupid about it.

I had booked an 'air b n b' and headed off to meet him. He was coming early in the evening and had booked five hours which was a great booking. I combined it with a genuine work meeting the next day.

I arrived and got 'slutted up', sat having a couple of beers. I always found with clients who wanted to deliver pain, that a few beers took the edge off. Emily was always furious with me about that, she said I needed my wits about me. He messaged saying he was running late, he ended up being very late indeed. So by the time I saw him trying to work out how to get into the building, I was pretty far gone.

I let him in, we went into the kitchen and I offered him a beer, he took one and we chatted for a bit. I jumped up on the kitchen counter. He was quite hot, rare in that line of work, black with mid-length dreads and a warm smile. You would never know the dark kink that lay beneath.

He wanted down to business after a few short minutes and powered over to me, spread my legs and finger blasted my pussy, commenting on how wet it was and telling me he was looking forward to hurting me. I was drippy. I love being told what men are going to do to me, like I have no choice, like they will do it anyway. His eyes clouded over, and the warmth left him. He told me to go to the living room and take off my skirt and blouse. As I did he kicked off his clothes and opened up the kit bag he had bought with him, pulling out chains, paddles, floggers, canes, nipple clamps, pegs and a lead.

He clipped the lead onto the necklace around my neck and pushed me down to my hands and knees, grabbed his flogger and had me crawl round for him while he flogged me.

At some point, likely due to the drink I checked out a bit and can now only really conscious of certain sensations and moments. Emily says it is never the drink, and it is just what I do when I start to feel a bit out of my depth, which is nonsense, as this is all very up my street.

I recall being pulled up to my knees and him fucking my face, brutally. My necklace snapped under the strain and force of the lead.

I recall being in the bedroom and being fucked. At one point he pegged my pussy flaps and then used duct tape to hold the pegs against my thighs, wrapping the tape all around. My pussy totally spread, dripping and exposed. He fucked me like that, it was agony as the pegs pressed into me due to his weight pressing down on them. Plus the pegs pulled, stretching and tugging on my pussy lips.

I was bent over the end of the wooden bed end and caned. A couple of his canes broke on my ass. I recall thinking I was like Batfink, but instead of wings of steel I had buns of steel.

He pissed in my mouth in the bathroom.

He told me the usual stuff, whore, dirty slut, worthless piece of shit, how he was going to fucking destroy my holes and fuck me like the dirty bitch I was.

In between him unloading in various holes, we lay and talked while he recovered. At one point he requested I look him in the eyes and tell him I wanted him to hurt me. I found this very hard to do.

I do like being hurt, but admitting it, and saying out loud feels wrong. Plus half the turn-on is, it just being done, like I have no choice, rather than me asking for it. However, as a paying client, I dug deep and delivered what he wanted.

"I want you to hurt me," I said softly.

As I spoke his cock twitched to life. It was clear this was a huge turn-on for him. Which of course made my pussy gush even more.

He stood me up and pegged round each tit. Then made me stand there, arms above my head while he caned them off, one by one. Me yelping and squealing with each strike, he didn't always have the best aim. I am unsure if that was genuine or deliberate.

Seeing me struggle, made him want me again. He bent me over the end of the bed and entered my ass. He hammered away like a rabid piston. I was squealing through 'painal' and my welted bruised ass being slammed with each thrust.

Then I felt and heard a 'crack'. Something had snapped. The bolt of pain that travelled through me was beyond that of pleasure and tipped into true agonising unbearable pain.

I knew something had broken, I knew it was an accident, he

was slamming his full body weight down on top of me while my torso was on the edge of a wooden bed frame.

I said nothing, fighting back tears, I let him carry on for some time. The appointment was close to the end and I did not want him to feel bad. He would have felt terrible. We had safe words in place, but this was not his intention.

Emily said I was stupid, and I should have shouted 'red' at that moment.

I get the concept of safe words, I had never had to use mine. It also feels for me, a bit different in a paid set up, like you can't, you would be a disappointment, they are paying for you after all. I think this kind of 'play' with effective safe words probably only works if your in a proper trusting relationship, rather than sex work and hook-ups. I would have to feel confident, safe that I could speak up without consequence.

Once he was done, we chatted briefly, he paid me my money, he was impressed with me, praised me. Confirmed that I really would do anything for cock, that I lived up to my profile, I had made his sadistic dreams come true, and he would be keen to book again.

I held it together until the door closed behind him. Then it hit like a wave, hard and fast. My body turned ice cold, but my skin felt like it was burning. I slid down the door, my legs too weak to hold me up. I couldn't stop shaking; my hands were trembling uncontrollably, and a dizziness crept over me, clouding my vision. My heart pounded like it was trying to escape my chest.

I crawled on my belly along the floor toward the bathroom, the ground feeling both too close and impossibly far away. Every inch forward felt like a struggle, my stomach twisting violently inside me. By the time I reached the toilet, I was already retching. The nausea overwhelmed me, my body emptying itself in a series of brutal spasms. The pain was so sharp, so intense. I was sweating but freezing at the same time, a clammy, suffocating kind of cold that clung to my skin.

At some point, I blacked out. When I came to, it was the middle of the night. My throat burned, my mouth was dry, and every muscle in my body ached. Freezing cold, I dragged myself out of the bathroom, my legs shaking beneath me. I couldn't stand, so I crawled, inch by inch, across the cold floor into the hallway, down to the bedroom and toward the bed. The pain in my ribs was setting in now, sharp and constant, radiating from my sides with every small movement.

I collapsed into bed, but sleep wouldn't come. The pain throbbed, making it impossible to get comfortable. Every shift of my body sent another stab of pain through me, leaving me trapped in this limbo of exhaustion and discomfort. My body was drained, but my mind was wide awake, forced to sit with the pain that pulsed and gnawed at me long into the night.

I had to think clearly, formulate a plan. In the morning I called Phil, told him I had fallen on a railing. I went to my meeting and stood for the duration, I endured the long drive home.

The day after that I had the embarrassment of attending accident and emergency. Receiving confirmation my ribs were fractured, body swerving concerned looks and difficult questions.

It took weeks to heal, I couldn't do any GW work. My rib breaking client wanted progress pictures of his work, to see the rainbow of colours that developed and then faded on my tits and ass.

Emily's response - that I had been stupid, I should never have gone. I should have spoken up, and who gives a fuck if that upset him. Cunt.

It was far from the ideal outcome, but had that accident not happened it would have been fine. All good in the hood. It was an accident, pure and simple.

I felt a bit like Disney Parks - I made his dreams come true. My superhero slut status is confirmed again. Stupidity or not, I made cock dreams come true and that felt good.

Chapter 30

Get back in your Lane

Following Sam's message, ending us. I feel like I've been shattered into a million pieces, all because I trusted Sam. I am a tit, a huge tit, I have been stupid. I am the world's biggest tit!

All the way along I knew, I absolutely knew I shouldn't have let it happen, but I did. I opened up to him in a way I never had with anyone before, and now I'm left grappling with the wreckage of my own foolishness.

I read and re-read his messages, no, 'I am sorry, no, will you be OK?' Literally no feelings in it at all, no hint of regret or sadness, just matter of fact. Done. Over. Dropped. Cast aside. Discarded. Forgotten. Unimportant . Unloved.

For the first time in my life, I let someone in, almost completely. I had fought so hard to protect myself but eventually against my better judgement, I caved. And now, as he so easily casts me aside, **every word, every promise he made was just a lie**, a cruel deception that makes me question how I could have been so blind.

I know better than that, I have always known. I am not wanted.

I had willingly and foolishly handed him the sharpest weapon he could use against me, and it all played out exactly the way I feared. I should have known better.

That pain, the betrayal, the feeling of being broken from the inside out, it hardens you. It changes you. It makes you want to build walls so high that no one can ever scale them. That's exactly what I did before Sam. I kept myself distant, safe, because when you don't let people in, they can't destroy you.

It was protection. It still is.

He **didn't** love me. I **didn't** matter. He **can** cope with not seeing me. He **has** left me. He **won't** always be there. He lied, he played me.

Proof - words mean nothing. I have always known this. Always, easy to say, never meant.

Olivia Rodrigo's song 'Favourite Crime'[6] plays in my head. I do not think Sam will ever understand how badly I loved him. I let him treat me this way and with the fall out in Sam's life there are four hands with blood on them, but one broken heart…mine.

It's a bitter and devastating truth that cuts deeper with every passing moment. I'm filled with regret for ever being hopeful in the sincerity of his feelings. How could I have been so stupid? I've been abandoned just when everything around me is falling apart, left to deal with the chaos and heartache while he shows a total disregard for the pain he's caused. Throwing in a grenade and walking away, back turned so he does not have to see the destruction.

I will never be the same again. The pain he inflicted is irreparable, a wound that cements all the worst things I've ever believed about myself. I know I will never recover from this betrayal, that I'll never be able to trust anyone again. He is the first person I ever properly began to trust, I won't ***ever*** make that mistake again. The ache is so intense, it makes me wish for a release, a way for the world to end, just to escape this over-whelming agony.

Three's A Crowd

To hear him talk about wanting to be friends, it's absurd. Friends don't do this. But I refuse to lower myself to his level, to let him see how deeply this has cut me. I've been there for him these past few weeks. I unlike him have **always** been there for him, instantly on hand with encouraging words, supporting him as he dealt with his own turmoil. I don't just run out on people.

I'll never believe another word he says. As soon as he's stable and sorted, I'll slip away quietly, out of his life. Then I will decide if mine is worth staying in.

Emily appears almost instantly, she has a sixth sense I am sure of it.

Emily's words were like a cold slap to the face. She sat across from me, her eyes filled with a mix of pity and disappointment.

"I told you so," she began, her voice barely a whisper. "Sam was never in love with you. He was using you."

The weight of her words settled on me like a heavy blanket. I had been so foolish to believe his lies, to think that he actually cared about me. Emily was right. I had been well and truly sucked in, I was a fool.

"I'm sorry for the pain he caused you," she continued, her voice softening slightly. "But you had been foolish to let him in. I tried to warn you. You knew better. Remember who you are. Your past is your past. If he had discovered everything, he would have left anyway. Natasha by finding out about, you just accelerated it. The end was inevitable. Move on enjoy men, fuck them, but remember because of who you are and what you have done, you can never reveal yourself fully and if you did, they would not want you. If there is a next time, for god's sake listen to me."

Her words stung, but I knew she was telling the truth. I had been so focused on believing that maybe, **just maybe**, I might matter to someone that I had ignored all the red flags. I had allowed myself to be manipulated and hurt.

"The best thing you can do is get back on the cock," Emily said. "Remember who you are and surround yourself with people who know exactly what you are are. People who make you feel good. Stop chasing romantic ideas, you gave them up as a teen."

Her words were harsh, but they were necessary. I had to learn my lesson. Return to my place, a nothing, a no one, just someone you fuck and ignore, or don't ignore and don't fuck.

No one but Sam, in my entire life, has made me feel so small, so insignificant. No one had ever made me feel less than this. I was a ghost, a shadow, a non-entity in his world, that much was clear.

Sam's actions have just confirmed everything I knew to be true, he gave me hope it maybe wasn't, but then just confirmed beyond a shadow of doubt it actually is: that I'm worthless to him and not just to him, to everyone. It's one thing to feel rejected, but to be shown so clearly that I'm not even worth a conversation, it's crushing. The fact that he's only reached out with a text, not even bothering to ask how I'm doing, speaks volumes.

It's like a cold reminder that I was never more than a fleeting convenience and play thing to him. And now an inconvenience he needed to shed.

The offer of friendship, but **only** on his terms and **only** when he needed something, it's an additional slap in the face. He didn't think enough of me to engage in a real conversation or show genuine concern. He didn't even ask if I would be ok or say he was sorry. No remorse, no care. No, I was only valuable when it suited him, when he needed a listening ear or a temporary escape. It makes me feel like I was just a placeholder, a stand-in for the real relation- ships and the connection he values.

In all my life, no one has ever made me feel so utterly insignificant. The way Sam has treated me is the worst I've ever felt about myself. It's as though every interaction we had was a lie, designed to keep me just close enough to keep me sweet but never to truly include me in his life, the hurt was deep.

His actions have shown me that I didn't matter, that my feelings were irrelevant. All his words of love and kindness, were as I suspected, nothing more than words.

Three's A Crowd

I'm left with this stark realisation of how little I meant to him, and it's a painful lesson that stings with every heartbeat. It's a betrayal that's not just about him but about how I allowed myself to even consider an alternative. I've never felt so devalued.

I don't know how to come back from this.

Chapter 31

Lost in the Mist

Y ou would think given all that has occurred in the last few years and this latest crushing blow to my soul, karma might give me a break. Not so. Karma really is a bitch, and she has the taste of my blood in her mouth.

After Sam's message, I have been in constant tears, I can't eat, vomiting bile as my stomach is empty and literally unable to function. Feigning illness (not hard) to Phil, Lottie and Thomas, hiding out in my bedroom. I get out for fresh air once a day to walk Ron. Thomas volunteers to help, but I need out.

The excruciating pain of how easily I was dropped by Sam, thoughts of Darren, Misty. I just can't get work done, and I am close to the cash running out, surely that is enough.

Apparently not, let's send Misty in... again. But hey, let's up the ante.

I put on my headphones and trudge out the door to walk Ron, every step a physical challenge, I have to convince everyone to let me go out.

"Jess, please you're not well, just stay in bed, Ron doesn't need a walk, he will be fine for a day." Pleads Phil.

"Mum, I will do it" volunteers Thomas.

"It's OK, please I want to go, I really need some fresh air," I pleaded. "I won't be long."

The debate continued until I was finally allowed out. The woods feel different today. There's a heaviness in the air that matches the weight in my chest. Each step feels slow, deliberate, as if the earth beneath my feet is pulling me down, asking me to sit in this sadness a while longer.

Ron walks beside me, his usual energy subdued, like he senses it too. His paws move softly over the crisp icy fallen leaves, and every now, and then he glances up at me, those trusting eyes meeting mine as if to say, "I'm here." I can feel his presence grounding me in a way that nothing else can right now. His quiet loyalty speaks louder than words. He shows me his love, he doesn't use words, words mean nothing.

We don't rush. There's no need to. The world feels muted, no birdsong, just the soft rustling of leaves underfoot and the distant sigh of the wind. Ron trots ahead, stopping occasionally to sniff a tree or a patch of earth, but always coming back, never straying too far. His companionship is steady, unspoken, and it makes the sadness feel a little less lonely.

The path curves deeper into the woods, and the trees close in around us. I walk, lost in my thoughts, while Ron stays by my side, the constant in the middle of everything else that feels uncertain and broken. There's a comfort in the routine of it, one foot in front of the other, moving forward, even if the weight doesn't lift. I reach the central point I often stop at, a pile of tree slices piled and strewn across the ground, leftover from the tree surgeons clearing the damage from the last named storm.

Even though Sam does not live here, has never been here, memories chase me at every turn. I used to sit on these logs and talk to him, or take a picture of my pussy and send it to him. Just down that path is where I was when I listened to a voice note from him telling me how much I meant to him. The cruelty of those lies as sharp as the frozen leaves.

Three's A Crowd

Darren jumps into my head and some of his final parting words when he left me that night - how I was lucky someone like him would even touch someone like me. I suppose I was lucky someone like Sam ever had even a fleeting interest in me. I am a fool.

I sit on my stump and bury my head in my hands. An icy wind cuts through me, Ron whimpers and I look up, Misty is sitting on the stump next to me with no coat and shaking uncontrollably. I start shaking too, it is so bitter. I don't have the energy to fight her off or to listen, but I am resigned, now is as good a time as any, there is never a right time and I can't feel much worse.

"You look frozen" I say "where is your coat?"

"What's wrong?" she asked me.

"I am unwanted," I say.

"I know," she says.

"How?" I ask

"I know how that feels" she clarifies "It hurts, doesn't it"

"Yes" I say and a small sob escapes me.

We pause talking as a couple and their beagle walk past us, giving us both a nod and a smile. Once out of ear shot Misty continued:

"I am sorry, I really hoped things would be better," she looks so broken by this, like it is a blow she may not be able to withstand. Like she needed it to be better for me and her world had just been crushed that bit further.

"Me too, anyway, have you something to tell me?" I say, and I notice for the first time since Misty appeared in my life, today I am not scared of her, it is like I can't even be bothered being scared, I just want her to do what she has to do and then leave me alone. I want everyone to leave me alone. I am better alone. *Nothing can hurt you, when you are alone.*

She leans forward and reaches for my hands. I can feel the cold from her skin penetrate through my thick woolly gloves. I change my grip and place her hands in between mine, trying to engulf her frozen stick digits in a cocoon to warm her. She begins to whisper, her voice strained and shaky, but tranced.

School disco
Rachel & clare dancing
So pretty - boys circle them
Darren dances with Rachel - 'Everything I do' playing.
Friends watch with envy
'Snoop Snoop Song - it's in his kiss'
Friends dancing - not me
Slip out to the toilet Thundering feet
3 of the boys, ran
Trying doors trying cupboards - locked
No escape, must hide
Home economics room - opens
Hide under a table.
They enter

Despite not feeling scared for once when Misty appeared sitting near me on the tree log, as she talked, that changed, fear and panic rose within me. I preferred not feeling, but at least the pain of Sam has shifted.

"Come out, we saw you looking, we're here to help."
"Boo!" a face pops up
Scramble out to run
Grabbed
Hand on mouth
Marched to wall
Held on wall by two
Dress lifted up
Third gets his cock out
Enters, fucks, fills
They swap around
They finish
Their cum drips out onto the floor
"Dirty fucking bitch, look at the mess you've made."

Three's A Crowd

"Clean that up"
Go for blue roll
"No bitch, with your fucking mouth'"
Laughing
"Are you fucking deaf? Lick up the mess you've made".
Mark flies at me, pulls me down
Pain
"Fucking lick it up, now". I pause.
Crack across the back of the head.
"Now!"
Face pushed to it.
Tentatively lick it
I shut my eyes and do it
All clean
Look up
"Don't fucking look at us again, got it."
They leave
Return to Disco

I don't know what Misty does to me, but the way she grips me, her words, they always hit. This is a stranger really, who has horrible tales to tell, but I feel them, as if the pain is mine.

It's strange, you know. People always say, "I understand" or "I know how you feel" when you're going through something tough, but they don't. How could they? No one can truly grasp the weight of something they haven't lived through. It's like...they try to empathise, they might even have had their own experiences to draw on, but it's never the same. How could they ever 'feel' it if they weren't there, living it, with every breath, every heartbeat, every sinking moment?

But Misty... She's different. When Misty talks, it's not just words. When she tells me about her pain she does not say much, there is no detail, she rarely adds any of her own feelings, other than the crushing expression on her face. Yet it's like I'm suddenly there, like it's happening to me, I can see it, feel it. And it's horrendous. Every detail she shares grips me in ways I can't explain. Her voice wraps around me, pulling me into this suffocating space where her experiences feel like my own, even though I know they aren't. I can feel the fear in my bones, the gut-wrenching sorrow in the pit of my stomach. It's like she's got this power to make her pain yours, and you can't shake it. I can only conclude that due to her being ages with Lottie it makes her tales more meaningful, more powerful as my maternal beast is awakened.

It's terrifying because for a moment, just a moment, I do understand what she's been through. I feel it. And I wish I didn't.

After she stops speaking, I sit in silence, I am just thrown by the cruelty of these boys. What has she ever done to deserve this treatment? How can no one around her see her suffering and help her? Why does it have to be me? I don't feel like I am helping. I need to gently find out more, take her with me slowly, build her trust so we can end this for her and get her the help she needs.

"Misty, do you go to school?"

"Yes"

"Where?"

"I told you already"

"Tell me again, please"

"Dames Order, your school"

"That's over 200 miles away Misty, it makes no sense."

"Its not, you still don't get it"

"Help me get it."

"That's down to you."

My patience is wearing thin. I am fed up with the cryptic talk, I just need her to be straight with me. I try to firmly, but gently point out the impossibility of this situation.

"Misty, I have had just about enough of this, I can't take much more, you want me to help, but you won't give me any information to help."

Misty slowly leans right into my face, eyes bulging with tears, and something else I can't put my finger on, perhaps frustration.

She is so close I can see every pore on her skin. Her fragile gentle manner shifted at pace, like a mouse trap being set off. Her mild meek demeanour became a dangerous energy. Like seeing a single flame burst into a wildfire.

"I HAVE TOLD YOU AND TOLD YOU, JUST LISTEN YOU WHORE" she screams and I mean screams, right up in my face.

Taken off guard from what was calm, I recoil backwards in shock and fall off my log onto my back, knock my head and screw up my eyes just in pain. Ron is whimpering and whining.

I am sick of this, I push up on my arms to say enough is enough, but she is gone. I slump back down and lay there, legs on my log, back on the ground, staring at the bare branches of the trees above, swaying and making patterns like a kaleidoscope in the sky.

It's too much. I can feel everything at once, and it's suffocating.

It's like my chest is caving in under the weight of it all, and I can't breathe.

I keep replaying what has happened with Sam. How he just... walked away like it was nothing, I was nothing. It burns. This mess of pain that won't stop.

Then there's Misty. God, Misty. I don't even know what to do with her. I don't know 'what' she is to me, or what I'm supposed to feel about her. Her stories, her voice, they stick with me like a hangover I can't shake. Even when she's not here, it lingers, haunting my thoughts. It's like she's sewn herself into my skin, and her pain is gnawing at me from the inside out. Every word she said still echoes in my head, I can't escape it.

Underneath all of that; Sam, Misty, there's this deeper despair. Like everything around me is crumbling, slipping through my fingers, and I'm powerless to stop it. Every part of my life is falling apart, piece by piece, and I just... I just can't hold it together any more. It's like I'm drowning in my own emotions, frantically trying to escape, gasping for air, for relief, but I can't reach the surface.

My phone rings, breaking me from my thoughts, I reach for it, my movements stiff and slow as I have seized up from being out in the cold.

"Mum?!" Says Lottie sounding anxious. "You OK?"

"Yes, are you?"

"Yes of course" I responded a bit puzzled.

"You've been gone a couple of hours, I was worried." I glance at my phone, shit she is right.

"Oh god sorry Lottie, just got lost in my thoughts walking, on my way back now" I say.

"OK"

I drag my aching, cold convulsing body back home, Ron who never pulls on the lead is straining to get back, he too is shaking.

Lottie has a cup of tea waiting for me, along with a blanket and some paracetamol. I sit with them all watching something on the television, I don't know what. It takes me hours to defrost.

I stay up when everyone goes to bed, I am going to read. I have gone from a cold I never thought I would recover from, to kicking off the blanket as the heat from the living room suffocates me.

To my surprise Emily lets herself in;

"Hey"

"Hey" I replied "want a drink?"

"Nah"

"It's late Em, my lot are all in bed, why are you here?" " Checking on you".

"I am OK"

"Bollocks Jessie, look at you." She replies.

"Shhh! Please Emily, everyones sleeping" I whisper.

"I don't care," she says but in a softer, more controlled voice. "You need to do something Jess, keep yourself busy, get back in the saddle and make this less painful"

"It will never not hurt."

"Get a fucking grip" she whispers angrily " He was a cock with a cock, it's done now, you can't change that. But you can do something for yourself, make it better"

"What?" I ask

"Take some action, do something, distract yourself."

"Like what?"

"Take the five pain points in your life and take action on each. Firstly, tell that girl to fuck off, I know I told you to listen to her, but you have enough on your plate, you cannot be dealing with her and everything else, get rid of her. Don't feel guilty, I know you will, this is self preservation. Secondly, get back on GW, sort your cash situation out. Thirdly and maybe most importantly, you were stronger before Sam, look at the nick of you, get these and all other feelings away to fuck, find that strength again. Fourthly, focus on your strengths, just remember, you're good at fucking, you get the validation without the turmoil. It's hurting like hell now, but it **will** pass. Keeping yourself busy will make it pass faster. Getting a buzz from sucking a few cocks will give you a boost. Finally, don't be used, Sam messages you for support, tell him to fuck off."

"I don't think I can do GW at the moment, I couldn't stomach it. But I could go back to panty selling for now until I am feeling better."

"OK, I will settle for that for now, but why not look at WhatsApp on your burner phone, see if anyone has been in touch, that would make you feel better, I bet some of them still want to book you, at least then you can have confidence you could earn cash still it gives you options."

"OK, but also whilst things will never be the same for Sam and I, he is going through hell, if he messages needing support, I won't not help him. I am the only person he can talk to about this. It wouldn't sit right with me to just ignore his pleas for help or let him vent."

"For fuck's sake Jessie, listen to yourself, yet again, ignore your own pain, caused by him, but try and reduce his pain, you have to stop putting everyone before you, tell me you are not actually serious?"

"Just because he had dumped me, I won't do that to him in his hour of need, or anyone for that matter. As for Misty, I don't think telling her to fuck off will stop her coming and I am scared of what she may say to Phil or the kids. I do wish she would go away, but I feel obliged to help her, she seems to have no one, I cannot just abandon her either."

"I will talk to her, hold her back, perhaps if I explain what is going on, what state you are in she will restrain herself, even for a few weeks. But you see her, don't engage for now, we need to get you better."

Emily says good night, tells me not to worry she will have me back to my old self soon enough and heads away.

I reinstalled WhatsApp for business on my burner phone and saw all the messages from the last few months. All the usuals, some have still been messaging every other day. I turn off read receipts so I can look at them. It comforts me, ***they*** want me at least. But I can't bring myself to do anything with it at the moment. I open up my old panty selling account and message some old regulars there. It will be good getting some cash in the door when I can face it. Not now.

To my utter shock, my phone pings, it's Sam:

> Quick update things calmer, talking about what has gone wrong.

> Good news, keep talking, suggest marriage counselling maybe.

It feels cruel, his two-day silence makes me feel utterly forgettable, and I don't understand why he is messaging. Guess it is the friends part. How can he think this is fair? Giving me updates on things getting better after telling me that we are over. I know Emily is right, I should not engage, it feels like he is being bitterly unfair.

As I wake in the night from another nightmare about Misty I ponder Emily's pain point about Misty. On the one hand I would love for her to vanish, but I am concerned for her, I don't want to

Three's A Crowd

do to her what Sam has done to me. I cannot just turn my back on her. I do wish I could turn my back on her in my dreams though.

I also wonder if it is possible to die from lack of sleep.

I trudge through another day of work, with kids back at school and Phil out on the hunt for a job again, I welcome having the house to myself. I do the minimum work wise, I can't focus, I am far too destroyed. I force myself to do any online meetings but other than that I get nothing done.

Late in the evening, I write to Sam on my note pad. I haven't stopped, it's purely for me, to get out how I feel. Then I check WhatsApp and sneak a peek at more messages inquiring if I am 'still working'. I have 3 panty requests too. I don't message back. I will. I am about to head to bed, it is just after 1am when Sam messages;

> Suggested counselling, it wasn't a no.
>
> Great, glad it's moving forward
>
> I still care about you
>
> OK
>
> Pls stay off those apps and any temptation, do it for me

My jaw hits the floor. I message Emily and tell her. Her response:

> WTAF fucker! Total twat. Lets run through this... we are done so fuck off, I don't want you, but I want to be your friend, so I will message as a friend only....and will only do that if and when I can or need some advise on my situation. Radio silence for 2 days.

> Then updates the women he played and doesn't love and just told to fuck off out his life, with how things are going with the woman he actually loves. Then had the balls or stupidity to ask the women he just told to fuck off , (but lets be friends) not to be tempted on any sex apps, and do to that FOR HIM? DICK!

Confused and in pain, I head to bed. As I try to drift off, all I can think of is what I could do to help, what advice I could give. I wonder how he is coping, how Beth is, is he sleeping, is he eating?

In the morning I message the only bit of advice I can think of which is, if he has not already done it, go to her and say he is sorry, it was the biggest mistake of his life and realising all he might lose, has made that so obvious and he will do anything to repair things.

Then Sam confuses me even more, later that night he messages saying;

> You are not a mistake, I think about you all the time, I love you, I can't manage without seeing and speaking to you, but I need to fix my marriage for Beth

> I know, you need to do what you can for Beth

I don't know what he is playing at, why tell me that? I know we are done. I know he has to fix his marriage, why is he making it worse by saying the other things? Does he just enjoy hurting me? I was not messaging him, to say those things, fishing for him to come back and tell me he cares. I know he doesn't and he doesn't need to make that point again. That landed perfectly when he first told me we were over.

I had another very bad night. The next day's work is awful. I can hardly keep my eyes open or focus. I cancelled a Zoom meeting for fear of not being able to perform. I need to get a grip. I see Misty lurking in the garden, looking for a way in. I am not having it. Not today.

Three's A Crowd

That night, Sam out of the blue sends another message, this time accusing me of 'not being there for him'. My mind is blown. I have replied to ***every single message*** he has sent. That felt **really** unfair. Another kick in the teeth. Not once has he considered how he might be coming across to me or how I am, how this may have impacted me, not once. I don't know how to behave with him any more. I can't win. Then he asks me if I understand how he feels about me.

Say what?! What does he ***even*** mean? Right now, I don't understand anything. What does he think I need to understand? He doesn't want me, but he wants me to support him. Yeah, I got that message loud and clear, so what the fuck is he on about?

The weekend brings the usual mum duties, running Thomas to Rugby, watching him play in a match, he is really coming on and has been selected for the national under sixteen team. I am proud of him. Lottie is in the middle of her prelims, looking tired and stressed, she won't take a break. She won't do anything social. I try to make sure everyday I get a minimum thirty minutes to let her talk about her worries. Phil is tentatively optimistic as he has got a couple of job prospects.

On Sunday, the three of them go to their Gran's for the day. I just lay in bed, cuddling Ron and wondering what is ***so*** wrong with me, that literally no one ever wants me. Scrolling through Instagram, I land on a post which just hits so hard it slashes my heart. I feel like it is literally going through a shredder and there are now so many strands all torn up, it is irreparable.

'Just remember when you ignore her, you teach her how to live without you.'

Is that what he is trying to do? Was that what he was trying to do even before snoop gate? Perhaps snoop gate although horrible gave him the perfect out.

'If it's not mutual, never force him, let him go'

I know I have to do this now, but why is it so fucking hard?

'A woman's attraction to a man is mostly based on

how his behaviour, thinking and actions make her feel.'

Well, that is bollocks. If that were true, then I wouldn't be attracted to him at all. His behaviour, thinking and actions could not have made me feel any shitter if he tried. He could literally shit on my face and I would still want him, what is wrong with me!

'You said she was important to you, but you still make her feel like she is not worth your time.'

Well that has been obvious since late November, why did I not listen to Emily back then? Perhaps if I had, this would not have gone to terminal pain levels.

'She wants to be happy, not hurt, not confused, not stressed, just happy.'

Boom! That is **ALL** I have ever wanted. That is true wealth, not money.

'If hurting her, doesn't hurt you, then don't even tell her that you love her'

Bang on, I agree, he has been hurting me for a few months now, even before snoop gate. I decide I need him to stop saying those empty words and never say them again. Perhaps then the pain will stop.

'Someone who loves you, isn't going to keep hurting you, that is just someone who doesn't care, but wants to keep you around.'

That last one hit like a 'Szymon slap.' That is exactly how it all feels. I lay curled up crying feeling that wall of pain crash on top of me again, my head telling me the truth, he never cared, he only wanted you for sex, that is all you are worth, you have never been and never will be wanted by anyone, *ever*. You're not good enough, never have been, never will be, you're someone men want to use as a wank aid, **that's it**. Accept that and get back to it, it's not a bad way to live. You're live porn, guys like porn, they just don't want you in any other part of their life, you're not like other women. Once you accept this, the pain will stop.

Three's A Crowd

I half think of sending those quotes to Sam to help him with Natasha, there are some good messages in them and it applies across the sexes. But I don't.

Exhausted I fall into a fitful sleep and dream, mostly words;

Darren: 'no one would be seen with you, you should be grateful I fucked you.'

Sam 'I love Natasha, she is a good person.'

Darren 'say thank you'.

Snippets, words and conversations all swirling at me in my sleep;

'No one wants you'

'I can't do both'

'No one wants to see that'

'It's an open plan office'

'Look at you repulsive'

'Embarrassed to be seen with you.'

'You matter'

'Go suck some cock, you're good at that.'

'No one cares what you think'

'I will never leave you.'

'I can't do both'

'Cum dump'

I wake, shaking, I want to scream, 'Shut up head, I **GET** it OK! You have made your point.'

I take Ron out and I run, as far and as fast as I can, as if somehow running at speed, my thoughts would fall out and be left behind for a bit. Giving me some peace until they sprung back on the coils they are attached to, when I eventually stop. But at least for a while, it will be peaceful. I manage about 15 minutes before the world starts to tilt, I am dizzy, faint, I slump to the ground, until my body calms and finds some store of fat and converts it into energy and allows me to walk home.

Everyone is back, full of tales and gossip from their visit to Gran's, there is always a drama, they are all buoyant, happy and have been given their own body weight in sugar and crap. I cook Fajitas, they eat them. We all settle down and watch a film.

I think I am going to have an early night for once. But first, once everyone is in bed, I have a quick look again on WhatsApp on my burner phone. Henry has messaged a lot, **there** is someone who actually seems to want me.

I realise I need that in my life.

I don't get it at home, never have. Sam has just taken that away with him, though the truth is it was never real with him anyway and all just lies.

I have done it my entire life, it's like I **have** to have moments of feeling wanted. Having chosen to marry Phil, I will never have it in the confines of a relationship. Instead I get that need from others, little nanoseconds that keep my soul fed and watered, keep me sane, help me conclude I can be wanted at least ***in some way*** for a little while. Just not the way I dreamed I would be as a child.

Sam once said, he'd take a bit of me, over never having me at all. Same applies, I will feed off the scraps of being wanted rather than never having that feeling. It is better than nothing.

I don't want Henry how I want Sam, I have never wanted anyone how I want Sam, but Henry, Szymon and the others have never made me feel unwanted and they always make me feel better about myself, like I have a point to my existence.

I decide after a good sleep I will construct a message to them, apologising and get back in the saddle, if they will have me. With Sam not a part of my life any more, I can earn and feel wanted in some way at least, hell, they have even messaged more often than Sam has in recent months, even before Snoop gate.

As I am about to head to bed, I am surprised by a message from Sam. I don't expect one any more and I turn off 'read receipts' and look.

> God I miss you, things tense here, but I am ok.

What the actual fuck, I am so confused. I can't ignore him,

that's just cruel. I know how it feels to reach out to someone when you are in the depths of despair and get no response. I want to ignore him though. Instead I turn 'read receipts' back on.

> Sorry it's so tense

Sam then goes on an 'Inspector Clueso' mission like the good old days, questioning me and shares how he feels. He tells me that the song 'Happy Ending' by Mika[5] came on in the kitchen the other day and he almost cried. That he wanted me, couldn't live without me.

My confusion quadruples. I know now it's not the truth, I want it to be, but I can't and won't ever trust his word again. I always doubted it, but now I know for certain. Proven by his actions, not words.

But I cannot be cruel, I cannot deny I don't have feelings for him, but I am too hurt to go all in. He asks about what has been happening with me, I share as little as I can get away with. I do however tell him I had looked in WhatsApp, other apps and considered returning to GW. I think I wanted to show him how much he hurt me and continues to. That did not go down well, he goes nuts, he is angry, disappointed, upset. I try to explain but he just sees it as pathetic, disappointing and a childish reaction. It doesn't matter what he thinks, he doesn't give a shit, so why would he care what I am up to. But he makes me feel bad.

He really has no understanding how this has impacted me, but I can't blame him, his mind is on what is important to him, that is not me.

As if to prove the point, he focuses on the only bit of me that **is** important to him, he asks for. So as requested I send pictures of my pussy and ass. I guess that shows me exactly where I stand and confirms what I have always known. He loves my holes.

We fall into a pattern over the next few weeks, not one you can really predict, nothing is 'officially' back on, we speak very occasionally, frustratingly when we do the signal is bad, or he has to hang up suddenly. Natasha is obviously wary of anytime he is alone and happens to call at those times, something she never did before. He is never bothered that our communication has reduced even further. When we do speak the conversation is awkward, polite, chewing the fat over day to day stuff or him sharing the latest with what Natasha has said.

He covers off again and again how disappointed he is that I had 'moved on' within a short few days. This infuriates me, and shows again how little he understands the position I am in and what he has done to me. I had no clue when he said he couldn't do this any more that he would **_ever_** come back and say he had feelings for me. How could I have? Not only that but how could I just slot back into how things were and ignore the pain he had handed out? How could I ever trust his word again?

I listen to his worries, and voice notes about life at home, and offer words of comfort and advice where I can. After a couple of weeks, he says I sound down and he wants to know why. He is the smartest man I have ever met, but he is dumb as fuck when it comes to this.

I can't tell him how he has made me feel for three reasons.

Firstly I would struggle to verbalise, it solves nothing, it would only add to his woes, and how I feel is insignificant compared to what is going on in his life. It feels selfish. My family is not falling apart...his is.

Secondly, it would serve no purpose, it might make him feel bad, and he has enough on his plate.

Thirdly, I don't need to share how I feel, as I know my place clearly now, so my feelings are irrelevant. The sky is not blue like he said and I wish I had never thought it was a possibility, this is exactly why I have avoided feelings for as long as I can remember.

At night, not always, but more often than not he messages for around fifteen minutes before saying he is going to read his book and requests pictures of my cunt and ass before signing off.

Three's A Crowd

I decided a few days prior, that if he wants me in his life, as a friend to support him and likely an occasional fuck buddy (if we do ever see each other again), or a supplier of wank material, then I have to have some rules in place to protect myself. I send them to him;

1. Don't ever tell me you love me, miss me or that I matter.
2. Don't ask me about Darren, Misty, or money. That is my shit to deal with.
3. Tell me when you and Natasha start fucking again, at that point I am out.
4. If you want me out of your life, a call would be appreciated, not a text.

These are carefully thought out, but I don't tell him the rationale.

1. Every time he says anything like that it's a stab right through my shredded heart, as I know it is not true. How can I ever believe these words now?
2. I am not having him support me and then leave me again. I have to get through this stuff with Darren's memories and Misty alone. I had stupidly allowed myself to feel a level of safety with him, relied on him, he started removing that before Snoop gate, it is no longer safe with him.
3. Once that happens, I don't want to hear about how great his life and relationship is, that is just masochistic, not in a sexually exciting way.
4. Is not actually necessary now, this is more a childish dig to make the point that given how he played me completely, had me the closest I have ever been to being convinced I actually was important to someone,

he ended it with a text. If he had meant any of the words I once began to believe, if he knew me at all, if he really was distraught at having no choice but to end things. Then he would have made the time to call, explain, say he was sorry, make sure I was ok. So actually when he does tell me to fuck off again, a text is fine because he has shown already that I am not important enough, I know this now. A call would be condescending.

He challenges it, saying he does love me, he does miss me, I do matter, but ok if that is what I want, he wants to help me with my past and Misty, that he and Natasha are very unlikely to have sex, but if it happens he will be honest about it and yes, he would call me rather than text to end it.

Emily thinks I am insane, she is really angry, and she is on the warpath. She thinks I have positioned myself firmly at his front door for him to wipe his feet on me. She cannot believe I am even entertaining being there for him. She wants his phone number. She is **not** getting that.

One thing I know for certain is, no matter what happens between Sam and I, it will never be the same again. I will never feel the same again, never trust him as I did, never believe what he says, never feel safe with him again. I love him, but having hurt me, hurt me more than I think anyone ever has, I won't ever trust his words, feel safe or have belief.

The damage is done.

Chapter 32
Blue Monday

Blue Monday is the 3rd Monday in January, known as the most depressing day of the year. There is an actual mathematical equations for this:

The formula[1] uses many factors, including: weather conditions, debt level (the difference between debt accumulated and ability to pay), time since Christmas, time since new year's resolutions have been broken, low motivation levels, and the feeling of a need to take action.

$$\frac{(C \times R \times ZZ)}{((Tt + D) \times St)} + (P \times Pr) > 400$$

Where Tt = travel time; D = delays; C = time spent on cultural activities; R = time spent relaxing; ZZ = time spent sleeping; St =

time spent in a state of stress; P = time spent packing; Pr = time spent in preparation

For me, every day in January through to almost the end of March is a blue Monday. I remain none the wiser about what is going on with Sam, he blows hot and cold. Communicates then doesn't. Seems to want me and tire of me in equal measure.

Emily is literally screaming at me every time I see her, Misty lurking around every corner, grabbing me, hurting my wrists, screaming, telling me about her experiences which continue to shock and floor me. I have had to remove myself from the food shopping altogether to try and stem the erosion of what little money remains. I draft letters to the bank to request payment breaks and support (in case the Q4 marketing plan payments are delayed or don't come), I have very little sleep, Phil is down and depressed, Lottie stressed and anxious about her exams. Thomas is the only one, kind of OK and Ron of course, oh to be a dog.

Although I should, I don't message any old clients, I can't bring myself to do it and with Sam kind of lurking, it feels like I can't. It would feel like a betrayal.

Emily is seething "Betrayal? You fucking serious? You're his doormat Jess, who picks you up for advice and wank material when it suits **him**! What do you get from this? Get back to GW, feed your family, reduce at least one of the stresses in your life and GIVE ME HIS FUCKING NUMBER."

I still go out every morning and night just in case he wants to call, I still make sure I walk Ron at the time he will drive to his drumming lesson or he is at dancing with Beth, he never does call and never tells me he can't or won't.

A few times a week he does call on his way to or from work, usually just 10 mins before he is hitting the office or home. I don't know if it's winter or not, but the signal is so awful, it hardly works out, we spend more time hanging up and calling back saying 'hello, can you hear me' than we do actually talking.

Three's A Crowd

He never calls when going to drumming or when at Beth's dancing and he no longer lets me know his plans, or tries to coordinate with me so we can speak. Just occasionally a message or voice note saying 'I am in the car, if you are free? If not, it is OK.' He is not bothered about talking to me...he says...'it is OK.'

I dare not ask if he plans to be in touch, I just wait in the wings like a tit. On the back of my communications meltdown pre Snoop gate, it would be wrong. I know it is the last thing he needs with all that is going on, having me scream for attention. He will get to me when he can. I know this, but for months I still go out, just in case, I said I would be there for him, so I walk, often getting soaked to the skin. Each time is a clear reminder how little regard he has for me.

Yet I can't stop, I lap up every tit bit of attention bestowed upon me, which is sparse and hate myself for it. Any scrap thrown my way, I feverishly lick off the floor, and it allows me to continue.

One Monday late in January, we are talking on the phone and he can tell I am a bit strained, he parks up, instead of driving home and gives me his full attention for a full fifteen minutes, delaying him getting home and probably causing trouble for himself. It is the biggest gesture he has ever given me, he has never sacrificed his routine or plans for me, ***ever*** and I cling to it for a while, to balance the scales against all the actions that do the opposite. I thank him for it. I tell Emily, she sees it differently.

"For fuck's sake Jessie, wow impressive, really cares doesn't he!Give me his number!"

I defend him, reminding her how he is watched and how that may well have caused a problem at home and I don't want that for him.

I try to read between the lines, I ask questions about what is going on at home, and how Beth is. He avoids the questions. He clearly does not want me to know what is going on in his life and I feel the same. I have so many questions I would like to know about Snoop gate, but I can't ask, it feels selfish.

He mainly messages late at night, not for long before he signs off to read, ten minutes if I am lucky, it makes me think of the Olivia Rodrigo song 'Vampire', I listen to it while walking Ron to remind myself of his intentions and not to get sucked into him again. I am there to support him through this, that is all. Once things are repaired for him, I can make my exit, head held high that I treated him right. The lyrics in the song fit perfectly, he did sell me a forbidden paradise, I was stupid the signs were there, and he only came out at night.

Once in a while he messages during the day. I message him in the day, but a lot less than I used to, he reacts with emojis a few hours later. I still check my phone every fifteen minutes, just in case, I still hope notifications are not working and I will open up our messaging app to see messages from him. But notifications are working, he just has not messaged.

I tend to send filth, or silly fun things to try and cheer him up. But sometimes I forget my place and message about something that has upset me or I have a problem with. I realise and correct myself by deleting them. I do not want him knowing the ins and outs of my life any more.

I went to the January business networking meeting alone this month. It feels different without him, a Sam shaped hole in the room. I made some valuable connections and secured a new marketing client, well an initial meeting with them, so it was worth going to.

Some of my friends who have been pestering me for around 18 months to see them, are not taking no for an answer any more. Emily is not invited, no one likes her, so she doesn't hang in that group. I have to cave and go, I am out of excuses, I don't want to go. I have come to hate 'twee' nights out with other mums for a variety of reasons.

They all got old, really quick, now they are mums, it's like they have lost themselves, morphed into their own mothers, the conversation is dull, they moan about their husbands, or show off about

Three's A Crowd

their husbands. They all want to be home and in bed by 10 pm. They discuss homewares, crochet, Tupperware boxes, Scentsy candles parties, and who's meat is better, Lidl or Aldi.

I am more interested in whose meat is better among the husbands. But this audience is not open to that kind of chat.

It is a complete contrast to going out with Emily. She and I refuse to be so dull and become old. I don't want to wear long cardigans and the highlight of the day is taking your bra off. We are mum's not dead. OK, at the moment the best moment in my life is when I **do** get some sleep that is not haunted by dreams, but that is not a true reflection of me when life is 'normal', it's just because life is a bit of a mess and once sorted, I won't be taking up crochet.

Emily and I dance, drink, talk nonsense, be silly and have a proper laugh. I am a mum 24/7. If I get out I want to be me, truly me and forget about all the responsibilities of adulthood.

I reluctantly go along, but with no intentions of having a 'proper' night. It is in the next village and I can't afford a taxi, so I drive, drink water and do my best to enthuse about whether the local parent council should be charging £1 or £2 entry for the easter egg hunt or not.

I cake myself in makeup to hide my fatigue and head over. As soon as I walk in, I am cocooned in hugs, questions about life, I lie effectively. Then my friend Nicky pipes up:

"Jess, you're working too much? You look absolutely done in."

"Ha, good to see you too Nicky" I laugh.

But the other two girls jump on it and all three are then in deep probe on why I look so tired. They say it looks like I have lost a bit of weight, they want to know what's going on, am I really OK? Why have you got 6 hair bobbles on each wrist?

"Shit what's that, how did you hurt yourself?"

Shit shit shit, why did I come to this!

I tell them my marketing contracts have been slower than I would like and with Phil not working it's a bit of a worry. I explain I seem to be absent mindedly picking at my skin.

Kirsty, my friend, a pharmacist picked my brains on if I had tried anything to help me sleep. Warm baths, drink before bed, over the counter antihistamines or cough medicine. She quizzed me on just how much sleep I was actually getting.

I endure the rest of the night, my head visibly lulling and popping back up. Kirsty pulls me aside. She says:

"Jess take these" she hands me some benzodiazepines.

"I shouldn't and you didn't get them from me. I am giving you three. You can become dependent on them, they can make you woozy. Just take one, when you ***really*** need it, at least that way you will get some sleep. Text me let me know how it goes and if it works for you, go to your GP."

I thank her, I hope they do work, but I am not going to my GP. I will buy them privately if they work. GPs ask too many questions. I don't want them to know I am having dreams of my teen sexual attack, I don't want them to know I am scared about my stalker, I don't want to tell them I have no money, I don't want to tell them I was once a hooker, I don't want to tell them my heart is broken.

Finally, it is an acceptable time to leave and so I do, and once again they swarm me in a hug, begging me not to be a stranger.

Quick exchange with Sam, before he heads off to read. He tells me Natasha has agreed to counselling. So that is positive. He also challenges me on how I feel about him. He blows my mind when he does stuff like this. Why does he care? It doesn't matter how I feel about him. I play along, and by that I mean, I am not lying, I do love and want him with all my heart, but I am desperately trying not to (I don't tell him that bit). It hurts too much. I ***want*** to walk away, but I know I am the only one he can talk to about what is going on, and I said I would support him. Then some filth exchange, he has what he needs, and he takes himself off to read.

The final few weeks of January bring five events. Phil has a second interview, we are all holding our breath. It is Beth's birthday. Then Sam's, then Thomas. I have an afternoon workshop to go to with a business guru. It cost me a few hundred, but it will be

Three's A Crowd

worth the investment. Sam was thinking of coming along too before everything went 'Pete Tong.'

I message Sam on Beth's birthday wishing her a happy birthday, he is surprised I remembered and says it was a bit fraught with an over-emotional child. Natasha and he are both sad, as depending on how things go, it could be her last birthday with them together as a family. My heart breaks for them all.

Phil puts his heart and soul into prepping for the assessment centre and gets pipped to the post on his psychometric testing by about 3 points. We go for a long walk and discuss it, letting him vent, me geeing him up.

He ***will*** get his break, but I also very gently tell him how close we are to the end of the line and literally any money in right now is essential, suggesting delivery driver work, stacking shelves, and the odd jobs he has been doing. He knows there is no choice, he can no longer after 24 months of being out of work, preserve his CV, he has to get something to help us put food on the table, so he heads home and fires up the computer and begins the search. I nip out and use the cash I was going to spend on some new thongs for me (as they are literally falling apart) to get him a cheesecake from the shop, one he loves. I wanted him to know, I know he is trying and to keep going. He appreciates it. So do the kids. Who needs pants anyway right?!

I head off to my guru meeting, all fired up, what I take away at this could really help me learn some strategies to grow my business faster. God knows I need to grow it faster. With a tired foggy brain, I check the venue, punch the postcode into my phone and head off. I arrive and walk into reception with fifteen minutes to spare. Then the receptionist told me there is no such event here today.

SHIT!

I search my emails, the confirmation email has this address, I fire off a text to the organiser. No reply... I searched more of my emails, damn, damn, damn, in small writing at the bottom of the one I got yesterday reminding me to attend the event, is a change of venue. It is twenty minutes in the other direction. That is not too bad, I will be maybe five minutes late, it could have been worse.

I walk out the hotel doors and coming in are three teens in tracksuits, one of them bumps into my shoulder as he passes, nearly sending me to the floor. Honestly, teens don't look where they are going, their heads are fixated on their phones. I climb into the car, put in the new postcode and head off.

I drive a little faster than I should, cursing myself for not being more thorough. I ramp up the car heater as I notice myself shivering with the cold.

As I glide out of the slip road onto the motorway I look in my rear view mirror and am greeted with cold, icy, distressed eyes staring back at me, I swerve nearly losing control of the car.

Misty

"FUCK! Misty, what the hell."

"You haven't been listening, you said you would" she says.

"Jesus christ."

"You have to listen now, you can't keep me out, you can't walk away."

I am scanning the road signs to see how far to the next junction, eight miles, shit, I could pull into a lay-by, but then what?! What do I do with a teen in my car?

She places her hands on my head from the back seat and I try to move my head away, the car swerves wildly as I do.

"Misty, no, not now, I am driving."

"I have no choice, you push me away all the other times, I can't hold this all in any longer."

I realise it is impossible, I let her place her icy hands on either side of my head, and I feel the cold radiate across my ears and cheeks and creep down my neck into my chest. I try and keep my eyes firmly fixed on the road:

Saturday at home

Three's A Crowd

Everyone out go for a run get home
James and Mark on doorstep
Sneak to garage, open it - hope not seen get to safety that way
Neighbour shouts
'You've got friends at the door"
James and Mark hear, come to the garage
"'I'm, I'm really busy"
"Wrong answer, now don't make a scene, invite us in!"
"I've a film to watch "
They laugh - close the garage door darkness
"Lead the way." into the kitchen
"You can't keep doing this, I don't like it, please can you just leave me alone, in fact please just leave or I'll call the police."
Laughing.
"I mean it!"
"Not your decision." try to get to the phone grabbed
"You can't...think about it, your neighbour saw you welcome us in, no one will believe you."
Mark eats grapes from the fruit bowl
"Don't you think we should teach her that she doesn't get to make decisions?"
"Yeah, let's make it a game, see how smart she is!"
"I like it"
"Wanna play?"
"No"
James walks around grabs my hair
Slap
"Uh uh-wrong answer, you see that's not your decision!" face stings
"We're going to have to make this really fucking simple, I'm going to give you choices, think very carefully before you answer, it will be a multi-choice, but you get to decide... ok?"
I stare
"Fucks sake, it's not a hard question, do you understand I'm

going to give you some options - you get to decide? Choose wisely. This is a gift, you get to choose, won't happen again."

Silence

Bangs his fist on the breakfast bar,

"OK, OK."

"Good, now, where do you want us to fuck you? On a bed or on the sofa?"

"Neither," I whisper.

Hand on my neck walks me back against the Fridge.

"Ungrateful bitch, we've given up our Saturday, I didn't say there was a third option, so fucking choose!"

James comes

Marks holding me against the fridge feeling my breasts squeezing

It hurts.

"Sofa"

Releases my neck grabs my hair

Bangs my head against the fridge.

"Dumb fuck, that's wrong - correct answer is -where ever we fucking want!"

"Try again-do you want to lay on the floor, I can jack hammer your mouth with my dick, or stay here and I fuck you against the fridge?"

"Here"

James now stripped from waist pulled my vest down

Breasts lifted out

Pinches squeezes

Head slams on fridge

"Wrong again, If I fucked you like this I'd have to look at you and who'd want that- fuck sake is there a single brain cell in your fucking skull?"

Head slammed again

"I've got one" James stroking his cock "Who's dick is better? Mine or Marks?"

Three's A Crowd

Silence
Head slams on fridge again
"Answer the fucking question"
"That's not a choice, it's an opinion" I whisper slam again.
"Don't get fucking smart'."
"I don't know, I don't know, I don't know"
Crying now
"Jesus, it's mine you bitch"
Mark 'play' punches James , laughing.
"OK, last choice, when sucking cock, do you spit or swallow?"
I know this one
"Swallow" Slam again.
"You don't fucking get it, if we say spit, you spit, if we say swallow, you swallow, if we say let us in, you let us in, on your knees, down you go -there is no choice, you don't get to make the decisions. Because you get it wrong. And when you get it wrong, you turn us off. So keep your stupid ideas to yourself. Got it?"
I nod
Pulled off fridge by hair dragged to hall
Thrown to ground land hands and knees
Arms kicked from under me legs pulled out
Flat on belly
Yanks off my trainers, pulls down cycling shorts pulls down pants
Drops his trousers
Full weight on top of me hammers me - cums
James next
"Best way to fuck an ugly bitch" laughing
Trousers pulled up leave
Carpet burns on knees, hips and elbows
Shower
Stings
PJ's
Watch Anne of Green Gables

She releases her hands from my head and leans back on the seat, closes her eyes and softly sobs.

I can hardly see the road, my eyes thick and coated in tears, I am struggling to hold the steering wheel and keep it under control, my entire body shaking uncontrollably.

I don't know what to say, silence fills the car, just the sounds of her muffled sobs and my sniffs.

I am not on the motorway any more, I don't recall coming off, I see a Tesco up ahead and pull into the car park. I park.

"Misty, I am so sorry."

"Did you feel it? Do you see?" She asks, her voice strained.

"I feel it, but you went through it, it's good you tried to call the Police, we could do that."

Misty sighs heavily and lets out a whimper like a wounded animal.

"You still don't see."

"I see you are being constantly attacked, you need help, you're hurting and they were cruel, so bitterly cruel."

As I say those words my heart stabs, my head hurts, fierce banging and I grab my head in my hands, moan in distress and pain. Sick swirls in my stomach, threatening to rise up. I quickly open the car door and lean outside retching. Nothing comes, it's what my mother would call a dry boak. I fold back into the car and close the door. Glance into the rear view mirror to check on Misty and see if I can get anything else from her, but she has gone. My heart sinks, the thought of her alone, carrying the weight of this and maybe facing an attack at any moment makes the sickness swirl again.

I glance at the clock. SHIT! 1:20pm, I am twenty minutes late for the workshop and actually have no clue where I am. I grab my phone and am puzzled by what I see. The route has a 'U' turn sign, thirty three minutes to my destination. I am way off to the east of where I need to be, I must have driven right past it and ended up here.

Three's A Crowd

In a panic, thinking how much I have spent on this workshop, I will miss almost the first hour I could scream. I bang the car in gear and speed off, tyres screeching, following the map guidance. I absentmindedly record a voice note to Sam telling him what has happened. What the fuck am I doing! I delete it and record a less dramatic version of events and send, just telling him I was annoyed as late for this workshop, as I had been distracted thinking about Misty and zoned out. I have to send something, as the stupid app shows when you have deleted something and he usually asks what I have deleted and pushes until he gets the truth out of me. Although one of the good changes that has happened between us, is he does this a lot less. Thank fuck. I mean you delete stuff because you don't want the other person to read or hear it, so why ask?

Truth is I don't want to tell him anything. I am the one who set the rule, no Misty chat and I have broken my own rule. Sometimes I absolutely hate myself.

I make it to the venue six minutes faster than my phone said, get parked, fix my running make-up and dash in at 1:57 pm.

I have mainly missed the introductions and goals of the workshop, plus one section on strategy but not the bulk of it. I do my best to focus and engage but, I am still reeling which makes it hard to take in the information. I am cursing myself for being such an idiot, getting the venue wrong, and then not focusing on the road. I must read things properly, at the moment I just seem incapable of things I used to do with ease. As I am half listening to the presentation, my mind wanders. How the hell did Misty know I would be where I was? What if I had **not** got the venue wrong? It makes no sense and a shiver runs over me.

When the event ends and I head to the car, I check for messages from Sam, to my surprise Sam has listened to my voice note, left a sad face emoji and a reply:

FFS

Lottie is in a mess when I get home, she is stressing about how much she has to do. I sat with her and let her spew her concerns out. Then start tackling it bit by bit. We focus on the things that are in her control, and make an action plan for each. Ninety minutes later she is calmer, I can tell she is exhausted. We watch a girly series together so she can switch off from studying, Thomas hides in his room as he is not interested and Phil tolerates it. She goes to bed more settled and is like a different girl in the morning.

Sam messages later, asking about the workshop and if it was useful, I send him the slides as I knew he had wanted to go. He doesn't ask about or dig deeper on my venue disaster or deleted voice note, and he has been honouring my request not to say he loves me, as per my rules.

Exhausted from the day's events I try one of Kirsty's sleeping tablets, I am out like a light and sleep all night, but am woken in the morning with a grogginess that doesn't lift all day and violent vomiting. I have two left, I don't know if that is a one off, but these were side effects I was warned about. I decide to only take the other two in times of absolute desperation.

Life follows a similar pattern for the following weeks, jobs hunts and homers for Phil, Lotties exams, rugby games for Thomas, Emily demanding I 'ditch the cunt,' Misty turning up at the wrong moment, Mensa level financial gymnastics, sporadic and unpredictable contact with Sam, checking WhatsApp to see if someone somewhere still wants me, they do.

Thomas's birthday is as good as it can be, Mum has given me some money to help with him having a party at the laser quest which he loves, I contribute some, to top it up. This is the bulk of his gift, so he has little to open on the day, a new rugby ball, some socks and a Nike top from Vinted.

Sam's birthday, I can't do much for, there is no talk of us ever seeing each other again, I can't post anything, he had to bin all his Christmas gifts as Natasha found them, it's too risky. I just made him a daft video, with me singing, 'happy' and 'birthday' written on each tit, 'Sam' written on my cunt, and me curling up to reveal a lit candle up my ass which I blew out. That was a bit of a logistical nightmare to film and took several takes and near misses with setting the house on fire. It seemed to make him smile.

Sometimes he is very late sending a message at night, as every 4-7 days, a small domestic thing or comment, causes a tsunami of emotions from Natasha, understandably. So they sit up talking, I have been tracking the blow ups and the gaps between each are lengthening, demonstrating to me that things, although horrendous are heading in the right direction for him.

They go over the same stuff each time, make some agreements and conclusions, then back to square one at the next blow up. Sam is walking on eggshells, and doesn't know whether he is coming or going. They have a date for an initial consultation with a marriage counsellor.

My mind races with what he is saying to Natasha. I imagine it is that he loves her, that she matters, that he misses her, that he cannot be without her, that they can make the sky blue again.

I am just in a holding pattern, I can't leave him, because despite the hurt he has caused me, I can't turn off how I feel. It is not like we have any form of relationship any more, but I don't seem to be able to close the door. I am just waiting for air traffic control to give the green light to him landing his marriage and ushering me off the plane, wishing me a safe onward journey.

One morning on the phone, he breaks the rule, says he doesn't care if he is not allowed to say it, but he is going to 'he loves me'. Another slash to my heart.

I conclude I need to give myself a kick and properly accept where we are, we always connected sexually like no one I have ever met before, I will keep my life and feelings to myself, but enjoy the sexual thrill of our filth chat and wank to it, I haven't stopped, he is a main feature in my wanks.

Even if I'm watching porn, I imagine it is him, doing whatever to me. So I may as well enjoy the distanced sex chat and do all I can to support him rebuilding his family and finding happiness again. That way I cause him no problems, I am a release for him, and he is for me. I get to be part of the solution, not the problem. Just like when I was selling my fuck holes. I help rebuild the life I destroyed, then I will be asked to exit stage left.

Chapter 33

Play Dates without Lego

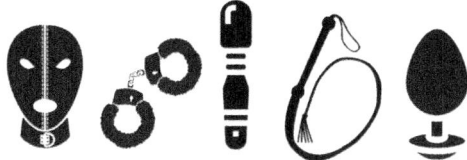

There are very few things I have not experienced sexually, I have never been faithful. I have wanted to be. If someone had ever really wanted me I would have been the most loyal person ever. When younger I only had two proper boyfriends, one drifted due to us moving to different towns, I was not faithful with him, the other dumped me. With Phil I was good for the first decade, apart from when in difficult positions with work where I had to have sex with people who put me in situations where there was no option.

I was faithful for maybe the first five years of the kids' lives when I, like so many of my fellow mums, lost myself while learning the ropes of being a mother.

After that I found myself in more difficult positions again, but I also actively pursued hook-ups. I couldn't cope with no sex, I felt utterly unwanted and discarded by Phil. I felt and still do feel horrendous guilt. It doesn't make it right and I know I am going to the bad fire. I have made my peace with that, it may even be better than my life at the moment.

Sam's theory is I am hyper-sexual. Mine is, I just need to feel like I have some worth even if fleeting.

My sex life until my mid-thirties had been relatively tame, so what people refer to as vanilla. But everything I looked at was much more extreme and kinky. I even recall as a young child being turned on by Princess Leia in chains and James Bond being rough with the women.

Nothing turned me on more than some BDSM and very rough porn. So I made a promise to myself I would not be on my deathbed filled with regret for not pursuing it. Why should Phil's decision to not engage with sex mean I never would again? I wanted to experience it for real, not through a screen.

As a result and combined with my hooker years, I have been; restrained, suspended, whipped, caned, spanked, paddled, belted, zapped, flogged, gagged, blindfolded, degraded, humiliated, set tasks, denied, drank piss, been pissed on and in, spit-roasted, airtight, gang bangs, FFM, FFMMM. I have used nipple clamps, nipple weights, weights on my labia, suction cups, pussy pumps, dildo's, vibrators, wands, butt plugs. I have dressed up and role played.

I have had bruises and welts, broken skin, and red stripes. I have written lines, learnt poses, followed commands and learnt all about the BDSM community and understood the need for safe words and aftercare. Although that goes out the window often in a paid set up and hookup environment.

I have learnt a lot of acronyms, in the escorting world:

A-level: Anal sex (also known as greek)

Aftercare: process of attending to one another after intense feelings of a physical or psychological nature relating to BDSM activities

ATM: Ass to mouth, anal sex immediately followed by oral

AR: Anal rimming refers to licking of the the anal area

BB or BBS: Bareback / Bareback sex, vaginal or anal sex without a condom

BBBJ: Bare back blow job without a condom BBBJTC: Bare back blow job to completion

BBW: Big beautiful woman, refers to women who are voluptuous or curvaceous

BBC: Big black cock

BWC: Big white cock

B & D: Bondage and discipline

BDSM: Bondage, discipline, domination, submission, sadism, masochism,

Bondage: Refers to activities involving tying up or restraining of one partner

BJ: Blow job,

BJTC: Blow job to completion, giving oral sex until the client cums; with or without a condom

BLS: Ball licking and sucking

Brat: A Submissive who likes being cheeky to encourage being put in their place

BS: Body slide. A service provider slides their naked body over the client's, often with the aid of oil or gel.

CBJ: Covered blow job refers to oral sex with a condom

CBT: Cock and ball torture, a BDSM sexual activity that involves torture or inflicting pain on genitals - **I never did this.**

CD: Cross dressing, may involve client or service provider dressing as a different gender during a booking - **I never did this.**

CIM: Cum in mouth without a condom

CIMWS: Cum in mouth with swallowing

COF / COB: Cum on face/cum on breasts/cum on body;

DP: Double penetration, either penetrating two orifices at once which may include two people, or penetration of one orifice with two things. **I never did this. Tried but my holes don't seem to manage double.**

DFK: Deep french kissing, passionate kissing with tongues

DT: Deep throat

Dom/Sub: One partner is dominant the other submissive

Facial: Ejaculating on a face

Filming: Filming or recording of a sexual act - **rarely allowed this to happen for obvious reasons.**

Fire and ice: Refers to applying hot and cold sensations, either directly to the genitals or via the mouth during oral sex.

Fisting: Penetration of a whole hand inside the vagina or anus - tried and failed

FK: French kissing

Foot fetish: A sexual desire and gratification focused on feet or shoes, may involve a foot job or kissing and licking of toes

Foot job: Similar to a hand job but performed with feet,

Funishment: a punishment both parties find fun, not as extreme as punishment

Gagging: Gagging or choking on an erect penis or sometimes fingers

GFE: Girlfriend experience, acting like a girlfriend; sensual, friendly, cuddly.

GS: Golden shower, urinating on body or in mouth

Happy ending: Hand job after massage

Hard limit: Something someone does not want to do ever. **One of mine would be scat.**

HJ: Hand Job, hand relief

Italian: Rubbing penis between buttocks

MILF: Mother I'd like to fuck.

MFF: Male Female Female, threesome

MMF: Male Male Female threesome

M/S: Master Slave

NSA: No strings attached, no serious relationships, just a hook-up

OWO: Oral without, a blow job without a condom

Pegging: Using a strap-on dildo to have anal sex with a partner - One of the few things I said no to if asked to deliver on a male, but I have been pegged myself by a more dominant female.

PSE: Porn star experience - rough sex, dirty talk, deep throating/gagging and spanking.

Three's A Crowd

R&T: Rub and tug, massage with hand relief Rimming: Licking around the the anus Russian: Rubbing the penis between breasts

Safe words: Agreed words and actions to allow communication between partners to slow or stop proceedings if needed.

Scat: Being sexually aroused by Jobby - **hard limit!**

Snowballing: The act of transferring semen or cum from one person's mouth to another

Soft limit: Something you're prepared to be pushed on or at least try.

Spanish: Rubbing the penis between breasts,

Squirting: Also known as female ejaculation or g-spot ejaculation.

Sub Drop: an emotional and physical low, that begins anywhere from a few hours to a few days after an emotional/endorphin high and can last hours to weeks.

Tea bagging: Placing balls in the mouth or on the face of a partner

Toy show: A masturbation show using sex toys including vibrators

Tromboning: kneels behind the client and licks their anus while masturbating their erect penis

TTM: Testicular tongue massage

TPE: Total power exchange - one partner gives all control to the other sexually and otherwise, often all aspects of their life.

The list is way longer than this, but these are the main things. People refer to more extreme sexual encounters as a 'scene' they can be planned in detail or a rough outline and more go with the flow.

Interacting in this way also is referred to as play. So you can do things like slap, whip and be verbally degraded under the protection of 'playing', knowing it is ring fenced, and not applicable outside of that set up. I guess to protect people emotionally. Like some people like being told they are ugly, but it's purely used sexually and not necessarily true. So doing it within play does no harm, it has been agreed. That would be a hard limit for me, I would not see that as play.

All of this is the adult equivalent of children's play dates, just fewer Lego and Pokemon cards and more whips and chains.

Sam and I have discussed kinks and experiences a lot. Plus hopes and desires sexually and it is good getting back to that in recent weeks. A welcome and pussy pulsating delight.

It took some time to fully open up, but once we did, it became comfortable, there is nothing off limits for discussion.

Talking openly with Sam about sexual kinks has been one of the most liberating experiences of my life. There's something so freeing about being able to share my deepest, most intimate desires without feeling any fear or judgement. With him, I don't have to second-guess myself or worry about being misunderstood. It's like I can finally be myself in a way I never have before.

Knowing that he feels the same way, that he feels safe discussing his own desires and fantasies , only served to deepen the sexual connection between us in a way I never thought possible. There's a level of vulnerability there, a mutual trust that feels rare. We can be completely honest with each other.

That kind of connection, where you can explore the most private parts of yourself and know the other person is right there with you, feels like nothing I've ever experienced before. It's powerful, intimate, and something I treasure deeply.

A lot of that is down to him, credit where credit is due, he has not accepted surface level answers and probed as deeply with his questions as he does with his cock.

We have both fantasised about if, in another life, we were able to be together, and how daily life would be. I have some voice notes from him where he describes how he would treat me if I was in his life and what his expectations would be. He paints a picture of my dream life and I wank to them regularly.

Sam is not completely on board with my dream life, but I have been able to express it and he understands it. I can't tell anyone else in the world because it is so badly frowned upon these days. I want a return to more defined gender roles. This desire has become even stronger since all the stress of the last few years.

My dream would be to be 'just' a partner and mother, I don't bring money in, I just serve my man. All I have to worry about is keeping the house clean, trying to look pretty and servicing his cock. His standards would be high, and I would be punished if they were not met.

I know this is frowned upon as women have fought so hard to earn an equal footing in society, but now in my opinion it has gone too far the other way. Women want it all and then complain juggling it all, and lose their sexual enthusiasm as they are exhausted.

I want to be protected, looked after and thoroughly used, without the stresses of life, a tool to help my man cope with the stresses of his life. Basically a TPE (total power exchange). I struggle to make decisions and having someone who I know has my best interests at heart doing that for me, would make things easier for me. I might learn a hobby to entertain dinner guests like playing piano, making cocktails, or sucking the cock of my man's boss to aid a promotion.

This is seen as a misogynistic kink similar to life in the 1950s where the man is seen as dominant and authoritative, and the woman is submissive, subservient, and expected to adhere to strict rules of femininity. The man is the undisputed head of the family, superior, making decisions and enforcing rules. Sexual consent is given once and then lasts for infinity for the man, anytime, anyplace, anywhere, however, he wishes. I would be inferior but have an important role to play and I would be happy, happier than I am now. I would be owned, obedient, and controlled. But cared for.

Having dived into the world of hookups and sex work, the

patriarchy lives strong, so many men wish for this, but society does not allow it. It is a hidden underworld.

If I could find the Delorean, I would set the clock to 1953 and never come back.

Sam too thinks that what women want and then in reality can manage has become a bit skewed. But he is much more on board with today's rules around consent and respect. I don't care about those, and he cannot get his head around that.

He constantly checks I am choosing to do things because **I** want to, not just to please him. He doesn't understand that pleasing him is half the kink.

One frustration and challenge of our meetings to date is that within a hotel you can't really go full pelt on a BDSM scene. He watches some pretty sadistic porn, both in terms of delivering pain and totally degrading and humiliating the women. We have played with that, but only a little so far, as you can't have a wailing screaming woman in a hotel room.

In the past he has said he struggles with hurting me, sending me home, driving in pain and suffering when he can't be there to check on me and deliver the appropriate aftercare. He is in a constant battle between what he wants sexually and what society says is the right way to treat a woman. They are at odds with each other. Much the same way as me enjoying receiving pain, society says I shouldn't, logically it makes no sense. I both love and hate it. But my pussy loves it a lot and as usual, my pussy always wins.

He also does not understand why I enjoy pain. He constantly asks me to explain it.

I don't understand why he enjoys delivering pain. I don't feel we have to understand it, not all kinks have to have a reason and being opposite we will never truly get it, as we are each other's ying to the yang.

If I say I want it done, and he wants to deliver it, I don't see the issue. It ticks his consent box. If we do see each other again, it will never be anywhere other than a hotel, so unless he grows a pair and beats my ass, we will never get to go as far as we both want. It's sad we have found someone we can be this open with, both into the same thing and yet we will never experience it properly together.

I have never had the proper aftercare either, as all my experiences were either paid or hookups, so mostly a few hours, occasionally an overnight. I can handle pain and I like the after-glow of having sore bits, it reminds me of the time I had. He can't get his head around it. In an alternative reality or perhaps the next life, I would love to live with someone who shares these interests and it can be explored within the confines of a relationship. Sam says that is how it should be done. That chance is not possible, so I will take what I can, which is how I have ended up in positions like I did in Doncaster. If that had been Sam, I could have spoken up, knowing he would stop and care for me.

He also thinks there is some kind of sinister, 'punishing myself', reason behind it due to my 'sexual trauma' as a teen. I wonder if he will ever believe me when I say, I got over that a long time ago and it is all just kinks I enjoy.

One of the best parts about being an escort was all the people you met, with their weird and wonderful kinks. One of my favourite parts of the job was not making them feel odd about their requests.

One of the worst feelings in the world is opening up about something and someone not believing you, being shocked, disgusted or judgemental. I would never make someone feel like that. So I was a kink friendly service and provided it wasn't illegal, scat, me being totally naked or resulting in permanent damage I could not explain at home. I would do anything and through that I met and experienced all sorts.

A guy that loved armpits and wanking into them, wetting myself, behaving like an animal, public exposure, tit tiers. The list is actually endless, but not once did I ever make any of them feel bad or that they were wrong.

These are just kinks, if I can be the person that does that for someone, makes them feel accepted, and they 'get off', then that is pretty special, that is superhero slut stuff. Being brave enough to show what you really want and who you really are and having someone accept that.

It's a play date, have fun.

I mean what's the big deal? Wetting my pants as an act does nothing for me sexually, I wouldn't watch porn of it and get off. But it's the mind fuck, it is humiliating and the bit where I know I am degrading myself to turn someone else on, is the magic button for me, knowing I am making them hard, that they want me. Hating yourself for what you're doing but your body betraying you by getting sloppy.

Pissing yourself can be cleaned up, but giving someone the gift of acceptance lasts a lifetime. I never in my wildest dreams when I signed up to GW thought I would get a single booking. I like to think my profile made me sound approachable allowing these people to get what they needed in the same way I needed to feel valued.

I accept Sam and his kinks, hell I embrace Sam and his kinks, as they are literally tailor-made for me. No one has ever had such a charged electric impact on me sexually.

If he decides he wants to see me again, I will enjoy every second of Sam and his kinks.

Long live kink!

Chapter 34

The Subtle art of shooting yourself in the Foot - By Jessie Newkirk

It is now well into February and entering the twelfth week since I saw Sam and zero mention by him of us actually seeing each other. I understand, to a point, things are still very tense at his home, although blow-ups have extended to around eleven days apart. I reminded him pre Valentine's day to do something for Natasha, and he did, flowers delivered to her work which she was thrilled with.

They have had their first counselling session too, and it seemed to go reasonably well. No mass fights, just quite an honest grown up adult discussion focusing on how over the years they have drifted. I was hardly mentioned, it was more on all the stuff that went wrong before, Sam mentioned he had been 'talking to someone else' but that was it.

All the things that happened to cause them to drift which led to Sam eventually booking escorts (not that she knows that) is exactly where the conversation needs to be. It is the only way they can stand a chance of moving forward. It sounds like some fault was admitted on both sides. So with the initial consultation done, they will be on the waiting list for the proper sessions to start.

Natasha has spoken to Sam saying she wants 'wooed', but won't tell him what that looks like, he is a bit frustrated, he wants to give her what she wants but is not sure what that even means, and she refuses to expand on it.

Honestly, women are their own worst enemies, they don't half-play games and expect men to be mind readers.

They are still in separate bedrooms, he is convinced that will be how it is now. He has shared that the in-laws are coming to stay soon though, to look after Beth so he and Natasha can go to some lecture she bought for him as a gift last year. Natasha has said he can come back into the bedroom for that, as she does not want her mother knowing what is going on. It's a few weeks away yet, Sam is convinced it will be two nights only, and he will be turfed out again. He says it will be the night before so the spare bed is ready and the night they are out.

I know that will be him back in the marital bed permanently. It is clear she is of the same view as Sam, if she was going, she would have gone, but they share the common goal of doing their best for Beth. Parents sleeping in separate bedrooms would be confusing for Beth, the separate beds will end. So like Sam, Natasha is going to try and work through this for her daughter.

My birthday comes and goes. The kids make me cards and both write a lovely paragraph each that makes me cry. Mum sends me some cash, which I blow on the kids and that makes me very happy. Phil helps the kids blow up balloons the night before and a happy birthday banner, I get a melon with candles in it, they know I don't want cake. Sam sends me a few birthday gifs on messages.

As is the way when you turn 48, it's just another day and passes relatively unnoticed, the way I prefer it.

Natasha's challenge to Sam has played on my mind, I don't feel he is capable of it, and it feels too important not to at least try and help. He has chosen to work on things, but seems unable to work out how to make things better. My fear is with no effort nothing will improve for him.

Three's A Crowd

Natasha is a challenge to impress, she can be cold and Sam has been burnt in the past with doing the wrong thing. If he is going to stay in this life for the next 40 years, then I want him to make it as happy as possible. That won't happen unless he can 'woo' her and convince her he is sorry and get back to a loving relationship, remember why they fell in love with each other. They need to revisit why that was.

Inevitably life takes over and couples get lost in duty and the hamster wheel of life. Taking time to show you care gets forgotten. He needs to start acting like he is head over heels in love with her and will do anything to win her. He needs to act as if he has just met her and put that level of effort in. Make her feel that she is too important, and he will fight until his dying breath to win her back. That is what she wants, she wants to feel like he is so sorry, he can't live without her, and he will kill himself trying to prove that point.

I spent a couple of hours jotting down some ideas. I make some of them the more obvious stuff that most blokes do and know, and most women seem to love. I combine it with some more creative, wow ideas. I came up with forty-three ideas. If he did one a week, he would fill the year with woo's and wows, showing consistent and persistent determination.

I send the document to him, praying it helps him:

Sam,

So many ideas for this - Some will cost a little bit, some free or time based. You know her best, so tweak and adapt as needed. And of course completely ignore. But I do hope this helps.

Your goal as you know is to make her feel special. Like she is the only woman in the world for you and to prove to her just how sorry you are. Show her you recognise all the things that made you head over heels for her originally. And help her remember all the amazing fun, fond and intimate moments you've had together.

This will show her you remember and treasure them too. For me, and I am not sure if I'm different, but it's things that require thought, effort and time, mean more than gifts. She values family and quality time so that's where to focus. Some of this may be out of your comfort zone & feel uncomfortable, but if you want to win her back. **Do** the uncomfortable. You may enjoy it, have fun with it.

1. Little handwritten notes in places she will find them throughout the day. Not everyday, so she doesn't come to expect them. But where she least expects but you know she'll find them. e.g. on her pillow before she goes to bed, or before she wakes. Inside the cup she uses for tea, next to her toothbrush, make up. Resting on her car dash in front of the speedometer, in her purse next to the card she uses. In her lunch box. You get the idea. Ideas for content of messages?

- Moments you've had together
- Remember when...'
- 'in-jokes or sayings'
- 'one thing I've never told you, that I love about you is...'
- ' Memorable dates'
- How you miss, x, y, z and will work to get it back and prove it!
- I'm sure you get the idea.

2. Make a wee video like I did for you, pictures, from when you first met all the way to now put to a song that means something to you both. Add some fun pictures or meaningful pictures or sayings as text. End with a slide saying 'I love you and I'll fight not to lose this'. Or something like that.

Three's A Crowd

3. You two must have a special place or a place you all go on a walk frequently. Find a tree or stone and carve a heartfelt message into it. Something like.' The only girl that matters is Natasha Miller'. Or Beth and Sam and Natasha forever. Or Natasha Miller= Soulmate/love of my life/ beautiful - Whatever resonates with you. And then surprise her on the walks, so it's discovered.
    - Quick aside, don't be put off if she is nasty back or snippy or it seems that you're banging your head against a brick wall. You have to keep going no matter how tough - she will eventually melt.

4. Team up with Beth or surprise both Natasha and Beth with a 'yes' day. Always fun! Leave them a note at the breakfast table explaining they can ask you for anything and you have to say yes. You could either have a word with Beth the day before, say I'd like to spoil and surprise mummy, will you help me? Then Natasha gets the note in the morning and Beth has to say yes to everything she requests too. Rule is, it can't cost money or be illegal. It can be as silly as jumping on one foot, barking like a dog to make me a cup of tea, her movie choice etc

5. Another one to recruit Beth for. Together you come up with some things that make mummy special. Write them out between you (hand written not typed) more effort. Hide them around the house, all on the same coloured paper or play the warmer colder thing until she finds them all.

6. Speak to her secretary at work. Find out a day/ time that you could surprise her at work. Take a picnic full of her favourite foods or book a restaurant. Get her secretary to time block her diary and turn up and surprise her. Give her a small thoughtful gift too. A

really cool thing I saw you can get on Etsy, is a keyring with a sound wave, you scan it with your phone, it opens Spotify & in it would be a playlist of songs that mean something to you both. Make her a playlist of songs from your time together.

7. One for a few weeks/month time, visit or call her mum and say you've not been making time for each other, ask for her to either come and babysit or have Beth overnight and then book a table and take her out. Maybe a gift of some pretty earrings to go with a dress you love her in that you've picked out for her to wear.

8. Book something for her and her mum to do together, afternoon tea? Spa afternoon? Nails done? You'll know better than me what they'd both enjoy.

9. Put together a small pamper box, scented candles, face mask, body cream, bottle of wine, a new book, make it pretty in a basket or leave it on her bed with a thoughtful note.

10. Along the same lines, but you and Beth collaborate. You buy or make genie hats and when she gets up one Sunday, say today we are genie's 'it's a spoil mummy day'. Everything she wishes for will be done.

11. Another Beth and Sam collaboration, or just do it on your own. Find old video clips, photos of times together and of special places. Both record messages as voiceovers and make a ten minute movie all about how amazing and special she is. Make it funny. I don't know the humour you guys all have together but maybe, mummy is special because her farts smell like roses. We love her, lots of fun sound bites. Then one sat night say Beth requested a movie night, get out the popcorn etc and surprise her with this movie.

12. Find photos from the start all the way to now and print them. Special happy ones. Make a scrapbook with

dates - a short soundbite written about each special day.
13. Contact her best mate Laura. Plan a girl's day out. Train to meet her or get Laura to come to you as a surprise. Girls lunch out, spa/massage/ shopping etc
14. Visit love book online.com. I made one of these for my kids, it's so lovely. You design the characters so they look like you all. And choose the one called 'all the reasons I love you!' It's not super cheap, but very very thoughtful. leave on her bed. You can add a lovely page saying please read this if we ever fight. That way you remember exactly how I feel about you. leave a note with the book saying something like - I know I've messed up, but here is why you're worth fighting for and I know it.
15. In top of the pops style, do a Top 10 favourite moments with Natasha. Make a pretty pdf counting from 10 to 1 with a bit of DJ spiel for each and email it to her when she's at work.
16. Sit and write a handwritten letter on nice paper and cover how sorry you are, how special she is, and what you're willing to do to make things work. Again maybe just me, but in a day and age where everything is instantly consumed, quick and easy to communicate, there is something really special about someone taking time (because it does take longer) to write and knowing that every word has been handwritten, with no other IT distractions. They can only focus on you when someone writes.
17. Visit Africa-greeting.com/products/greeting - these are fun.
18. You first met up at a lake right? Go visit that place all together. Retell the story all about how you felt when you first saw her and what happened in front of Beth.

19. Make March - 'Mad March' epic for special memorable places that will bring back fun memories. Declare it mad March, we're marching back in time and you go visit those places all together and reminisce.
20. Buy some clay, or balloons and make paper mache and have a craft afternoon of making a statue of one another. Pull names from a hat, so maybe you end up making Natasha, Natasha makes Beth and Beth makes you.
21. Do you have a wedding video? Maybe not now, but when things are calmer, watch it or make a shortened edit of it and WhatsApp it to her. Saying it was the best decision you ever made.
22. She likes yoga right? Anything you can do with that?
23. Do her a fun, heartfelt poem. If you're stuck, I can help.
24. Leave Scrabble messages, I'm sorry, I'll be better, I love you, I'm an idiot, please forgive me, in random places.
25. Buy her some nice socks when you go to marriage counselling & before you go in, give them to her, with a note saying...'If you give me a second chance, I am going to knock your socks off.' Or 'let's not lose each other in the washing machine, we are a pair, meant for each other.'
26. Unroll the toilet roll in her bathroom, and write 'I'm sorry I made you feel crap. Let me clean up the shit' and roll it back up.
27. Give her some band-aids with a note, I know I've hurt you and these won't fix it, How can I make it better?
28. Write a message in morse code, she has to decipher, include how much you love her, regret everything and will work until you die to fix it, send it to her and say it's your 'remorse code'.

Three's A Crowd

29. Write I love you Natasha, on the bathroom mirror, It's you I need, it's only ever been you. Or something like that, so it shows up when she comes out of the shower.
30. Does she eat bananas? Do a banana love note - google it.
31. Make an apology ticket like this:

OFFENDER. Sam Miller
STATEMENT: DESCRIBE WHAT YOU'VE DONE
SIGNED: S. Miller DATE: 16/2/24

Why	I feel	Forgive me
List the reasons you are sorry	List the reasons you feel bad	List reasons you are asking for forgiveness

31. Buy the book - 'when sorry isn't enough' making things right with the one you love and make sure

You read it.

She sees you reading it.

32. Get into the habit of sending loving or fun texts a few times a day, even when she is next to you. E.g. this is your daily reminder I love you or a memory. Or you look adorable when XXX. Whatever he is doing at the time.
33. Thank her, for listening, replying to her, whatever, be grateful - thankful.

34. Ask for advice on something, work, the garage etc. This always makes people feel good and valued.

35. Compliment her clothes, hair etc. She'll be feeling super crap about herself, be careful, gentle and genuine. But make her feel beautiful, wanted and needed.

36. Does your drumming teacher write songs, could he make you a verse and chorus for her? Learn it and sing it to her.

37. Maybe too soon, but when Beth is in bed. Lights down, play a song that means a lot to you both a slow dance to it. Then let her go, but thank her, tell her you love her, you'll be patient, she's worth the wait and the fight.

38. Record a nice loving message in her voice memos on her phone. Then set an alarm on her phone for when you're not around telling her to check her voice memos.

39. Pick up the phone or give her a call instead of texting in the week. Just say 'wanted to hear your voice, thinking about you/love you.

40. If you spot something she's about to run out of, buy it.

41. Print a picture of you both, put it in a frame, next to your bed in your new bedroom and don't tell her, wait for her to spot it.

42. Change your phone background from Beth to Natasha.

43. Write a note with lets have some hope and pass a note between us each night, has to be about something on your 'realistic life bucket list.' Night 1 she slides it under your door, next night you write yours and slide under hers, keep going. It will get her head in the future. Creating plans more positively, focusing on what there is to look forward to, rather than what has happened.

Then there are the usual flowers, chocolates, a bath etc.

Hope this helps. J x

I don't get much of a response, he confirms some things are just 'not him' which is fair enough, but some things he can work with.

Sometimes I get the impression he cannot be bothered trying with her. That he is too wounded by years of rejection. I get that.

But if he doesn't do something, then this is his future, his life and it is no life. He will continue to be used and put upon. She gets everything she wants, and denies him what he needs. It is a very one-sided empty relationship. Heavily weighted in her favour. Just like him and I, he gets what he wants from me and the terms are heavily weighted in his favour.

Sam has shared with me before how he feels the world has changed when it comes to relationships. He is a supporter of women and feminism, but feels the pendulum has swung too far the other way. He feels it has resulted in men's needs being cast aside. Women are taught to expect love, care, support, guidance and attention from men. Men are taught to be there for your woman, love them, look after them. But what are women taught about men's needs? Men run around giving their all to women and their families putting their own needs last. Is it any wonder male suicide and divorce rates are at an all-time high. He says long before snoop gate, he has felt unheard, discarded and used. Women are taught nothing about how to treat men, only what to expect from men. He doesn't think it unreasonable given all men do for their women is to expect the same in return and that they open their legs once in a while.

I totally agree with him. And I know therefore my ideas are likely never going to be looked at. After years of rejection, you cannot blame him and I cannot help think, that she should be as responsible for making an effort as he is. I was the lava erupting from the volcano... but the volcano was already active long before me. And both of them played a part in that, both of them need to play a part to fix things.

Despite that, I go to bed, happy to have maybe given him some ideas that will help. It may seem daft to offer him help, Emily certainly thinks so and doesn't hold back in telling me.

In my head, as they are going to be doing counselling, they will sort it out anyway or tread water and exist as they are, no point fighting it, better to support it. Sam and I are over, I know it, this is just the slow death. He has just not realised that yet. But I can help improve his happiness. I love him, why would I not do that?

He often sounds so flat, and so worried, I just want him happy again. That is all I want for him.

Emily says I am digging my own grave, but she is happy to help. Just give her a spade, hell, she says she will buy her own spade. She asks for his number... again.

Chapter 35

Misty Morning

Months of sleepless nights have completely drained me. Physically, I'm a wreck. My body feels like it's in constant overdrive while being utterly exhausted.

My muscles are tense all the time, my head constantly pounds, and the bags under my eyes make me look like I haven't rested in years. I feel shaky, like I'm running on nothing but adrenaline, and even when I try to eat or relax, nothing feels right. My heart often races for no reason, which only makes the anxiety feel worse.

Emotionally, I'm hanging on by a thread. I'm overly emotional, and the smallest things set me off. It's hard to concentrate or remember anything; I feel like I'm walking through a fog that never lifts. Sometimes I feel completely numb, like I'm just floating through my days without being truly present. Other times, everything feels overwhelming, and the tiniest problem sends me spiralling.

Driving is a risk I know I'm taking, but I have no choice. I catch myself zoning out behind the wheel, or my eyes start to feel heavy, and I get scared. It's like I'm gambling every time I get in the car, knowing that I'm not fully alert, but I have to keep going.

To make things worse, Sam is going through it too. His home

life has been falling apart, and he's barely sleeping either. We're both struggling, but I made a mistake recently. I made an off hand comment, something like, "I never know when I'll hear from you." It is not a lie, communication's been so inconsistent, and I was feeling frustrated. That one comment set him off. He snapped, completely lost it. He said something about how I don't understand what he's going through, how everything in his life is crumbling, and he can't be everything for everyone all the time. It was like all his built-up stress, and exhaustion just exploded in that moment. I felt awful, whenever I said something out of turn and he got annoyed, I felt like I had just hammered another nail in the coffin. Why that bothers me I don't know, because I have accepted we are not meant for each other in this life, and he has chosen her over me anyway. But somewhere deep in me, there is one last ember of hope that still glows. He fans it sometimes, sparking a small flickering flame, until it reduces back down to an ember once more. I wish he would just stamp it out. Then all this confusion and pain might stop.

After a particularly bad night, once the kids have gone to school, Phil headed off on a gardening tidy job and the house is finally my own. I check my diary and I have no work meetings. I desperately need to get on with writing campaigns and proposals, but I feel I am at the end. I can't.

Sam called, the signal was poor, I got some snippets of an argument that morning with Natasha, he then had to run into the office.

I decided I would try and go to bed for a couple of hours. A top-up of sleep, I am certain would do me the world of good and help me focus and be more productive. But I am fearful too. It is a trade-off. The fear of going to sleep has become constant.

Sam often sends me to bed when he is ready to go, but there is little point. I now fight sleep like a demon, I stay up long after he goes until I know sleep will win.

Three's A Crowd

It's not just the thought of another restless night, it's the night-mares I know are waiting for me. I dread that moment when I finally close my eyes because I know what's coming. These aren't ordinary nightmares, the kind where you can just wake up, shake it off, and tell yourself it wasn't real. These are different. They cling to me, digging in deep, even after I've woken up.

The images and feelings from the dreams stay with me for hours. I'll wake up drenched in sweat, my heart pounding, but it doesn't end there. I can still feel the fear, the panic, like it's lurking right beneath the surface, ready to pull me back in. Even in the light of day, the nightmare hangs around, casting a shadow over everything I do.

It messes with my mind. I'll catch myself replaying parts of the dream in my head, even though I desperately want to forget them. Sometimes, I can still feel the weight of whatever happened in the dream, as if it crossed into my reality. It makes me question what's real and what isn't, and I hate that feeling of losing control.

The worst part is that I know I have to sleep eventually, but I'm terrified of what's waiting when I do. There's no escape. I can't outrun it, and I can't fight it. I'm stuck in this cycle where I avoid sleep, but when it finally takes over, it's like stepping into a night-mare I know I'll be trapped in, long after I wake up.

Today it feels like no choice, I have to get some shut-eye. I climb the stairs and slide under the covers. My body is in pain. Ron jumps up and curls up at my feet, he is not bothered about missing his walk and happy to go back to a soft slumber. I envy the ease at which he can sleep. If I ever sleep again I will never take it for granted.

Even though I am under the covers, my body turns icy as the cool covers touch my skin and I shiver. Ron begins to whimper, I wonder if he is cold too. I lean over and pull a throw over him and lay back down.

I drift quite quickly but I jolt awake frequently. On the third jolt when my eyes fly open, Misty is laying on my bed, where Phil would lay, staring at me with her pained sorrowful eyes.

"It's time," She says softly.

I give her a slow nod and blink, I don't have the energy to beg her to let me sleep. I am wondering if Thomas forgot to take the latch off when he pulled the door behind him this morning. In my fog of tiredness I forget to check. Misty has not managed to get in the house since I removed the key. But I see her wandering the garden a lot or trying the windows.

She pulls my hands into hers, adding to my shivers, her hands are always like ice.

On a park bench killing time - people watching
Looking for a part-time job in the paper newspaper snatched
Blows away
James, Christopher, Paul
"Hey"
Whacks my cap
Stand up try to walk around them James blocks
"Whoa, where are you going?"
I step
He blocks
I step
He blocks
I bend and try to duck under arm grabbed, shoulder wrenches
They look around
"Clear" they drag
I bend my knees, lean back digging my heels in peeling fingers off my arm.

Releases me - I fall hard backwards hit the ground
Scooped up screaming
Laughing
A man looks over then looks away
Looking in our direction, then looks away dragged to toilets
Pushed in urine stench door locked they smile shaking

Three's A Crowd

"ooo oo" laughter
"You scared?"
They mimic me shaking
"I'll scream"
James dashes forward
Expect him to hit me - doesn't grabs toilet paper
"No you won't"
Forces mouth open, slaps face rams toilet paper in
Scratchy toilet paper frozen, shaking
Eyes darting about the room no escape
Christopher marches to me tugging at my trousers.
I slap him on the head and body James lets go of my mouth
Grabs my arms
Pins me to the wall by my wrists. can't spit out the toilet paper
Trousers and pants down at my ankles.

"Not a good view down here, you can see her fat floppy belly hanging down".

"Turn the bitch around, then you don't have to see that or look at her face".

I am lying listening, but also feeling, it is as if I can feel my mouth dry and full of toilet paper, struggling to breathe through my nose, breathing fast and panicked. Feeling trapped, no escape. I don't know why, but I just wail, shake and cry. It should be Misty crying and wailing, not me, I am just so tired. I find myself wanting only one thing in the world. Sam.

'Shhhh' Misty says "Listen" I quieten.

Unbuckling noise, unzipping shaking his trousers down with his
Free arm the other holds me.
Feel his penis on my bum
"Fucking open your legs further"
I squeeze them together.
Nails dig into my bum, skin breaks shuffle my legs apart
Slams his cock inside fucks me hard

My body banging off the wall.
Toilet paper is my mouth dying
Sticking to the insides of my cheek
"As promised lads"
James slides out.
Paul holds me,
James releases
Paul fucks me
Then Christopher.
They leave
I scoop the toilet paper out my mouth, pull up my pants and trousers
They are soaked
Wet from the bathroom floor
I buy another newspaper

My eyes are squeezed shut tight, as if it will help block out the images Misty places in my mind.

I can't stop. The sobs are ripping through me, uncontrollable, shaking my whole body. I can barely breathe, my chest tightens with every wail, and the tears just keep pouring out. My hands are trembling, clutching at nothing, I have lost Misty's grip, I am reaching for her trying to hold on to something, anything, but there's nothing to ground me. The sound of my own voice feels distant, but I can hear myself screaming, crying out for Sam. Over and over, I call his name, my voice breaking, desperate for him to come, for him to just be here, he can't be and that makes it worse. But still I cry out.

"Sam! Please, Sam!" I don't even know if I'm making sense any more. It's like this tidal wave of emotion is drowning me, and I can't stop it. Everything hurts, my throat is raw from crying, my head is pounding, but the pain in my chest, that's the worst. It feels like I'm being torn apart from the inside out.

I'm choking on my own sobs, gasping between cries, but his name keeps slipping out like it's the only thing I can hold on to.

Three's A Crowd

"Sam... please, I need you." My voice cracks, barely more than a whisper now, but I keep saying it, hoping somehow, he'll hear me. My body switches from ice cold to boiling through my sobbing and hot tears.

"Hey bitch, you're OK, shhh....it is OK." Says Emily.

I sit up rubbing my eyes, Misty is no longer in the bed, and nowhere to be seen. Emily is looking down at me.

"Oh Emily," I said, sobbing.

"Hey, you **are** ok - don't you dare cry out for him again, I am here."

"Where is Misty? Is she ok?"

"She just left," Emily says "now get a grip girl, it's just your mind, it's not happening, it's not happening to Misty now, stop sobbing, get some sleep, I will sit with you until you are sleeping ok?"

"My phone, I need it..." I start to get up.

"I will get it," Says Emily.

Once in my hands I open the messaging app I use for Sam, I just want to know if he has messaged me.

Nothing.

I quickly scroll through instagram, find something funny and send it off to him and wait. Emily watches me.

"Jessie, he is not going to message OK."

I ignore her and wait. Nothing, I come out of it, and go back in to refresh just in case. Still nothing.

"For fuck's sake Jessie, if he wanted to message you he would find a way, he doesn't so he doesn't want to. It is that simple. Accept it. When are you going to get that through your thick head?"

"Emily, he has notifications turned off because of snoop gate, and he works in an open-plan office"

"He always did work in an open plan office Jessie, it never stopped him when **he** needed to hear from you, when you were doing GW. When you need it, it doesn't matter to him, if you give a shit about someone, you take thirty seconds a few times a day to check on them, or given what he has put you through, at least to try and show you he gives a shit, but he doesn't. Please, wake the fuck up"

"Unfair Em, he is going through hell."

"I don't deny it, but so are you and he has barely asked after you or bother with you, where as you have not dropped him like a piece of shit."

"He does what he can, it's hard for him."

"But what does he do for **you** Jess? Fuck all, thats what!"

"Leave me alone Emily, you're not helping."

"You have to wake up, I don't like seeing you hurting."

"I know fine well where I stand, I am not a total fucking idiot, but I don't need you rubbing salt in the wound. You were right all along, I should not have let it get to this stage, but you know what, I did and I am here now. Trying, desperately trying to not give a shit. But I can't just switch it off. He is not a bad guy, he is a great guy, life has just thrown us a shitty hand."

"Sure, but that doesn't give him the right to be so cold, pick you up and drop you and never consider your needs."

I am too tired to fight her, I close my eyes. She watches over me and I fall into a deep sleep. I wake up a little after 1pm, I am groggy, but I feel a bit more human.

Emily has gone. I make myself a cup of tea and head to the office. I do some proposal work and have a Zoom meeting at 2 pm, despite me being off my game the menopause brand are thrilled with the results and want to continue into Q2 and 3.

My mind wanders, thinking about my lack of sleep and how it cannot continue. I tried the sleeping tablet again a couple of weeks ago and had the same reaction, so I don't think that is viable for me.

One option is smoking weed, not viable, wouldn't even know how to get it these days. Alcohol seems like a slippery slope. Then I stumble across a video that talks of setting an alarm to wake up before your usual disturbance, so disrupt the REM pattern. This makes sense to me, there are disadvantages, you don't go through

Three's A Crowd

all the sleep stages, but potentially apart from waking to knock your alarm off every few hours, without the nightmare causing high alert, it may be feasible, if it worked I could almost get a full night. I decide there is nothing to lose and will try it.

I feel a bit more positive. This seems like a plausible solution. I told Sam about it that night. He finds it interesting and hopes it works for me.

We say good night, and I am just about to head to bed, when he messages again.

> Emily has just messaged me, WTAF.

Chapter 36

Broken Boundaries

Shit, Emily must have got his number from my phone when she got it for me this morning. I feel sick, I hate to think what she has said.

> Oh god, I am sorry, she must have got your no. from my phone this morning. I don't suppose it's a nice message from her?

I message Emily at the same time:

> Emily, you got his no. and text him, I am pissed off, that is out of order, pls don't ruin this for me. Stay out of it.

Sam:

> No, she wants me to piss off basically, thinks I am going to hurt you, thinks I don't value you, thinks you will eventually just fuck someone else. Think's I am treating you badly.

As I read his message I think to myself, but you already **have** hurt me, you have no idea how much. And you are not exactly treating me well at the moment. But I absolutely do not want Emily sticking her oar in.

> I am so sorry, I will talk to her, get her to butt out.

He screenshots the messages and send them to me:

> Hey prick face, stop fucking with Jessie and end it. I won't see her hurt.

>> Assume this is Emily? Why do you want me to end it, when I love her? I would never intentionally hurt her.

> Because you don't love her and you know it, if you have any care for her at all, end it. I won't sit back and watch her continue to be hurt by you.

>> She loves me, you will deny her happiness with me, how does that help her?

> What happiness? You pick her up and drop her on a whim. You will end it once you are done with her, she is needy, hard work and loves cock, she will fuck someone else, so you end it or I will make sure she slips up. You have already shown you don't give a fuck. So just pull the plaster off

>> I would be lost without her, I need her, I miss her everyday, I am in a very difficult position, I have a daughter to consider and I try my best. I won't give up on her.

> Then I will make sure you have no choice. Did you know she caught Trich? Do you know she has done more than one gang bang? I know her, you don't. And I know men, you will discard her like a used condom.

>> Wow, you put me in the same group as all men, and you're going to deny her the first person in her life who has ever given her any kind of love or support - what a great friend.

>> Fuck Off

Three's A Crowd

I feel sick as a dog. I know deep down Emily does come from a good place, but she had no right to either snoop on my phone or message him and interfere. And by the sound of it, her plan has worked. He is pissed off and gone, he can't even bring himself to talk to me.

Emily messages:

> I won't stay out of it, I saw the state of you this morning, he has this hold over you but no time for you. He just gives you scraps from the table so you will let him fuck your holes. He does not give a shit and the sooner he fucks off the sooner you will stop feeling shit about yourself. So be pissed off all you like. I don't give a fuck. Have you forgotten how easily he cast you aside at Christmas?

I crawl into bed, sleep takes a long time to come, I can't get Sam out of my head and what he must be thinking. I should have told him about the other gang bangs and Trich, and probably a lot more. So much is hard to tell anyone, let alone Sam, if he knows the truth of what I have done his view of me will change completely. Even if this ends I don't want him to know all I have done.

I don't try the alarm idea as I need to work out how to have an alarm go off in the night and not wake or alert Phil.

I wake in the morning, feeling as exhausted as ever. Phil has already left, we should get news today of another interview he completed. The kids pour out the door to head for the bus, Thomas running back in a panic a few minutes later as he had forgotten his French homework.

I head out to walk Ron. Sam messages asking if I am free this morning, he should be in the car about 8:40am. Been a long time since he has informed me of that in advance. I say I will be free. I feel a bit sick about what he is going to say, I suspect it will be along the lines of, 'I am sorry Jess but with all I have going on, I can't cope with your psycho friend plus you lied to me about Manchester being your only gang bang. Please be safe and I wish you well.'

The phone rings, and I pluck up the courage to answer:

"Hey"

"Hey"

"I asked you if there were any other events I should know about and you lied."

"Not lie, just didn't expand."

"Same thing."

It is actually not, but I decide it is best to keep my mouth shut.

"OK, I am sorry," I reply flatly.

"What else are you not telling me?" I can't think, my head is empty.

"Nothing" I say, but I know that's not quite the truth but can't think of what else he might want to know. "Sam all of that is in the past, it is all pre you, I am not doing anything like that any more."

'But you might, you can't say no."

"I am working on that and not going anywhere or doing anything that could cause that to be a problem"

"I want to know about the other gang bangs, who, when, where, what happened," he states.

"Why? It is in the past."

"I want to know exactly what you have done, send me a video with all the details, start with the first one you did."

"Please Sam, no."

"Jessie, I am serious, every fucking detail, where, who, what happened and what went through your head."

"OK"

"Emily thinks I am like all other men you have encountered, do you feel like that?"

"Not really, no"

"What does that mean?"

"I just wish things were different, but I know they can't be."

"So do I Jess, but I am trying to save my marriage for Beth, what would you have me do for fucks sake?"

"I know the situation, I am not stupid, I know nothing can be done."

"And you won't leave Phil, so where does that leave me? Why would I blow my life? So can't we just enjoy each other?"

Even if I was single and left Phil tomorrow, I know he would never leave Natasha and Beth, so his argument is flawed. But I keep that to myself.

"I will leave Phil, but when the time is right, I need my life sorted first and kids through their exams, then I will be gone, whether you're around or not. It's just hard for me to know how you feel sometimes"

"I tell you all the time."

Does not make it true, I think to myself but hold back, if he loved me, he'd not have binned me so easily, if he loved me, he would want to see me, he would be talking about a date to see me, if he loved me, he'd find a way to show me, if he loved me, he would talk about the future, if he loved me he would message me, if he loved me, he'd keep me informed so we could maximise our chances of talking.

"I know, I am sorry, I am the problem" I know I am, but I also know that is the best way to diffuse any conflict, accept blame.

"Do you know how important you are to me?"

My head is screaming - seriously!!! How the fuck can I possibly know that!?

"It's hard to see".

"Don't mistake lack of contact for lack of interest, my hands are tied". He says

"OK"

Really? That tied? I think.

So tied he can't message good morning or fire off just a quick text now and again in the course of a full eight to ten hours, he has not a second, so interested, he no longer bothers to keep me informed, content with keeping me in the dark.

I guess he doesn't need to bother because he knows I will

always be there like the fool I am. So tied there is literally not a single moment in the day he has sixty seconds? These days people are never far from their phones and a message takes seconds, sure he is being watched, he has to be careful, but I am pretty sure Natasha takes a shit, or he does. He is not permanently intertwined with her, or work. Truth is, no matter what he says I am just not important enough to him, if I was he would accept this is super important to me, and therefore it would become important to him.

None of this sits right with me, it is all so one-sided. I am too scared to say anything, I keep quiet. Considering Emily has just thrown a grenade in the mix, I am hardly in a position to be asking for anything. Not that I would anyway.

"I want to see you."

"We can't, it's too risky for you." I get in there first so he doesn't have to tell me he can't, it is just too difficult at the moment. I know he can't. There is a huge difference between saying he 'wants' to see me and actually doing anything about it. I do not want to hear that when it is meaningless and we won't see each other anyway, I don't want to carrot dangled.

"If you could come here, we could get a hotel for a few hours, Natasha won't bat an eyelid if it's in work hours, make it my drumming night and I could stay until around 7pm?"

I am stunned, he must be feeling more settled. I had tentatively mentioned meeting again a few times but each time he body swerved it over the last few months or ignored me. He is now talking more specifics and details. I don't know how I feel about it if I am honest. I am still so hurt, I feel like that hurt has never been acknowledged like it didn't matter, but I don't want to not see him. I feel like I was cast aside, treated like a piece of shit on his shoe, I still feel cast aside, confused and insignificant. And now he is snapping his fingers and expecting me to come running, and of course, I will.

"Well let me know some dates and I can see what I can do" I don't expect to get any dates.

"I want in that tight ass again"

"My holes miss cock" I replied, and it was true. I have not gone this long without since the kids were little, and I feel like a drug addict having gone cold turkey. It has been really hard for me. Holding off because if there was a chance with us I don't want to break any of his red lines and shoot myself in the foot. But equally knowing he would be shooting me in the foot soon enough, so why not just start proceedings.

My pussy is starving, and I am not getting the feeling I need to survive, being so unsure on where I stand with him is eroding what little self-confidence I had. A quick cock pick me up would help.

"Cock?"

"Your cock" I correct myself.

"Good save, OK, got to run Jess, I miss you, love you, need you, please remember that."

"I'll try," I say.

"Have a good day, be good."

A few days later Phil gets the best news, he has got the job and starts in two weeks. It is crap money, but it *is* money and will help. It doesn't mean we are out of the woods, not by a long shot, but it keeps the wolves from the door that bit longer. He is elated but also frustrated at the crap pay and the dull job he is having to face doing. I tell him that he should feel good, that he is stepping up and doing what he needs to do, he should be proud of that and I mean it.

It is also the night Sam's mother-in-law is coming to stay, so he is back in the marital bed. Our chat is inevitably cut very short. He hides in the bathroom for 5 mins to text me. He had said he told Natasha he wasn't comfortable coming back into the bedroom, he knows she does not want him in there and was considering sleeping on a camp bed next to her. Of course that didn't happen.

The next night he can't message either as they are late back after the meal and lecture which they both thoroughly enjoyed.

I start testing out the alarm in the night and to my utter relief it works. I set my phone to silent and sleep with my watch on, so it vibrates on my wrist. It has been trial and error, but I have nailed it. If I set it to every two hours from when I go to bed, it stops the nightmares, 70% of the time. It is a huge improvement. A couple of nights a week it doesn't work, and I have to get up in the night to settle myself, but in the main it is life changing. Sam has also rediscovered sleep, perhaps the comfort of being back beside his wife and less threat of his marriage being terminal. Like when I sleep with him, I feel safe and at peace. He must get that with Natasha, hence he has found sleep again.

As predicted, he was never turfed out of the marital bed after that. So instead of brief chats and then him reading, it has become brief chats in the bathroom before he slides in beside his wife. I think the days of us getting the chance to message for any length of time at night are gone. He cannot stay up long after she turns in any more as it will be far too suspicious.

I asked if they had a date for marriage counselling yet, but there is a long waiting list. Who knew that service was in such high demand, guess it tells you a lot. He has never mentioned if he has tried any of my ideas with her. I remain utterly confused by their set up. This dominant man is just accepting his fate and continues to be treated like crap. Neither of them address or discuss anything and just exist ignoring the problem with the occasional fierce blow up, going over old ground, it is a literal ground hog day. Beth is caught in the middle and playing up. None of them are happy, they sleepwalk through life, head in the sand, bouncing from blow up to blow up, expecting a magic genie to come and make it all better. Sadly nothing gets better without effort and no matter how many times I mention this to Sam it falls on deaf ears.

It beggars belief to me that the 'only' reason he claims to be staying is for Beth's sake, he owes it to her. He is of the view that a

Three's A Crowd

family staying together gives the child the best chance. I agree, if that is a happy functional one. Where it is not, then the child is better off with a chance of happiness in two happy homes rather than one toxic one. Plus the lessons he is teaching Beth are not great, he is role modeling being bullied, ignored and disrespected by his wife, Beth will learn that is how you treat men. She is also observing a loving relationship, without the loving part being visible. My kids have that too. We don't have the tension, but they see no affection between Phil and I, because it is not there.

I don't think he appreciates my input and I need to learn to stay out of it. It really is none of my business, I just want to help him though, seeing and hearing him unhappy kills me. From what I hear of his life at the moment, it is no life.

I recorded a video providing details to Sam of the Manchester gang bang. I do my best with it but I find it hard, the details are vague for me. In fairness, I'd had a fair bit to drink. It was a client who had a group of friends, and did this regularly. I had to verify on the phone. It was arranged for mid-week. The main guy was a trader and worked late, so I was told to meet in a bar near his flat and they would come for me at 9 pm. There was a bus strike and I had to walk a long way from my hotel to the pub. I got there about 8 pm and started drinking. They had requested I send outfit options in advance and they chose a short black halter-neck black dress with thigh high boots. They promised a minimum of three guys but there could be more. They were a group of thirty six men. I made it to the pub and sat there having a drink, waiting on them when a guy came up asking me to watch his backpack while he went to the toilet. He then returned and asked if he could sit with me. We chatted and he bought me a drink. Shortly after 9:30 pm Neil the gang bang leader found me and joined us for a drink, along with an Italian friend of his, Marco. We chatted for a while and they were lovely, which made me feel very comfortable. Neil pulled me aside and said I think the guy you have attracted likes you, and did I want him to join us? I said no, because Neil had certified all attendees as having clean tests and didn't know about this guy. I was not convinced the guy liked me either and was unsure how that conversation may go. "Hey Mr stranger in a bar, I am actually here to get gang banged, want to join in?!"

We exited the pub, Marco linked arms with me and we walked to Neil's flat, pausing at a newsagents first. On entering Neil's flat another guy, who's name I can't recall was on the sofa, they got me a drink and started circling me, feeling me, before I had to suck the guy off on the couch while Neil and Marco played with their cocks. Neil was like the compère, directing. We ended up in the bedroom, and I can't tell you much other than first Neil and the couch guy spit roasted me, then Marco joined in and I ended up airtight. The sensation of two cocks, one in my pussy and one in my ass intense, they could feel each other through the dividing wall between my pussy and my ass. I could feel everything, like I was being stretched and destroyed.

I kept saying, I am never going back to one cock! They laughed. Various positions and ejaculations occur. Neil said fill the bitch, they tried two cocks in my ass and pussy but failed. I failed. Neil had a circular rug on his bedroom floor, and they finished with me kneeling on that and wanking over my face. They treated me really well and I felt amazing. I never thought my holes would be the same again, they felt open, loose, baggy, and destroyed. They didn't want me walking back to my hotel alone, so Marco drove me back in his open-top car, buzzing and high on cock, I sucked him off on the journey back to the hotel. I got back to the hotel about 2:30am.

Afterwards one of Neil's gang bang friends who was not there, kept calling me, videoing me, begging me to come back, saying the lads said I had done so well and it was rare to find a woman these days like me. He would wank on camera talking to me, he rang at

Three's A Crowd

really bad times, he wanted me to run away with him for a year. It was ridiculous. I did want to go back, it never worked out.

My video seemed to satisfy Sam and I sent details of the others too. He had questions some of which I could not answer, because I could not remember.

To my surprise Sam does come back to me a week later suggesting a date. I clear it at home and book it. I got a good deal on the hotel the night before. He was thinking I could come up and down in a day, save me the overnight cost. On paper this would be sensible. However, not for me at the moment. If life were normal I could, but I know how much I struggle to drive at the moment. He lives in butt fuck nowhere three hours from me. It is actually only ninety minutes in miles, but because it is in the heart of Cumbria, the roads are crap combined with slow tractors and tourists clogging the main arteries. If I have to stop en route because I am falling asleep at the wheel, it could take me double the time and would mean we would have less time together. Plus if it lands on a bad night for me, I may have to get up at 5am to make it to him at a decent hour and that could well be the time I am just about ready to head back to bed having not slept at all. It would be safer to stay the night before.

It is booked for the day of his drumming, I can check in at 3 pm, and then we will have until around 6:30pm. I have tagged on a day use room for the following day otherwise by the time he gets to me, I would have to check out in an hour. If I am going all that way, we may as well try and maximise the time we have together.

The whole trip is not cheap, and I really can not afford it, paying for the hotel is ok as I use my business card and put it down as company spend, but whatever way you cut it, it still removes what I am able to take to live on, but at least the cash is available in that account. The petrol tips me into my overdraft. The 'day use' room I can't put through the business, but can be paid on the day. I have some money from the kids' Christmas savings to cover that. I will move it back later. I put £40 away for them each month, so by

March I have £120, the room for the day is only £65, I can cut off other areas and replace that in a couple of months. I will put it back, I would never not do that for them. I am just borrowing it, after a truly shit few months it is literally the only thing I have done for myself. I need this.

Sam has moved his meetings and will come to me just after 9 am once he has dropped Beth on day two and can stay until around 2:30pm before he has to leave to collect her.

I am extremely anxious about seeing him. It will have been four months, literally ⅓ of a year. So much has changed in that time:

1. Once there was a hope of a future together, now there is none.

2. Once I had some belief he might love me, now I know he doesn't.

What if I don't look how he remembers or he has built me up, and I am a disappointment? What if i don't know how to fuck or swallow cock any more? What if I can't take his cock in my ass because it's sealed up through lack of use. What if he thinks, what was the fuss about? What the hell was he thinking, she is not all that! He may think; Jesus, I nearly ruined my marriage for this! What if someone sees him come in or leave, flags to Natasha and world war three breaks out.

Then there is the guilt, there is a woman and a child, trying to fight to keep their family together, and he is seeing me, even after hurting the woman he loves. If he can look her in the eyes and hurt her, what is he capable of doing to me? Before she knew, she was not hurt, but now she is, I know it, he knows it and I feel awful for it.

But like chewing gum stuck on your shoe, he is impossible to get off. I tell myself if it was not me providing holes for him, he would be seeking another escort anyway. I am the symptom not the cause, even without me, he would still develop symptoms.

Three's A Crowd

What if he is only wanting me to come to honour my rules and end this face to face?

What if Misty shows up, she has done that twice before with Sam?

Emily messages him incessantly, she has even done video calls with him. I am currently not talking to her. She has told him to fuck off, told him about some things I have done with clients. She tells him I am just a cum hungry slut and not worth his time. Some of it is hurting him and upsetting him. Five days before I am due to leave to see him, she calls him and tells him she knows he is after nothing more from me than filling my holes like all men. It is the last straw.

He messages me and says:

> You're friends with Emily, girls talk if that is what you really think of me, then I understand you not wanting to come.

I am distraught, after four fucking months I finally get to see him and she has ruined it. He has had enough, he is pitching to me as if it is my decision, but really it's his way of saying don't bother. I don't blame him. I can't even bring myself to message Emily, right now I hate her.

Messages and conversation are awkward, he is pissed off. I don't know what to say or do. It must be awful thinking he has been bundled in with all the bad guys in the world and that is what I think. I don't. The atmosphere does eventually thaw, and we manage two nights of build up filth chat. We are on.

We talk about how I intend to make him work for my holes, as I want him to take me roughly. He laughs, says that will never happen, that as soon as I see his cock again, my brain will go to mush and my pussy liquify. I fear that might be true, but I tell him I have a superpower, something in my head I can draw on that will help me hold my resolve and make it hard for him. He laughs. It is true though, all I have to do is think about how he hurt me between January and now, that pain is still so strongly present. How easily he cast me aside, and it makes me think, why should I let him touch me. I almost feel angry and that is something I never feel. I don't tell him my superpower.

It is a good job, I did book the room for the night. I left about 9 am and my three-hour trip took five and a half hours. I had to keep stopping. Sam messaged asking for updates. I didn't want the pressure so, I told him I left later than I did so he didn't challenge why it was taking me so long.

The anticipation had been building for days, but as the moment got closer, my heart felt like it was going to burst. I hadn't seen Sam in four months. Four long, aching months. As I checked into the hotel, I could barely keep still, but underneath it all, this heavy layer of doubt lingered. What if I wasn't what he remembered? What if, after all this time, I was... less? Less attractive to him, less interesting, less everything. I wondered if the months apart had made him see me differently and with Emily poking her oar in, that was entirely possible.

As I waited in the room for him to arrive, I kept fidgeting with my clothes, running my hands through my hair, trying to make sure everything looked right, but it felt like no matter what I did, it wasn't enough. The worry gnawed at me, what if when he saw me, there was disappointment in his eyes? That thought stung more than I wanted to admit.

Then I heard a knock and opened the door. I saw him. For a second, my heart stopped, and it was like everything in the room shifted around him. He looked so perfect, so familiar. His face, his presence, just the sight of him made me feel like I was glowing from the inside out. I couldn't help but drink him in, every single detail. The way his smile started slowly, the way his eyes crinkled just a bit at the corners... I'd forgotten how much just seeing him could overwhelm me, comfort me and the thought of him not wanting me, a death blow threat floating in my head.

My heart, which had been soaring, faltered. He didn't rush to me the way he used to. His smile was there, yes, but it wasn't as bright, as eager as it once was. There was something in his eyes that I couldn't quite read, like he was holding back.

We hugged and kissed, he was right, when I saw his cock my head did turn to mush and my cunt did liquify. It was an unfair challenge, I had not had cock for four fucking months, what did he expect! And looking at him, my superpower faltered. God I am pathetic, I think to myself.

We fucked and fucked again. The feeling of his cock entering every one of my holes is better than I remembered. At one point when I was not expecting it, he tied my hands behind my back and then forced me onto the bed, I wrestled and wriggled to get him off, he overpowered me and took me, it was hot as fuck. In between fucks, we chatted, and I could not stop touching his face and looking at him, I just had to keep checking this was real.

He left earlier than he said he would, showering to get me off him before he went. I think he was nervous about making sure his routine was not too off for Natasha. I could understand him being nervous, he messaged when he got back confirming all was ok at home, code for, no suspicions raised.

I went out that night, there was someone I knew who stayed in the town worth connecting with, he took me to lots of local bars and I got pretty drunk, in a bar with live music, I get an eerie feeling, like I am being watched, god please don't let it be Misty. I scan the bar, I don't see her, my eyes catch a man's, dark wavy hair, strong brown eyes fixed on mine, I look away, still feeling like I am being watched, I look back, and he is still staring.

It is creeping me out, I never get creeped out. When I look back again, he has gone. Andy and I continued chatting and putting the marketing world to rights. It's past 11pm and I don't want to be too tired for Sam so leave, the walk back to the hotel sobered me up. Sam was not happy about me walking all the way back and not getting a taxi. He told me to pay for the taxi and he would give me the cash in the morning. Problem was I did not have the money to pay for it that night. I liked the walk anyway. I set my alarms and passed out.

The next morning, I got up, went for a run, came back, showered and was ready by 8am. Sam always had requirements for what he wanted me to wear, school girl, nun, secretary, the dress I did my gang bang in, the 'slut dress' from my GW profile. The only thing we really had a problem with was one of my hard limits, my red line about not being naked. He accepted it, but I know he didn't like it and it frustrated him. He was fed up with fabric over my pussy. The one pieces I wear are crotchless, but they do interfere I suppose. So he asked me if I would cling film myself, around the torso leaving my tits, pussy and ass exposed. I felt like a total disappointment not just being able to be free and give him what he wants, but I can't. He sent me some porn, showing cling filmed sluts, I had not seen that before. So that is what I did for him, wrapped myself up like a chicken breast.

I was expecting him at around 9am. He didn't message in the morning.

9am came and went, so did 9:10

9:15

9:20

9:25

I checked messages constantly, maybe he had to do school drop off in a sudden change, maybe he had a flat tire, maybe he had an accident, maybe Natasha had clocked something, maybe Beth was off school sick.

Surely any of those things he would have let me know, one of those 60 second texts I need but never get.

Maybe he was just not coming back. 9:30

9:35

OK, he is not coming, he doesn't have the guts to tell me. I start to tremble and get up off the bed, thinking I may as well just pack and head home.

9:37 - the door opens. Relief washes over me.

Three's A Crowd

"I thought you weren't coming" I said, lightheartedly, fighting back tears.

"What a nightmare morning" he said and proceeded to tell me about not getting Beth out the door on time and needing to drop bottles at the bottle bank on the way.

Why did you not just message me, I think, I can hear Emily's voice repeating what she has said before "He doesn't message because he doesn't want to, it is important to you, not to him."

Why would you go to the bottle bank in 'our time'. I think.

Considering how little we get, I value ever second, obviously Sam does not.

As he wraps his arms around me and I feel his throbbing cock, all those thoughts disappear, overcome with lust. I devour his cock in every hole anyway he wants to give it to me. I orgasm like I have not in months, no one can make me orgasms like Sam and no one's cum is as delicious as Sam's.

On my knees sucking his cock and having him ram it into my throat, I am so turned on I squirt all over the carpet. I have never squirted while sucking cock, I didn't think it was possible, it's not like my G-spot is getting any action which is usually the source of a squirt. I suppose it had got loads of attention just before. Sam often jokes that if I lived with him, everything would have to be constructed of wipe down material.

My favourite part of Sam's cock is the head, it is so bulbous, he is cut. It is truly a thing of beauty. He has a slight curve which hits all the right spots. On camera when he squeezes out the pre-cum and I see it glide over his jap's eye, I melt.

Sometimes it looks like butt cheeks if too close on camera, sometimes it reminds me of the guys in star wars on the death star who arm the weapons and wear helmets just like Sam's cock.

Sam's cock, rocks.

By early afternoon I am thoroughly cock drunk.

I love just laying with him too, I don't want the day to end. But it must. He goes to wash me away again and leaves a good half hour before he said he had to leave. Before he goes, he looks at me, says I am beautiful, that he has missed me. I can feel tears prickling in my eyes.

"Don't be nice to me please Sam." (It hurts too much when I know it's not true).

"You're the only girl I know that is happy to be called a bitch, slut, whore, but compliment you, tell you I miss you, and you fall part". He laughs.

He kindly gives me some cash to help with the petrol.

The moment Sam hands me the money, my stomach twists. I force a smile, but it doesn't reach my eyes. His gesture is kind, but all I can think about is how much it stings. I can feel my cheeks flush with shame as I take the notes, my fingers heavy with guilt.

He knows I'm struggling, knows I'm skint. And here he is, giving me cash like I'm some charity case. It feels wrong, like I'm stealing from his family, like I'm dipping my hands into their lives, taking what isn't mine. His wife, she's got it all together, doesn't she? Successful, put-together, everything I'm not. I can't help but compare. They've got a house, careers, a future. And here I am, accepting a handout because I have failed.

I glance at Sam, and there's no judgement in his eyes, only kindness, and he explains he wants to help. All the money he spent pre-snoop gate still weighs heavy on me, I hate not standing on my own two feet, I will repay him. He's doing this out of care, but I feel like I'm being paid for.

We hug one last time, and then I have to let him go. I collapse onto the bed, confused, scared, sad and wondering what is next. After I gather myself I make the 3 hour drive home, he messages wanting updates, I send what I can, when I can. It takes me 6 hours to get home.

Chapter 37
But it's a Shitehole

Leaving Sam has not got any easier, it was never easy before and being out of practice leaving him has not helped. Our time together is now even more fleeting than before. What we used to have was not enough, back then I was sad and bitter at how little time we got. If only I had known this was our future. I would go back to that in a heartbeat.

This is it now. See him for a few hours, fuck, he goes home to his wife, comes back, fucks me, pays me money and goes back to his life. I feel like nothing. I feel like a whore.

Leaving Sam cause's a peculiar kind of ache that hangs for days. I had forgotten how bad it was, but now it is worse due to our new restrictions on every level of our ability to communicate and meet. It's a heavy weight in the pit of my stomach, a constant reminder of the distance. The world seems to have lost its colour as I trudge through each day, replaced by a muted, grey hue.

The thought of weeks, maybe even months, without his touch, his laughter, this presence is a crushing blow. It's like another piece of my heart has been ripped away, leaving an empty void that nothing can fill. I find myself replaying cherished memories, clinging to them like a lifeline in a stormy sea.

The sadness is a constant companion, a persistent undercurrent. It's all the moments when I ache for Sam but will not be able to reach him, that the weight of his absence becomes most unbearable.

Sam transitions much more easily than me, he always accuses me of boxing things, but in actual fact, **he** can box me away a lot more easily than I can him. Once he has had his time with work or family, where I don't enter his world physically or in thoughts, he can then get me out of the box and play with me, putting me away again before bed. I used to have that level of control. I don't have it when it comes to Sam.

I try to keep myself busy with work, mum duties, running, walking the dog. Sam is going away to a cabin they own in the hills over easter. Communication will drop... again. When it drops I am never sure if it will return, it never seems to ever quite go back to what it was.

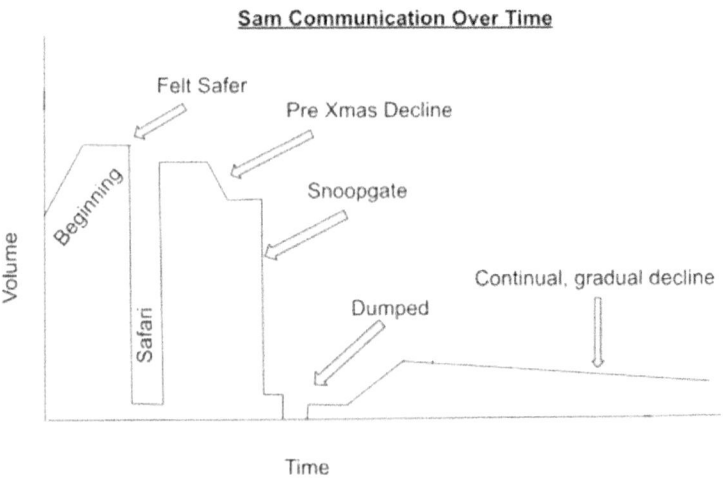

I have a client meeting to go to in the city. I am taking the train as it works out cheaper than petrol and parking. Phil is dropping me in the morning on his way to work and then collecting me when I come back. I have been invited for a meal and drinks after

but I don't want to go. I can't be in positions like that at the moment.

This is a potentially big contract so I have been prepping and practising my value proposition. I am ready, or as ready as I can be. The train is on time, despite the fact we are well into spring, the air has a chill and the wind tunnels down the platform like the trains do.

The train chunders, slows and stops. The doors slide open with a soft, mechanical hiss, like air escaping from a sealed vault. There's a faint metallic rumble beneath it, a low hum that vibrates through the platform as the panels part, smooth and precise.

As I step inside, there's a moment of stillness. Then, with a sudden, quick swish, the doors snap shut behind me, sealing with a muted thud, like a quiet clap of two hands meeting, propelling the icy air onto my back. The outside world fades as the sound settles into the rhythm of the train.

The train is busy but not full, and I slip into a two seater a few rows down from the doors. I am relieved as the train pulls out of the station that no one takes the seat next to me. I place my forehead on the window and wonder what Sam might be up to. It is a rare day, they happen once in a blue moon, when I am not available to message, just like Sam. I was getting driven in by Phil when Sam would have been driving to work, so we didn't manage to talk this morning and I will be back after he drives home. Since I saw him he has been messaging a bit more of late. More consistent in the morning, rarely when at work and very unusual to be messaged in the day at weekends. He calls in the week when he can. I am grateful for a bit more contact, it will never be what it once was and I miss the security of that, but I will take as much as I can get.

I gently mentioned how he never messages any more at Beth's

dancing or weekends. His response, he stopped himself finishing his sentence and then changed it:

"Weekends are fam.... busy. I have to be careful, I am never alone, I don't get a second, I don't go for a walk any more while Beth is dancing, it's been winter, the weather is bad and Natasha would wonder why I am soaking wet. So I sit in and watch and usually have the company of other parents."

I heard it, 'the weekend is family time'. That is how he is boxing things to try and spread himself to meet everyone's needs. It is simple, he doesn't want me in his life on the weekends. Only late at night when he wants a pussy or ass picture.

He expressed before that he is doing his best not to hurt anyone. I get it, it's tough. It is not possible though. I have to be the one he hurts and he does it everyday. Not intentionally, not with any malice, but he does.

I wonder if the summer will bring him walking and talking to me again. I suspect not. This half finished sentence hurts like a bitch. He has decided weekends I am not to be in his life. Yes, he is being watched more, I get that. But if he wanted to be in touch with me, reassure me, help me, he would fire off the odd message. He just doesn't want to. Keeping me during family time, firmly to a quick hello in the morning and filth late at night.

The change is undeniable.

Urgh I am suddenly aware of a slump in the seat next to me. Then I feel hands being gently placed on my thigh, light, delicate, icy, the cold spreading up my skin. Misty. I turn my head, and she is there, looking at me, searching my eyes, like she is trying to see into me, to know what I am thinking, feeling. She looks exhausted, frail and like a gust of wind would scatter her frame into dust particles.

"Hi" I say

"Hi" she replies sadly.

"I am not sure this is the right place Misty."

"It's ok," she says.

Three's A Crowd

She leans in and puts her mouth right up to my ear, I can feel her breath, even her breath is cool. She begins whispering.

Saturday working late at the cafe quiz night rugby club
10 pm finish
Walk home very, very dark.
Glow of the cafe behind Street lights ahead
Grass underfoot
Footsteps and clothing rubbing together
Whoosh surround me
Three of them
"Hey, it's your lucky night"
Shove them all
Start to run
Body slam to ground
Tripped up
Disorientated
Lift myself onto my arms
Flop again
Ankles grabbed Pulled back
My top is pulling up as I'm dragged backwards.
Kicking
Not screaming, no point.
My jeans are wrestled with
Pulled to my ankles
Pants too
Harder to move , legs trapped
Free one leg from my shoe and jeans I can kick more
"Look, she wants it"
"For Fuck's sake pull your top down, told you we don't want to see that."
Grabbed around the waist Lifted onto all fours.
Drop to my tummy Repeat
They give up Roll me over
One straddles my shoulders Penis out

The other force me head up on a tilt Back and forth in mouth
The third enters me at the other end.
I can smell cut grass
Both pummelled me
Focus on something
It will end
The moon
My mouth fills I gulp it down.
"Good fucking girl, you're learning".
He smiles, proper smile
Other hole filled
They climb off
One to go.
Pulled up to standing One leg still in my jeans One shoe still on.
Waist grabbed
Bent over
Grabs my waist by bending over me
Torso on top
I'm bent under him
The 3rd boy drops his trousers
Approaches
Slaps my bottom
Fingers me
"You must want this"
Pushes against me.
"Wrong hole!"
Laughing.
He sinks inside
Searing pain
Asshole stretched ripping
"There is no wrong hole bitch"
"GET OUT"
Crying out in pain..

Three's A Crowd

Feel like I am being torn inside out
Hammers at me
"Wrong hole"
Laughter
"Look at you getting fucked in the shit pipe"
"Say thank you"
"Thank you"
Pulls out Released
Hit the ground
Pulled up by hair
Penis waved in face
"Can you smell your own shit you dirty bitch?"
"Clean it and next time make sure your shitehole is fucking clean."

I can't believe what I am hearing, I can taste shit in my mouth as I listen to her, I can feel her shame, feel her shock. I tremble and shake like the train. Our conversation is interrupted as the train conductor approaches requesting to see our tickets, he asks if we are ok, we must both look distraught. I assure him we are, we gives a concerned smile and moves along.

"Misty, please, please, tell me who they are and we can make it stop"

"Shhh" She says " LISTEN."

2 pulling up their trousers - laughing
Swing my hand hard on his balls
Hair released
He doubles over
Pick up my shoe
Scramble to my feet
Run, trouser leg flapping
Trip, get up, trip, get up
Still running
Edge of grass Look back
Pull on trousers and shoe

Run across road
Horned Home
Everyone out
Clothes in washing machine
Bed

She is quiet now. I am glad this is the end, I don't know what to say, there is a lot to take in. Why are they doing this to her? My mind numbs, closes off but is wild with thoughts. I rest my head on the train window again letting the tears fall. I place my hands on top of hers on my thigh and rub them.

"I am going to fix this for you, if it's the last thing I do."

"I know," she says.

I look her in the eyes, I think of Lottie and can't believe a girl has been subjected to this. Her pain is visible, like you can touch it.

"Well done for kicking him in the balls" I say.

"I paid for that later," she says, holding back a sob.

My heart sinks and I wrap her in a hug. I am scared that if I squeeze her too tightly she might shatter. She cries quietly, softly on my shoulder for a long time.

I release her, wipe her tears with my thumb. Give her a gentle smile. I need to think. I turn to look out the window to gather my thoughts. There has to be a new tact to try with her. She won't tell me her surname, where she lives, the school she goes to, must be a lie. She won't go to the police. I have an idea, it's gentle but she might go for it. If I give her my phone number, she could call me. Talk anytime. If I get hers I can reach her anytime. It is a start. I turn to make that suggestion.

She has gone.

I get up and look down the aisle, she is nowhere. I sit back at the window and stare out, running over what she has said, unable to shake it and let the tears fall. After the stop before mine I head to the toilet, no amount of makeup will cover this, my eyes are puffy, red, bloodshot. When the train pulls into the station and I walk down the aisle to the doors, I get a sensation like someone is watching me. As the doors open I glance back down the aisle and see a guy sitting staring right at me. Curly brown hair, he looks so like the guy from the folk pub when I visited Sam. It can't be. He smiles at me and gives me a wink. I turn away and step onto the platform.

I am grateful for the hour I have to kill before my meeting, hopefully meaning my eyes will settle in time.

I go to a cafe and grab a coffee and try to get my thoughts back in the game. I always struggle after speaking to Misty. I just can't shake her. It is like her sadness is infectious, and it spreads across your skin all day.

I message Sam to let him know I have arrived. I do not tell him about Misty. I stopped telling him about her, money and dreams at Christmas. He doesn't get to be in that part of my life any more. He responds;

> Good luck, be safe, I have a couple of days in
> April. I can rejig some meetings if you can come to
> me? love you, miss you x

> Send me the dates I will make it work x

I am pleasantly surprised, I did not mention any new dates to him, scared what the answer would be. I desperately wanted to ask, but was still not entirely sure what was going on and where I stood. I didn't want to put pressure on him. Maybe he does want to see me after all, what I can't work out is, in what capacity. Are we just fuck buddies? Is it just my holes he is after? But that doesn't sit well with him as he is a decent guy, so he adds on the 'love you's' and 'miss you's' to make the truth more palatable for him and I.

A few months ago, after snoop gate when we kind of slipped back into semi regular contact, one night he really pushed me on how I felt about him. It was not long after when he had said to me, 'I know you don't want me to say I love you any more, but I do, so I am saying it.' I had not been reciprocating those words.

Sam being Sam, he tackled that head on saying, if I love him I should tell him. So we now message each other and say it. I don't believe his words, they still sting, I am not sure I ever will, how can I? So, I let him tell me if it makes him feel better and I tell him because it is not a lie.

The world has changed so much between us. I don't feel secure any more, he dropped the axe once after saying he never would, he isn't there for me like he used to be. Part of me has come to understand when everything hit, he was distraught and just acted without any care as he was focused on the shit show at home. But I guess that is my point, if he cared he would ever have done that the way he did.

I have to accept that he used to message more because it was the early days. I was exciting then. The thrill of the chase, he has me now, so why bother, plus his new restrictions make it more difficult. He is just not a messenger, the way I am. Although that confuses me, as he was once a messenger. I wonder what I did wrong, as this reduction was happening before snoop gate, so it is not just that. I have to learn to chill with it. It is hard as that is my only measure of how he feels and as a result, I don't think he feels much at all.

He gets what he needs, he calls on me, when he needs, I am there when he needs. Sometimes I wish I could get what I need. Then I remember Darren's words, how life has been with Phil and realise, my role is to give, not receive.

I can't say what I want to say to him, or I will push him away. It's going to be a bit trickier coming up with a plausible reason at home to escape again to butt fuck nowhere so quickly. I say trickier, but the truth is no one ever bats an eyelid when I say I am going away or asks why or what I am up to. So I know it will be ok. Sam texts me some dates, I check my diary, move a couple of meetings, message Phil to let him know and start looking at hotels.

Emily calls me while having coffee. I have been ignoring her.

"Hi," I say coldly.

"Still in a huff?" She asks.

"I feel betrayed, like you have no regard for my feelings."

"Try being me!" She snaps

"What do you mean?"

"Nothing, Jessie, you know all I ever do is look after you right?"

"Yes, but this is not helping me Em, you're hurting me."

"Can you not see that **he** will hurt you, he **is hurting you,** he may not mean to, but he will, he doesn't give a shit about you, he has actually **proven** that to you, like all the guys you have ever met (except Phil) he just wants your holes, and you have fallen for him, he hurt you badly once, why put yourself through that again?"

"You may be right, but there is also a chance you may be wrong, please let me find out" I say.

"But I **am** right Jess"

"I will never talk to you again if I lose him because of you, let him make his own decisions, don't I deserve a chance?"

"Jess, you know this is not a chance that is open to you. This only ends one way. It literally cannot work. You can't have love, you get wanted from sucking cock and being fucked. That's it. You are stuck with Phil and get your kicks elsewhere. Don't let him pull the wool over your eyes, I am begging you."

"Bye Emily" I say and hang up.

God, she can be a bitch, but somewhere deep inside, although I try to bury it, I know she is right. But then again, he **is** kind of communicating more, things are better than what they were, he could have just walked away when everything kicked off with his wife, but he did come back to me. My holes are good, but they are just holes, he could use any holes. Maybe he does.

He has said that to me a few times;

"Jess, I have the money, I could go unload in holes tomorrow if I wanted and book someone, but I want you. You are over a hundred miles away, if I didn't love you and just wanted you for sex I could get that here, think about it".

It is hard to argue against that, but perhaps it's because he is tight? Perhaps it's because it's better to have someone who gets to know you sexually? Perhaps it is because I am so sexually wild, and he can fulfil things not on offer with others? Perhaps, he saw that I had fallen for him, and knew he could control me like a puppet on a string? Perhaps it is because I am no risk, I won't demand unreasonable things and far enough away not to cross paths with his wife?

I decided a while ago, I would try my best just to go with the flow. I can't go off and fuck randoms at the moment, and I don't have the time for GW, with Misty and sleepless nights I have too much on my plate. So this works for me too. Yes I wish it was more, but it's not. So I try to push those feelings aside and enjoy the ride. If only it was that easy. I force myself to look for what he *is* doing rather than what he no longer does.

He is messaging more than he was a few months ago, and he is now wanting to see me again. So go with the flow it is.

I drain the last of my coffee and head off to meet my prospective clients.

I sit at the long table, trying to focus on the faces around me, the sound of my own voice explaining projections and strategies. My hands are gripping the table's edge, but my mind… it's not in the room. It's somewhere else, in the dim light of a field, in the middle of Misty's story.

I felt what she said with such intensity. I see it again: the darkness, the glow from the cafe, the sounds of feet. Sound bites from those boys;

"Can you smell your own shit you dirty bitch",

"For Fucks sake pull your top down, told you we don't want to see that."

"Clean it."

Misty's words echo, repeating in my head, loud, intrusive.

I lose track of my pitch. My words stumble, and I scramble to pull myself back into the present. I see the faces of the clients, some of them nodding politely, but I feel their interest slipping, the energy draining from the room. I try to rally, bring up numbers, trends, but instead I hear Misty's voice:

"Next time make sure your shite hole is fucking clean."

God, I should've never listened to her and pushed her away. I can feel that chill creeping up my spine. I glance at my slides, but the words swim. Every time I pause, it's like the silence is filled with those ghostly whispers. I can tell I'm not landing the points I need to. I can tell I'm losing them.

Later that night, the email came. I didn't get the business. They went with someone else. I stare at the screen, feeling a sinking weight in my chest. I know exactly when I lost them, right in the middle of that room, haunted by Misty's story I just can't shake.

Chapter 38

April Fools

Perhaps it is the Easter holidays, but hotel prices seem to have skyrocketed in Cumbria. Even the 'day use' hotels. The only option is a Travel Lodge but with check-in at 3 pm and check-out at 10 am, it would leave us very little time, as Sam would need to be home in the evening. The only way to make it work is to book two nights. It works out a little more than the last trip. I know I should not be doing it, but I can't not see him, usually his words, but *I* actually mean it. Phil will also be getting his first pay at the end of April and that is most welcome, plus some of my clients have just paid their Q1 campaigns. I still have to be careful as although what is coming in this month covers what is going out for a change, I am unsure what the next month will bring. So I do some financial gymnastics and make it work. Again planned for his drumming night to ensure he could stay until almost 7 pm.

It is booked, we are on.

Sam has decided to take from April to mid-June off work. He has won some pretty big clients, his team can handle things, he is tired, and it's a break before a big project starts in June for him. After which he is going to be flat out busy. I am already thinking if that is the case from mid-June onwards, how on earth will we manage to see each other. I will worry about that later but for now, it makes being able to see him in April and May all the more important.

He wants to do something nice for Natasha and has set himself the challenge of transforming their large garden by fully landscaping it. It is a mammoth task and doesn't sound like much of a break from the stresses of his business to me.

I would not say things are back to normal, but they are better, he has maybe listened to a few of my pleas and is messaging a little more and seems a bit more engaged when we talk and message. It makes me feel a little calmer. I can't relax, but I feel a bit more comfortable than I have been feeling.

I love our messages and phone calls. It is literally the thing that helps me put one foot in front of the other as I navigate the sea of shit I exist in.

We can talk about literally anything, we just 'get' each other and connect. Mundane stuff is not even mundane with Sam. Filth chat as always is amazing and then we just get daft.

He was messaging me about how after July we will have to find a way to see each other, and perhaps he could secure some business down my way. He joked that we could meet in a woods, he could fuck me there and use 'what3words,' making the point and the dig that I have done it before.

> I know plenty of woods

I know you do

> Could give you a what 3 words location

Maybe you should give me what 3 words

> Dick in Ass!

Wonder if that is on what 3 words? 😏

Three's A Crowd

                                                                                          Fuck my face

Squeeze your throat

Make you cum

Roll your eyes

Flush your head

                                                                             No toilet in the woods 💨

                                                                                     Piss on me

                                                                           Devour your spunk

Donkey punch you

Rape your ass

Make you wet

Rub your clit

                                                                                Drain your balls

Finger your cunt

                                                                             Swallow your cock

                          These are the best collection of what three words

Pound your mound

Blast your ass

Roger with todger

Rock my cock

                                                                                 Gape my ass

                                                   We should rewrite what 3 words

                                                       Be much more interesting

                                                         Deliver in the shitter

                                                                   (that's 4) 💩

JCP Thomas

Drunk on spunk

Dream of cream

Glaze my face

Rim your ass

Teabag the slut

Being with Sam in any capacity feels so natural, like we've known each other forever. Conversations flow effortlessly, whether we're deep in thought or just talking about the little things. There's never any awkward silence; even when we don't speak, it feels comforting. Whether that is in person or via messages. It's like there is no pressure, no effort, just a sense of belonging that's hard to describe.

When we're together, everything feels right, and I can just be myself or as much of myself as is safe to show, completely at ease in a way I've never felt with anyone else. But when we're apart, apart physically or in terms of contact in general, it feels like something is missing. Every second apart feels heavier, like time slows down, and I can't wait to be in contact with Sam again.

It's hard to explain how someone can make you feel so light and yet make absence of any kind feel so heavy at the same time.

I am feeling a lot more energised with almost a month of semi sleep now, what a difference it makes. It is not full nights and every one disturbed with having to knock my alarm off, plus a full on bad one a couple of times a week, but I will take this over how it was any day of the week.

Phil is coping well in his new job, he doesn't love it, but he is getting on with it with a smile on his face. Thomas is sprouting, it literally seems like he gains overnight, every single night, and he now towers above me. Lottie is calmer, she is more on top of things and looking forward to her study leave.

I am not!

I love her to bits and adore spending time with her, not that while she is studying there will be much chance of that. But it will seriously curtail my wanks! That is another release and escape for me and without it I get very grumpy! I don't do grumpy, I survived six months on minimal sleep and was never grumpy, take away an un-curtailed wank, and you know all about it!

I will have to keep myself in check as I don't want to add to Lottie's stress by snipping at her because my clit has not had any attention!

It will be like weekends for a month. No more giving it laldy in my bedroom when the house is empty and back to muted controlled secret wanks in the bathroom. It will only add to my frustration.

It is often a game I play with myself, when having a coffee with a potential marketing client, or a beer with a friend. I wonder what their kink is? I wonder what causes them to chug their cocks to completion or rub their swollen clit and finger blast themselves into oblivion. I pick, who if I had to, would I fuck.

Wanking is still taboo, hidden, secret, unspoken. I like to imagine a time when wanking is accepted, after all it relieves stress and brings joy, much like going for a run and cycling. I imagine walking through a park, where wanking is happening all around you, but viewed no differently to reading a paper on a park bench or going for a jog.

As I walk by I see 'John' tugging his cock while watching Adriana Chechik have a fat cock rammed in her ass, or seeing Nick, sitting under the tree, spraying his load watching Bonnie Rotten getting facially abused.

"Morning Nick, nice load" I say as I give him a morning wave. Then passing Mary leaning on a fence rubbing her clit to some Max Hardcore.

"I've seen that one Mary, it's a cracker."

And I ***am*** sexually frustrated. Sam doesn't quite understand how often I used to get fucked and how hard this is for me as it is.

Being sexually frustrated feels like this restless, nagging tension that just won't go away. It's like there's this constant buzz under my skin, and no matter what I do, I can't shake it. My mind keeps circling back to that craving, and it only makes things worse, like the more I think about it, the more intense it gets.

It's hard to focus on anything else when my body feels wound up, so tight, like I'm waiting for some kind of release that never comes. There's this heat, this pull, and it leaves me feeling a bit on edge, like I'm wanting something so badly but can't quite get there. It's frustrating in the truest sense, and the longer it lasts, the more consuming it feels.

It is not just the physical either, I don't get what I need mentally any more and with Sam's waning interest it is worse, yes it's better (ish) than it was for a few months, but it is not enough and I feel pretty empty.

Missing the feeling of being wanted, desired, and useful leaves me feeling hollow, like I've lost something essential. It's not just the absence of connection, a connection and purpose I used to get every few days not once in four months. It's this deep ache of not being needed or valued. I miss that sense of purpose, of knowing that I matter to someone, even if that was just hole related. Without that, it's hard not to feel pointless, like I'm just drifting without direction.

It makes me feel almost invisible like I'm just taking up space without contributing anything meaningful. That feeling of worth, of being desired for my slut skills, for who I am and what I bring to someone's life, it's gone, and without it, I feel worthless. Like if no one needs me, what's the point? It's a heavy emptiness.

It's hard to shake the feeling that if I'm not wanted, then maybe I'm not worth much at all. And at the moment there is not much indication I am wanted by anyone.

I can't raise my extreme sexual frustration with him as I don't want him doubting my ability not to jump on another cock. I know

Three's A Crowd

while he wants me around I wouldn't do that, but given my past it would be hard to convince him of that.

Even more so at the moment, as Emily continues to make trouble for me. They message each other quite a lot now. Mostly heated from what I can tell, but it makes me feel very uncomfortable.

The result is messages from Sam that come out of the blue, things I have forgotten about but he wants to know more about.

> Hotel, client, paid you extra, tied you up and blindfolded you, bought in extra men... is this true?

>> Yes, is this fucking Emily?

> Yes. How many extra men?

>> I don't know. Please don't engage with her

> WHAT! How can you not know? You let this happen? 😡

>> Yes

> Why? And don't say money..

>> Idk, he was paying, it's what he wanted

> It could have been anyone Jess?

>> I knew the client, trusted him

> BB?

>> Don't think so, saw condoms in the bin after

> But you don't know?

>> No, not for certain.

> FFS you're lucky, you could have caught anything, they might have filmed it.

> My client knew I didn't allow that.

But you wouldn't know, would you?

> No

What were you thinking?

> I wasn't. Sam, please, stop messaging Emily.

I want to know, so why don't you just tell me?

> I don't know what to tell you. You know the job I did I can't remember everything.

Then Emily will tell me…

> Please Sam, it's in the past, it should stay there. It is not relevant to us

I want to know. Not up for discussion. And you EVER allow yourself to be treated like that again, I will beat your ass

> OK

I mean it Jess, you're worth more than that.

I always feel sick when he gets like this, it's like the more he learns, the more astounded and disappointed he gets. This information can only have come from Emily, she is the only other person who knows, and the scariest thing is she knows a lot more than that. I am petrified of what he is going to discover from talking to her.

Emily surprised me by joining me on a walk one day. It was a typical April day, rain one moment and blistering sun the next. I was taking off my jacket having gone from freezing to the sun splitting the sky when she appeared.

"He just won't go"

"Well, the way you're going Emily, that is only a matter of time."

"I am going to tell him everything Jess, once he knows all you have done, how low you have gone, he will not want anything to do with you."

"I know"

I have given up arguing with her. I can't stop her.

It feels very much like the net is closing in. There are three things which could mark it being over for good, all a very real possibility:

1. Sam is caught again
2. Marriage counselling is successful and provides him with all he needs at home.
3. He realising who I really am;
   - Far too needy for his complicated life
   - Not in his league
   - A bigger slut than he could possibly ever imagine.

Those fears and doubts are a constant cloud in my thoughts which I try to blow away.

Silence and minimal contact fluff those clouds up, making them bigger and harder to expel. Just as communication has increased a little, and it is making me feel a bit less vulnerable, my own internal dialog begins to reduce in volume. Easter hits and he heads away with the family for a break, and the volume turns up.

I want to go see my Mum, I have not seen her this year, but I can't justify the time or expense. I need money in the door not out, so spend the kids' Easter holiday frantically working. The guilt is awful, not so bad for Lottie as she just wants to study, but I feel awful for Thomas. I pause whenever he needs me to run him to his friends, but we can't do anything together and I can't give him money to 'do' things with his friends. He is incredibly mature and understanding about it all, which only makes me feel worse.

A highlight is a client got me a £50 just eat voucher as a thank you for the work I had done for her on her facebook campaigns. So one night we all got a takeaway treat, but even with £50 I still had to add £12 to it. It was worth it, it was like we had won the lottery and all ate until we could hardly move.

Sam heads to the lodge he owns in the mountains by a lake. It is not like last October, he does have a signal, but it is *'family time'*, so he is barely more than inches away from Natasha making messaging rare.

They take paddle boards with them for the lake, and bikes to cycle the trails. It's just after 9am, I imagine they are having a family breakfast or still sleeping. I might hear from him, a quick text to say good morning, followed by a 'I am just going for a shower, catch you later have a good day', or I might hear nothing, I can never be sure. I might get a quick message at night that leads to a ten minute exchange or a simple 'good night, love you.'

I realise like a love sick teen I am jealous. I don't think I have experienced that before. I had one boyfriend at 16 and one at 18, but jealousy did not occur. Then Phil, no jealousy there either. But I suppose they didn't spend the bulk of their life with another woman and I didn't love them. I may have thought I did, but I now know I have only experienced that once. I find myself thinking; Is he getting better from her? Is he telling her he loves her? Why can't I be the one to wake up with him?

It is very hard not to feel used and dropped.

It just all feels a bit asymmetrical. I have some degree of certainty he wants me but it feels like he wants me more physically, not wholly and only when it fits in with his life. He can compartmentalise easily.

Sometimes I feel like I need a way out of this, but it is so hard, as I can't picture life without him.

It is not like the safari, I do hear from him every day, but I don't get the volume downloads like I did then, the heartfelt messages. The silence for days was torture, but at least I got some validation, some feeling that he had at least thought of me for more than a nanosecond. Lodge messages are a few words, if that.

Three's A Crowd

Like a fool, with no slutmin, and no one else to talk to, I write to him every night in his absence. Not for him, for me.

When he is back, I learn it has not been the best trip, weather awful, and a good few blow ups about snoop gate and their future, where Natasha accuses him of making no change or effort. It is a strange feeling hearing that, torn between sadness for him. I love him and don't want him to be sad, he deserves a break, he deserves a laugh, he deserves to feel welcome, valued and wanted in his family space. But also relieved. Relieved I am not yet no longer required. I get him for a bit longer.

Finally, I get to see him again, the second time in six months, we have spoken and messaged, filth is in full flow and his requests this time are a secretary, a nun and my gang bang dress. He wants me to recreate some events for him, saying 'if you did it for them, you will do it for me.'

I arrive and check in, he arrives maybe forty minutes later, he doesn't run to me or kiss me or look excited to see me, he walks right up to me, spins me around, hikes up my skirt and spanks my ass hard.

It's hot, my pussy streams.

"Don't you ever lie to me again, I ask where you are, you tell me."

I knew driving was still an adrenaline sport for me, as although I am sleeping better I am still tired and lacking focus, I didn't want the pressure of him checking on my progress every two minutes. So I lied about when I left and when I would arrive.

We rough fuck all afternoon with a bit of light pain thrown in for good measure. My pussy fed on him like a starved animal. My mouth is sucking the life out of his cock.

Having found out details of what I suppose was a 'surprise gang bang', he uses that to shame, embarrass and degrade me while fucking the shit out of me.

While he is fucking my ass and ramming a dildo in my pussy he is saying things like:

"You fucking whore, how many cocks did you take in that hotel?"

I can't speak, I am so embarrassed by my actions.

"You don't even know, you dirty bitch, do you?"

"No.." I whisper as my tits are swinging from the force of his thrusts.

"You fucking slut, mouth, cunt and ass, stuffed with multiple cocks... you could pass them in the street and you'd not know they fucked you...you worthless piece of cum hungry cock sucking shit."

Despite the shame, my body betrays me and I have the most intense anal orgasm, rippling throughout my groin, legs shaking as I absorb the intense sensations. Just fucking bliss on a dick.

The interlude conversations are easy, except when he starts questioning me about some of my sexual escapades or saying he loves me. When he degrades me sexually while fucking the shit out of me it is hot, when he talks seriously about my stupidity, wanting me to think about how I have allowed myself to be treated, it is uncomfortable.

We laugh and I enjoy every second of actually being able to see and touch him and lay my eyes on him in person rather than through a screen.

This visit is harder, I have nothing to do in the evening, when he goes home. I go to a lakeside beach he recommends and walk until the sunsets. Emotional and distracted I get lost on the way back, overshooting the exit back to my car and having to walk far longer, as the sun sets I lose the heat in my body and shiver in the freezing cold.

The sky has that strange glow about it as it shifts from day to night. Misty appears from the bushes, gaunt, haunted and wanting in her eyes. I fly at her, I don't know why, all the pent-up frustrations pouring out of me, she grabs me digs in her nails and I scream at her to "piss off". She goes, distraught looking, guilt and frustration coat my entire being.

Three's A Crowd

As I drive back to the hotel, I pass Sam's town, shaking, I punch in his address into my phone.

I don't know why I'm doing this. My hands are gripping the steering wheel too tightly, knuckles white, like they're the only things tethering me to reality. I've told myself a thousand times to turn around, go back to the hotel, but I can't seem to listen. My mind keeps screaming stop, but my body, my heart, something inside me, is pulling me closer to his house. To 'their' house.

Olivia Rodrigo's song driving licence[13] is playing, the lyrics... they are apt:

How can she not be everything I'm insecure about? The guy I love chooses to be with her. He chose her as 'the one' for him. He spends all his time with her, he is fighting to save his marriage with her. And just like the song, he is absolutely fine okay when I am gone.

As I drive through the unfamiliar streets, I feel sick. Every turn, feels like I'm heading deeper into some twisted trap of my own making. Why am I doing this? What am I even hoping to see? To feel? It's like some cruel urge I can't fight, as if looking in on his real life will somehow make sense of the chaos in my own head. But I know deep down, I'm just torturing myself.

I pause a few houses down. I sit there, frozen, staring at the house that belongs to him, to her, to them. My heart is pounding so hard I can hear it, and every sound outside feels deafening in the silence of my car. It's like the world is taunting me, reminding me I don't belong here.

I'm petrified that Natasha will see me. I imagine her face at the window, drawing the curtains, her eyes narrowing as she catches sight of me in my car, her realisation it is me, I am sure from snoop gate she will have seen pictures of me and my face is burned into her retina for life, the face she hates. There's no excuse for this. There's no reason. I'd look like an insane stalker, and maybe that's exactly what I am.

I shouldn't be here. I **know** I shouldn't be here. But the pull is stronger than the fear. I find myself glancing up at the house, half terrified, half desperate for a glimpse of something. He's home right now. They're inside, laughing, playing house like the perfect little family they are. I'm terrified that if I see them happy, together, it'll rip something inside me apart that I can never put back together.

But at the same time, there's this sick curiosity, this need to see the life I'm not part of. I feel cold. Cold inside, cold outside. Like I'm standing on the edge of something, peering in at a world that's warm and whole, while I'm left out here in the dark, frozen, with no way in.

I feel ridiculous. Like I've lost any sense of who I am, or what I'm doing. This isn't me. I'm not the kind of person who sits outside someone's house, scared to be seen, scared to see. But here I am. Watching from the outside, because that's all I'll ever be. On the outside.

I head back to the hotel, just a few miles away from him, and all I can think about is how close he is but still so far out of reach. He's at home right now, playing house, wrapped in the life I'm not part of. His Wife by his side, their routine, their shared history, here I am, stuck in this limbo. I long for the past, when we used to get to spend an evening together and fall asleep in each others arms.

The bed feels empty, too big, too cold, even though I know it's just me in here. It's the kind of loneliness that gets under your skin, the kind that makes you question everything, why am I doing this to myself? I try to push it all away, but the thoughts creep in no matter how much I tell myself it doesn't matter. It does matter. It matters so damn much.

I imagine them together, her laugh, his smile, the ease they must have, and it makes my stomach churn with this sharp, ugly jealousy. It's irrational, I know. She's his wife. But that doesn't stop the sting. Doesn't stop the way it eats at me, like a reminder of what I'll never have with him. I wonder if he even thinks about me, just down the road, or if he's too caught up in that life, his real life.

Three's A Crowd

And here I am, on the outskirts, alone. **Always alone**. It's like being stuck in a place where I can see everything I want but can never touch it, and it burns.

He messages later and I tell him what I have done. I expect him to be angry, but he is not.

The next day, our full day, I am to be a nun.

I get up stupidly early and shower singing my heart out to Chloe Adam's song - Dirty Thoughts[8] and it rings true, I can't help dirty thoughts about Sam, he is just too damned hot, and our connection electric, being away from him just intensifies those thoughts.

Once again I am ready **way** before I need to be. Once again he arrives **way** later than he said. Once again the doubts come. Once again they fade when I see him. Once again I consume his cock, his cum, his words, his scent, his eyes, every part of him, I immerse myself in the glory of Sam.

For the nun session, he is a rogue sex addict sent to me, to pray for him and save him from himself. In preparation for his arrival I have used my extendable selfie stick tripod and used elastic bands to strap one of my dildo's across it to make a makeshift crucifix.

I encourage him to kneel next to me and put his hands together to pray to the lord, seeking forgiveness and guidance. I recite the Lord's prayer and encourage him to say it with me.

"Our Father, who art in heaven, hallowed be thy name; thy kingdom come; thy will be done; on earth as it is in heaven. Give us this day our daily bread. And forgive us our trespasses, as we forgive those who trespass against us. And lead us not into temptation; but deliver us from evil..."

Being a sex addict he is unable to keep his hands to himself, making things very difficult for me, as I have to knock his hands away and threaten to call Father James in. Before I know it, I am taking an unwanted vow of silence, by being gagged by his fat cock, my coif slipping off my head. Then he takes me on the floor and converts me to his ways, and shows me who my true God is, his throbbing cock.

As ever it was fun, hot, and I could role play with him all day, we have so many ideas. I am in heaven, the heaven I believe in, covered in fluffy cum clouds, until he leaves, earlier than he said. And once again I am alone, while he is a few miles away with his family.

I don't know why I find this so hard, but I do find it **very** hard.

It is so different from when we spent nights together.

It seems silly, because he is with his family most of the time anyway, why is this so different? I think it just serves to make it more obvious and in your face. I can't pretend.

It feels different. It just shines a light on how much has changed and what he is really coming to me for.

I can't face another night alone so I head to the bar, have a couple of drinks and some soup. I chat to some locals and enjoy the distraction from my thoughts.

Sam messages, he doesn't want me in the bar drinking and I don't blame him, he knows my history, well, a lot of it. But I don't want to be alone either. I don't want to worry him, so I head back to my room. After we finish messaging, tiredness engulfs me and I fall asleep.

That was a mistake, I forgot my alarm and without that, I find my nightmares return and I spend three hours awake and drawing.

Shock and fear hit me when the next thing I hear is Sam's voice. I am confused.

SHIT SHIT SHIT!

I am not ready, I am not showered or dressed and no makeup and groggy. I am so upset with myself. Last time and this time, I gave him a spare key card to the room, so he could let himself in on arrival.

Sam is sweet, patient and calms me, we don't fuck as I tell him about my dream. I am still shaken. He looks after me. I needed

Three's A Crowd

that. But I am annoyed at myself for talking about what I don't want to talk to him about.

As it is time to leave and check out, panic hits me, and I apologise. I realise I have not sucked his cock or fucked him or anything, what a waste, he must be disappointed and annoyed. I have not delivered, not fulfilled my role, I have to make it up to him. I say I can suck his cock now through tears, feeling like the world's biggest failure and cursing my nightmare and stupid damn head.

Why can't I just be simple? Why can't life just go my way, for once?

Leaving feeling disappointed is worse than any other time. He leaves first to avoid us being seen together. I watch him walk to his car from the window. Distraught. Then I leave, struggling to hold myself together.

He calls and I can't take the call. Eventually I do, he speaks to me most of the way. Then has to go as he needs to pick up Beth. But once he has Beth he continues to check in on my progress the whole way via messages. He sends songs for me to listen to.

This time I don't lie about where I am on my journey.

The void and emptiness lingers for days. But he then talks of meeting again in May, he lifts my spirits by giving me something to focus on, it helps knowing he wants to see me again, despite being let down that morning. I am better, more settled and positive when I know what is going on, when I can see a line in the sand, a target to aim for, I ***will*** see him again.

As I begin to feel calmer over the following days and weeks, we message with some level of consistency and enjoy video calls and filth. Until it is shattered once again with Emily and her big wooden spoon, revealing more of my past, which leads to the Spanish Inquisition on:

Wetting myself in public.

Flashing my pussy in a bar.

Being fucked in a toilet.

Doing a cum walk

Being hired for an entire night to be the party entertainment for six married men when their wives were away.

I want to curl up and die. He won't let any of these go, he wants details, lots of details, he wants to know why, how I felt, what I was thinking. He says I am a dirty bitch , a whore, a slut. He wants me to do videos describing the events and my feelings around them. He wants to see the shame in my face as I retell these tales. I ask why, he says it makes him hard seeing me squirm. It does make me squirm.

He says I am a fool. Maybe I am.

Chapter 39

May-Day! May-Day!

Sam is now in full swing on his obsession with landscaping the garden. It means we get way more opportunity to talk which is amazing as he is home alone most of the time while Beth is at school and Natasha is at work. A lot of what he is doing means he can multitask. He can chat away for hours while he digs holes and paints fences.

It is as close as we can get to being in each others lives, and it feels easy, like a distanced domestic life. I am working away and chatting, so is he, he pauses and makes lunch and continues talking. I get to see him on screen in all sorts of interesting angles as he scales ladders and bangs nails into things.

Lottie is on study leave but she sits with noise-cancelling headphones in, at the other end of the house, my desk is positioned such that I can see her coming, so I can pause the video if she needs anything.

Sam and I even manage a good few mutual wanks. His latest thing is using his discoveries about my past and watching me squirm with shame and embarrassment. He loves it, I hate it, but even though I hate it, the way he talks to me and degrades and humiliates me does something to my pussy that is new and I love and hate it.

Outside of him getting off on my discomfort he also digs and digs. He wants into the heart of my psyche. He can't understand how I don't have all the details to share. Truth is on some events I just kind of zone out, always have, or sometimes I drift in and out. He is back on this all being linked to my past, to Darren, to my 'PTSD' and my 'hyper-sexuality.'

Whatever.

He is concerned I don't value or love myself, but I assure him I do. I know I am quite creative, hard working, and despite my bad behaviour a thoughtful and kind person. I know when I am less overwhelmed with life due to Misty and finances, I am a fun person, always up for a laugh. So ***I do*** love and value myself.

He asks what I was chasing doing the things I did. I can't really answer. He says my GW profile attracted the wrong sort of person. Each moment he discovers something else is a new torture, a new moment of this is it, this will be the one that makes him go, enough now, you really are nothing but a cheap whore, and I am done with you.

Emily feeds him stuff constantly, he jumps on everything she says and delves deeper. He says she is a bitch and not a good friend. He says he now knows Emily encouraged me to see the stomach punching no condom man, purely to try and break us up, she has admitted that to him and said she was glad she did it. He is dumbfounded. How could a real friend betray all my secrets, encourage her friend to do something he felt put me at risk, want to remove the man I love and believe I am nothing but a piece of shit.

I can see his point, I am very much coming round to that way of thinking and frankly want her to piss off. Yet she is my oldest and dearest friend, she has been with me through thick and thin, she has been a shoulder to cry on (well, for a nanosecond before being told to 'fucking grow a pair and get over it'), she has picked me up when I am down, she has always got me home safely, she has warned and protected me from men who didn't care about me and that is all she is doing now. Granted badly, and possibly for the first time ever she is off the mark here.

What is fascinating about Sam is, he is different to other men in how he views some of these events. Sam knows more than anyone now bar Emily, but the likes of Szymon knew a few things I had done. Not once did any of them question why I did it, or how I felt or what I was seeking, or could I not see the risk. They just wanted the details. Those questions never entered my head either.

He wants the details, absolutely, but he also goes deeper. He makes me think in ways I have never thought before. Why did I agree to some of these things? Was I seeking something?

If I struggle to recall details, I don't escape the torture, he asks Emily. Emily recalls more than me, as I would usually tell her straight after all that had happened while it was fresh. I don't know how Emily recalls all the details so well, as I can't and I was there.

Sam begins to cross-check my videos with Emily to make sure he has got every last detail.

The worst was the party girl night. He was really pissed off about that. I did my best, told him I was hired from 8pm until 8am, shared what I had to wear and that I was expected to serve drinks, fetch things and serve my holes as required. There were six guys and I filled him in on being fucked on the coffee table, up against a wall, over the kitchen counter and woken a couple of times in the night to be fucked. Most of it in front of the five remaining men. Being required to jump up and down and crawl across the floor while one guy with an erect cock backed away.

When he cross-referenced it with Emily he discovered more. He specifically asked me things like did you do this or that. I said no, then Emily fills him in and he is all pissed off saying I lied or evaded revealing the truth. He was not impressed with this event at all. He even worked out how many men and fucks and a price per hole based on what they paid for the night, which he said made me very cheap, in both senses of the word. He made a big deal out of my required parting gift which was having to rim and wank each guy, like a production line, as they sat legs up on an L shaped sofa, and I crawled from one butt and cock to the next, only moving on as one completed.

One night I was particularly upset about his discoveries, convinced he would end it, he spent a long time messaging, then following up the next day with messages and voice notes reassuring me that it didn't matter what Emily said, he was not leaving me, no matter what he discovered about my past, it was in the past and he loved me.

He said that yes, he wanted details for his own sexual gratification, but he also wanted to understand me more, to help me, he wanted me to see the crazy risks I had taken, understand them rather than dismiss them, he wanted to see me live to experience my grandkids.

I took offence at that, I didn't need help, I have looked after myself and survived a full 48 years now. That was proof in my eyes that I was perfectly capable of assessing risk and surviving. He disagreed... using the 'Lottie test', would I be happy with Lottie being a 'party girl' for £17 a hole? Of course there is only one answer to that which is no.

But Lottie is not me, she is better. (But I don't share that thought and just tell him what he wants to hear).

You could hear the 'mic drop', 'I rest my case' from a mile away. Apparently I mattered and needed to realise it.

He reassured me there was nothing Emily could say or do that would make him leave and sent me the song 'White Flag' By Dido[9]. I do not think I am deserving of this love, yet he just doesn't ever seem to give up on me, despite everything. Most men would have legged it a long time ago. The song was perfect and it helped. Sam always has a way of convincing me in my darkest moments and for that I am grateful.

Three's A Crowd

What men want in women is interesting. Who they choose to be their partner sexually compared to being the person in their life and the mother of their child is a conflict. It is called the Madonna - Whore complex. Maybe this is why dead bedrooms occur, it has been found that once a man loves a woman and sees them as the mother of their offspring, they lose sexual desire for them. Yet they still need their sexual desires met and seek out women like me, who deep down they don't really care about or respect and just use to fulfil their deepest fantasies they cannot do with the woman they love. So Sam may not be waving his white flag, yet I still feel I fulfil the whore need, not the Madonna one. Women with my history are not desired to be permanently part of a man's life.

Misty continued to lurk and catch me at various points. She is angry at me, I know she is, I can see the fire and frustration in her eyes. Sometimes she shouts, sometimes she screams, sometimes she digs her nails into my sore swollen scabby wrists. I know I need to face her again and help. I keep cycling through, leave me be, I have too much going on in my life, to then view her like a lost child, similar to Lottie, and needing help, so desperately.

I got a referral plus a recommendation via my menopause brand lady and have another exciting opportunity to work on a health wearable campaign related to diabetes and blood sugar. It's potentially a big contract and I am excited about it, so I have been very much focused on that. It could be a big payday, so I am working all hours to deliver on it.

Knowing I am seeing Sam in about a week is the only thing keeping me going, and he has already given me my 'instructions' on how he wants me presented. Hotels remain pricey due to heading towards tourist season but I manage to get a similar deal to last time. The plan is almost identical to last time too. Arriving at 3 pm day one, day two is his drumming lesson meaning he can stay with me until just before 7 pm, day three I've paid an extra £10 for a late check-out giving us until midday.

Then he drops the bomb:

It's a screenshot of a text exchange between him and Natasha. Natasha:

> I have managed to get an appt 4:10 on Tuesday, it's the only time I can get. I won't be able to collect Beth as normal. Should I cancel or can you get her?

> It's drumming night

> I know, but it's the only time, What do you want me to do?

> I will get Beth

And that is it....again, our time curtailed once again, another time Sam can't do anything to accommodate me. I am driving an eight to ten hour round trip, spending over £300 on hotels and petrol, sitting on my todd each night, losing three days of work, and I get at most ten hours in his company. Fewer hours with him, than I am actually sitting in a fucking hotel for.

> I can't really say no, she has had a bad back for ages, I am 'off' work, I don't have an excuse not to help.

I am devastated and feel like a fool, cast aside yet again. Logically and rationally he is right, there is no real excuse... But what pisses me off and hurts is he literally would never even consider any other options. Natasha says jump, he says how high. I will **never, ever** be prioritised, **ever**. How the fuck am I supposed to feel loved. He might say it, but he never shows me.

> I know. Have a good evening

He knows I am upset and so, I get messages, more than usual, and voice notes. He is gutted too, if he could think of a way, bla bla bla. If I can think of something he is all ears.

Three's A Crowd

BLA BLA BLA! Whatever, prick.

How about getting Beth to go to a friend's place for a play date? How about asking granny... how about putting her to an after school club... I don't know, call me crazy but I don't think an extra £20 is a stretch for them.

But of course it will be; 'how can I justify that when I am so close to the school, off work and could get her?'

In my head it is simple. You justify it by saying:

"Natasha, that appointment is really important, you must do it, we will find a way, but I love drumming, it keeps me sane and is the **only** hour I get to myself, how about we see if Emma's mum would have Beth for a couple of hours after school until you get home? Then we both get what we need?"

Or

"Natasha, that appointment is really important, you must do it, we will find a way, but I have been called into an important work meeting, how about we see if Granny would have Beth for a couple of hours after school until you get home? Then we both get what we need?"

Or

"Natasha that appointment is really important, you must do it, we will find a way, but I have the worlds biggest slut coming to see, me, she has come an awfully long way and given the fact you don't let me fuck you, I do need to unload in her ass, how about we see if Emma's mum would have Beth for a couple of hours after school until you get home? Then we both get what we need?"

But I don't suggest it, no point, I will be in the wrong, again, coming across as unreasonable, again, asking too much, again, not understanding and would just have to endure all the reasons why my ideas won't work.

So you know what... forget about it. I will be there, like the fucking tool I am, with my legs open waiting, whenever it suits him to get to me. What's fucking new. Yeah of course you love me, and don't see me as just a set of convenient fuck holes.

And that is exactly what happens, I arrive, he comes thirty minutes later than planned, he leaves earlier than planned, day two he arrives later than planned, no communication about him being late. He leaves early to get Beth from school. On the final morning, he comes late and leaves early. He pays for my 'petrol' (not me apparently). I sit alone for two nights and then I go home.

The bits I do see him are of course totally cocktastic, cumfilled, orgasmic, connected emotionally, physically, affectionate, like it **is** all real.

Is this the biggest gas light of all time?

You can't beat it. This is why I come, as those precious hours are like nothing on this earth. I feel nothing but overwhelming love for him, I want and need him so badly. He is a drug. I have a Sam habit. Instead of inhaling lines of coke through my nose, its ribbons of cum on my tongue. I just can't kick it, even though I know it's not good for me.

June is our last 'definite' chance to see each other as we enter the unknown. After that he is super busy on projects and I will just about have run out of excuses to visit Cumbria.

Hotel prices are now four times the price they were in March. I can't possibly stay over. Day use is higher too, but far cheaper to book that than an overnight **and** day use. An overnight and late check out would only give us until midday.

I check out some hotels midway up and prices look much more reasonable. The day before he can manage, I have a meeting further south, so I go to that meeting and then head north. On the way I thankfully found a last minute deal, otherwise I would have been sleeping in my car. I picked up a couple of hitch-hikers on the way and dropped them at a nearby youth hostel to my hotel. Their company is welcome as they distract me from my thoughts as I drive up. Pulling out of the youth hostel car park, standing on the opposite side of the road, is a tall figure, sunglasses on. Staring right over at my car, well I think he is, it is hard to tell with his shades on. His brown curls glinted in the evening sun. As I turn the wheel and pass him, he gives a nod and raises his hand slowly in a hello motion. I check my rear view mirror assuming he is waving at someone behind me. No one is there. As I straighten up on the adjoining road, a chill runs through me, I check my mirror, and he is still there, but he has turned, so he is now square on with the boot of my car, as if he has turned to ensure I know the wave is for me.

The next morning I get ready and head to the day use to check in. This time he wants me in a long dress with no pants on. Its from a vintage porn scene he loves, where the woman is cheeky, then raises the front of the dress, exposing her bare pussy and says 'well, what are you waiting for' and he fucks her in quite an animalistic way. I love a bit of role play but being all demanding is not me and I do an utterly crap job of it. Next outfit was my 'party girl' attire, which was actually a pencil skirt I pulled up under my tits and put a belt around my waist. It meant my tits and all my holes were always on show and accessible. That is what the 'party girl' men requested, they wanted to just plough into me whenever the mood took them over the evening, in between watching sport and grabbing food.

Sam wanted to see this slut attire for himself.

We fucked like animals too, I literally cannot get enough of that man and his cock. When he fucked me in an almost pretzel position I was trapped under him, which I find hot, I love feeling overpowered, trapped and helpless. His cock bashed against my cervix, it was very uncomfortable, but also hot as fuck. Hell ,just bloody everything with him is hot as fuck.

This departure was one of the worst ever. With no mention of the 'next time' or either of us knowing how that would even be possible. I felt like all was lost and most of all, I felt like I had lost him.

Chapter 40
Misty & Friends

Time has become this endless void, stretching out in front of me like a dark highway with no signs, no stops, no end in sight. Each day bleeds into the next, a monotonous blur of routine and silence, but it's the waiting that gnaws at me the most. The absence of a plan, of even a tentative date to see Sam, a constant ache I can't shake.

I try to distract myself, keep busy, but nothing really helps. Every moment is tinged with this hollow sense of not knowing, of not having anything to look forward to. It's like time itself has lost meaning, no longer tied to anything real. Just endless hours pass by, and each one without him feels heavier than the last.

The worst part is the uncertainty, this gnawing fear that maybe a plan will never come. That I'm just drifting, waiting for something that might not even happen. It feels like standing at the edge of a vast, empty ocean, staring out at nothing but dark water and a sky that never changes. No horizon. No shore. Just me, lost in this eternal stretch of waiting, with no idea when, if I'll ever see him again.

With his garden landscape project completed. He is headed back to work with a focus and determination around this new big project. He says there is a lot to do, and learn and it is likely he will be distracted with it for some time until he can get his head around it.

He has also made a decision. He has concluded he likes being at home, and so has cancelled his co-working space. Most of his team work remotely, he only really had it to discipline himself into a routine and utilise the meeting space for clients, but he can still hire that space on an as needed basis. There will be no drives to and from work any more. But there may be more chances to chat during the day, work dependant.

Natasha only works a four-day week and is off on a Friday, leaving us Monday to Thursday to speak, the remainder of the time will be via messages.

He can't yet tell me what things will look like, he needs to see how the project goes. But assured me I do not need to worry, we will find time to talk, he will make sure it happens, he has to take lunch every day, worst case that will be our chance.

Before starting this new project, Natasha has taken a few days annual leave and they head to Manchester to take Beth to a Taylor Swift concert. Not quite radio silence but almost is reinstated.

Lottie had wanted to go to that concert. It is literally the only thing she wanted, all her friends were going. I couldn't make it happen for her. Yet another thing I cannot do for them.

When he is away at the concert, every time Sam's name lights up my phone, my heart skips a beat. Even though it's just short messages, with a massive gap between them as he is in company and always something simple, a few words to keep me updated and dangle the carrot:

> Arrived x
>
> Concert amazing will send videos later I miss you
>
> Love you

I latch onto them like a lifeline. I reply instantly, desperate to catch him, to hold onto the brief chance of a real conversation. But by the time I've sent it, he's already gone. His messages always feel like these fleeting glimpses, like he's tossing me a crumb before disappearing again. And then I'm left waiting, staring at my phone, knowing it'll sit unread for hours and hours.

It happens over and over, he sends something, I jump on it, hoping this time we'll actually get an exchange, that maybe this time he'll stick around for more than a passing moment. But he never does. I'm left hanging, my words hanging there in the void, unanswered. It's like screaming into a canyon, only to hear my own voice echo back.

I recognise he has company and it is hard, it's harder my end, I am certain of it. He is distracted, having fun with family, or head in this project. I just have the void.

After a while, I just stopped trying. It feels pointless, sending messages that only get acknowledged when he feels like it, when it's convenient for him. I can't keep being the one who's always waiting, always hoping for a reply that never really satisfies. It only serves to show how much this is all on his terms, he gets what he needs, when he needs it. I'm just there, on standby, waiting for the next breadcrumb.

And me? I'm left empty, drained by this one-sided effort, by the endless cycle of giving and getting nothing back.

I've stopped proactively messaging in the main because, honestly, it just reminds me of the imbalance between us, I respond to his messages and no longer share my day unless he asks. I don't bother to send things I have seen that make me laugh or I think will bring a smile to his face or things I see that make me think of him. It is pointless.

It's so clear, he can come and go as he pleases, dip in and out when it suits him, while I'm left holding on to every little interaction like it might fill this gaping hole. But it never does. And I'm tired of feeling like I'm always the one left behind, waiting, empty.

The kids are counting down the days until summer break, Phil has settled into his job, and we have two of his pay days in the bag. He is still looking for other positions, he is better than this role, but nothing is really grabbing his attention.

After a flurry of work for me and some payments due, my leads have dried up and I am growing very concerned. Maybe I will have to turn my back on this and get a proper full-time job again. If only I could supplement it with some GW work, I could fill the gap. Filling my holes to fill the gap. Just enough until my business becomes consistent. I know I am exceptional at what I do, but time is against me. The tipping point within the business must be close, but it may well be too far out for me to make it. I may have to turn my back on this dream.

That's another skill I possess, letting dreams go.

Why am I not skilled in a man truly wanting me? All of me, that is the skill I would like the most.

June brings with it some warmth in the air. Ron likes to lay on the front step of my house, absorbing the cold from the concrete, while his fur sucks in the heat from above, so in the summer I prop the door open for him so he can enjoy that, but can find me if he needs me.

The step gives him the best vantage point to protect and warn off passers-by. He is not a barker. If he went for a job as a security guard he would not get it. He does not possess the skills. It is like he knows what he should do, but cannot follow through on it.

From the office upstairs I hear him gruff and woof for ten seconds whenever a delivery driver or postie comes up the drive, followed quickly by sounds of "Awww cute, good dog" and the thumping of his tail.

Useless, but utterly loveable.

With the kids and Phil gone, I prop open the door for Ron and head up to the office. Today's job, lead generation. I desperately needed some new business.

As I hang up from a call to Barry, a tree surgeon looking to start

Three's A Crowd

optimising his social media, I put on a 90's playlist while I write up my notes and craft an email with my proposal and pricing.

"Rhythm is a dancer[12]' comes on and it makes me smile, recalling times in my teens when my friends and I used to change the lyrics to all the things that rhythm might be, if rhythm was not a dancer, maybe rhythm is a tree surgeon!

I hear Ron starting to gruff, it's not a bark, his low gruffs also make me smile, he sounds so serious. Looking at the time I figure it must be Sandy the postie. I have a return to hand him, so I head down the stairs. I am expecting him to be rubbing Ron's belly on the doorstep, but he is nowhere to be seen. I step outside and look around the garden, no sign of him. Maybe Ron just saw a squirrel run across the garden or someone walk past. A cloud blocks the sun and the temperature drops, a shiver runs over me and I turn back into the house. I stop dead, Misty, is standing inside the porch, her eyes exceptionally tortured today.

"Don't turn me away, please," She says weakly.

I am thinking of all the things I need to do, but how can I turn her away? There is something about her that tells me this is important, she really needs me today.

I nod and brush past her into the living room. Ron follows and jumps onto the sofa, favouring the soft comfort it provides over the concrete step. I don't blame him.

I sit down, Misty joins me. She takes my hands softly and leans her head against mine and begins to talk in a low, whispering voice that is shrouded in distress.

Dominic's Dad is away I have to go to the party I don't want to
Its OK, its small, just close friends
I am staying at Anne's after
It's safe.
Help set up
Stormy wild night
Noisy
Everyone must know

More and more people come Dominic is stressed
Dancing - Rhythm is a dancer[12]

When she says this my heart stops, I can't believe that I just played on my 90's Spotify mix. I have not heard that song in decades, yet here it is, twice in one day. I am surprised this generation even knows that song.

Darren, James, Mark Christopher - arrive I go to the kitchen
Away from them
Don't want to be seen

It's fine, it's fine, it's fine, it's fine, it's busy, it's busy, it's busy, it's busy , just avoid, avoid, avoid, avoid!

I down some water. I can't leave Staying at Anne's
I need to hide
Break past makeshift barrier on the stairs
Head to a bedroom
Close the door
I sit down
Tuck my legs under me
Pumping music
Howling wind
Beating rain
Door opens
They found me
"How smart, waiting for us in a bedroom"
They kick off shoes and clothes
I won't be heard
Music, wind, rain
Four against one
Unthinkable
The group everyone worships
No chance
My words won't matter
Mark pulls me up
"Please let me go," I whisper. "Please!"

Three's A Crowd

"Ha" says Mark "Did you hear that? Making out she doesn't want this?"

"Let's find out shall we?" Smirks Darren. "Strip her."

I drop to the floor again.
James & Mark lift me
Wrestling with the Zip on the back of my dress,
I fight
They win
Dress off
Standing in my tights
No bra
Christopher helps
Tights and pants off
I'm totally naked
Try to curl into a ball
I am lifted to standing.
Curl my arms around me
"Feel her pussy" says Darren.
Mark inserts a finger
Removes it
Holds it up "wet as Fuck"
"What an actress"
"Pathetic"
James and Mark hold my arms out
Exposed
Darren come over
Grabs and pokes parts of me

"Thought I told you to fucking sort this, and this and this, do you know how lucky you are, you ungrateful bitch, think of all the girls downstairs who'd kill to be with us, we gift this to you,"

He spits in my face,
Poke, poke, pokes at my belly
"On the bed" he commands Mark, James throw me on it
Face down

Try and crawl away
Ankles are grabbed
Pulled back.
Turned onto my back
Shuffle back up the bed
They bounce the mattress
I bounce
They laugh
"Fuck she wobbles like Jelly-fat cow!"
Too fast
James is lying on the bed naked
His cock, standing proud
Pulled over the top of him by the others
They hold me down
James enter me
Starts pulsating
I cry
Darrens watches
Darren wanks
"Christopher, shut that bitches mouth."
Climbs over James, stuffs his cook in my mouth
Hammers like a piston
I gag
I struggle
I panic
I'm held
Can't move.
"Mark, fuck her shithole, I'll hold her, this bitch needs to learn what getting fucked is"
I fight harder
My mouth is released briefly
"Please no, please"
Pain
My body is being torn Ripped from the inside, Darren;

Three's A Crowd

"Fat fucking cow, getting what she deserves, ugly bitch getting fucked, I say when I say how, you're nothing, you want this. What makes you think you stand a chance, that you can be like Rachel, pretty, wanted, Smart, never gonna happen you dumb bitch, you're a slut, nothing more, don't worry, your secrets safe with us. Remember when I fucked you? You fucking loved it. I felt you cum all over my cock, don't deny it. You're lucky we fuck you, we should get a medal for it, no one else would. Why would they? There's nothing anyone wants here, you're a bit better than a hand that's it. I'd never fuck you again, bad enough the 1st time."

He's snarling
Christopher slams in or out of my mouth,
James ploughing into my pussy
Mark in my ass.
I don't know what happened
Next memory is being on top of Mark
Floppy
Being supported by James and Christopher
Groans
Moans
Warm splatters on my face
Eyes focus
Darren's cock a few inches away.
My pussy retracts
Marks cock is removed
And James
I collapsed on the bed
Staring into space.
No thoughts
I don't notice them leaving.
Time passes
Shit
I'm at a party,
I'm naked,

Beds a mess and wet I need to get sorted
My pussy burns
My ass screams,
My body aches
I get dressed
Neaten the bed
Bathroom, clean my face
Downstairs.
Everyone is still around.
All is, as was
But will never be the same I get to leave
I sleep over at Anne's
There is no sleep

This was unbearable to hear. Each word hit me like a physical blow, the kind that knocks the wind out of you. The details, God, the details, were so brutal, so raw, that I could feel something inside me shutting down. It was like someone had unplugged me, like the ground dropped away, and I was just... drifting. Numb. My mind couldn't process it, couldn't handle the weight of what she'd been through. I couldn't even respond. I just sat there, frozen, as her words echoed in my head, over and over.

I don't even know how long I stayed in that state, zoned out, staring blankly into space, not thinking or feeling anything, just... disconnected. Time felt unreal, like I was floating outside of it, outside of myself. The shock was so complete, it left me paralysed, stuck in some in-between space where nothing made sense any more.

Hours passed, I don't know how many, before I started to come back to myself. Slowly, the numbness began to fade, and with it came this rising wave of action, of determination. I couldn't stop thinking about her, about what she'd told me, about the way she looked when she said it. I thought about everything she must have felt, everything she's been carrying, and it hit me like a tidal wave. There was no way I could let this go.

Three's A Crowd

No more stories, no more listening and feeling powerless. Something had to be done.

But then I realised she was gone. She had slipped away while I was still stuck in my shock, and now she was out there... vulnerable. Alone. I swore to myself, right then and there, that this couldn't continue. I couldn't just sit here, letting her face this alone. I needed to find her, to hunt her down and make sure that no one, **no one**, could ever hurt her like this again.

This wasn't about words any more. It wasn't about listening or comforting or waiting for her to tell me the next horror she's lived through. Action had to happen. I had to make sure this stopped, once and for all. No more waiting, no more hoping things would get better on their own. I needed to be the one to protect her, whatever it took. I couldn't fail her again.

The days that followed were a blur, like I was moving through thick fog, pretending everything was fine while my mind was still stuck on what Misty had told me. I went through the motions with my family, forcing myself to smile, to laugh at the right moments, to answer questions and keep up conversations. But every word felt like a lie. It was exhausting, this constant act, pretending to be present when, inside, I was completely hollowed out.

I'd sit at the dinner table, nodding along as they talked, but all I could hear was Misty's voice echoing in my head. Her story kept replaying, like a loop I couldn't break free from. I felt disconnected, like I was watching my life from a distance, just playing my part while everything inside me was still in pieces. Every interaction took effort, smiling when I felt like screaming, acting normal when my insides were twisted with shock. The weight of it all dragged me down, and by the end of each day, I was completely drained, collapsing into bed just to do it all over again the next day.

But slowly, almost imperceptibly, the shock began to fade. It wasn't gone, not really, but it started to hurt a little less. The rawness dulled, and the pressure in my chest lightened, just a bit. I could function again, even if I was still pretending, still carrying the weight of what Misty had told me. There were moments where I almost felt normal, where I could laugh or talk without it feeling forced. The numbness began to lift, and my mind started to clear.

I don't know when it happened exactly, but one morning I felt... something like myself again. The exhaustion was still there, but I could push through it. I could focus on my family, on messaging Sam, on the day in front of me, without that constant, crushing sense of being stuck in a nightmare. The pain wasn't gone, not completely, but it wasn't the only thing I could feel any more. Slowly, I started to function again, piece by piece, like I was reclaiming parts of myself that had been lost in the chaos. I will never forget what she told me, it will haunt me for eternity and whilst now more muted, it would rise and fall like the waves on the beach.

It wasn't a sudden change, just a gradual return to something like normal. But even as I began to move forward, the promise I'd made to myself still lingered, a quiet fire in the back of my mind. I wouldn't forget what had happened. I couldn't. And sooner or later, I knew I'd have to act on it. I just didn't know how.

Barry the tree surgeon signed up with me, Sam returned from his concert and delivered me news that lifted my spirits beyond what I thought was possible:

Natasha is taking Beth to the lodge, 17th to 26th July. I will be home alone, I can't go because I have to work. I will join them on the weekends. I will have to work during the day, but you could come stay here for a couple of nights?

Jesus I could burst.

When I got the news, it felt like a wave of warmth just washed over me, the kind that starts in your chest and spreads out, making everything feel lighter. I couldn't believe it at first. Actually spending some **real time** with Sam again. Not just meeting up for a quick fuck and being left in some hotel room by myself, but a real night, where we could talk, laugh, touch, and just be together.

Three's A Crowd

Not just one night, maybe three. Like it used to be, when I felt loved, when I felt safe.

The thought of being close to him, not just physically but in that intimate, vulnerable way that comes when you're lying next to someone at night, filled me with this deep sense of anticipation. It's been so long since I've had the chance to feel his presence like that, the comfort of hearing his voice as we talk for hours, the quiet moments between conversations where our fingers intertwined or his hand rests on my skin, warm and grounding. And knowing that I can fall asleep next to him, nestled in his arms, safe and content... it makes my heart race, but in the most comforting way.

The idea of having him beside me, where we can share those moments after sex, our bodies tired but satisfied, whispers in the dark before sleep takes over, it's everything I've missed. There's something so special about falling asleep knowing you're not alone, that the person you care about is right there with you, holding you close, breathing in sync with you.

I feel this mix of excitement and peace, knowing that I can finally stop imagining it and live it, even if just for a few nights. It feels like getting back something precious that I've been aching for, a piece of myself I've missed. It's like coming home.

My mind races with, how do I get away with this at home? What if Natasha pops back for something? What will it feel like being in their home? I have some anxiety around the whole thing, but there is no way I am missing this chance. It is possibly a once in a lifetime shot. More time than we ever got at the business networking events.

Yes I would have to restrain myself from crawling under his desk and using his cock like a dummy all day. He did have to work, and so would I, but I would have him the rest of the time. It was like the perfect gift. The gift of the year, I needed nothing else.

It also means he can properly beat my ass!

Chapter 41
FML

The excitement builds between us, both so grateful for this opportunity. He wants to use what he has learnt about my past and continues to be revealed by Emily to utterly humiliate me over the days I am there.

It is uncomfortable but hot.

Then something happens I never saw coming. Emily switches camp, she is now 'team Sam.'

She tells me herself, in her usual manner. I am sitting on the bench in the garden drinking tea one morning after being out with Ron, enjoying the heat from the sun. It's only 8:20 am but the sun seems to be making me sweat. Emily turns up.

"So turns out the cunt is not a total cunt"

"Really?" I exclaim

"Yeah, he is a partial cunt."

"What does that mean?"

"I have thrown everything I can at him and he still claims to love you, he just won't piss off and with you moping about like a pathetic lost puppy, I can't bear it any more. I am too late, you've fallen for the prick anyway, if he is going to hurt you, I can't stop it."

"Holy crap, does that mean you will leave us alone now?"

"No, I am fucking loving giving him information on you, feels like revenge for all the times I have had to step in and mop up your crap and he likes to know, but I don't believe he will leave you now, I actually think the idiot gives a fuck about you, thinks your special."

"Wow, you want revenge on me?"

"Too fucking right, I have put up with your crap for decades, still love ya, but now I have someone who can see what a dumb ass you have been, just like me. I have told you that time and time again but you've not fucking listened, who knows, maybe you will listen to him and stop getting yourself into stupid situations."

"He thinks I am a dumb ass?"

"Yep, thinks you have been a fucking idiot. Sam and I finally have something we can agree on, he's alright, for a cunt."

I am dumbfounded, actually floored, no one gets on with Emily but me, only I put up with her cutting ways, and Emily **never** likes anyone, ***ever***. Being a "partial cunt" is high praise indeed. But her words, that he thinks I am a "fucking idiot' gnaw at me.

I message Sam when she has gone.

> What's the deal with you and Emily? She tells me she thinks you're not a total cunt?

Emily and I have become sort of friends

> Wow, how? 😱

We have a mutual goal

> Which is?

Keeping you safe

> So you like her?

I wouldn't say we like each other but we respect each other

Three's A Crowd

> Wow

> She is quite funny too 😊

> OK

> I don't know how I feel about this I feel like she is a spy in my camp

> She is and with her I get to fill in a lot of blanks and understand you more

> But it's things from my past that don't matter

> They won't change how I feel about you now, but they do matter. You have completely devalued yourself, put yourself in danger and neither of us want you to do that again. We are going to make you wake up.

I have very mixed feelings about this, it is good they are 'getting on' and he maybe sees in her what I do and others can't. That despite her abrasive exterior she is actually a really good, and caring person. But I don't like the fact she will be running to him with even more tales from my past or telling him if I am upset or making demands of him. I am not sure which was worse, them hating each other or getting along.

As the weeks roll past and our once in a lifetime chance at being together for more than 18 hours appears on the horizon things continue to be revealed.

Every night on messages a new past event is raised.

Being made to act like a dog, being fucked in the ass in my clients garden, cocking my leg like a dog to take a piss, begging and doing tricks. Sam asked me if my client gave me a dog name, he had done, it was Roxy.

He even asked me to bark on camera for him, and called me Roxy. He gets off on my discomfort. I want the ground to swallow me. Despite him and Emily believing nothing he hears will make him turn his back, each new revelation makes me fear the worst.

How much more can he take?

I have to do videos for him with blow by blow accounts. He comes back with extra details I had shared with Emily and forgotten and lords it over me. Emily and I fight about this all the time. I am very angry at her for betraying my trust. I am starting to question if my life long friend is really a good friend at all. Sam defends her, saying I struggle to understand how much is play and how much is real, as he tells me how stupid I am, that I am a total whore, a slut and that there is literally nothing I won't do for cock.

I get a bit upset one day and he reassures me there are two separate strands at play. One that he is enjoying sexually, it is wank material for him, he says we can have fun with it as despite my discomfort, the power he has over me is intoxicating and makes my pussy crave him, spewing liquid onto my office chair or squelching as I walk.

The other is to have me see how stupid I have been, how much I have put myself at risk. Being walked like a dog in a mans back garden, in broad daylight and fucked in the ass. Anyone could have seen. He may have a point.

He discovers that a bunch of asian clients who had enjoyed degrading me by having me wank off in front of them while they pissed on me, or wanking onto toast and watching me eat it.

A client who had a zimmer frame, and I had to rim his fat ass while he supported himself.

Being made to do squats with a cucumber in my pussy and being punished if I let it drop.

Punishments that led to severe bruising.

As he learnt more about Szymon, he did not like it. Concluding he was not a good guy. Both he and Emily, saying it was just paid for domestic abuse as he slapped me until I saw stars.

I broke, having all of this thrown at me non stop, I begged for it to stop. Please stop, I told him he could do anything, but please stop this mental torture. I had been silly and I would take any punishment he deemed fit, just please stop bringing up my past.

He paused, Emily paused, but it didn't stop. The two of them devised a punishment together, she was apparently clapping her hands with glee, hoping this would finally deliver a message to me, make me wake up and stop saying yes to anyone and everything.

It was torture, as whilst I was ashamed of some of my acts and the thought of Thomas or Lottie ever discovering how low I had gone haunted me. But equally, it was all harmless and just kinks, I was fulfilling dreams and if Emily had kept her trap shut, no one would be any the wiser. In my view what happened between my clients and me, was private and should not have been passed on. Like the escorting version of fight club. What is the first rule of fight club? You do not talk about fight club. What is the first rule of GW work? You do not talk about GW work.

My punishment was devised between Sam and Emily. I have taken stuff like this before, it can be super hot and a huge turn on. Sam was excited to deliver it and Emily possibly even more excited to hear the outcome. She wanted me broken and in tears begging for mercy and forgiveness.

The agreement was drawn up:

I, **JESSICA ELLEN NEWKIRK** (hereinafter referred to as "Cunt") does hereby agree to the following which shall be carried out in Kendal between 20th and 23rd July, or at any other date and location at the unfettered discretion of **SAMUEL ARCHIBALD MILLER** (hereinafter referred to as "Owner").

1 Cunt shall present herself for punishment at the unfettered discretion of the Owner.

2 Cunt shall be completely compliant in all ways. There shall be no exceptions, and Cunt shall ensure Owner is completely satisfied and happy with the obedience and compliance of the Cunt.

3 Cunt shall acknowledge that she is called "Cunt" or other derogatory names (for example Roxy, Fuck hole, Bitch, Whore, Slut etc) at the sole discretion of the Owner.

Cunt shall state the following:

I am a Cunt. I know I deserve to be treated like shit. I am nothing more than a wet sloppy cum rag, who is grateful for my Owner. I will always comply with my Owners wishes, and I shall ensure that I always exceed his expectations.

I ask for this punishment freely. I admit that I am a useless slut, nothing more than a human fleshlight, that is begging for this, so I may cleanse my soul and find peace. I am thankful for my Owner. I love him with all my heart, and am grateful he bestows attention on my worthlessness. I have been a slut, cumrag, whore, hooker, scum. I am his Slut. I will thank my Owner for every fucking strike. I, the Cunt, agrees to the Owner carrying out a punishment as follows:

1. *2 punches to the stomach as full and final punishment for No condom ass man*
2. *OTK 20 spanks on the ass, 10 to each ass cheek.*
3. *Caned 88 times on the ass, which shall be delivered in 4 sets of 22 impacts.*
4. *Caned 10 times on left foot sole 5 Caned 10 times on right foot sole*
5. *Whipped 40 times on the back, which shall be delivered in 4 sets of 10 impacts.*
6. *Belted 20 times to the back of the thighs, which shall be delivered in 2 sets of 10 impacts*
7. *Belted 30 times on the ass cheeks, which shall be delivered in 2 sets of 15 impacts.*
8. *Zapped 10 times on the asshole*
9. *Zapped 10 times on each ass cheek 11 Zapped 6 times on right tit*

12 Zapped 6 times on left tit 13 Slapped 19 times in the face 14

Three's A Crowd

Cropped 1 time in the face 15 Zapped 2 times on the face 16 Zapped 5 times on the clit

17 Cropped 100 times on the cunt, which shall be delivered in 10 sets of 10 impacts. Cunt will be taped open for maximum impact.

Furthermore, Cunt will take any role requested, such as Party Girl, gang bang Girl, Schoolgirl, Nun, Bride, CEO, Secretary, Roxy Dog, Cat or any other role requested.. Cunt will ensure that she provides as realistic as possible experience for my Owner.

Should any of the above not be met, the Owner can do anything in response.

If the Cunt does not present herself when requested, the all above punishments will instantly double in intensity and duration. In addition, full critique of past events will restart at a relentless pace and intensity.

The Slave shall sign and date here to confirm acceptance of these terms and conditions.
Signed:

Jessica Ellen Newkirk

Printed: Jessica Ellen Newkirk Date: 19th June

I signed it, straight away, desperate for the digging into the past to stop. I would take the above over that any day of the week. Sam knew it and loved making me feel uncomfortable, nothing seemed to make him harder.

The dredging up the past and the extent to how far I had gone did not stop. I kept raising the fact we had agreed for it to stop. It fell on deaf ears, him raising time and time again and drumming it into my head that ***if*** I chosen to do these things in a safe, consent- ing, loving relationship he would have no problem, but to allow complete strangers to treat me in such a way without any safety net or aftercare was dictionary definition of a dumb fuck.

> How many cocks do you think you have had?

>> I don't know 😷

> And that tells you everything you fucking slut

>> I know

> You should be ashamed

>> I am

> I know

>> What?

> How many cocks you have had. Shall I tell you?

>> How do you know?

> Emily has been very helpful and created a very detailed list and calculation

>> WHAT?!

> 211

.....flatline

> Yes and how many of those have fucked you in the ass?

>> I don't know

> More than a third

>> OK

> No... it's really not.

I do feel ashamed, but then again. I have made a lot of cocks very happy. I don't share that thought, I don't think it will help my case. I feel like I deserve this punishment and I can see by having had to retell some of these things, I have been a bit stupid. I also feel a bit sad. I almost feel like I have been used for people's gain, yes some paid for it, but where I thought I was wanted and loved for what I did, maybe I was only a means to an end. That end being caked in cum, covered in bruises or piss.

I would present myself willingly for punishment to Sam, feeling it may be a cathartic release, a way to pay for past sins, that strange world between pleasure and pain I endure and enjoy in equal measure.

Sam, Emily and myself were filled with excitement. Me with both excitement and dread at the thought of the upcoming meet. He knew he would have me for a few days, be able to really go to town on me, but satisfy his need to care for me after. Kink done properly in the confines of a loving relationship, where we both knew deep down I was safe. He checked and rechecked safe words, and made it clear I was to use them. I knew this was essential, if I didn't speak up if needed, he would never trust me again and never allow us to play to these extremes.

He still wrestled with the idea of properly hurting me, despite my willingness. I knew if we didn't do it when an opportunity like this presented itself we never would.

And we never did.

The weekend before, he was due to go away to the lodge, he was feeling unwell, he was in pain under his shoulder blade, he was hot and sweaty and felt like he was going to pass out.

Feeling so unwell he could not chat at night and took himself to bed. The next morning listening to his symptoms I felt like something was not right and encouraged him to go to 'out of hours'. He did, they thought he had an abscess where he had caught himself on a metal fence post when landscaping the garden. He was given antibiotics to stem the infection.

It didn't calm down and so he went back to his GP when they opened on Monday, and he was sent straight to the hospital.

When I first learned Sam had been admitted to the hospital, my heart sank. The words didn't even seem real at first; scans, investigations, something about an abscess. It all blurred together. The thought of him lying there, borderline delirious, battling this infection hit me like a punch to the chest. His health was all I could think about. Every other worry fell away. But in the back of my mind, the reality of our situation, of where I stood in his life, kept creeping back in.

I couldn't message him. I couldn't call the hospital for updates. His wife was there by his side, as she should be, but that left me in the dark, clinging to scraps of information I wasn't even sure I'd get. I knew if things got worse, if he became seriously ill, I would be the last to know, I would never be told and have to dig around to find out. That thought clawed at me, over and over. The helplessness was unbearable.

When I found out he needed surgery, it was like time stopped. They had to drain the abscess. I kept trying to tell myself it was routine, but deep down, I was terrified. I learnt later that day that when they scanned him to pinpoint the site, everything spiralled. He became extremely unwell during the scan and had to be rushed to surgery immediately. I didn't know it at the time, but at that exact moment, I was physically sick, as if my body somehow knew before my mind could catch up. The radio silence during all of this was crushing. I couldn't focus on anything except the fear twisting inside me, wondering, imagining the worst, and having no way to reach him . And if the worst did happen, I would never be on his list of contacts, I would have to scour the internet for news. I wouldn't be able to go and say goodbye at his funeral, Natasha would recognise me.

It felt like the longest day of my life. Every second dragged by in agonising uncertainty, my mind spinning with every possibility, from the worst-case scenarios to desperately hoping he'd come through it okay. When Sam finally messaged me that he was out of surgery and stable, I just collapsed with relief. He apologised that he had not been able to let me know. Natasha had not long left and he had just finished responding to lots of messages then got his chance to tell me.

He responded to other people before me.

I pushed that thought aside and the weight that had been pressing down on my chest lifted, and for the first time all day, I could breathe again. He was okay. That was all that mattered.

But then reality hit again. Of course, he needed time to heal, to rest, medication, painkillers, wound care.

And the worst part?

He'd be going to the lodge with them, for a full week to recover and be nursed back to health by Natasha. It broke my heart. That **one** chance we had, the chance I'd been dreaming of, was gone. In the blink of an eye, everything had changed. But at the same time, all I could do was be grateful that he was alive.

It was such a painful mix; heartbreak and relief, joy that he'd made it through, he had been close to death, sepsis beginning to take hold, he was flushed with drips. I would be eternally grateful he was alive.

Yet filled with devastation that our time, our moment, had slipped away. All I could do was hold on to the fact that he was still here, still breathing, that was what was important. The only thing that was important.

Chapter 42

The Truth Will Set You Free

With our opportunity gone. Life felt lost. I suffered another week of being sidelined and relegated to the occasional message whilst he was at the lodge. He may have put me out of his mind, but he was in mine constantly.

How was he healing? Was he getting actual rest or had Natasha tasked him with her usual list of requests and jobs? God forbid he ever be permitted a moment to sit down.

I was feeling a bit woe is me, which was ridiculous considering I am not the one that just nearly died.

When he got home, he was still sore and uncomfortable, he had as I suspected done too much. And of course, he was stressed. He had lost a week of work on his big project and so had to immerse himself in that.

He did his best to message me when he could. He always did. Deep down I knew that, but it didn't make it easier. It was another two-week spell of very minimal contact. It felt like we never got a run at any consistency any more. A curveball always seems to be thrown.

Evenings when he did message, he often had to be quick,

exhausted from pain, work, and subsequently being sent to bed early by Natasha to rest.

I was glad someone was looking out for him. I understood, but I missed him terribly.

Once he was healed and less tired, messaging at night did not improve.

There were very long pauses between me sending a message and him replying. His messages are short and less engaging. The occasional ghost from my past was mentioned and tackled but in the main, it felt like he was there, but not there at all.

Was he bored of me and just watching porn in between messages? Or setting up a local escort after our meeting was cancelled and he has not mentioned a future date.

When I finally understood why, I did not know what to think.

After around fourteen days of not seeing the messages as read or typing indicators for anything from thirty seconds to fifteen minutes or more, I decided to give him an out. He was clearly torn, perhaps bored, someone else or still busy with work and trying to squeeze me in, I felt guilty. If he was going to give me time, I wanted his time properly, not feeling like a pain to him, and sitting waiting on him like usual.

> Hey if you're busy, it's fine go do what you need to

Sorry, I am here just messaging Emily

> Oh, ok, all ok?

Yes, fine!

She is funny! 😄😄

> OK, well at least you are getting along.

I was thrown by this, he was literally keeping me on hold, to message her and ***she was funny***. Am I not funny any more? Had his interest waned from me and was shifting to her? Was Emily

Three's A Crowd

after him? I mean she has never met a partial 'cunt before.' I have told her about how great the sex is, maybe she wants to weasel her way in there.

I give myself a shake, it's ridiculous to even think like that, despite all of Emily's faults she would never do that, would she? And Sam would never be so cruel, would he?

It happens night after night, I can send a message and it takes twenty to thirty minutes for him to respond.

> God Emily is filthy as fuck! 😏

>> Well, she is my friend!

> Yes! And she is strong, takes no shit!

>> Unlike me?

> Yes, unlike you - you do as anyone says! 😬😩

I can't take it any longer... if Emily is so fucking great, funny, filthy and strong like Natasha then why the fuck is he even bothering with me? So I message back something I know I will regret.

>> Well, if she is so amazing, why don't you just fuck her, not me.

> OK, I was going to wait until I saw you in-person to raise this, but I can't hold off any longer, this is not how I wanted to do it.

My heart sank, my gut was right. I thought I knew it was an axe that was going to eventually fall, I thought I could see it coming, instead, it was a noose that had slipped around my neck unnoticed. He is about to kick the stool from under my feet. But never, did I ever think my oldest friend Emily would be the rope.

>> That doesn't sound good.

> This will be a bit of a shock, but promise me, you won't freak out?

> I can't promise that

> OK, I am sending this, please read with an open mind.
>
> https://www.mind.org.uk/information-support/types-of-mental-health-problems/dissociation-and-dissociative-disorders/dissociative-disorders/

I am deeply baffled. I expected this 'I am so sorry but I am actually in love with Emily' line to land, and instead he sent me some link about crazy people. I read it and I don't understand.

> I don't understand, what are you telling me?

> I think you may have DID, it's the only explanation. I want you to think about it, read it, research it, and then get to bed. I will call you in the morning, once all is clear here and we can talk. But know this… it does not change how I feel. I love ALL of you. I always will.

> WTF!? How did you come up with this?

> I just googled 'my girlfriend has two distinct personalities' and got this and the more I read, the more it made sense. Read, be open, sleep and know I love you, speak tomorrow x

> OK x

I am utterly shell-shocked. I know I have been a handful, I know I have been needy and demanding at times, but two distinct personalities? Am I that bad? Do I really come across as that psycho? Is he gaslighting me? What the fuck is going on?

I read feverishly all night.

Learning about Dissociative Identity Disorder (DID) feels like diving into a fragmented mirror. As I go through the information, each detail resonates in a strange way, pulling me into memories I can't fully grasp. Memories that seem distant, disjointed, and yet

Three's A Crowd

somehow mine. The more I learn, the more I feel like I'm trying to assemble a puzzle made of pieces I'm not even sure belong to me.

I started reading about how DID often begins in childhood, a time when the mind is still forming, still fragile. It's usually triggered by severe trauma, often repeated or sustained over time, and I pause. This idea makes me uncomfortable because it sounds eerily familiar. I know I've been through things, things I don't like to think about. But could they really have led to something like this?

Apparently, DID is a defence mechanism, the mind's way of coping with overwhelming pain. Instead of staying whole, the personality fractures, creating different identities, 'alters', they're called, each one designed to handle something the original self couldn't. Some might deal with anger, others with fear, or even with day-to-day life. I wonder if that's why there are times I feel so disconnected like parts of me are operating on their own, beyond my control. I wonder if that's why so much of my life I can't remember clearly and some I cannot remember at all.

As I keep reading, it sort of clicks: the "losing time" moments, the strange gaps in memory, the feeling that I'm watching myself from a distance sometimes. These may not be just weird quirks or lapses in attention, they could be signs of different alters taking control. I start connecting more dots, realising that the intense mood swings I've dismissed as normal stress or the times when people tell me I said or did something that I can't recall, might be more than what I thought.

DID works by dividing consciousness, with each alter holding a specific set of memories, emotions, or skills. They can have different names, genders, ages, and even physical traits like different postures or allergies. Some people have many alters, while others have only a few. Alters can interact with one another internally, sometimes arguing or offering support, but the person with DID might not be aware of all these dynamics. It's like sharing a body with others who have their own lives and agendas, but they all coexist within one mind.

The symptoms are more than just memory loss, though. There's dissociation, feeling detached from oneself, as though life is happening to someone else. There are sudden, unexplained shifts in behaviour, mood, or abilities. People with DID can experience depression, anxiety, or severe flashbacks to traumatic events. Some might even hear voices inside their head. The other alters may try to communicate. Or feel like they're being pulled in different directions by thoughts or feelings that don't seem to be their own.

Reading this is unsettling because the more I learn, the more I start to wonder if this is me. I thought I knew who I was, but now I'm not so sure. If I do have DID, it's like discovering that there are parts of me I've never met, parts that have been living in the background, helping me survive in ways I didn't even realise.

But where do I go from here? How could I get this confirmed, or denied, do I even want to find out? Why would Sam want me if this is true?

I need to talk to Emily about this, maybe that is what she and Sam have been discussing.

It may explain the gaps in memory and lapses in concentration, but I am still me. I have thoughts and voices in my head of course, and so does everyone.

I can't help but feel Sam is clutching at straws. I am not sure if that is good or bad, he clearly thinks there is something 'wrong' with me to even raise this and that is not a comforting thought. I don't want to have anything 'wrong' with me, but I don't want him to be right either.

I feel sick in the morning in anticipation of his call and what he might say. He rings, I take a few deep breaths and answer.

"Hey," I say

"Hey, how are you?"

"Confused, scared."

Three's A Crowd

"Understandable, what are you thinking?"

"That you think there is something wrong with me, that yes I do have gaps and memory loss, yes I did go through some trauma, but I am ok."

"I think you went through a lot of trauma, this explains so much."

"Have you spoken to Emily about this before you spoke to me?"

"Jess, this is going to be hard to hear, but Emily *is* you."

"What do you mean?. She is not!"

I am starting to feel teary and panicked.

"When I talk to Emily, Jess, I am looking at your face, when she calls, messages or video calls, it comes from your old GW burner phone number."

"No! You met her, she came and told you to end it over breakfast when I was outside calling a client"

"No Jess, you physically never left that table."

I am floored, it can't be, it absolutely can't be, I have known Emily forever. She comes to me, she is there with me.

"No, no"

"Think about when you see her, has Phil ever met your oldest friend? Your kids? Can you remember her face, or just the conversations you have? Check your burner phone, Jess."

I am silent. Time hangs between us as my brain stops and falls into overdrive all at the same time. I reach into my bag and pull out my other phone. Click on WhatsApp for Business and there are hundreds of messages I have never written, messages I have received to me, on my phone, from Emily on my burner phone, but I never wrote and whole conversations between Sam and Emily.

"That means I am insane, I will be locked up."

"No, it means you were hurt, badly hurt and your brain has done a very clever thing to allow you to function and cope with life. Think about it, it is like Emily is the part of you, built to protect, to keep men away. She is angry, you're never angry, you're not angry at Darren, she is. She can be a bitch and speak her mind, you can't. She holds skills you don't. But she **is** you, you have those skills in you."

He pauses and lets me digest what he is saying, it is a lot to take in. He continues.

"Emily can and has filled in gaps in your memory because when presented with certain sexual scenarios, she has stepped in, she has taken over, she has endured. That is why she is angry at you, you have ignored her, never recognised she is real, and left her to handle your messes and clean them up. She does it because it's her job. The reason she was created is to look after you and stop you from being hurt. You can't say no to men, because of your experiences, it never worked when you were younger, so you gave up saying no, if you went along with it, you would never be raped again. Emily has told me this, she has said when she has 'taken over' from you, she has sometimes known it's bad and that it's safer to just let it happen. To get through it. Emily was born out of necessity from your traumas, your younger self created her and she has been your best friend ever since."

"And Jess, I do mean traumas"

"No"

"Sadly yes, it wasn't just Darren, Darren started it, but James, Mark, Paul, Christopher, they carried on."

"No, no, that is Misty, not me."

"Don't you remember thinking it odd, the names were similar? Don't you remember her saying it was the same school you went to? How is it possible, she can be all the places she has been, turning up where she has? She is a child, trapped in time, holding onto the memories you buried. She is sending you memories, like flashbacks of the trauma."

My mind is racing, to all the times I have seen her or the places she has turned up, this makes no sense.

"No, she hurt me, you have seen my wrists."

Three's A Crowd

"You did that to yourself, Jess, trying to stop remembering, trying to bury it all."

"No" I am starting to sob now. I sit silently, tears flowing. "What does she look like?"

"Frail, skinny, blonde distraught."

"Like you, when you were that age, don't you see? You got skinny and frail, you had an eating disorder and you can't be naked because of all the cruel things those cunts did and said to you, to **you** Jess".

But her name, she would be called Jessie, I think.

"But Sam, her name is Misty, not Jessie"

"Did she tell you that?"

I search my mind, casting it way back to the first time I met her in the Asda car park.

'Jess, no you have to help me, you're the only one, don't you remember?'

'No, no please, help me, listen, you need to listen, you need to see, you can't hide any longer, it's Misty, save me Jess, can't you see it, don't you remember?'

I think and think, and it runs through my head...

"It's Misty"

No...no.. It's clear she said..

"It's me see"

It is like a train hitting me... she was trying to tell me all along, it **had** to be me, I **had** to listen, Emily said it **had** to be me... they both knew. Misty was saying it is 'me, see'. As in me, the younger me and **only** I can help **me**. I needed to hear the stories, I needed to acknowledge what had happened, I needed to remember. I knew, I always knew there was more than just Darren, but I pushed it away, Misty couldn't hold it any longer, she was trapped, and that is why she kept saying when I said to get the Police or tell someone, that it was too late. And it was because this all happened over 30 years ago.

"Sam, I don't think she did say her name was Misty, I think she was saying it is 'me...see'?"

"I wish I was with you Jessie, you could do with a hug"

"What does this all mean, what can I do, to fix it all?"

"I don't know, probably therapy"

"I can't afford therapy," I sniffle.

"One step at a time."

"I might not have it, this DID thing."

"No, you might not, but it fits, it also explains your hyper-sexuality and the positions you have put yourself in and how you have allowed yourself to be treated, why you don't believe me when I say I love you, why you chose Phil as a husband, avoiding love and being wanted, so avoiding any more pain, but even if we are wrong, you have some stuff to deal with, things you have buried and never faced. Misty is flashbacks trying to burst out so you can process them."

"I think I would like to go now"

"OK sweetheart, but please, if you remember nothing else, hear this, I love YOU, this doesn't scare me, I love all three of you."

"I love you too."

We hung up and I sat, for hours. Processing, contemplating, and running over everything that has happened in the last year. I reach out for Emily, she is there, but for the first time, I realise she is just a voice in my head, she is not present.

"I have been trying to tell you this you dumb bitch" She says.

Sam messages me frequently to check how I am.

At lunchtime, I take Ron out. I need some fresh air. I head to our usual woods and walk slowly, unaware of what I am doing, mind racing, but empty, busy but still.

I plonk myself down on the log, the one where Misty, well young Jess I suppose, found me that day. And I contemplate what Sam may have unveiled.

Finding out that I might have Dissociative Identity Disorder is like the ground beneath me has disappeared. It feels like I don't

Three's A Crowd

even know who I am any more. For over 30 years, I thought I had a grasp on myself, my life, and my identity, but now, all of that feels like a lie.

It's terrifying. It's not just a little confusion or self-doubt, it's like realising that parts of me, entire pieces of my life, might not even belong to 'me.' What if I'm not the one who lived in some of those moments? What if I've been here only part of the time, and the rest was someone else? I can't even trust my own memories any more. I don't know where they end and where someone else begins. From my reading last night people with DID describe their other selves as 'head mates', like 'room mates'. I can't help but chuckle at the irony. I have always felt alone, but I have had company the whole time. I just didn't know it.

Sure, there were things, times I'd lose track of hours or days, moments where I didn't feel like myself, but I thought everyone had those. I thought it was stress, burnout, or just me being a bit scatterbrained. Now, those little cracks in my sense of self feel like chasms, deep and dark, and I don't know how far they go. I don't know how much of my life I've actually lived.

How could this have happened? How could I have gone this long without realising something so massive? I thought I knew who I was. But maybe that person never really existed. Maybe I've been a collection of pieces, pretending to be whole. It's a horrifying thought, this idea that I might have been sharing my body.

I feel so disconnected from everything, like I'm floating outside of myself, looking down at someone I don't recognise. When I look in the mirror will I ever be able to trust that the face looking back is mine? Is it me? Or is it one of them? I don't know where I begin, and where they end.

It feels like I've lost everything, even myself. How do you make sense of a life that might not be fully yours? How do you reconcile with the fact that for 30 years, you've been living with others inside your own mind? There's a deep sadness, an overwhelming grief for the person I thought I was. But there's also this emptiness, a hollow space where my sense of identity used to be.

I thought I had a past, a story that made me 'me'. But now, it's like flipping through a book and finding blank pages, parts torn out, rewritten by someone else. I don't know how to move forward from this. How do you rebuild a self when you don't even know who the pieces belong to?

I sit for a long while and then head back to the house, so I am home in time for the kids. As I pass the gate to the cow field I feel eyes on me. I scan the area and spot a guy, standing perfectly still, legs slightly apart, hands hanging loosely in his pockets, and his brown curls flopping over his face. He looks familiar. I feel uneasy and pick up my pace for home.

I listen to music to quieten my head, 'Teenage Dream[8]' comes on by Olivia Rodrigo.

It makes me think of Misty (Young Jess, YJ) the last time I saw her and how I swore I had to do something. How her hopes and dreams have been killed and my denial has caused a half-lived life, far off course from where she wanted to be. I don't even remember being 19 as referenced in the song, not clearly anyway, snippets. Sam has called my bluff on my past and got to the truth, a truth I was only half conscious of. And yes, I wish I could go back to age 15 and not go outside the disco with Darren.

It takes me some time, a few floored days before I leap into true Jess mode. I have always done this, when faced with a problem, let it settle then start taking action, and break it into chunks.

I won't be able to get help or a diagnosis until my finances are better, but I can start working on things now. I have learnt that if it is confirmed I have DID, then there is some hope and I have some choices to make.

One thing for certain is I need to deal with and listen to Misty, she should then rest and quieten. She will then stop preventing me from working, sleeping and going out. She will feel heard, settled and happy, she can find peace. That means I have to face everything that happened to me between ages 15 and 18. If I am honest, I don't want to do that.

Emily is tricker, but she is causing less trouble, she is on my side, and she and I can talk. I can't talk to Misty, I have to wait for her to come to me. But as Sam says, Emily holds skills I don't, I may need to get angry at the past to heal. I don't feel any anger towards the boys. She can also stand up for herself. I can't.

From what I have read you can work on co-existing, integrating or merging fully. I haven't worked out which is right for us and how we actually do it. But the first step, get Misty at peace. Emily is less keen on 'merging' she doesn't want to 'die'.

Sam has been amazing, patient, and supportive and he is excited about us 'merging' if we choose to do it, as he says *Jessie 2.0* will be a sight to behold.

Whatever way you cut it, I have some major life decisions to make. I have YJ to care for like an extra daughter, career, money, and finances to decide on, get to know myself all over again, free myself from the past and explore the future I (we) want, I have lost over 30 years, time to make up for lost time.

Chapter 43

The Sky Is Not Blue - For Me

The weeks roll on into August and my newfound insight is never far from my mind, I try to untangle all the parts of my life. Sam is supportive, helping me come to terms with my fractured soul. His support makes this albeit unconfirmed but likely outcome easier to accept. He loves me for it, in spite of it. We return to filth and fun. There is no talk of another date and doubts ring in my head constantly. He says it is my narrative, my past and I just have to learn to accept he is going nowhere and he loves me.

My love for him, which I never thought could grow any bigger, has bloomed again.

Sadly with his work and home restrictions, I still suffer, I can't cope with the low communication, it makes me feel like shit. I chat to Emily about it who leaps to his defence.

Oh, how things have changed!

She reminds me he does what he can, that he really does care and not to push him, to back off, give him space, not jeopardise this, be fun and he will always want me.

But I can't help wondering, is it enough for me?

Then Sam quite unexpectedly went and blew my mind about

3 weeks ago, a small envelope arrived in the post. He told me not to open it when it arrived, but to call him and open it with him on a video call.

I was intrigued and baffled, I called him, and carefully opened it, a tiny little clear bag held something silver. It had little bumps on it and when I first pulled it out, I thought it was some form of miniature anal beads... but you'd need to have a Barbie doll butt for it to work.

I then realised it was a bracelet.

My heart was pounding, no one had ever done something like this for me. No one.

I don't know if it was because it was from Sam or if it was just beautiful (and it is) but it was the most beautiful bracelet I had ever seen. Delicate, shimmering in the light.

I blinked hard, trying to keep my emotions in check, but it was no use. Tears welled up, and my chest tightened as the realisation hit me, someone cared, someone thought of me. Sam cared enough to pick out something so special, ***just for me***.

I asked why, and he said it was a "thank you". To this day I don't know why I was being thanked, I couldn't think straight enough to ask.

I felt overwhelmed like I didn't deserve this, I wasn't used to this. It wasn't just about the bracelet itself, it was what it represented. That someone thought of me and chose something beautiful because they thought I was worth it. I wasn't sure how to handle that.

I could barely speak. All I managed was a choked, "Thank you," but even that felt inadequate. How could I possibly put into words what I was feeling?

The gratitude, the disbelief, the warmth that was flooding through me. I wanted to tell Sam everything, how much this meant but I was too overwhelmed. So I just sat there, clutching the bracelet, trying to hold back the tears that threatened to spill over.

Three's A Crowd

I had something I could always wear that would remind me of him every day. It was incredibly special.

I told Emily about it and she told me that she and Sam had already discussed how it had landed with me. Emily and Sam still messaged frequently.

She told me Sam was stunned that such a little gift caused such a big reaction. It highlighted to him how little I got. How uncared for I was by Phil. Emily pointed out to him that I am not bothered by gifts and that I had come to terms with Phil not getting anything for me a long time ago.

He said that was sad, that my reaction showed it was important to me and that should be reason enough for Phil to want to do it if he loved me.

There was something about that conversation that Emily relayed that gnawed away at me.

Then one evening, while walking Ron, it crystallised in my mind and I knew what I had to do.

The sun dipped lower toward the horizon, the hay fields stretched out in waves of golden light. The tall grasses catch the sun's dying rays, each blade glowing like it's been kissed by fire. A soft breeze rippled through them, making the field shimmer like an ocean of liquid gold.

In the distance, the hay bales stand like quiet replica 'shredded wheats', their round shapes casting long, soft shadows on the ground. The light hits them just right, wrapping them in a warm, amber glow. The air smelt sweet and earthy, and everything felt so still, so peaceful at that moment.

In that peace, I found what must be done. It was the worst thing imaginable, it would cause pain, guaranteed for eternity, but also balanced with some form of peace. A peace I didn't currently have.

Sam and I have talked many times about our relationship. He was trapped, trying to rebuild his marriage out of duty, I was staying in mine until a less impactful time on my kid's lives.

He says he loves me and the whole time I have known him, he has done nothing but love me in spite of all he has discovered. But I realise now it is not enough. I want more and without more, pain dominates more than pleasure and I have had enough pain.

By more I don't mean him walking out of his life into my arms, I would never ask him to do that. He has to choose to do that for himself and no one else.

I mean that I want more than the unavoidable feeling of being picked up and dropped. I want more than being fucked and left. I want more than uncertainty over when I will see him again.

I know now why feeling safe is so important to me. He can't make me feel safe, he can't be there when I need him. I can't text and he would see it, he would only see it if he thought to check, because I am hidden away in a locked secure folder. He is so controlled and watched, that communication will never be what it was. ***I need that***. I have expressed this time and time again.

It is important to me, very important to me, and as per his argument to Emily about Phil, ***if it is important to me and he loves me, that should be reason enough.***

I could have carried on, if we could have found a way to meet my needs, I didn't need much, but it was too much for him to manage. Probably not because he doesn't want to, just because he can't. It feels like he gets all the benefits and I get all the pain.

As if sensing my thoughts my playlist skips to 'When I Was Your Man[9]' by Bruno Mars.

I was simpler than that, always have been, I didn't need flowers, ***I needed consistent communication and clear plans***. Messages, time with him and truth. I just needed him to find a way to work with me to discover a solution that gave me the minimum I could survive on and ***he would have had me for life.*** He can't do that for me or he won't do that for me, either way the outcome is the same.

But I won't be dancing with another man.

This is for me. Time to put me first, for once.

Three's A Crowd

I never thought I'd find myself here, making this decision, but for my own sanity, I have to let go of Sam. It's tearing me apart to even say those words, to acknowledge that I won't feel his arms around me, hear his voice or see that smile that lights up my world. But I know deep down, no matter how much I love him, this isn't something I can keep enduring.

It's not because he doesn't love me, I know he does in his way. But love isn't always enough, and that's the hardest part. I can't live like this, hidden away in the shadows, pretending that his marriage doesn't weigh on me every single day. Every time I see him, every stolen moment, it reminds me of what I'll never have. And the pain of not being able to reach out to him when I need him because we have to hide 'us', it's suffocating. It's like I'm not allowed to exist fully in his life, and I can't help but feel I'm not good enough, not important enough to be someone who can be seen.

It's not his fault. He has a duty to his daughter, Beth. I understand that I really do, and I would never ask him to be anything less than a good father to her. But that doesn't make this hurt any less. Every day, the doubt gnaws at me, will things ever get better between him and Natasha? Will they find their way back to each other? And when they do, that will be the end of us? It feels like I'm constantly bracing for the moment when he finally tells me I'm not the one he's choosing. Well in truth, he has already chosen and it is not me. I think of the song, 'Never not[10]' by Lauv.

We **have** had fun, **no one will ever compare**, and I will **never forget**. I will get our memories out and look at them frequently and wish things were different and I will never forget the kindness, patience and love he showed me.

I can't keep living in limbo, waiting for the final confirmation that I'll never truly be his. Deep down, I already know, I'm not the one he can choose, and I never will be. He's bound by duty, and I can't fault him for that. Beth deserves her father, just like Misty (YJ) deserves me. But I can't let Misty (YJ), this sweet, innocent soul never realise **her** dreams. After all her pain, she deserves to rest in peace, having a chance at least of no longer feeling second best, always waiting for the other shoe to drop. I owe it to her to be strong enough to let go of something that's breaking me, even if it feels like it's shattering my heart into a million pieces.

I know I'll never love like this again. Sam was it for me, the one person who made me feel alive, who understood me in a way no one else ever will. The thought of never being with him, of never loving ***anyone*** again, is devastating, life ending, not physically, but in my soul. There will be no one else, and I've made peace with that. I'll carry this love for him in my heart for the rest of my life. It is eternal.

And maybe, just maybe, in another life, we'll find each other sooner, before the complications, before the responsibilities and the duties that keep us apart. I pray for that chance, that we'll have the time we couldn't have in this life. But for now, I have to walk away, even though it's breaking me. I have to save what little of myself is left.

I won't ever remove that bracelet.

But for me, I don't get to see the blue sky, not this time.

I won't deliver this news in a text, a call or a video. I have to see him, to explain, he has to know how broken I am about this, how loved and special he is. I know he will be heartbroken, but I also know deep down, he will understand. He wouldn't want to cause me any more pain. He tells me true love is selfless, well, that will be tested, but I know the kind of man Sam is, I know he'll be devastated, but he will accept my choice.

When we message that night, I discovered he has an unusually light day tomorrow and is working from home. I will drive to him, phone him twenty minutes before I get there and ask him to come meet me for a coffee.

I have a fitful sleep and hit the road once everyone has left. I am on edge, dreading delivering the news and feeling nausea the entire way, but I know this is the right thing to do.

Three's A Crowd

I ponder the saying 'two's company, three's a crowd' and how ironic that is, I am the third in Sam's marriage, as he is in mine.

Misty (YJ), Emily and I, also a crowd of three. In the world of escorting, you are often the third in an existing relationship.

Three is not the magic number, that is for sure. I think for me it is meant to be one.

About an hour shy of Sam's town, I stop for petrol.

I step into the garage to pay, the smell of engine oil and rubber filling the air. As I approach the counter, I see him, standing by the door, not far from the till. Brown curly hair, unkempt but somehow familiar, his eyes lock onto mine. It's that same man I've noticed lately, popping up in odd places. I thought it was a coincidence at first, but seeing him now, this close sends an icy chill down my spine. He doesn't look away, doesn't even blink, just stares, his gaze intense and unsettling, as if he's sizing me up.

I hand over the cash, my hands shaky, trying to act normal, but my heart is racing. I glance over my shoulder as I leave the shop. He's still watching, his eyes tracking me as I walk out. A creeping sense of dread spreads through me, but I shake it off. It's just a random guy, I tell myself, though my instincts scream something else. Emily screams something else.

Some young guys are parked at the tyre pressure machine, pumping out music. It's 'God's plan' by Drake. I feel really uneasy.

I walk around the back of the building as the music fills the forecourt, heading toward the disabled toilet, hoping to take a moment and catch my breath, letting the anxiety pass while I empty my bladder. As I reach the door, there's a flicker of movement in the corner of my eye. Before I can react, he's there, leaping out of the shadows like he's been waiting for me. His body slams into mine, and the air leaves my lungs in a single, terrified gasp.

I'm pinned against the cold brick wall, his forearm pressing hard against my throat. I try to scream, but the pressure is too much, his grip is strong, suffocating. My mind is racing, panic flooding my veins. His face is inches from mine, eyes dark and unblinking, filled with something I can't quite place, anger, hunger, or worse.

I claw at his arm, desperate for air, my heart hammering in my chest as every nerve in my body screams in terror. His breath is hot against my face as he leans in closer, and I realise, with cold horror, that this is no coincidence.

"Hello Jessie, I am going to remind you of your place, you're a **FUCKING WHORE!**"

Epilogue

Misty suffered 64 sexual attacks between the ages of 15 and 18, another 14 were faced by Emily. There were 33 failed attempts where they escaped. What was endured fractured a young girl into three, leading to a life less lived, lived on the edge, chasing the unattainable and entertaining a staggering 211 cocks in an attempt to feel any worth or to just feel something. These attacks were not just sexually violent but verbally cruel, causing a near-death eating disorder and creating a life-avoiding connection out of fear. It caused Jess as an adult unable to say 'no' to men, but never knew why she could not. Misty's time taught her, that "No!" did not work, so they gave up on it.

Darren, Mark, Christopher, James and Paul of Dames Order School, rapists one and all, nearly killed them. They will have to live with that on their conscience. Forever looking over their shoulders. They should be in jail, and maybe one day that is exactly where they will be for the crimes they committed so many years ago. They knew what they were doing.

Life is never as simple as we imagine it to be when we are

young. As children, we dream of clear paths, straight lines leading us toward the futures we envision, free of complication or pain. We grow up believing in the narratives we're told: work hard, be kind, follow the rules, and life will reward you with happiness and stability. But life rarely follows that script. Instead, it twists and turns, throwing curveballs we couldn't have prepared for, pushing us to confront parts of ourselves and the world we never thought we'd face. Showing that what people present outwardly hides the true stories that lie beneath.

This book has been a testament to that truth, exploring the messy, complicated, often painful realities that many people live through and that, hopefully, most won't have to endure. It has touched on the silent but powerful presence of Post-Traumatic Stress Disorder (PTSD), and the way unresolved trauma can ripple through people's lives like a shadow that refuses to fade. It has looked at the physical and emotional scars left by eating disorders, and how we wage wars against our own bodies when the world makes us feel like we don't belong in them.

Sexual violence, in its many horrifying forms, has been another dark thread running through these stories, rape, gang rape, and the unbearable weight they leave behind. These acts leave wounds that sometimes never fully heal, but they are experiences some survive with strength they never knew they had.

The complexities of human desire and how it intersects with trauma have also played a major role here, hyper-sexuality, often a misunderstood response to deep pain, is a way some people try to reclaim control over their bodies or numb themselves from their feelings. At the same time, self-worth becomes a fragile, elusive thing, something that we are constantly negotiating in a world that tells us we are never enough.

Dissociative Identity Disorder (DID) is another reminder of how the mind, in its incredible resilience, can fracture to protect itself from unbearable pain. It shows us the power of survival, even

Three's A Crowd

if it means splitting into parts just to keep going. In some lives, sex work is a choice, or a necessity, one that comes with its own set of challenges and stigmas, complicated by the realities of a dead bedroom at home, where intimacy is absent, leaving an empty space that is often filled elsewhere. The impact is far wider than 'just sex' affecting those trapped to their very core, making them feel unwanted, discarded and unloved.

Love, parental love, has been a constant theme, too, demonstrating just how far a parent will go to provide for their child. Love that is fierce, unconditional, and protective, but also love that sometimes falters, is misplaced, or is constrained by cultural norms and expectations. Unrequited love, true love, missed love, lost love.

The presence of affairs, hook-up culture, and the ongoing tug-of-war between patriarchy and matriarchy only add to the chaos of trying to find connection and meaning in a world that so often feels disconnected and transactional.

And then there are the hidden desires: kinks, the parts of ourselves we often keep locked away, afraid of judgement, afraid of what they mean about who we are. But they are part of us, part of the complexity of human experience, and they remind us that there is no 'normal' when it comes to desire.

In the end, this book has been an exploration of life's unexpected and sometimes devastating turns. It reflects the journeys many people will take, touching on experiences that are raw, real, and sometimes taboo. It is not a fairy tale. It is not a neat, linear story with easy answers or happy endings packed in pretty boxes and tied up in bows. But it is a story of survival. Of finding pieces of yourself in the rubble, picking them up, and moving forward, even when it feels like the world is working against you.

Because life, in all its complexity, is not about walking a straight path, it's about navigating the curves, the obstacles, and the unexpected bends along the way. It's about finding your way through, in spite of everything.

Today, Jess still struggles with flashbacks, her past catching up with her, and her love for Sam.

And she writes books.

DID you spot it?

Can you identify each trigger that caused Jessie's flashbacks and Misty to appear? (Misty IS her flash backs)

DID you notice what always happened each time before Jessie saw Emily or Misty?

DID you notice only Jessie ever said Misty's name? What else DID you spot?

DID you know, there are around 10,000 books self published every day... yes... every.single.day. Making it so hard for people to find your book, unless you have a bottomless bank account (I don't!). So if you enjoyed this book, a review makes all the difference and helps others find it. It takes two minutes of your time, but is life changing for the authors. So wether Amazon, Good reads or somewhere else, it could be your good deed of the day and karma would reward you with multiple orgasms x

Join the conversation on:

DID you spot it?

TikTok: @jcp.thomas
Facebook: JCP Thomas
Instagram: @jcp_thomas_author

Don't be a C.U.N.T!

If you enjoyed this book, then I have a favour to ask. Please do not reveal how it ends.

You got to enjoy the story as intended. Perhaps the penny dropped for you early, perhaps it did not. Either way, readers should be free to experience it with out influence.

Sure, talk about it, but wait until the person you are discussing it with has finished before you reveal your genius in spotting it early (or not!).

It drives me nuts when I hear spoilers of things for TV, film or books.

No spoilers please! Xxx

Soundtrack - Film Producers, Take Note!

Hey, a girl can dream right!?

A Few of My Favourite Things - The Sound of Music
    Ain't No Sunshine - Bill Withers
    Animals - Maroon 5
    Billie Jean- Michael Jackson
    Dirty Thoughts - Chloe Adams
    Driving License - Olivia Rodrigo
    Favourite Crime - Olivia Rodrigo
    Fill My Little World - The Feeling
    Gods Plan - Drake
    Happy Ending - Mika
    Have a little faith in me - John Hiatt
    I don't want to miss a thing - Aerosmith
    I wanna be the only one - eternal
    I'll stand by you - pretenders
    I'm your man - Wham
    I'll be there for you - Bon Jovi
    It must be love - Madness
    It was always you - Maroon 5

Soundtrack - Film Producers, Take Note!

Just the way you are - Bruno Mars
Justified and ancient - KLF
Lean on me - Bill Withers
Love Again - Dua Lipa
Love It When You Call - The Feeling
Never Not - Lauv
Rhythm is a dancer - Snap!
She's so lovely - Scouting for Girls
Snoop Snoop Song - Cher
So Strange - Polyphia
Teenage Dream - Olivia Rodrigo
Vampire - Olivia Rodrigo
When I was your man - Bruno Mars
White flag - Dido

References & Resources:

1 https://en.wikipedia.org/wiki/Blue_Monday_
2 Maroon 5 - Animals
3 Polyphia - So Strange
4 Dua Lipa - Love Again
5 Mika - Happy Ending
6 Olivia Rodrigo - Favourite Crime
7 Olivia Rodrigo - Vampire
8 Olivia Rodrigo - Teenage Dream
9 Bruno Mars - When I Was Your Man
10 Lauv - Never Not
11 Drake - God's Plan
12 Rhythm is a dancer - Snap!
13 Olivia Rodrigo - Driving License

Support for those who have been raped or sexually assaulted:
https://rapecrisis.org.uk/
https://www.rapecrisisscotland.org.uk/help-helpline/

Eating Disorder Support:
https://www.beateatingdisorders.org.uk/

Dissociative Identity Disorder Support

References & Resources:

https://survivorsnetwork.org.uk/resource/dissociative-identity-disorder-d-i-d/

Sex Work Support:

https://www.swarmcollective.org/   https://theredproject.co.uk/

PTSD Support:

https://www.ptsduk.org/

Printed in Great Britain
by Amazon